CHILDREN'S CLASSICS

# The Hound of the Baskervilles

Sir Arthur Conan Doyle

# The Hound of the Baskervilles

PARRAGON

The Hound of the Baskervilles
A Parragon Classic

---

This is a Siena Book
Siena is an imprint of Parragon

First published in 1902

This edition published in 1999 by
Parragon
13 Whiteladies Road
Clifton
Bristol BS8 1PB



Printed and bound in the UK

## CHAPTER 1

# MR. SHERLOCK HOLMES

Mr Sherlock Holmes, who was usually very late in the mornings, save upon those not infrequent occasions when he was up all night, was seated at the breakfast table. I stood upon the hearth-rug and picked up the stick which our visitor had left behind him the night before. It was a fine, thick piece of wood, bulbous-headed, of the sort which is known as a "Penang lawyer." Just under the head was a broad silver band, nearly an inch across. "To James Mortimer, M.RC.S., from his friends of the C.C.H.," was engraved upon it, with the date "1884." It was just such a stick as the old-fashioned family practitioner used to carry—dignified, solid, and reassuring.

"Well, Watson, what do you make of it?"

Holmes was sitting with his back to me, and I had given him no sign of my occupation.

"How did you know what I was doing? I believe you have eyes in the back of your head."

"I have, at least, a well-polished, silver-plated coffee-pot in front of me," said he. "But, tell me, Watson, what do you make of our visitor's stick? Since we have been so unfortunate as to miss him and have no notion of his errand, this accidental souvenir becomes of importance. Let me hear you reconstruct the man by an examination of it."

"I think," said I, following as far as I could the methods of my companion, "that Dr. Mortimer is a successful, elderly medical man, well-esteemed, since those who know him give him this mark of their appreciation."

"Good!" said Holmes. "Excellent!"

"I think also that the probability is in favour of his being a country practitioner who does a great deal of his visiting on foot."

"Why so?"

"Because this stick, though originally a very handsome one, has been so knocked about that I can hardly imagine a town practitioner carrying it. The thick iron ferrule is worn down, so it is evident that he has done a great amount of walking with it."

"Perfectly sound!" said Holmes.

"And then again, there is the 'friends of the C.C.H.' I should guess that to be the Something Hunt, the local hunt to whose members he has possibly given some surgical assistance, and which has made him a small presentation in return."

"Really, Watson, you excel yourself," said Holmes, pushing back his chair and lighting a cigarette. "I am bound to say that in all the accounts which you have been so good as to give of my own small achievements you have habitually underrated your own abilities. It may be that you are not yourself luminous, but you are a conductor of light. Some people without possessing genius have a remarkable power of stimulating it. I confess, my dear fellow, that I am very much in your debt."

He had never said as much before, and I must admit that his words gave me keen pleasure, for I had often been piqued by his indifference to my admiration and to the attempts which I had made to give publicity to his methods. I was proud, too, to think that I had so far mastered his system as to apply it in a way which earned his approval. He now took the stick from my hands and examined it for a few minutes with his naked eyes. Then with an expression of interest he laid down his cigarette, and, carrying the cane to the window, he looked over it again with a convex lens.

"Interesting, though elementary," said he as he returned to his favourite corner of the settee. "There are certainly one or two indications upon the stick. It gives us the basis for several deductions."

"Has anything escaped me?" I asked with some self-importance. "I trust that there is nothing of consequence which I have over looked?"

"I am afraid, my dear Watson, that most of your conclusions were erroneous. When I said that you stimulated me I meant, to be frank, that in noting your fallacies I was occasionally guided to wards the truth. Not that you are entirely wrong in this instance. The man is certainly a country practitioner. And he walks a good deal."

"Then I was right."

"To that extent."

"But that was all."

"No, no, my dear Watson, not all—by no means all. I would suggest, for example, that a presentation to a doctor is more likely to come from a hospital than from a hunt, and that when the initials 'C.C.' are placed before that hospital the words 'Charing Cross' very naturally suggest themselves."

"You may be right."

"The probability lies in that direction. And if we take this as a working hypothesis we have a fresh basis from which to start our construction of this unknown visitor."

"Well, then, supposing that 'C.C.H.' does stand for 'Charing Cross Hospital,' what further inferences may we draw?"

"Do none suggest themselves? You know my methods. Apply them!"

"I can only think of the obvious conclusion that the man has practised in town before going to the country."

"I think that we might venture a little farther than this. Look at it in this light. On what occasion would it be most probable that such a presentation would be made? When would his friends unite to give him a pledge of their good will? Obviously at the moment when Dr. Mortimer withdrew from the service of the hospital in order to start in practice for himself We know there has been a presentation. We believe there has been a change from a town hospital to a country practice. Is it, then, stretching our inference too far to say that the presentation was on the occasion of the change?"

"It certainly seems probable."

"Now, you will observe that he could not have been on the staff of the hospital, since only a man well-established in a London practice could hold such a position, and such a one would not drift into the country. What was he, then? If he was in the hospital and yet not on the staff he could only have been a house-surgeon or a house-physician—little more than a senior student. And he left five years ago—the date is on the stick. So your grave, middle-aged family practitioner vanishes into thin air, my dear Watson, and there emerges a young fellow under thirty, amiable, unambitious, absent-minded, and the possessor of a favourite dog, which I should describe roughly as being larger than a terrier and smaller than a mastiff"

I laughed incredulously as Sherlock Holmes leaned back in his settee and blew little wavering rings of smoke up to the ceiling.

"As to the latter part, I have no means of checking you," said I, "but at least it is not difficult to find out a few particulars about the man's age and professional career." From my small medical shelf I took down the Medical Directory and turned up the name. There were several Mortimers, but only one who could be our visitor. I read his record aloud.

"Mortimer, James, M.R.C.S., 1882, Grimpen, Dartmoor, Devon. House surgeon, from 1882 to 1884, at Charing Cross Hospital. Winner of the Jackson prize for Comparative Pathology, with essay entitled 'Is Disease a Reversion?' Corresponding member of the Swedish Pathological Society. Author of 'Some Freaks of Atavism' (Lancet, 1882). 'Do We Progress?', (Journal of Psychology, March, 1883).

Medical Officer for the parishes of Grimpen, Thorsley, and High Barrow."

"No mention of that local hunt, Watson," said Holmes with a mischievous smile, "but a country doctor, as you very astutely observed. I think that I am fairly justified in my inferences. As to the adjectives, I said, if I remember right, amiable, unambitious, and absent-minded. It is my experience that it is only an amiable man in this world who receives testimonials, only an unambitious one who abandons a London career for the country, and only an absent-minded one who leaves his stick and not his visiting-card after waiting an hour in your room."

"And the dog?"

"Has been in the habit of carrying this stick behind his master. Being a heavy stick the dog has held it tightly by the middle, and the marks of his teeth are very plainly visible. The dog's jaw, as shown in the space between these marks, is too broad in my opinion for a terrier and not broad enough for a mastiff. It may have been—yes, by-Jove, it is a curly-haired spaniel."

He had risen and paced the room as he spoke. Now he halted in the recess of the window. There was such a ring of conviction in his voice that I glanced up in surprise.

"My dear fellow, how can your possibly be so sure of that?"

"For the very simple reason that I see the dog himself on our very door-step, and there is the ring of its owner. Don't move, I beg you, Watson. He is a professional brother of yours, and your presence may be of assistance to me. Now is the dramatic moment of fate, Watson, when you hear a step upon the stair which is walking into your life, and you know not whether for good or ill. What does Dr.James Mortimer, the man of science, ask of Sherlock Holmes, the specialist in crime? Come in!"

The appearance of our visitor was a surprise to me, since I had expected a typical country practitioner. He was a very tall, thin man, with a long nose like a beak, which jutted out between two keen, gray eyes, set closely together and sparkling brightly from be hind a pair of gold-rimmed glasses. He was clad in a professional but rather slovenly fashion, for his frock-coat was dingy and his trousers frayed. Though young, his long back was already bowed, and he walked with a forward thrust of his head and a general air of peering benevolence. As he entered his eyes fell upon the stick in Holmes's hand, and he ran towards it with an exclamation of joy. "I am so very glad," said he. "I was not sure whether I had left it here or in the Shipping Office. I would not lose that stick for the world."

"A presentation, I see," said Holmes.

"Yes, sir."

"From Charing Cross Hospital?"

"From one or two friends there on the occasion of my marriage." "Dear, dear, that's bad!" said Holmes, shaking his head.

Dr. Mortimer blinked through his glasses in mild astonishment. "Why was it bad?"

"Only that you have disarranged our little deductions. Your marriage, you say?"

"Yes, sir. I married, and so left the hospital, and with it all hopes of a consulting practice. It was necessary to make a home of my own."

Come, come, we are not so far wrong, after all," said Holmes. "And now, Dr.James Mortimer

"Mister, sir, Mister—a humble M.RC.S."

"And a man of precise mind, evidently."

"A dabbler in science, Mr. Holmes, a picker up of shells on the shores of the great unknown ocean. I presume that it is Mr. Sherlock Holmes whom I am addressing and not—"

"No, this is my friend Dr. Watson."

"Glad to meet you, sir. I have heard your name mentioned in connection with that of your friend. You interest me very much, Mr. Holmes. I had hardly expected so dolichocephalic a skull or such well-marked supra-orbital development. Would you have any objection to my running my finger along your parietal fissure? A cast of your skull, sir, until the original is available, would be an ornament to any anthropological museum. It is not my intention to be fulsome, but I confess that I covet your skull."

Sherlock Holmes waved our strange visitor into a chair. "You are an enthusiast in your line of thought, I perceive, sir, as I am in mine," said he. "I observe from your forefinger that you make your own cigarettes. Have no hesitation in lighting one."

The man drew out paper and tobacco and twirled the one up in the other with surprising dexterity. He had long, quivering fingers as agile and restless as the antenna of an insect.

Holmes was silent, but his little darting glances showed me the interest which he took in our curious companion.

"I presume, sir," said he at last, "that it was not merely for the purpose of examining my skull that you have done me the honour to call here last night and again to-day.?"

"No, sir, no; though I am happy to have had the opportunity of doing that as well. I came to you, Mr. Holmes, because I recognized that I am myself an unpractical man and because I am suddenly confronted with a most serious and extraordinary problem. Recognizing, as I do, that you are the second highest expert in Europe

"Indeed, sir! May I inquire who has the honour to be the first?" asked Holmes with some asperity.

"To the man of precisely scientific mind the work of Monsieur Bertillon must always appeal strongly."

"Then had you not better consult him?"

"I said, sir, to the precisely scientific mind. But as a practical man of affairs it is acknowledged that you stand alone. I trust, sir, that I have not inadvertently—"

"Just a little," said Holmes. "I think, Dr. Mortimer, you would do wisely if without more ado you would kindly tell me plainly what the exact nature of the problem is in which you demand my assistance."

## Chapter 2

# THE CURSE OF THE BASKERVILLES

"I have in my pocket a manuscript," said Dr.James Mortimer.

"I observed it as you entered the room," said Holmes.

"It is an old manuscript."

"Early eighteenth century, unless it is a forgery."

"How can you say that, sir?"

"You have presented an inch or two of it to my examination all the time that you have been talking. It would be a poor expert who could not give the date of a document within a decade or so. You may possibly have read my little monograph upon the subject. I put that at 1730."

"The exact date is 1742." Dr. Mortimer drew it from his breast pocket. "This family paper was committed to my care by Sir Charles Baskerville, whose sudden and tragic death some three months ago created so much excitement in Devonshire. I may say that I was his personal friend as well as his medical attendant. He was a strong minded man, sir, shrewd, practical, and as unimaginative as I am myself Yet he took this document very seriously, and his mind was prepared for just such an end as did eventually overtake him."

Holmes stretched out his hand for the manuscript and flattened it upon his knee.

"You will observe, Watson, the alternative use of the long s and the short. It is one of several indications which enabled me to fix the date."

I looked over his shoulder at the yellow paper and the faded script. At the head was written: "Baskerville Hall," and below, in large, scrawling figures: "1742."

"It appears to be a statement of some sort."

"Yes, it is a statement of a certain legend which runs in the Baskerville family."

"But I understand that it is something more modern and practical upon which you wish to consult me?"

"Most modern. A most practical, pressing matter, which must be decided within twenty-four hours. But the manuscript is short and is intimately connected with the affair. With your permission I will read it to you."

Holmes leaned back in his chair, placed his finger-tips together, and closed his eyes, with an air of resignation. Dr. Mortimer turned the manuscript to the light and read in a high, cracking voice the following curious, old-world narrative:

"Of the origin of the Hound of the Baskervilles there have been many statements, yet as I come in a direct line from Hugo Baskerville, and as I had the story from my father, who also had it from his, I have set it down with all belief that it occurred even as is here set forth. And I would have you believe, my sons, that the same Justice which punishes sin may also most graciously forgive it, and that no ban is so heavy but that by prayer and repentance it may be removed. Learn then from this story not to fear the fruits of the past, but rather to be circumspect in the future, that those foul passions whereby our family has suffered so grievously may not again be loosed to our undoing.

"Know then that in the time of the Great Rebellion (the his tory of which by the learned Lord Clarendon I most earnestly commend to your attention) this Manor of Baskerville was held by Hugo of that name, nor can it be gainsaid that he was a most wild, profane, and godless man. This, in truth, his neighbours might have pardoned, seeing that saints have never flourished in those parts, but there was in him a certain wanton and cruel humour which made his name a byword through the West. It chanced that this Hugo came to love (if, indeed, so dark a passion may be known under so bright a name) the daughter of a yeoman who held lands near the Baskerville estate. But the young maiden, being discreet and of good repute, would ever avoid him, for she feared his evil name. So it came to pass that one Michaelmas this Hugo, with five or six of his idle and wicked companions, stole down upon the farm and carried off the maiden, her father and brothers being from home, as he well knew. When they had brought her to the Hall the maiden was placed in an upper chamber, while Hugo and his friends sat down to a long carouse, as was their nightly custom. Now, the poor lass upstairs was like to have her wits turned at the singing and shouting and terrible oaths which came up to her from below, for they say that the words used by Hugo Baskerville, when he was in wine, were such as might blast the man who said them. At last in the stress of her fear she did that which might have daunted the bravest or most active man, for by the aid of the growth of ivy which covered (and still covers) the south wall she came down from under the eaves, and so homeward across the moor, there being three leagues betwixt the Hall and her father's farm.

"It chanced that some little time later Hugo left his guests to carry food and drink—with other worse things, perchance— to his captive, and so found the cage empty and the bird escaped. Then, as it would seem, he became as one that hath a devil, for, rushing down the stairs into the dining-hall, he sprang upon the great table, flagons and trenchers flying be fore him, and he cried aloud before all the company that he would that very night render his body and soul to the Powers of Evil if he might but overtake the wench. And while the revellers stood aghast at the fury of the man, one more wicked or, it may be, more drunken than the rest, cried out that they should put the hounds upon her. Whereat Hugo ran from the house, crying to his grooms that they should saddle his mare and unkennel the pack, and giving the hounds a kerchief of the maid's, he swung them to the line, and so off full cry in the moonlight over the moor.

"Now, for some space the revellers stood agape, unable to understand all that had been done in such haste. But anon their bemused wits awoke to the nature of the deed which was like to be done upon the moorlands. Everything was now in a uproar, some calling for their pistols, some for their horses, and some for another flask of wine. But at length some sense came back to their crazed minds, and the whole of them, thirteen in number, took horse and started in pursuit. The moon shone clear above them, and they rode swiftly abreast, taking that course which the maid must needs have taken if she were to reach her own home.

"They had gone a mile or two when they passed one of the night shepherds upon the moorlands, and they cried to him to know if he had seen the hunt. And the man, as the story goes, was so crazed with fear that he could scarce speak, but at last he said that he had indeed seen the unhappy maiden, with the hounds upon her track. 'But I have seen more than that,' said he, 'for Hugo Baskerville passed me upon his black mare, and there ran mute behind him such a hound of hell as God forbid should ever be at my heels.' So the drunken squires cursed the shepherd and rode onward. But soon their skins turned cold, for there came a galloping across the moor, and the black mare, dabbled with white froth, went past with trailing bridle and empty saddle. Then the revellers rode close together, for a great fear was on them, but they still followed over the moor, though each, had he been alone, would have been right glad to have turned his horse's head. Riding slowly in this fashion they came at last upon the hounds. These, though known for their valour and their breed, were whimpering in a cluster at the head of a deep dip or goyal, as we call it, upon the moor, some slinking away and some, with starting hackles and staring eyes, gazing down the narrow valley be fore them.

"The company had come to a halt, more sober men, as you may guess, than when they started. The most of them would by no means advance, but three of them, the boldest, or it may be the most drunken, rode forward down the goyal. Now, it opened into a broad space in which stood two of those great stones, still to be seen there, which were set by certain forgot ten peoples in the days of old. The moon was shining bright upon the clearing, and there in the centre lay the unhappy maid where she had fallen, dead of fear and of fatigue. But it was not the sight of her body, nor yet was it that of the body of Hugo Baskerville Iying near her, which raised the hair upon the heads of these three dare-devil roisterers, but it was that, standing over Hugo, and plucking at his throat, there stood a foul thing, a great, black beast, shaped like a hound, yet larger than any hound that ever mortal eye has rested upon. And even as they looked the thing tore the throat out of Hugo Baskerville, on which, as it turned its blazing eyes and drip ping jaws upon them, the three shrieked with fear and rode for dear life, still screaming, across the moor. One, it is said, died that very night of what he had seen, and the other twain were but broken men for the rest of their days.

"Such is the tale, my sons, of the coming of the hound which is said to have plagued the family so sorely ever since. If I have set it down it is because that which is clearly known hath less terror than that which is but hinted at and guessed. Nor can it be denied that many of the family have been unhappy in their deaths, which have been sudden, bloody, and mysterious. Yet may we shelter ourselves in the infinite goodness of Providence, which would not forever punish the innocent beyond that third or fourth generation which is threatened in Holy Writ. To that Providence, my sons, I hereby commend you, and I counsel you by way of caution to forbear from crossing the moor in those dark hours when the powers of evil are exalted.

"This from Hugo Baskerville to his sons Rodger and John, with instructions that they say nothing thereof to their sister Elizabeth."

When Dr. Mortimer had finished reading this singular narrative he pushed his spectacles up on his forehead and stared across at Mr. Sherlock Holmes. The latter yawned and tossed the end of his cigarette into the fire.

"Well?" said he.

"Do you not find it interesting?"

"To a collector of fairy tales."

Dr. Mortimer drew a folded newspaper out of his pocket.

"Now, Mr. Holmes, we will give you something a little more re cent. This is the Devon County Chronicle of May 14th of this year. It is a short account of the facts elicited at the death of Sir Charles Baskerville which occurred a few days before that date."

My friend leaned a little forward and his expression became in tent. Our visitor readjusted his glasses and began:

"The recent sudden death of Sir Charles Baskerville, whose name has been mentioned as the probable Liberal candidate for Mid-Devon at the next election, has cast a gloom over the county. Though Sir Charles had resided at Baskerville Hall for a comparatively short period his amiability of character and extreme generosity had won the affection and respect of all who had been brought into contact with him. In these days of *nouveaux riches* it is refreshing to find a case where the scion of an old county family which has fallen upon evil days is able to make his own fortune and to bring it back with him to restore the fallen grandeur of his line. Sir Charles, as is well known, made large sums of money in South African speculation. More wise than those who go on until the wheel turns against them, he realized his gains and returned to England with them. It is only two years since he took up his residence at Baskerville Hall, and it is common talk how large were those schemes of reconstruction and improvement which have been interrupted by his death. Being himself childless, it was his openly expressed desire that the whole countryside should, within his own lifetime, profit by his good fortune, and many will have personal reasons for bewailing his un timely end. His generous donations to local and county charities have been frequently chronicled in these columns.

"The circumstances connected with the death of Sir Charles cannot be said to have been entirely cleared up by the inquest, but at least enough has been done to dispose of those rumours to which local superstition has given rise. There is no reason whatever to suspect foul play, or to imagine that death could be from any but natural causes. Sir Charles was a widower, and a man who may be said to have been in some ways of an eccentric habit of mind. In spite of his considerable wealth he was simple in his personal tastes, and his indoor servants at Baskerville Hall consisted of a married couple named Barrymore, the husband acting as butler and the wife as housekeeper. Their evidence, corroborated by that of several friends, tends to show that Sir Charles's health has for some time been impaired, and points especially to some affec tion of the heart, manifesting itself in changes of colour, breathlessness, and acute attacks of nervous depression. Dr.James Mortimer, the friend and medical attendant of the deceased, has given evidence to the same effect.

"The facts of the case are simple. Sir Charles Baskerville was in the habit every night before going to bed of walking down the famous yew alley of Baskerville Hall. The evidence of the Barrymores shows that this had been his custom. On the fourth of May Sir Charles had declared his intention of starting next day for London, and had ordered Barrymore to prepare his luggage. That night he went out as usual for his nocturnal walk in the course of which he was in the habit of smoking a cigar. He never returned. At twelve o'clock Barry more, finding the hall door still open, became alarmed, and, lighting a lantern, went in search of his master. The day had been wet, and Sir Charles's footmarks were easily traced down the alley. Halfway down this walk there is a gate which leads out on to the moor. There were indications that sir Charles had stood for some little time here. He then proceeded down the alley, and it was at the far end of it that his body was discovered. One fact which has not been explained is the statement of Barrymore that his master's footprints altered their character from the time that he passed the moor gate, and that he appeared from thence onward to have been walking upon his toes. One Murphy, a gypsy horsedealer, was on the moor at no great distance at the time, but he appears by his own confession to have been the worse for drink. He declares that he heard cries but is unable to state from what direction they came. No signs of violence were to be discovered upon sir Charles's person, and though the doctor's evidence pointed to an almost incredible facial distortion—so great that Dr. Mortimer refused at first to believe that it was indeed his friend and patient who lay before him—it was explained that that is a symptom Which is not unusual in cases of dyspnœa and death from cardiac exhaustion. This explana- tion was borne out by the post-mortem examination, which showed long-standing organic disease, and the coroner's jury returned a verdict in accordance With the medical evidence. It is well that this is so, for it is obviously of the utmost importance that Sir Charles's heir should settle at the Hall and continue the good work which has been so sadly interrupted. Had the prosaic finding of the coroner not finally put an end to the romantic stories which have been whispered in connection with the affair, it might have been difficult to find a tenant for Baskerville Hall. It is understood that the next of kin is Mr. Henry Baskerville, if he be still alive, the son of sir Charles Baskerville's younger brother. The young man when last heard of was in America, and inquiries are being instituted with a view to informing him of his good fortune."

Dr. Mortimer refolded his paper and replaced it in his pocket. "Those are the public facts, Mr. Holmes, in connection with the death of sir Charles Baskerville."

"I must thank you," said Sherlock Holmes, "for calling my attention to a case which certainly presents some features of interest. I had observed some newspaper comment at the time, but I was exceedingly preoccupied by that little affair of the Vatican cameos, and in my anxiety to oblige the Pope I lost touch with several interesting English cases. This article, you say, contains all the public facts?"

"It does." "Then let me have the private ones." He leaned back, put his finger-tips together, and assumed his most impassive and judicial expression.

"In doing so," said Dr. Mortimer, who had begun to show signs of some strong emotion, "I am telling that which I have not confided to anyone. My motive for withholding it from the coroner's inquiry is that a man of Science shrinks from placing himself in the public position of seeming to endorse a popular superstition. I had the further motive that Baskerville Hall, as the paper says, would certainly remain untenanted if anything were done to increase its al ready rather grim reputation. For both these reasons I thought that I was justified in telling rather less than I knew, since no practical good could result from it, but with you there is no reason why I should not be perfectly frank.

"The moor is very sparsely inhabited, and those who live near each other are thrown very much together. For this reason I saw a good deal of Sir Charles Baskerville. With the exception of Mr. Frankland, of Lafter Hall, and Mr. Stapleton, the naturalist, there are no other men of education within many miles. Sir Charles was a retiring man, but the chance of his illness brought us together, and a community of interests in science kept us so. He had brought back much scientific information from South Africa, and many a charming evening we have spent together discussing the comparative anatomy of the Bushman and the Hottentot.

"Within the last few months it became increasingly plain to me that Sir Charles's nervous system was strained to the breaking point. He had taken this legend which I have read you exceedingly to heart—so much so that, although he would walk in his own grounds, nothing would induce him to go out upon the moor at night. Incredible as it may appear to you, Mr. Holmes, he was honestly convinced that a dreadful fate overhung his family, and cer tainly the records which he was able to give of his ancestors were not encouraging. The idea of some ghastly presence constantly haunted him, and on more than one occasion he has asked me whether I had on my medical journeys at night ever seen any strange creature or heard the baying of a hound. The latter question he put to me several times, and always with a voice which vibrated with excitement.

"I can well remember driving up to his house in the evening, some three weeks before the fatal event. He chanced to be at his hall door. I had descended from my gig and was standing in front of him, when I saw his eyes fix themselves over my shoulder and stare past me with an expression of the most dreadful horror. I whisked round and had just time to catch a glimpse of something which I took to be a large black calf passing at the head of the drive. So excited and alarmed was he that I was compelled to go down to the spot where the animal had been and look around for it. It was gone, however, and the incident appeared to make the worst impression upon his mind. I stayed with him all the evening, and it was on that occasion, to explain the emotion which he had shown, that he confided to my keeping that narrative which I read to you when first I came. I mention this small episode because it assumes some importance in view of the tragedy which followed, but I was convinced at the time that the matter was entirely trivial and that his excitement had no justification.

"It was at my advice that Sir Charles was about to go to London. His heart was, I knew, affected, and the constant anxiety in which he lived, however chimerical the cause of it might be, was evidently having a serious effect upon his health. I thought that a few months among the distractions of town would send him back a new man. Mr. Stapleton, a mutual friend who was much concerned at his state of health, was of the same opinion. At the last instant came this terrible catastrophe.

"On the night of Sir Charles's death Barrymore the butler, who made the discovery, sent Perkins the groom on horseback to me, and as I was sitting up late I was able to reach Baskerville Hall within an hour of the event. I checked and corroborated all the facts which were mentioned at the inquest. I followed the footsteps down the yew alley, I saw the spot at the moor-gate where he seemed to have waited, I remarked the change in the shape of the prints after that point, I noted that there were no other footsteps save those of Barrymore on the soft gravel, and finally I carefully examined the body, which had not been touched until my arrival. Sir Charles lay on his face, his arms out, his fingers dug into the ground, and his features convulsed with some strong emotion to such an extent that I could hardly have sworn to his identity. There was certainly no physical injury of any kind. But one false statement was made by Barrymore at the inquest. He said that there were no traces upon the ground round the body. He did not ob serve any. But I did—some little distance off, but fresh and clear."

"Footprints?"

"Footprints." "A man's or a woman's.?"

Dr. Mortimer looked strangely at us for an instant, and his voice sank almost to a whisper as he answered:

"Mr. Holmes, they were the footprints of a gigantic.hound!"

## CHAPTER 3

# THE PROBLEM

I confess that at these words a shudder passed through me. There was a thrill in the doctor's voice which showed that he was himself deeply moved by that which he told us. Holmes leaned forward in his excitement and his eyes had the hard, dry glitter which shot from them when he was keenly interested.

"You saw this?"

"As clearly as I see you."

"And you said nothing?"

"What was the use?"

"How was it that no one else saw it?"

"The marks were some twenty yards from the body and no one gave them a thought. I don't suppose I should have done so had I not known this legend."

"There are many sheep-dogs on the moor?"

"No doubt, but this was no sheep-dog."

"You say it was large?"

"Enormous."

"But it had not approached the body?"

"No."

"What sort of night was it?"

"Damp and raw."

"But not actually raining?"

"No."

"What is the alley like?"

"There are two lines of old yew hedge, twelve feet high and im penetrable. The walk in the centre is about eight feet across."

"Is there anything between the hedges and the walk?"

"Yes, there is a strip of grass about six feet broad on either side." "I understand that the yew hedge is penetrated at one point by a

"Yes, the wicket-gate which leads on to the moor."

"Is there any other opening?"

"None."

"So that to reach the yew alley one either has to come down it from the house or else to enter it by the moor-gate.?"

"There is an exit through a summer-house at the far end." "Had Sir Charles reached this.?" "No; he lay about fifty yards from it"

"Now, tell me, Dr. Mortimer—and this is important—the marks which you saw were on the path and not on the grass?"

"No marks could show on the grass."

"Were they on the same side of the path as the moor-gate?"

"Yes; they were on the edge of the path on the same side as the moor-gate."

"You interest me exceedingly. Another point. Was the wicket gate closed?"

"Closed and padlocked."

"How high was it?"

"About four feet high."

"Then anyone could have got over it?"

"Yes."

"And what marks did you see by the wicket-gate?"

"None in particular."

"Good heaven! Did no one examine?"

"Yes, I examined, myself"

"And found nothing?"

"It was all very confused. Sir Charles had evidently stood there for five or ten minutes."

"How do you know that?"

"Because the ash had twice dropped from his cigar."

"Excellent! This is a colleague, Watson, after our own heart. But the marks?"

"He had left his own marks all over that small patch of gravel. I could discern no others."

Sherlock Holmes struck his hand against his knee with an impatient gesture.

"If I had only been there!" he cried. "It is evidently a case of extraordinary interest, and one which presented immense opportunities to the scientific expert. That gravel page upon which I might have read so much has been long ere this smudged by the rain and defaced by the clogs of curious peasants. Oh, Dr. Mortimer, Dr. Mortimer, to think that you should not have called me in! You have indeed much to answer for."

"I could not call you in, Mr. Holmes, without disclosing these facts to the world, and I have already given my reasons for not wishing to do so. Besides, besides—"

"Why do you hesitate?"

here is a realm in which the most acute and most experienced of detectives is helpless."

"You mean that the thing is supernatural?"

"I did not positively say so."

"No, but you evidently think it."

"Since the tragedy, Mr. Holmes, there have come to my ears several incidents which are hard to reconcile with the settled order of Nature."

"For example?"

"I find that before the terrible event occurred several people had seen a creature upon the moor which corresponds with this Baskerville demon, and which could not possibly be any animal known to science. They all agreed that it was a huge creature, luminous, ghastly, and spectral. I have cross-examined these men, one of them a hard-headed countryman, one a farrier, and one a moor land farmer, who all tell the same story of this dreadful apparition, exactly corresponding to the hell-hound of the legend. I assure you that there is a reign of terror in the district, and that it is a hardy man who will cross the moor at night."

"And you, a trained man of science, believe it to be super natural?"

"I do not know what to believe."

Holmes shrugged his shoulders.

"I have hitherto confined my investigations to this world," said he. "In a modest way I have combated evil, but to take on the Father of Evil himself would, perhaps, be too ambitious a task. Yet you must admit that the footmark is material."

"The original hound was material enough to tug a man's throat out, and yet he was diabolical as well."

"I see that you have quite gone over to the supernaturalists. But now, Dr. Mortimer, tell me this. If you hold these views, why have you come to consult me at all? You tell me in the same breath that it is useless to investigate Sir Charles's death, and that you desire me to do it n

"I did not say that I desired you to do it."

"Then, how can I assist you?"

"By advising me as to what I should do with Sir Henry Baskerville, who arrives at Waterloo Station" —Dr. Mortimer looked at his watch— in exactly one hour and a quarter."

"He being the heir?

"Yes. On the death of Sir Charles we inquired for this young gentleman and found that he had been farming in

Canada. From the accounts which have reached us he is an excellent fellow in every way. I speak now not as a medical man but as a trustee and executor of Sir Charles's will."

"There is no other claimant, I presume?":

"None. The only other kinsman whom we have been able to trace was Rodger Baskerville, the youngest of three brothers of whom poor Sir Charles was the elder. The second brother, who died young, is the father of this lad Henry. The third, Rodger, was the black sheep of the family. He came of the old masterful Baskerville strain and was the very image, they tell me, of the family picture of old Hugo. He made England too hot to hold him. fled to Central America, and died there in 1876 of yellow fever. Henry is the last of the Baskervilles. In one hour and five minutes I meet him at Waterloo Station. I have had a wire that he arrived at Southampton this morning. Now, Mr. Holmes, what would you advise me to do with him?"

"Why should he not go to the home of his fathers?"

"It seems natural, does it not? And yet, consider that every Baskerville who goes there meets with an evil fate. I feel sure that if Sir Charles could have spoken with me before his death he would have warned me against bringing this, the last of the old race, and the heir to great wealth, to that deadly place. And yet it cannot be denied that the prosperity of the whole poor, bleak countryside depends upon his presence. All the good work which has been done by Sir Charles will crash to the ground if there is no tenant of the Hall. I fear lest I should be swayed too much by my own obvious interest in the matter, and that is why I bring the case before you and ask for your advice."

Holmes considered for a little time.

"Put into plain words, the matter is this," said he. "In your opin ion there is a diabolical agency which makes Dartmoor an unsafe abode for a Baskerville—that is your opinion?"

"At least I might go the length of saying that there is some evidence that this may be so."

"Exactly. But surely, if your supernatural theory be correct, it could work the young man evil in London as easily as in Devon shire. A devil with merely local powers like a parish vestry would be too inconceivable a thing."

"You put the matter more flippantly, Mr. Holmes, than you would probably do if you were brought into personal contact with these things. Your advice, then, as I understand it, is that the young man will be as safe in Devonshire as in London. He comes in fifty minutes. What would you recommend?"

"I recommend, sir, that you take a cab, call off your spaniel who is scratching at my front door, and proceed to Waterloo to meet Sir Henry Baskerville."

"And then?"

"And then you will say nothing to him at all until I have made up my mind about the matter."

"How long will it take you to make up your mind?"

'Twenty-four hours. At ten o'clock to-morrow, Dr. Mortimer, I will be much obliged to you if you will call upon me here, and it will be of help to me in my plans for the future if you will bring Sir Henry Baskerville with you."

"I will do so, Mr. Holmes." He scribbled the appointment on his shirt-cuff and hurried off in his strange, peering, absent-minded fashion. Holmes stopped him at the head of the stair.

"Only one more question, Dr. Mortimer. You say that before Sir Charles Baskerville's death several people saw this apparition upon the moor.?"

"Three people did."

"Did any see it after?"

"I have not heard of any."

"Thank you. Good-morning."

Holmes returned to his seat with that quiet look of inward satisfaction which meant that he had a congenial task before him.

"Going out, Watson?"

"Unless I can help you."

"No, my dear fellow, it is at the hour of action that I turn to you for aid. But this is splendid, really unique from some points of view. When you pass Bradley's, would you ask him to send up a pound of the strongest shag tobacco Thank you. It would be as well if you could make it convenient not to return before evening. Then I should be very glad to compare impressions as to this most inter esting problem which has been submitted to us this morning."

I knew that seclusion and solitude were very necessary for my friend in those hours of intense mental concentration during which he weighed every particle of evidence, constructed alternative theories, balanced one against the other, and made up his mind as to which points were essential and which immaterial. I therefore spent the day at my club and did not return to Baker Street until evening. It was nearly nine o'clock when I found myself in the sitting-room once more.

My first impression as I opened the door was that a fire had broken out, for the room was so filled with smoke that the light of the lamp upon the table was blurred by it. As I entered, however, my fears were set at rest, for it was the acrid fumes of strong coarse tobacco which took me by the throat and set me coughing. Through the haze I had a vague vision of Holmes in his dressing-gown coiled up in an armchair with his black clay pipe between his lips. Several rolls of paper lay around him.

"Caught cold, Watson?" said he.

No, it's this poisonous atmosphere."

"I suppose it is pretty thick, now that you mention it."

"Thick! It is intolerable."

"Open the window, then! You have been at your club all day, I perceive."

"My dear Holmes!"

"Am I right?"

"Certainly, but how—?"

He laughed at my bewildered expression.

"There is a delightful freshness about you, Watson, which makes it a pleasure to exercise any small powers which I posses at your expense. A gentleman goes forth on a showery and miry day. He returns immaculate in the evening with the gloss still on his hat and his boots. He has been a fixture therefore all day. He is not a man with intimate friends. Where, then, could he have been? Is it not obvious?"

"Well, it is rather obvious."

"The world is full of obvious things which nobody by any chance ever observes. Where do you think that I have been?"

"A fixture also."

"On the contrary, I have been to Devonshire."

"In spirit?"

"Exactly. My body has remained in this armchair and has, I regret to observe, consumed in my absence two large pots of coffee and an incredible amount of tobacco. After you left I sent down to Stamford's for the Ordnance map of this portion of the moor, and my spirit has hovered over it all day. I flatter myself that I could find my way about."

"Large-scale map, I presume?"

"Very large." He unrolled one section and held it over his knee. "Here you have the particular district which concerns us. That is Baskerville Hall in the middle."

"With a wood round it?"

"Exactly. I fancy the yew alley, though not marked under that name, must stretch along this line, with the moor, as you perceive, upon the right of it. This small clump of buildings here is the ham let of Grimpen, where our friend Dr. Mortimer has his head quarters. Within a radius of five miles there are, as you see, only a very few scattered dwellings. Here is Lafter Hall, which was mentioned in the narrative. There is a house indicated here which may be the residence of the naturalist—Stapleton, if I remember right, was his name. Here are two Moreland farmhouses, High Tor and Foulmire. Then fourteen miles away the great convict prison of Princetown. Between and around these scattered points extends the desolate, lifeless moor. This, then, is the stage upon which tragedy has been played, and upon which we may help to play it again."

"It must be a wild place."

"Yes, the setting is a worthy one. If the devil did desire to have a hand in the affairs of men—"

"Then you are yourself inclining to the supernatural explanation."

"The devil's agents may be of flesh and blood, may they not? There are two questions waiting for us at the outset. The one is whether any crime has been committed at all; the second is, what is the crime and how was it committed? Of course, if Dr. Mortimer's surmise should be correct, and we are dealing with forces outside the ordinary laws of Nature, there is an end of our investigation. But we are bound to exhaust all other hypotheses before falling back upon this one. I think we'll shut that window again, if you don't mind. It is a singular thing, but I find that a concentrated atmosphere helps a concentration of thought. I have not pushed it to the length of getting into a box to think, but that is the logical out come of my convictions. Have you turned the case over in your mind.?"

"Yes, I have thought a good deal of it in the course of the day."

"What do you make of it?"

"It is very bewildering."

"It has certainly a character of its own. There are points of distinction about it. That change in the footprints, for example. What do you make of that?"

"Mortimer said that the man had walked on tiptoe down that portion of the alley."

"He only repeated what some fool had said at the inquest. Why should a man walk on tiptoe down the alley?"

"What then?"

"He was running, Watson—running desperately, running for his life, running until he burst his heart and fell dead upon his face."

"Running from what?"

"There lies our problem. There are indications that the man was crazed with fear before ever he began to run."

"How can you say that?"

"I am presuming that the cause of his fears came to him across the moor. If that were so, and it seems most probable, only a man who had lost his wits would have run.7m the house instead of towards it. If the gypsy evidence may be taken as true, he ran with cries for help in the direction where help was least likely to be. Then, again, whom was he waiting for that night, and why was he waiting for him in the yew alley rather than in his own house?"

"You think that he was waiting for someone?"

"The man was elderly and infirm. We can understand his taking an evening stroll, but the ground was damp and the night inclement. Is it natural that he should stand for five or ten minutes, as Dr. Mortimer, with more practical sense than I should have given him credit for, deduced from the cigar ash?"

"But he went out every evening."

"I think it unlikely that he waited at the moor-gate every evening. On the contrary, the evidence is that he avoided the moor. That night he waited there. It was the night before he made his departure for London. The thing takes shape, Watson. It becomes coherent. Might I ask you to hand me my violin, and we will postpone all further thought upon this business until we have had the advantage of meeting Dr. Mortimer and Sir Henry Baskerville in the morning."

## CHAPTER 4

# SIR HENRY BASKERVILLE

Our breakfast table was cleared early, and Holmes waited in his dressing-gown for the promised interview. Our clients were punctual to their appointment, for the clock had just struck ten when Dr. Mortimer was shown up, followed by the young baronet. The latter was a small, alert, dark-eyed man about thirty years of age, very sturdily built, with thick black eyebrows and a strong, pugnacious face. He wore a ruddy-tinted tweed suit and had the weather beaten appearance of one who has spent most of his time in the open air, and yet there was something in his steady eye and the quiet assurance of his bearing which indicated the gentleman.

"This is Sir Henry Baskerville," said Dr. Mortimer.

"Why, yes," said he, "and the strange thing is, Mr. Sherlock Holmes, that if my friend here had not proposed coming round to you this morning I should have come on my own account. I under stand that you think out little puzzles, and I've had one this morn ing which wants more thinking out than I am able to give it."

"Pray take a seat, Sir Henry. Do I understand you to say that you have yourself had some remarkable experience since you arrived in London?"

"Nothing of much importance, Mr. Holmes. Only a joke, as like as not. It was this letter, if you can call it a letter, which reached me this morning."

He laid an envelope upon the table, and we all bent over it. It was of common quality, greyish in colour. The address, "Sir Henry Baskerville, Northumberland Hotel," was printed in rough characters; the post-mark "Charing Cross", and the date of posting the preceding evening.

"Who knew that you were going to the Northumberland Hotel?" asked Holmes, glancing keenly across at our visitor.

"No one could have known. We only decided after I met Dr. Mortimer."

"But Dr. Mortimer was no doubt already stopping there?"

"No, I had been staying with a friend," said the doctor. "There was no possible indication that we intended to go to this hotel."

"Hum! Someone seems to be very deeply interested in your movements." Out of the envelope he took a half-sheet of foolscap paper folded into four. This he opened and spread flat upon the table. Across the middle of it a single sentence had been formed by the expedient of pasting printed words upon it. It ran:

> As you value your life or your reason keep away from the moor.

The word "moor" only was printed in ink.

"Now," said Sir Henry Baskerville, "perhaps you will tell me, Mr. Holmes, what in thunder is the meaning of that, and who it is that takes so much interest in my affairs?"

"What do you make of it, Dr. Mortimer? You must allow that there is nothing supernatural about this, at any rate?"

"No, sir, but it might very well come from someone who was convinced that the business is supernatural."

What business?" asked Sir Henry sharply. "It seems to me that all you gentlemen know a great deal more than I do about my own affairs."

"You shall share our knowledge before you leave this room, Sir Henry. I promise you that," said Sherlock Holmes. "We will confine ourselves for the present with your permission to this very interesting document, which must have been put together and posted yesterday evening. Have you yesterday's Times, Watson?"

"It is here in the corner."

"Might I trouble you for it—the inside page, please, with the leading articles?" He glanced swiftly over it, running his eyes up and down the columns. "Capital article this on free trade. Permit me to give you an extract from it.

"You may be cajoled into imagining that your own special trade or your own industry will be encouraged by a protective tariff, but it stands to reason that such legislation must in the long run keep away wealth from the country, diminish the value of our imports, and lower the general conditions of life in this island.

What do you think of that, Watson?" cried Holmes in high glee, rubbing his hands together with satisfaction. "Don't you think that is an admirable sentiment?"

Dr. Mortimer looked at Holmes with an air of professional interest, and Sir Henry Baskerville turned a pair of puzzled dark eyes upon me.

"I don't know much about the tariff and things of that kind," said he, "but it seems to me we've got a bit off the trail so far as that note is concerned."

"On the contrary, I think we are particularly hot upon the trail, Sir Henry. Watson here knows more about my methods than you do, but I fear that even he has not quite grasped the significance of this sentence."

"No, I confess that I see no connection."

"And yet, my dear Watson, there is so very close a connection that the one is extracted out of the other. 'You,' 'your,' 'your', 'life,' 'reason,' 'value,' 'keep away,' 'from the.' Don't you see now whence these words have been taken?"

"By thunder, you're right! Well, if that isn't smart!" cried Sir Henry.

"If any possible doubt remained it is settled by the fact that 'keep away' and 'from the' are cut out in one piece."

"Well, now—so it is!"

"Really, Mr. Holmes, this exceeds anything which I could have imagined," said Dr. Mortimer, gazing at my friend in amazement. "I could understand anyone saying that the words were from a newspaper; but that you should name which, and add that it came from the leading article, is really one of the most remarkable things which I have ever known. How did you do it?"

"I presume, Doctor, that you could tell the skull of a Negro from that of an Esquimau?"

"Most certainly."

"But how?"

"Because that is my special hobby. The differences are obvious. The supra-orbital crest, the facial angle, the maxillary curve, the—"

"But this is my special hobby, and the differences are equally obvious. There is as much difference to my eyes between the leaded bourgeois type of a Times article and the slovenly print of an even ing half-penny paper as there could be between your Negro and your Esquimau. The detection of types is one of the most elementary branches of knowledge to the special expert in crime, though I confess that once when I was very young I confused the *Leeds Mercury* with the Western Morning News But a Times leader is entirely distinctive, and these words could have been taken from nothing else. As it was done yesterday the strong probability was that we should find the words in yesterday's issue."

"So far as I can follow you, then, Mr. Holmes," said Sir Henry Baskerville, "someone cut out this message with a scissor—"

"Nail-scissors," said Holmes. "You can see that it was a very short-bladed scissors, since the cutter had to take two snips over 'keep away.'

"That is so. Someone, then, cut out the message with a pair of short-bladed scissors, pasted it with paste—"

"Gum," said Holmes.

"With gum on to the paper. But I want to know why the word 'moor' should have been written?"

"Because he could not find it in print. The other words were all simple and might be found in any issue, but 'moor' would be less common."

"Why, of course, that would explain it. Have you read anything else in this message, Mr. Holmes?"

"There are one or two indications, and yet the utmost pains have been taken to remove all clues. The address, you observe, is printed in rough characters. But the Times is a paper which is seldom found in any hands but those of the highly educated. We may take it, therefore, that the letter was composed by an educated man who wished to pose as an uneducated one, and his effort to conceal his own writing suggests that that writing might be known, or come to be known, by you. Again, you will observe that the words are not gummed on in an accurate line, but that some are much higher than others. 'Life,' for example, is quite out of its proper place. That may point to carelessness or it may point to agitation and hurry upon the part of the cutter. On the whole I incline to the latter view, since the matter was evidently important, and it is unlikely that the composer of such a letter would be careless. If he were in a hurry it opens up the interesting question why he should be in a hurry, since any letter posted up to early morning would reach Sir Henry before he would leave his hotel. Did the composer fear an interruption—and from whom?"

"We are coming now rather into the region of guesswork," said Dr. Mortimer!

"Say, rather; into the region where we balance probabilities and choose the most likely. It is the scientific use of the imagination, but we have always some material basis on which to start our speculation. Now, you would call it a guess, no doubt, but I am almost certain that this address has been written in a hotel."

"How in the world can you say that?"

"If you examine it carefully you will see that both the pen and the ink have given the writer trouble. The pen has spluttered twice in a single word and has run dry three times in a short address, showing that there was very little ink in the bottle. Now, a private pen or ink-bottle is seldom allowed to be in Such a state, and the combination of the two must be quite rare. But you know the hotel ink and the hotel pen, where it is rare to get anything else. Yes, I have very little hesitation in saying that could we examine the waste-paper baskets of the hotels around Charing Cross until we found the remains of the mutilated Times leader we could lay our hands straight upon the person who sent this singular message. Hello! Hello! What's this?"

He was carefully examining the foolscap, upon which the words were pasted, holding it only an inch or two from his eyes.

"Well?"

Nothing," said he, throwing it down. "It is a blank half-sheet of paper, without even a water-mark upon it. I think we have drawn as much as we can from this curious letter; and now, sir Henry, has anything else of interest happened to you since you have been in London?"

"Why, no, Mr. Holmes. I think not."

"You have not observed anyone follow or watch you?"

"I seem to have walked right into the thick of a dime novel," said our visitor. "Why in thunder should anyone follow or watch me?"

"We are coming to that. You have nothing else to report to us before we go into this matter?"

"Well, it depends upon what you think worth reporting."

"I think anything out of the ordinary routine of life well worth reporting."

Sir Henry smiled.

"I don't know much of British life yet, for I have spent nearly all my time in the States and in Canada. But I hope that to lose one of your boots in not part of the ordinary routine of life over here."

"You have lost one of your boots?"

"My dear sir," cried Dr. Mortimer, "it is only mislaid. You will find it when you return to the hotel. What is the use of troubling Mr. Holmes with trifles of this kind?"

"Well, he asked me for anything outside the ordinary routine."

"Exactly," said Holmes, "however foolish the incident may seem. You have lost one of your boots, you say?"

"Well, mislaid it, anyhow. I put them both outside my door last night, and there was only one in the morning. I could get no sense out of the chap who cleans them. The worst of it is that I only bought the pair last night in the Strand, and I have never had them on."

"If you have never worn them, why did you put them out to be cleaned.?"

"They were tan boots and had never been varnished. That was why I put them out."

"Then I understand that on your arrival in London yesterday you went out at once and bought a pair of boots.?"

"I did a good deal of shopping. Dr. Mortimer here went round with me. You see, if I am to be squire down there I must dress the part, and it may be that I have got a little careless in my ways out West. Among other things I bought these brown boots—gave six dollars for them—and had one stolen before ever I had them on my feet."

"It seems a singularly useless thing to steal," said Sherlock Holmes. "I confess that I share Dr. Mortimer's belief that it will not be long before the missing boot is found."

"And, now, gentlemen," said the baronet with decision, "it seems to me that I have spoken quite enough about the little that I know. It is time that you keep your promise and gave me a full account of what we are all driving at."

"Your request is a very reasonable one," Holmes answered. "Dr. Mortimer, I think you could not do better than to tell your story as you told it to us."

Thus encouraged, our scientific friend drew his papers from his pocket and presented the whole case as he had done upon the morning before. Sir Henry Baskerville listened with the deepest at tcntion and with an occasional exclamation of surprise.

"Well, I seem to have come into an inheritance with a vengeance," said he when the long narrative was finished. "Of course, I've heard of the hound ever since I was in the nursery. It's the pet story of the family, though I never thought of taking it seriously be fore. But as to my uncle's death—well, it all seems boiling up in my head, and I can't get it clear yet. You don't seem quite to have made up your mind whether it's a case for a policeman or a clergyman."

"Precisely."

"And now there's this affair of the letter to me at the hotel. I sup pose that fits into its place."

"It seems to show that someone knows more than we do about what goes on upon the moor," said Dr. Mortimer.

"And also," said Holmes, "that someone is not ill-disposed to wards you, since they warn you of danger."

"Or it may be that they wish, for their own purposes, to scare me away."

"Well, of course, that is possible also. I am very much indebted to you, Dr. Mortimer, for introducing me to a problem which presents several interesting alternatives. But the practical point which we now have to decide, Sir Henry, is whether it is or is not advisable for you to go to Baskerville Hall."

"Why should I not go?"

"There seems to be danger."

"Do you mean danger from this family fiend or do you mean danger from human beings?"

"Well, that is what we have to find out."

"Whichever it is, my answer is fixed. There is no devil in hell, Mr. Holmes, and there is no man upon earth who can prevent me from going to the home of my own people, and you may take that to be my final answer." His dark brows knitted and his face flushed to a dusky red as he spoke. It was evident that the fiery temper of the Baskervilles was not extinct in this their last representative. "Meanwhile," said he, "I have hardly had time to think over all that you have told me. It's a big thing for a man to have to understand and to decide at one sitting. I should like to have a quiet hour by myself to make up my mind. Now, look here, Mr. Holmes, it's half past eleven now and I am going back right away to my hotel. Sup pose you and your friend, Dr. Watson, come round and lunch with us at two. I'll be able to tell you more clearly then how this thing strikes me."

"Is that convenient to you, Watson?"

"Perfectly."

"Then you may expect us. Shall I have a cab called?"

"I'd prefer to walk, for this affair has flurried me rather."

"I'll join you in a walk, with pleasure," said his companion.

"Then we meet again at two o'clock. Au revoir, and good-morn ing!"

We heard the steps of our visitors descend the stair and the bang of the front door. In an instant Holmes had changed from the languid dreamer to the man of action.

"Your hat and boots, Watson, quick! Not a moment to lose!" He rushed into his room in his dressing-gown and was back again in a few seconds in a frock-coat. We hurried together down the stairs and into the street. Dr. Mortimer and Baskerville were still visible about two hundred yards ahead of us in the direction of Oxford Street.

"Shall I run on and stop them?"

"Not for the world, my dear Watson. I am perfectly satisfied with your company if you will tolerate mine. Our friends are wise, for it is certainly a very fine morning for a walk."

He quickened his pace until we had decreased the distance which divided us by about half Then, still keeping a hundred yards behind, we followed into Oxford Street and so down Regent Street. Once our fiends stopped and stared into a shop window, upon which Holmes did the same. An instant afterwards he gave a little cry of satisfaction, and, following the direction of his eager eyes, I saw that a hansom cab with a man inside which had halted on the other side of the street was now proceeding slowly onward "gain.

"There's our man, Watson! Come along! We'll have a good look at him, if we can do no more."

At that instant I was aware of a bushy black beard and a pair of piercing eyes turned upon us through the side window of the cab. Instantly the trapdoor at the top flew up, something was screamed to the driver, and the cab flew madly off down Regent Street. Holmes looked eagerly round for another, but no empty one was in sight. Then he dashed in wild pursuit amid the stream of the traffic, but the start was too great, and already the cab was out of sight.

"There now!" said Holmes bitterly as he emerged panting and white with vexation from the tide of vehicles. "Was ever such bad luck and such bad management, too? Watson, Watson, if you are an honest man you will record this also and set it against my successes!"

"Who was the man.7"

"I have not an idea."

"A spy?"

"Well, it was evident from what we have heard that Baskerville has been very closely shadowed by someone since he has been in town. How else could it be known so quickly that it was the Northumberland Hotel which he had chosen? If they had followed him the first day I argued that they would follow him also the second. You may have observed that I twice strolled over to the window while Dr. Mortimer was reading his legend."

"Yes, I remember."

"I was looking out for loiterers in the street, but I saw none. We are dealing with a clever man, Watson. This matter cuts very deep, and though I have not finally made up my mind whether it is a benevolent or a malevolent agency which is in touch with us, I am conscious always of power and design. When our friends left I at once followed them in the hopes of marking down their invisible attendant. So wily was he that he had not trusted himself upon foot, but he had availed himself of a cab so that he could loiter behind or dash past them and so escape their notice. His method had the additional advantage that if they were to take a cab he was all ready to follow them. It has, however, one obvious disadvantage."

"It puts him in the power of the cabman."

"Exactly."

"What a pity we did not get the number!"

"My dear Watson, clumsy as I have been, you surely do not seriously imagine that I neglected to get the number? No. 2704 is our man. But that is no use to us for the moment."

"I fail to see how you could have done more."

"On observing the cab I should have instantly turned and walked in the other direction. I should then at my leisure have hired a second cab and followed the first at a respectful distance, or, better still, have driven to the Northumberland Hotel and waited there. When our unknown had followed Baskerville home we should have had the opportunity of playing his own game upon himself and seeing where he made for. As it is, by an indiscreet eagerness, which was taken advantage of with extraordinary quickness and energy by our opponent, we have betrayed ourselves and lost our man."

We had been sauntering slowly down Regent Street during this conversation, and Dr. Mortimer, with his companion, had long vanished in front of us.

"There is no object in our following them," said Holmes. "The shadow has departed and will not return. We must see what further cards we have in our hands and play them with decision. Could you swear to that man's within the cab?"

"I could swear only to the beard."

"And so could I—from which I gather that in all probability it was a false one. A clever man upon so delicate an errand has no use for a beard save to conceal his features. Come in here, Watson!"

He turned into one of the district messenger offices, where he was warmly greeted by the manager.

"Ah, Wilson, I see you have not forgotten the little case in which I had the good fortune to help you?"

"No, sir, indeed I have not. You saved my good name, and per haps my life."

"My dear fellow, you exaggerate. I have some recollection, Wil son, that you had among your boys a lad named Cartwright, who showed some ability during the investigation."

"Yes, sir, he is still with us."

"Could you ring him up?—thank you! And I should be glad to have change of this five-pound note."

A lad of fourteen, with a bright, keen face, had obeyed the summons of the manager. He stood now gazing with great reverence at the famous detective.

"Let me have the Hotel Directory," said Holmes. "Thank you! Now, Cartwright, there are the names of twenty-three hotels here, all in the immediate neighbourhood of Charing Cross. Do you see?"

"Yes, sir."

"You will visit each of these in turn."

"Yes, sir."

"You will begin in each case by giving the outside porter one shilling. Here are twenty-three shillings."

"Yes, sir."

"You will tell him that you want to see the waste-paper of yesterday. You will say that an important telegram has miscarried and that you are looking for it. You understand?"

"Yes, sir."

"But what you are really looking for is the centre page of the Times with some holes cut in it with scissors. Here is a copy of the Times. It is this page. You could easily recognize it, could you not?"

"Yes, sir."

"In each case the outside porter will send for the hall porter, to whom also you will give a shilling. Here are twenty-three shillings. You will then learn in possibly twenty cases out of the twenty-three that the waste of the day before has been burned or removed. In the three other cases you will be shown a heap of paper and you will look for this page of the Times among it. The odds are enormously against your finding it. There are ten shillings over in case of emergencies. Let me have a report by wire at Baker Street before evening. And now, Watson, it only remains for us to find out by wire the identity of the cabman, No. 2704, and then we will drop into one of the Bond Street picture galleries and fill in the time until we are due at the hotel."

## CHAPTER 5

# THREE BROKEN THREADS

Sherlock Holmes had, in a very remarkable degree, the power of detaching his mind at will. For two hours the strange business in which we had been involved appeared to be forgotten, and he was entirely absorbed in the pictures of the modern Belgian masters. He would talk of nothing but art, of which he had the crudest ideas, from our leaving the gallery until we found ourselves at the Northumberland Hotel.

"Sir Henry Baskerville is upstairs expecting you," said the clerk. "He asked me to show you up at once when you came."

"Have you any objection to my looking at your register?" said Holmes.

"Not in the least."

The book showed that two names had been added after that of Baskerville. One was Theophilus Johnson and family, of New castle; the other Mrs. Oldmore and maid, of High Lodge, Alton.

"Surely that must be the same Johnson whom I used to know," said Holmes to the porter. "A lawyer, is he not, gray-headed, and walks with a limp.?"

"No, sir, this is Mr.Johnson, the coal-owner, a very active gentleman, not older than yourself"

"Surely you are mistaken about his trade?"

"No, sir! he has used this hotel for many years, and he is very well known to us."

"Ah, that settles it. Mrs. Oldmore, too; I seem to remember the name. Excuse my curiosity, but often in calling upon one friend one finds another."

"She is an invalid lady, sir. Her husband was once mayor of Gloucester. She always comes to us when she is in town."

"Thank you; I am afraid I cannot claim her acquaintance. We have established a most important fact by these questions, Watson," he continued in a low voice as we went upstairs together. "We know now that the people who are so interested in our friend have not settled down in his own hotel. That means that while they are, as we have seen, very anxious to watch him, they are equally anxious that he should not see them. Now, this is a most suggestive fact."

"What does it suggest.?"

"It suggests—hello, my dear fellow, what on earth is the matter?"

As we came round the top of the stairs we had run up against Sir Henry Baskerville himself His face was flushed with anger, and he held an old and dusty boot in one of his hands. So furious was he that he was hardly articulate, and when he did speak it was in a much broader and more Western dialect than any which we had heard from him in the morning.

"Seems to me they are playing me for a sucker in this hotel," he cried. "They'll find they've started in to monkey with the wrong man unless they are careful. By thunder, if that chap can't find my missing boot there will be trouble. I can take a joke with the best, Mr. Holmes, but they've got a bit over the mark this time."

"Still looking for your boot?"

"Yes, sir, and mean to find it."

"But, surely, you said that it was a new brown boot?"

"So it was, sir. And now it's an old black one."

'What! you don't mean to say_ ?"

"That's just what I do mean to say. I only had three pairs in the world—the new brown, the old black, and the patent leathers, which I am wearing. Last night they took one of my brown ones, and to-day they have sneaked one of the black. Well, have you got it? Speak out, man, and don't stand staring!"

An agitated German waiter had appeared upon the scene.

"No, sir; I have made inquiry all over the hotel, but I can hear no word of it."

"Well, either that boot comes back before sundown or I'll see the manager and tell him that I go right straight out of this hotel."

"It shall be found, sir—I promise you that if you will have a little patience it will be found."

"Mind it is, for it's the last thing of mine that I'll lose in this den of thieves. Well, well, Mr. Holmes, you'll excuse my troubling you about such a trifle

"I think it's well worth troubling about."

"Why, you look very serious over it n

"How do you explain it?"

"I just don't attempt to explain it. It seems the very maddest, queerest thing that ever happened to me."

"The queerest perhaps—" said Holmes thoughtfully.

"What do you make of it yourself?"

"Well, I don't profess to understand it yet. This case of yours is very complex, Sir Henry. When taken in conjunction with your uncle's death I am not sure that of all the five hundred cases of capital importance which I have handled there is one which cuts so deep. But we hold several threads in our hands, and the odds are that one or other of them guides us to the truth. We may waste time in following the wrong one, but sooner or later we must come upon the right."

We had a pleasant luncheon in which little was said of the busi ness which had brought us together. It was in the private sitting room to which we afterwards repaired that Holmes asked Baskerville what were his intentions.

"To go to Baskerville Hall."

"And when?"

"At the end of the week."

"On the whole," said Holmes, "I think that your decision is a wise one. I have ample evidence that you are being dogged in London, and amid the millions of this great city it is difficult to dis cover who these people are or what their object can be. If their intentions are evil they might do you a mischief, and we should be powerless to prevent it. You did not know, Dr. Mortimer, that you were followed this morning from my house?"

Dr. Mortimer started violently.

"Followed! By whom?"

"That, unfortunately, is what I cannot tell you. Have you among your neighbours or acquaintances on Dartmoor any man with a black, full beard?"

"No—or, let me see—why, yes. Barrymore, Sir Charles's butler, is a man with a full, black beard."

"Ha! Where is Barrymore?"

"He is in charge of the Hall."

"We had best ascertain if he is really there, or if by any possibility he might be in London."

"How can you do that?"

"Give me a telegraph form. 'Is all ready for Sir Henry?' That will do. Address to Mr. Barrymore, Baskerville Hall. What is the nearest telegraph-office? Grimpen. Very good, we will send a second wire to the postmaster, Grimpen: 'Telegram to Mr. Barrymore to be delivered into his own hand. If absent, please return wire to Sir Henry Baskerville, Northumberland Hotel.' That should let us know before evening whether Barrymore is at his post in Devon shire or not."

"That's so," said Baskerville. "By the way, Dr. Mortimer, who is this Barrymore, anyhow.?n

"He is the son of the old caretaker, who is dead. They have looked after the Hall for four generations now. So far as I know, he and his wife are as respectable a couple as any in the county."

"At the same time," said Baskerville, "it's clear enough that so long as there are none of the family at the Hall these people have a mighty fine home and nothing to do."

"That is true."

"Did Barrymore profit at all by Sir Charles's will?" asked Holmes.

"He and his wife had five hundred pounds each."

"Ha! Did they know that they would receive this?"

"Yes; Sir Charles was very fond of talking about the provisions of his will."

"That is very interesting."

"I hope," said Dr. Mortimer, "that you do not look with suspicious eyes upon everyone who received a legacy from Sir Charles, for I also had a thousand pounds left to me."

"Indeed! And anyone else"'

"There were many insignificant sums to individuals, and a large number of public charities. The residue all went to Sir Henry."

"And how much was the residue?"

"Seven hundred and forty thousand pounds."

Holmes raised his eyebrows in surprise. "I had no idea that so gigantic a sum was involved," said he.

"Sir Charles had the reputation of being rich, but we did not know how very rich he was until we came to examine his securities. The total value of the estate was close on to a million."

"Dear me! It is a stake for which a man might well play a desperate game. And one more question, Dr. Mortimer. Supposing that anything happened to our young friend here—you will forgive the unpleasant hypothesis!—who would inherit the estate?"

"Since Rodger Baskerville, Sir Charles's younger brother, died unmarried, the estate would descend to the Desmonds, who are distant cousins. James Desmond is an elderly clergyman in West Moreland."

"Thank you. These details are all of great interest. Have you met Mr.James Desmond?"

"Yes; he once came down to visit Sir Charles. He is a man of venerable appearance and of saintly life. I remember that he re fused to accept any settlement from Sir Charles, though he pressed it upon him."

"And this man of simple tastes would be the heir to Sir Charles's thousands."

"He would be the heir to the estate because that is entailed. He would also be the heir to the money unless it were willed otherwise by the present owner, who can, of course, do what he likes with it."

"And have you made your will, Sir Henry?

"No, Mr. Holmes, I have not. I've had no time, for it was only yesterday that I learned how matters stood. But in any case I feel that the money should go with the title and estate. That was my poor uncle's idea. How is the owner going to restore the glories of the Baskervilles if he has not money enough to keep up the property? House, land, and dollars must go together."

"Quite so. Well, Sir Henry, I am of one mind with you as to the advisability of your going down to Devonshire without delay. There is only one provision which I must make. You certainly must not go alone."

"Dr. Mortimer returns with me."

"But Dr. Mortimer has his practice to attend to, and his house is miles away from yours. With all the good will in the world he may be unable to help you. No, Sir Henry, you must take with you someone, a trusty man, who will be always by your side."

"Is it possible that you could come yourself, Mr. Holmes?"

"If matters came to a crisis I should endeavour to be present in person; but you can understand that, with my extensive consulting practice and with the constant appeals which reach me from many quarters, it is impossible for me to be absent from London for an indefinite time. At the present instant one of the most revered names in England is being besmirched by a blackmailer, and only I can stop a disastrous scandal. You will see how impossible it is for me to go to Dartmoor."

"Whom would you recommend, then?"

Holmes laid his hand upon my arm.

"If my friend would undertake it there is no man who is better worth having at your side when you are in a tight place. No one can say so more confidently than I."

The proposition took me completely by surprise, but before I had time to answer, Baskerville seized me by the hand and wrung it heartily.

"Well, now, that is real kind of you, Dr. Watson," said he. "You see how it is with me, and you know just as much about the matter as I do. If you will come down to Baskerville Hall and see me through I'll never forget it."

The promise of adventure had always a fascination for me, and I was complimented by the words of Holmes and by the eagerness with which the baronet hailed me as a companion.

"I will come, with pleasure," said I. "I do not know how I could employ my time better."

"And you will report very carefully to me," said Holmes. "When a crisis comes, as it will do, I will direct how you shall act. I suppose that by Saturday all might be ready?"

"Would that suit Dr. Watson?"

"Perfectly."

"Then on Saturday, unless you hear to the contrary, we shall meet at the ten-thirty train from Paddington."

We had risen to depart when Baskerville gave a cry of triumph, and diving into one of the corners of the room he drew a brown boot from under a cabinet.

"My missing boot!" he cried.

"May all our difficulties vanish as easily!" said Sherlock Holmes.

"But it is a very singular thing," Dr. Mortimer remarked. "I searched this room carefully before lunch."

"And so did I," said Baskerville. "Every inch of it."

"There was certainly no boot in it then."

"In that case the waiter must have placed it there while we were lunching."

The German was sent for but professed to know nothing of the matter, nor could any inquiry clear it up. Another item had been added to that constant and apparently purposeless series of small mysteries which had succeeded each other so rapidly. Setting aside the whole grim story of Sir Charles's death, we had a line of inexplicable incidents all within the limits of two days, which included the receipt of the printed letter, the black-bearded spy in the hansom, the loss of the new brown boot, the loss of the old black boot, and now the return of the new brown boot. Holmes sat in silence in the cab as we drove back to Baker Street, and I knew from his drawn brows and keen face that his mind, like my own, was busy in endeavouring to frame some scheme into which all these strange and apparently disconnected episodes could be fitted.

All afternoon and late into the evening he sat lost in tobacco and thought.

Just before dinner two telegrams were handed in. The first ran:

> Have just heard that Barrymore is at the Hall.
>
> BASKERVILLE.

The second:

> Visited twenty-three hotels as directed, but sorry to report unable to trace cut sheet of Times.
>
> CARTWRIGHT.

"There go two of my threads, Watson. There is nothing more stimulating than a case where everything goes against you. We must cast round for another scent."

"We have still the cabman who drove the spy."

"Exactly. I have wired to get his name and address from the Official Registry. I should not be surprised if this were an answer to my question."

The ring at the bell proved to be something even more satisfactory than an answer, however, for the door opened and a rough looking fellow entered who was evidently the man himself

"I got a message from the head office that a gent at this address had been inquiring for No. 2704," said he. "I've driven my cab this seven years and never a word of complaint. I came here straight from the Yard to ask you to your face what you had against me."

"I have nothing in the world against you, my good man," said Holmes. "On the contrary, I have half a sovereign for you if you will give me a clear answer to my questions."

"Well, I've had a good day and no mistake," said the cabman with a grin. "What was it you wanted to ask, sir?"

"First of all your name and address, in case I want you again."

"John Clayton, 3 Turpey Street, the Borough. My cab is out of Shipley's Yard, near Waterloo Station."

Sherlock Holmes made a note of it.

"Now, Clayton, tell me all about the fare who came and watched this house at ten o'clock this morning and afterwards followed the two gentlemen down Regent Street."

The man looked surprised and a little embarrassed. "Why, there's no good my telling you things, for you seem to know as much as I do already," said he. "The truth is that the gentleman told me that he was a detective and that I was to say nothing about him to anyone."

"My good fellow, this is a very serious business, and you may find yourself in a pretty bad position if you try to hide anything from me. You say that your fare told you that he was a detective.?"

"Yes, he did."

"When did he say this?"

"When he left me."

"Did he say anything more?"

"He mentioned his name."

Holmes cast a swift glance of triumph at me. "Oh, he mentioned his name, did he? That was imprudent. What was the name that he mentioned?"

"His name," said the cabman, "was Mr. Sherlock Holmes."

Never have I seen my friend more completely taken aback than by the cabman's reply. For an instant he sat in silent amazement. Then he burst into a hearty laugh.

"A touch, Watson—an undeniable touch!" said he. "I feel a foil as quick and supple as my own. He got home upon me very prettily that time. So his name was Sherlock Holmes, was it?"

"Yes, sir, that was the gentleman's name."

"Excellent! Tell me where you picked him up and all that oc curred."

"He hailed me at half-past nine in Trafalgar Square. He said that he was a detective, and he offered me two guineas if I would do exactly what he wanted all day and ask no questions. I was glad enough to agree. down to the Northumberland Hotel and waited there until two gentlemen came out and took a cab from the rank. We followed their cab until it pulled up somewhere near here."

"This very door," said Holmes.

"Well, I couldn't be sure of that, but I dare say my fare knew all about it. We pulled up halfway down the street and waited an hour and a half Then the two gentlemen passed us, walking, and we followed down Baker Street and along—"

"I know," said Holmes.

"Until we got three-quarters down Regent Street. Then my gentleman threw up the trap, and he cried that I should drive right away to Waterloo Station as hard as T could go. I whipped up the mare and we were there under the ten minutes. Then he paid up his two guineas, like a good one, and away he went into the station. Only just as he was leaving he turned round and he said: 'It might interest you to know that you have been driving Mr. Sherlock Holmes.' That's how I come to know the name."

"I see. And you saw no more of him?"

"Not after he went into the station."

"And how would you describe Mr. Sherlock Holmes?"

The cabman scratched his head. "Well, he wasn't altogether such an easy gentleman to describe. I'd put him at forty years of age, and he was of a middle height, two or three inches shorter than you, sir. He was dressed like a toff, and he had a black beard, cut square at the end, and a pale face. I don't know as I could say more than that."

"Colour of his eyes?"

"No, I can't say that."

"Nothing more that you can remember?"

"No, sir; nothing."

"Well, then, here is your half-sovereign. There's another one waiting for you if you can bring any more information. Good night!"

"Good-night, sir, and thank you!"

John Clayton departed chuckling, and Holmes turned to me with a shrug of his shoulders and a rueful smile.

"Snap goes our third thread, and we end where we began," said he. "The cunning rascal! He knew our number, knew that sir Henry Baskerville had consulted me, spotted who I was in Regent Street, conjectured that I had got the number of the cab and would lay my hands on the driver, and so sent back this audacious message. I tell you, Watson, this time we have got a foe who is worthy of our steel. I've been checkmated in London. I can only wish you better luck in Devonshire. But I'm not easy in my mind about it.

"About what?"

"About sending you. It's an ugly business, Watson, an ugly, dangerous business, and the more I see of it the less I like it. Yes, my dear fellow, you may laugh, but I give you my word that I shall be very glad to have you back safe and sound in Baker Street once more."

## CHAPTER 6

# BASKERVILLE HALL

Sir Henry Baskerville and Dr. Mortimer were ready upon the appointed day, and we started as arranged for Devonshire. Mr. Sher lock Holmes drove with me to the station and gave me his last part ing injunctions and advice.

"I will not bias your mind by suggesting theories or suspicions, Watson," said he; "I wish you simply to report facts in the fullest possible manner to me, and you can leave me to do the theorising."

"What sort of facts?" I asked.

"Anything which may seem to have a bearing however indirect upon the case, and especially the relations between young Baskerville and his neighbours or any fresh particulars concerning the death of Sir Charles. I have made some inquiries myself in the last few days, but the results have, I fear, been negative. One thing only appears to be certain, and that is that Mr.James Desmond, who is the next heir, is an elderly gentleman of a very amiable disposition, so that this persecution does not arise from him. I really think that we may eliminate him entirely from our calculations. There remain the people who will actually surround sir Henry Baskerville upon the moor."

"Would it not be well in the first place to get rid of this Barry more couple?"

"By no means. You could not make a greater mistake. If they are innocent it would be a cruel injustice, and if they are guilty we should be giving up all chance of bringing it home to them. No, no, we will preserve them upon our list of suspects. Then there is a groom at the Hall, if r remember right. There are two Moreland farmers. There is our friend Dr. Mortimer, whom I believe to be entirely honest, and there is his wife, of whom we know nothing. There is this naturalist, Stapleton, and there is his sister, who is said to be a young lady of attractions. There is Mr. Frankland, of Lafter Hall, who is also an unknown factor, and there are one or two other neighbours. These are the folk who must be your very special study."

"I will do my best."

"You have arms, I suppose?"

"Yes, I thought it as well to take them."

"Most certainly. Keep your revolver near you night and day, and never relax your precautions."

Our friends had already secured a first-class carriage and were waiting for us upon the platform.

"No, we have no news of any kind," said Dr. Mortimer in answer to my friend's questions. "I can swear to one thing, and that is that we have not been shadowed during the last two days. We have never gone out without keeping a sharp watch, and no one could have escaped our notice."

"You have always kept together, I presume?"

"Except yesterday afternoon. I usually give up one day to pure amusement when I come to town, so I spent it at the Museum of the College of Surgeons."

"And I went to look at the folk in the park," said Baskerville. "But we had no trouble of any kind."

"It was imprudent, all the same," said Holmes, shaking his head and looking very grave. "I beg, Sir Henry, that you will not go about alone. Some great misfortune will befall you if you do. Did you get your other boot?"

"No, sir, it is gone forever."

"Indeed. That is very interesting. Well, good-bye," he added as the train began to glide down the platform. "Bear in mind, Sir Henry, one of the phrases in that queer old legend which Dr. Mortimer has read to us and avoid the moor in those hours of darkness when the powers of evil are exalted."

I looked back at the platform when we had left it far behind and saw the tall, austere figure of Holmes standing motionless and gazing after us.

The journey was a swift and pleasant one, and I spent it in making the more intimate acquaintance of my two companions and in playing with Dr. Mortimer's spaniel. In a very few hours the brown earth had become ruddy, the brick had changed to granite, and red cows grazed in well-hedged fields where the lush grasses and more luxuriant vegetation spoke of a richer, if a damper, climate. Young Baskerville stared eagerly out of the window and cried aloud with delight as he recognized the familiar features of the Devon scenery.

"I've been over a good part of the world since I left it, Dr. Wat son," said he; "but I have never seen a place to compare with it."

"I never saw a Devonshire man who did not swear by his county," I remarked.

"It depends upon the breed of men quite as much as on the county," said Dr. Mortimer. "A glance at our friend here reveals the rounded head of the Celt, which carries inside it the Celtic enthusiasm and power of attachment. Poor Sir Charles's head was of a very rare type, half Gaelic, half Ivernian in its characteristics. But you were very young when you last saw Baskerville Hall, were you not?"

"I was a boy in my teens at the time of my father's death and had never seen the Hall, for he lived in a little cottage on the South Coast. Thence I went straight to a friend in America. I tell you it is all as new to me as it is to Dr. Watson, and I'm as keen as possible to see the moor."

"Are you? Then your wish is easily granted, for there is your first sight of the moor," said Dr. Mortimer, pointing out of the carriage window.

Over the green squares of the fields and the low curve of a wood there rose in the distance a gray, melancholy hill, with a strange jagged summit, dim and vague in the distance, like some fantastic landscape in a dream. Baskerville sat for a long time, his eyes fixed upon it, and I read upon his eager face how much it meant to him, this first sight of that strange spot where the men of his blood had held sway so long and left their mark so deep. There he sat, with his tweed suit and his American accent, in the corner of a prosaic rail way-carriage, and yet as I looked at his dark and expressive face I felt more than ever how true a descendant he was of that long line of high-blooded, fiery, and masterful men. There were pride, valour, and strength in his thick brows, his sensitive nostrils, and his large hazel eyes. If on that forbidding moor a difficult and dangerous quest should lie before us, this was at least a comrade for whom one might venture to take a risk with the certainty that he would bravely share it.

The train pulled up at a small wayside station and we all descended. Outside, beyond the low, white fence, a wagonette with a pair of cobs was waiting. Our coming was evidently a great even for station-master and porters clustered round us to carry out our luggage. It was a sweet, simple country spot, but I was surprised to observe that by the gate there stood two soldierly men in dark uniforms who leaned upon their short rifles and glanced keenly at us as we passed. The coachman, a hard-faced, gnarled little fellow, saluted Sir Henry Baskerville, and in a few minutes we were flying swiftly down the broad, white road. Rolling pasture lands curved upward on either side of us, and old gabled houses peeped out from amid the thick green foliage, but behind the peaceful and sun lit countryside there rose ever, dark against the evening sky, the long, gloomy curve of the moor, broken by the jagged and sinister hills.

The wagonette swung round into a side road, and we curved up ward through deep lanes worn by centuries of wheels, high banks on either side, heavy with dripping moss and fleshy hart's-tongue ferns. Bronzing bracken and mottled bramble gleamed in the light of the sinking sun. Still steadily rising, we passed over a narrow granite bridge and skirted a noisy stream which gushed swiftly down, foaming and roaring amid the gray boulders. Both road and stream wound up through a valley dense with scrub oak and fir. At every turn Baskerville gave an exclamation of delight, looking eagerly about him and asking countless questions. To his eyes all seemed beautiful, but to me a tinge of melancholy lay upon the countryside, which bore so clearly the mark of the waning year. Yellow leaves carpeted the lanes and fluttered down upon us as we passed. The rattle of our wheels died away as we drove through drifts of rotting vegetation—sad gifts, as it seemed to me, for Nature to throw before the carriage of the returning heir of the Baskervilles.

"Hello!" cried Dr. Mortimer, "what is this?"

A steep curve of heath-clad land, an outlying spur of the moor, lay in front of us. On the summit, hard and clear like an equestrian statue upon its pedestal, was a mounted soldier, dark and stern, his rifle poised ready over his forearm. He was watching the road along which we travelled.

'What is this, Perkins?" asked Dr. Mortimer.

Our driver half turned in his seat.

"There's a convict escaped from Princetown, sir. He's been out three days now, and the warders watch every road and every station, but they've had no sight of him yet. The farmers about here don't like it, sir, and that's a fact."

"Well, I understand that they get five pounds if they can give in formation."

"Yes, sir, but the chance of five pounds is but a poor thing compared to the chance of having your throat cut. You see, it isn't like any ordinary convict. This is a man that would stick at nothing."

"Who is he, then?"

"It is Selden, the Notting Hill murderer."

I remembered the case well, for it was one in which Holmes had taken an interest on account of the peculiar ferocity of the crime and the wanton brutality which had marked all the actions of the assassin. The commutation of his death sentence had been due to some doubts as to his complete sanity, so atrocious was his conduct. Our wagonette had topped a rise and in front of us rose the huge expanse of the moor, mottled with gnarled and craggy cairns and tors. A cold wind swept down from it and set us shivering. Somewhere there, on that desolate plain, was lurking this fiendish man, hiding in a burrow like a wild beast, his heart full of malignancy against the whole race which had cast him out. It needed but this to complete the grim suggestiveness of the barren waste, the chilling wind, and the darkling sky. Even Baskerville fell silent and pulled his overcoat more closely around him.

We had left the fertile country behind and beneath us. We looked back on it now, the slanting rays of a low sun turning the streams to threads of gold and glowing on the red earth new turned by the plough and the broad tangle of the woodlands. The road in front of us grew bleaker and wilder over huge russet and olive slopes, sprinkled with giant boulders. Now and then we passed a Moreland cottage, walled and roofed with stone, with no creeper to break its harsh outline. Suddenly we looked down into a cuplike depression, patched with stunted oaks and firs which had been twisted and bent by the fury of years of storm. Two high, narrow towers rose over the trees. The driver pointed with his whip.

"Baskerville Hall," said he.

Its master had risen and was staring with flushed cheeks and shining eyes. A few minutes later we had reached the lodge-gates, a maze of fantastic tracery in wrought iron, with weather-bitten pillars on either side, blotched with lichens, and surmounted by the boars' heads of the

Baskervilles. The lodge was a ruin of black granite and bared ribs of rafters, but facing it was a new building, half constructed, the first fruit of Sir Charles's South African gold.

Through the gateway we passed into the avenue, where the wheels were again hushed amid the leaves, and the old trees shot their branches in a sombre tunnel over our heads. Baskerville shuddered as he looked up the long, dark drive to where the house glimmered like a ghost at the farther end.

"Was it here?" he asked in a low voice.

"No, no, the yew alley is on the other side."

The young heir glanced round with a gloomy face.

"It's no wonder my uncle felt as if trouble were coming on him in such a place as this," said he. "It's enough to scare any man. I'll have a row of electric lamps up here inside of six months, and you won't know it again, with a thousand candlepower Swan and Edison right here in front of the hall door."

The avenue opened into a broad expanse of turf, and the house lay before us. In the fading light I could see that the centre was a heavy block of building from which a porch projected. The whole front was draped in ivy, with a patch clipped bare here and there where a window or a coat of arms broke through the dark veil. From this central block rose the twin towers, ancient, crenelated, and pierced with many loopholes. To right and left of the turrets were more modern wings of black granite. A dull light shone through heavy mullioned windows, and from the high chimneys which rose from the steep, high-angled roof there sprang a single black column of smoke.

"Welcome, Sir Henry! Welcome to Baskerville Hall!"

"A tall man had stepped from the shadow of the porch to open the door of the wagonette. The figure of a woman was silhouetted against the yellow light of the hall. She came out and helped the man to hand down our bags.

"You don't mind my driving straight home, Sir Henry?" said Dr. Mortimer. "My wife is expecting me."

"Surely you will stay and have some dinner?"

"No, I must go. I shall probably find some work awaiting me. I would stay to show you over the house, but Barrymore will be a better guide than I. Good-bye, and never hesitate night or day to send for me if I can be of service."

The wheels died away down the drive while Sir Henry and I turned into the hall, and the door clanged heavily behind us. It was a fine apartment in which we found ourselves, large, lofty, and heavily raftered with huge bulks of age-blackened oak. In the great old-fashioned fireplace behind the high iron dogs a log-fire crackled and snapped. Sir Henry and I held out our hands to it, for we were numb from our long drive. Then we gazed round us at the high, thin window of old stained glass, the oak panelling, the stags' heads, the coats of arms upon the walls, all dim and sombre in the subdued light of the central lamp.

"It's just as I imagined it," said Sir Henry. "Is it not the very picture of an old family home? To think that this should be the same hall in which for five hundred years my people have lived. It strikes me solemn to think of it."

I saw his dark face lit up with a boyish enthusiasm as he gazed about him. The light beat upon him where he stood, but long shadows trailed down the walls and hung like a black canopy above him. Barrymore had returned from taking our luggage to our rooms. He stood in front of us now with the subdued manner of a well-trained servant. He was a remarkable-looking man, tall, hand some, with a square black beard and pale, distinguished features.

"Would you wish dinner to be served at once, sir?"

"Is it ready"

"In a very few minutes, sir. You will find hot water in your rooms. My wife and I will be happy, Sir Henry, to stay with you un til you have made your fresh arrangements, but you will under stand that under the new conditions this house will require a considerable staff."

"What new conditions?"

"I only meant, sir, that Sir Charles led a very retired life, and we were able to look after his wants. You would, naturally, wish to have more company, and so you will need changes in your house hold."

"Do you mean that your wife and you wish to leave?"

"Only when it is quite convenient to you, sir."

"But your family have been with us for several generations, have they not? I should be sorry to begin my life here by breaking an old family connection."

I seemed to discern some signs of emotion upon the butler's white face.

"I feel that also, sir, and so does my wife. But to tell the truth, sir, we were both very much attached to Sir Charles and his death gave us a shock and made these surroundings very painful to us. I fear that we shall never again be easy in our minds at Baskerville Hall."

"But what do you intend to do?"

"I have no doubt, sir, that we shall succeed in establishing our selves in some business. Sir Charles's generosity has given us the nicans to do so. And now, sir, perhaps I had best show you to your rooms."

A square balustraded gallery ran round the top of the old hall, approached by a double stair. From this central point two long corridors extended the whole length of the building, from which all the bedrooms opened. My own was in the same wing as Baskerville's and almost next door to it. These rooms appeared to be much more modern than the central part of the house, and the bright paper and numerous candles did something to remove the sombre impression which our arrival had left upon my mind.

But the dining-room which opened out of the hall was a place of shadow and gloom. It was a long chamber with a step separating the dais where the family sat from the lower portion reserved for their dependents. At one end a minstrel's gallery overlooked it. Black beams shot across above our heads, with a smoke-darkened ceiling beyond them. With rows of flaring torches to light it up, and the colour and rude hilarity of an old-time banquet, it might have softened; but now, when two black-clothed gentlemen sat in the little circle of light thrown by a shaded lamp, one's voice became hushed and one's spirit subdued. A dim line of ancestors, in every variety of dress, from the Elizabethan knight to the buck of the Regency, stared down upon us and daunted us by their silent company. We talked little, and I for one was glad when the meal was over and we were able to retire into the modern billiard-room and smoke a cigarette.

"My word, it isn't a very cheerful place," said Sir Henry. "I suppose one can tone down to it, but I feel a bit out of the picture at present. I don't wonder that my uncle got a little jumpy if he lived all alone in such a house as this. However, if it suits you, we will re tire early to-night, and perhaps things may seem more cheerful in the morning."

I drew aside my curtains before I went to bed and looked out from my window. It opened upon the grassy space which lay in front of the hall door. Beyond, two copses of trees moaned and swung in a rising wind. A half moon broke through the rifts of racing clouds. In its cold light I saw beyond the trees a broken fringe of rocks, and the long, low curve of the melancholy moor. I closed the curtain, feeling that my last impression was in keeping with the rest.

"And yet it was not quite the last. I found myself weary and yet wakeful, tossing restlessly from side to side, seeking for the sleep which would not come. Far away a chiming clock struck out the quarters of the hours, but otherwise a deathly silence lay upon the old house. And then suddenly, in the very dead of the night, there came a sound to my ears, clear, resonant, and unmistakable. It was the sob of a woman, the muffled, strangling gasp of one who is torn by an uncontrollable sorrow. I sat up in bed and listened intently. The noise could not have been far away and was certainly in the house. For half an hour I waited with every nerve on the alert, but there came no other sound save the chiming clock and the rustle of the ivy on the wall.

## CHAPTER 7

# THE STAPLETONS OF MERRIPIT HOUSE

The fresh beauty of the following morning did something to efface from our minds the grim and gray impression which had been left upon both of us by our first experience of Baskerville Hall. As Sir Henry and I sat at breakfast the sunlight flooded in through the high mullioned windows, throwing watery patches of colour from the coats of arms which covered them. The dark panelling glowed like bronze in the golden rays, and it was hard to realise that this was indeed the chamber which had struck such a gloom into our souls upon the evening before.

"I guess it is ourselves and not the house that we have to blame!" said the baronet. "We were tired with our journey and chilled by our drive, so we took a gray view of the place. Now we are fresh and well, so it is all cheerful once more."

"And yet it was not entirely a question of imagination," I answered. "Did you, for example, happen to hear someone, a woman I think, sobbing in the night?"

"That is curious, for I did when I was half asleep fancy that I heard something of the sort. I waited quite a time, but there was no more of it, so I concluded that it was all a dream."

"I heard it distinctly, and I am sure that it was really the sob of a woman."

"We must ask about this right away." He rang the bell and asked Barrymore whether he could account for our experience. It seemed to me that the pallid features of the butler turned a shade paler still as he listened to his master's question.

"There are only two women in the house, Sir Henry," he answered. "One is the scullery-maid, who sleeps in the other wing. The other is my wife, and I can answer for it that the sound could not have come from her."

"And yet he lied as he said it, for it chanced that after breakfast I met Mrs. Barrymore in the long corridor with the sun full upon her face. She was a large, impassive, heavy-featured woman with a stern set expression of mouth. But her telltale eyes were red and glanced at me from between swollen lids. It was she, then, who wept in the night, and if she did so her husband must know it. Yet he had taken the obvious risk of discover,v in declaring that it was not so. Why had he done this? And why did she weep so bitterly? Already round this pale-faced, handsome, black-bearded man there was gathering an atmosphere of mystery and of-gloom. It was he who had been the first to discover the body of Sir Charles, and we had only his word for all the circumstances which led up to the old man's death. Was it possible that it was Barrymore, after all, whom we had seen in the cab in Regent Street? The beard might well have been the same. The cabman had described a somewhat shorter man, but such an impression might easily have been erroneous. How could I settle the point forever? Obviously the first thing to do was to see the Grimpen postmaster and find whether the test telegram had really been placed in Barrymore's own hands. Be the answer what it might, I should at least have something to re port to Sherlock Holmes.

Sir Henry had numerous papers to examine after breakfast, so that the time was propitious for my excursion. It was a pleasant walk of four miles along the edge of the moor, leading me at last to a small gray hamlet, in which two larger buildings, which proved to be the inn and the house of Dr. Mortimer, stood high above the rest. The postmaster, who was also the village grocer, had a clear recollection of the telegram.

"Certainly, sir," said he, "I had the telegram delivered to Mr. Barrymore exactly as directed."

"Who delivered it?"

"My boy here.James, you delivered that telegram to Mr. Barry more at the Hall last week, did you not?"

"Yes, father, I delivered it."

"Into his own hands?" I asked.

"Well, he was up in the loft at the time, so that I could not put it into his own hands, but I gave it into Mrs. Barrymore's hands, and she promised to deliver it at once."

"Did you see Mr. Barrymore?"

"No, sir; I tell you he was in the loft."

"If you didn't see him, how do you know he was in the loft?"

"Well, surely his own wife ought to know where he is," said the postmaster testily. "Didn't he get the telegram? If there is any mistake it is for Mr. Barrymore himself to complain."

It seemed hopeless to pursue the inquiry any farther, but it was clear that in spite of Holmes's ruse we had no proof that Barrymore had not been in London all the time. Suppose that it were so—suppose that the same man had been the last who had seen Sir Charles alive, and the first to dog the new heir when he returned to England. What then? Was he the agent of others or had he some sinister design of his own? What interest could he have in persecuting the Baskerville family? I thought of the strange warning clipped out of the leading article of the Times. Was that his work or was it possibly the doing of someone who was bent upon counteracting his schemes? The only conceivable motive was that which had been suggested by Sir Henry, that if the family could be scared away a comfortable and permanent home would be secured for the Barrymores. But surely such an explanation as that would be quite inadequate to account for the deep and subtle scheming which seemed to be weaving an invisible net round the young baronet. Holmes himself had said that no more complex case had come to him in all the long series of his sensational investigations. I prayed, as I walked back along the gray, lonely road, that my friend might soon be freed from his preoccupations and able to come down to take this heavy burden of responsibility from my shoulders.

Suddenly my thoughts were interrupted by the sound of running feet behind me and by a voice which called me by name. I turned, expecting to see Dr. Mortimer, but to my surprise it was a stranger who was pursuing me. He was a small, slim, clean-shaven, prim-faced man, flaxen-haired and lean-jawed, between thirty and forty years of age, dressed in a gray suit and wearing a straw hat. A tin box for botanical specimens hung over his shoulder and he carried a green butterfly-net in one of his hands.

"You will, I am sure, excuse my presumption, Dr. Watson," said he as he came panting up to where I stood. "Here on the moor we are homely folk and do not wait for formal introductions. You may possibly have heard my name from our mutual friend, Mortimer. I am Stapleton, of Merripit House."

"Your net and box would have told me as much," said I, "for I knew that Mr. Stapleton was a naturalist. But how did you know me?"

"I have been calling on Mortimer, and he pointed you out to me from the window of his surgery as you passed. As our road lay the same way I thought that I would overtake you and introduce my self I trust that Sir Henry is none the worse for his journey?"

"He is very well, thank you."

"We were all rather afraid that after the sad death of Sir Charles the new baronet might refuse to live here. It is asking much of a wealthy man to come down and bury himself in a place of this kind, but I need not tell you that it means a very great deal to the countryside. Sir Henry has, I suppose, no superstitious fears in the matter?"

"I do not think that it is likely."

"Of course you know the legend of the fiend dog which haunts the family?"

"I have heard it."

"It is extraordinary how credulous the peasants are about here! Any number of them are ready to swear that they have seen such a creature upon the moor." He spoke with a smile, but I seemed to read in his eyes that he took the matter more seriously. "The story took a great hold upon the imagination of Sir Charles, and I have no doubt that it led to his tragic end."

"But how?"

"His nerves were so worked up that the appearance of any dog might have had a fatal effect upon his diseased heart. I fancy that he really did see something of the kind upon that last night in the yew alley. I feared that some disaster might occur, for I was very fond of the old man, and I knew that his heart was weak."

"How did you know that?"

"My fiend Mortimer told me."

"You think, then, that some dog pursued Sir Charles, and that he died of fright in consequence?"

"Have you any better explanation?"

"I have not come to any conclusion."

"Has Mr. Sherlock Holmes?"

The words took away my breath for an instant, but a glance at the placid face and steadfast eyes of my companion showed that no surprise was intended.

"It is useless for us to pretend that we do not know you, Dr. Wat son," said he. "The records of your detective have reached us here, and you could not celebrate him without being known yourself When Mortimer told me your name he could not deny your identity. If you are here, then it follows that Mr. Sherlock Holmes is interesting himself in the matter, and I am naturally curious to know what view he may take."

"I am afraid that 1 cannot answer that question."

"May I ask if he is going to honour us with a visit himself?"

"He cannot leave town at present. He has other cases which engage his attention."

'That a pity! He might throw some light on that which is so dark to us. But as to your own researches, if there is any possible way in which I can be of service to you I trust that you will command me. If I had any indication of the nature of your suspicions or how you propose to investigate the case, I might perhaps even now give you some aid or advice."

"I assure you that I am simply here upon a visit to my fr.end, Sir Henry, and that I need no help of any kind."

"Excellent!" said Stapleton. "You are perfectly right to be wary and discreet. I am justly reproved for what I feel was an unjustifiable intrusion, and I promise you that I will not mention the mat ter again."

We had come to a point where a narrow grassy path struck off from the road and wound away across the moor.

A steep,, boulder sprinkled hill lay upon the right which had in bygone days been cut into a granite quarry. The face which was turned towards us formed a dark cliff, with ferns and brambles growing in its niches. Prom over a distant rise there floated a gray plume of smoke.

"A moderate walk along this moor-path brings us to Merripit House," said he. "Perhaps you will spare an hour that I may have the pleasure of introducing you to my sister."

My first thought was that I should be by Sir Henry's side. But then I remembered the pile of papers and bills with which his study table was littered. It was certain that I could not help with those. And Holmes had expressly said that I should study the neighbours upon the moor. I accepted Stapleton's invitation, and we turned together down the path.

"It is a wonderful place, the moor," said he, looking round over the undulating downs, long green rollers, with crests of jagged granite foaming up into fantastic surges. "You never tire of the moor. You cannot think the wonderful secrets which it contains. It is so vast, and so barren, and so mysterious."

"You know it well, then?"

"I have only been here two years. The residents would call me a newcomer. We came shortly after Sir Charles settled. But my tastes led me to explore every part of the country round, and I should think that there are few men who know it better than I do."

"Is it hard to know?"

"Very hard. You see, for example, this great plain to the north here with the queer hills breaking out of it. Do you observe any thing remarkable about that?"

"It would be a rare place for a gallop."

"You would naturally think so and the thought has cost several their lives before now. You notice those bright green spots scattered thickly over it?"

"Yes, they seem more fertile than the rest."

Stapleton laughed.

"That is the great Grimpen Mire," said he. "A false step yonder means death to man or beast. Only yesterday I saw one of the moor ponies wander into it. He never came out. I saw his head for quite a long time craning out of the bog-hole, but it sucked him down at last. Even in dry seasons it is a danger to cross it, but after these autumn rains it is an awful place. And yet I can find my way to the very heart of it and return alive. By George, there is another of those miserable ponies!"

Something brown was rolling and tossing among the green sedges. Then a long, agonised, writhing neck shot upward and a dreadful cry echoed over the moor. It turned me cold with horror, but my companions's nerves seemed to be stronger than mine.

"It's gone!" said he. "The mire has him. Two in two days, and many more, perhaps, for they get in the way of going there in the dry weather and never know the difference until the mire has them in its clutches. It's a bad place, the great Grimpen Mire."

"And you say you can penetrate it?"

"Yes, there are one or two paths which a very active man can take. I have found them out."

"But why should you wish to go into so horrible a place?"

"Well, you see the hills beyond? They are really islands cut off on all sides by the impassable mire, which has crawled round them in the course of years. That is where the rare plants and the butter flies are, if you have the wit to reach them."

"I shall try my luck some day."

He looked at me with a surprised face.

"For God's sake put such an idea out of your mind," said he. "Your blood would be upon my head. I assure you that there would not be the least chance of your coming back alive. It is only by remembering certain complex landmarks that I am able to do it."

"Hello!" I cried. 'That is that?"

A long, low moan, indescribably sad, swept over the moor. It filled the whole air, and yet it was impossible to say whence it came. From a dull murmur it swelled into a deep roar, and then sank back into a melancholy, throbbing murmur once again. Stapleton looked at me with a curious expression in his face.

"Queer place, the moor!" said he.

"But what is it?"

"The peasants say it is the Hound of the Baskervilles calling for its prey. I've heard it once or twice before, but never quite so loud."

I looked round, with a chill of fear in my heart, at the huge swelling plain, mottled with the green patches of rushes. Nothing stirred over the vast expanse save a pair of ravens, which croaked loudly from a tor behind us.

"You are educated man. You don't believe such nonsense as that?" said I. "What do you think is the cause of so strange a sound?"

"Bogs make queer noises sometimes. It's the mud settling, or the water rising, or something."

"No, no, that was a living voice."

"Well, perhaps it was. Did you ever hear a bittern booming?"

"No, I never did."

"It's a very rare bird—practically extinct—in England now, but all things are possible upon the moor. Yes, I should not be surprised to learn that what we have heard is the cry of the last of the bitterns."

"It's the weirdest, strangest thing that ever I heard in my life."

"Yes, it's rather an uncanny place altogether. Look at the hillside yonder. What do you make of those?"

The whole steep slope was covered with gray circular rings of stone, a score of them at least.

"What are they? Sheep-pens?"

"No they are the homes of our worthy ancestors. Prehistoric man lived thickly on the moor, and as no one in particular has lived there since, we find all his little arrangements exactly as he left them. These are his wigwams with the roofs off. You can even see his hearth and his couch if you have the curiosity to go inside."

"But is quite a town. When was it inhabited?"

"Neolithic man—no date."

"What did he do?"

"He grazed his cattle on these slopes, and he learned to dig for tin when the bronze sword began to supersede the stone axe. Look at the great trench in the opposite hill. That is his mark. Yes, you will find some very singular points about the moor, Dr. Watson. Oh, excuse me an instant! It is surely Cyclopides."

" small fly or moth had fluttered across our path, and in an instant Stapleton was rushing with extraordinary energy and speed in pursuit of it. To my dismay the creature flew straight for the great mire, and my acquaintance never paused for an instant, bounding from tuft to tuft behind it, his green net waving in the air. His gray clothes and jerky, zigzag, irregular progress made him not unlike some huge moth himself. I was standing watching his pursuit with a mixture of admiration for his extraordinary activity and fear lest he should lose his footing in the treacherous mire when I heard the sound of steps and, turning round, found a woman near me upon the path. She had come from the direction in which the plume of smoke indicated the position of Merripit House, but the dip of the moor had hid her until she was quite close.

I could not doubt that this was the Miss Stapleton of whom I had been told, since ladies of any sort must be few upon the moor, and I remembered that I had heard someone describe her as being a beauty. The woman who approached me was certainly that, and of a most uncommon type. There could not have been a greater contrast between brother and sister, for Stapleton was neutral tinted, with light hair and gray eyes, while she was darker than any brunette whom I have seen in England—slim, elegant, and tall. She had a proud, finely cut face, so regular that it might have seemed impassive were it not for the sensitive mouth and the beautiful dark, eager eyes. With her perfect figure and elegant dress she was, indeed, a strange apparition upon a lonely Moreland path. Her eyes were on her brother as I turned, and then she quickened her pace towards me. I had raised my hat and was about to make some explanatory remark when her own words turned all my thoughts into a new channel.

"Go back!" she said. "Go straight back to London, instantly."

I could only stare at her in stupid surprise. Her eyes blazed at me, and she tapped the ground impatiently with her foot.

"Why should I go back?" I asked.

"I cannot explain." She spoke in a low, eager voice, with a curi ous lisp in her utterance. "But for God's sake do what I ask you. Go back and never set foot upon the moor again."

"But I have only just come."

"Man, man!" she cried. "Can you not tell when a warning is for your own good? Go back to London! Start to-night! Get away from this place at all costs! Hush, my brother is coming! Not a word of what I have said. Would you mind getting that orchid for me among the mare's-tails yonder? We are very rich in orchids on the moor, though, of course, you are rather late to see the beauties of the place."

Stapleton had abandoned the chase and came back to us breath ing hard and flushed with his exertions.

"Hello, Beryl!" said he, and it seemed to me that the tone of his greeting was not altogether a cordial one.

"Well,Jack, you are very hot."

"Yes, I was chasing a Cyclopides. He is very rare and seldom found in the late autumn. What a pity that I should have missed him!" He spoke unconcernedly, but his small light eyes glanced incessantly from the girl to me.

"You have introduced yourselves, I can see."

"Yes. I was telling Sir Henry that it was rather late for him to see the true beauties of the moor."

"Why, who do you think this is?"

"I imagine that it must be Sir Henry Baskerville."

"No, no," said I. "Only a humble commoner, but his friend. My name is Dr. Watson."

A flush of vexation passed over her expressive face. "We have been talking at cross purposes," said she.

"Why, you had not very much time for talk," her brother re marked with the same questioning eyes.

"I talked as if Dr. Watson were a resident instead of being merely a visitor," said she. "It cannot much matter to him whether it is early or late for the orchids. But you will come on, will you not, and see Merripit House?"

" short walk brought us to it, a bleak Moreland house, once the farm of some grazier in the old prosperous days, but now put into repair and turned into a modern dwelling. An orchard surrounded it, but the trees, as is usual upon the moor, were stunted and nipped, and the effect of the whole place was mean and melancholy. We were admitted by a strange, wizened, rusty-coated old manservant, who seemed in keeping with the house. Inside, how ever, there were large rooms furnished with an elegance in which I seemed to recognize the taste of the lady. As I looked from their windows at the interminable granite-flecked moor rolling unbroken to the farthest horizon I could not but marvel at what could have brought this highly educated man and this beautiful woman to live in such a place.

"Queer spot to choose, is it not?" said he as if in answer to my thought. "And yet we manage to make ourselves fairly happy, do we not, Beryl?"

"Quite happy," said she, but there was no ring of conviction in her words.

"I had a school," said Stapleton. "It was in the north country. The work to a man of my temperament was mechanical and uninteresting, but the privilege of living With youth, of helping to mould those young minds, and of impressing them with one's own character and ideals was very dear to me. However, the fates were against us. A serious epidemic broke out in the school and three of the boys died. It never recovered from the blow, and much of my capital was irretrievably swallowed up. And yet, if it were not for the loss of the charming companionship of the boys, I could rejoice over my own misfortune, for, with my strong tastes for botany and zoology I find an unlimited field of work here, and my sister is as devoted to Nature as I am. All this, Dr. Watson, has been brought upon your head by your expression as you surveyed the moor out of our window."

"It certainly did cross my mind that it might be a little dull—less for you, perhaps, than for your sister."

"No, no, I am never dull," said she quickly.

"We have books, we have our studies, and we have interesting neighbours. Dr. Mortimer is a most learned man in his own line. Poor sir Charles was also an admirable companion. We knew him well and miss him more than I can tell. Do you think that I should intrude if I were to call this afternoon and make the acquaintance of sir Henry?"

"I am sure that he would be delighted."

"Then perhaps you would mention that I propose to do so. We may in our humble way do something to make things more easy for him until he becomes accustomed to his new surroundings. Will you come upstairs, Dr. Watson, and inspect my collection of *Lepidoptera*? I think it is the most complete one in the south-west of Eng land. By the time that you have looked through them lunch will be almost ready."

But I was eager to get back to my charge. The melancholy of the moor, the death of the unfortunate pony, the weird sound which had been associated with the grim legend of the Baskervilles, all these things tinged my thoughts with sadness. Then on the top of these more or less vague impressions there had come the definite and distinct warning of Miss Stapleton, delivered with such intense earnestness that I could not doubt that some grave and deep reason lay behind it. I resisted all pressure to stay for lunch, and I set off at once upon my return journey, taking the grass-grown path by which we had come.

It seems, however, that there must have been some short cut for those who knew it, for before I had reached the road I was astounded to see Miss Stapleton sitting upon a rock by the side of the track. Her face was beautifully flushed with her exertions, and she held her hand to her side.

"I have run all the way in o-der to cut you off, Dr. Watson," said she. "I had not even time to put on my hat. I must not stop, or my brother may miss me. I wanted to say to you how sorry I am about the stupid mistake I made in thinking that you were Sir Henry. Please forget the words I said, which have no application whatever to you."

"But I can't forget them, Miss Stapleton," said I. "I am Sir Henry's friend, and his welfare is a very close concern of mine. Tell me why it was that you were so eager that Sir Henry should return to London."

"A woman's whim, Dr. Watson. When you know me better you will understand that I cannot always give reasons for what I say or do."

"No, no. I remember the thrill in your voice. I remember the look in your eyes. Please, please, be frank with me, Miss Stapleton, for ever since I have been here I have been conscious of shadows all round me. Life has become like that great Grimpen Mire, with little green patches everywhere into which one may sink and with no guide to point the track. Tell me then what it was that you meant, and I will promise to convey your warning to Sir Henry."

An expression of irresolution passed for an instant over her face, but her eyes had hardened again when she answered me.

"You make too much of it, Dr. Watson," said she. "My brother and I were very much shocked by the death of Sir Charles. We knew him very intimately, for his favourite walk was over the moor to our house. He was deeply impressed with the curse which hung over his family, and when this tragedy came I naturally felt that there must be some grounds for the fears which he had expressed. I was distressed therefore when another member of the family came down to live here, and I felt that he should be warned of the danger which he will run. That was all which I intended to convey."

"But what is the danger?"

"You know the story of the hound?"

"I do not believe in such nonsense."

"But I do. If you have any influence with Sir Henry, take him away from a place which has always been fatal to his family. The world is wide. Why should he wish to live at the place of danger?"

"Because it is the place of danger. That is Sir Henry's nature. I fear that unless you can give me some more definite information than this it would be impossible to get him to move."

"I cannot say anything definite, for I do not know anything definite."

"I would ask you one more question, Miss Stapleton. If you meant no more than this when you first spoke to me, why should you not wish your brother to overhear what you said? There is nothing to which he, or anyone else, could object."

"My brother is very anxious to have the Hall inhabited, for he thinks that it is for the good of the poor folk upon the moor. He would be very angry if he knew that I had said anything which might induce Sir Henry to go away. But I have done my duty now and I will say no more. I must get back, or he will miss me and suspect that I have seen you. Good-bye!" She turned and had disappeared in a few minutes among the scattered boulders, while I, with my soul full of vague fears, pursued my way to Baskerville Hall.

## CHAPTER 8

# FIRST REPORT OF DR. WATSON

From this point onward I will follow the course of events by transcribing my own letters to Mr. Sherlock Holmes which lie before me on the table. One page is missing, but otherwise they are exactly as written and show my feeling and suspicions of the moment more accurately than my memory, clear as it is upon these tragic events, can possibly do.

*Baskerville Hall, October 13th.*

MY DEAR HOLMES:

My previous letters and telegrams have kept you pretty well up to date as to all that has occurred in this most God-forsaken corner of the world. The longer one stays here the more does the spirit of the moor sink into one's soul, its vastness, and also its grim charm. When you are once out upon its bosom you have left all traces of modern England behind you, but, on the other hand, you are conscious everywhere of the homes and the work of the prehistoric people. On all sides of you as you walk are the houses of these forgot ten folk, with their graves and the huge monoliths which are sup posed to have marked their temples. As you look at their gray stone huts against the scarred hillsides you leave your own age behind you, and if you were to see a skin-clad, hairy man crawl out from the low door, fitting a flint-tipped arrow on to the string of his bow, you would feel that his presence there was more natural than your own. The strange thing is that they should have lived so thickly on what must always have been most unfruitful soil. I am no antiquarian, but I could imagine that they were some unwarlike and harried race who were forced to accept that which none other would occupy.

All this, however, is foreign to the mission on which you sent me and will probably be very uninteresting to your severely practical mind. I can still remember your complete indifference as to whether the sun moved round the earth or the earth round the sun. Let me, therefore, return to the facts concerning Sir Henry Baskerville.

If you have not had any report within the last few days it is be cause up to to-day there was nothing of importance to relate. Then a very surprising circumstance occurred, which I shall tell you in due course. But, first of all, I must keep you in touch with some of the other factors in the situation.

One of these, concerning which I have said little, is the escaped convict upon the moor. There is strong reason now to believe that he has got right away, which is a considerable relief to the lonely householders of this district. A fortnight has passed since his flight, during which he has not been seen and nothing has been heard of him. It is surely inconceivable that he could have held out upon the moor during all that time. Of course, so far as his concealment goes there is no difficulty at all. Any one of these stone huts would give him a hiding-place. But there is nothing to eat unless he were to catch and slaughter one of the moor sheep. We think, therefore, that he has gone, and the outlying farmers sleep the better in consequence.

We are four able-bodied men in this household, so that we could take good care of ourselves, but I confess that I have had uneasy moments when I have thought of the Stapletons. They live miles from any help. There are one maid, an old manservant, the sister, and the brother, the latter not a very strong man. They would be helpless in the hands of a desperate fellow like this Notting Hill criminal if he could once effect an entrance. Poth Sir Henry and I were concerned at their situation, and it was suggested that Perkins the groom should go over to sleep there, but Stapleton would not hear of it.

The fact is that our friend, the baronet, begins to display a considerable interest in our fair neighbour. It is not to be wondered at, for time hangs heavily in this lonely spot to an active man like him, and she is a very fascinating and beautiful woman. There is some thing tropical and exotic about her which forms a singular contrast to her cool and unemotional brother. Yet he also gives the idea of hidden fires. He has certainly a very marked influence over her, for I have seen her continually glance at him as she talked as if seeking approbation for what she said. I trust that he is kind to her. There is a dry glitter in his eyes and a firm set of his thin lips, which goes with a positive and possibly a harsh nature. You would find him an interesting study.

He came over to call upon Baskerville on that first day, and the very next morning he took us both to show us the spot where the legend of the wicked Hugo is supposed to have had its origin. It was an excursion of some miles across the moor to a place which is so dismal that it might have suggested the story. We found a short valley between rugged tors which led to an open, grassy space flecked over with the white cotton grass. In the middle of it rose two great stones, worn and sharpened at the upper end until they looked like the huge corroding fangs of some monstrous beast. In every way it corresponded with the scene of the old tragedy. Sir Henry was much interested and asked Stapleton more than once whether he did really believe in the possibility of the interference of the supernatural in the affairs of men. He spoke lightly, but it was evident that he was very much in earnest. Stapleton was guarded in his replies, but it was easy to see that he said less than he might, and that he would not express his whole opinion out of consideration for the feelings of the baronet. He told us of similar cases, where families had suffered from some evil influence, and he left us with the impression that he shared the popular view upon the matter.

On our way back we stayed for lunch at Merripit House, and it was there that Sir Henry made the acquaintance of Miss Stapleton. From the first moment that he saw her he appeared to be strongly attracted by her, and I am much mistaken if the feeling was not mutual. He referred to her again and again on our walk home, and since then hardly a day has passed that we have not seen some thing of the brother and sister. They dine here to-night, and there is some talk of our going to them next week. One would imagine that such a match would be very welcome to Stapleton, and yet I have more than once caught a look of the strongest disapprobation in his face when Sir Henry has been paying some attention to his sister. He is much attached to her, no doubt, and would lead a lonely life without her, but it would seem the height of selfishness if he were to stand in the way of her making so brilliant a marriage. Yet I am certain that he does not wish their intimacy to ripen into love, and I have several times observed that he has taken pains to prevent them from being tete-a-tete. By the way, your instructions to me never to allow Sir Henry to go out alone will become very much more onerous if a love affair were to be added to our other difficulties. My popularity would soon suffer if I were to carry out your orders to the letter.

The other day—Thursday, to be more exact—Dr. Mortimer lunched with us. He has been excavating a barrow at Long Down and has got a prehistoric skull which fills him with great joy. Never was there such a single-minded enthusiast as he! The Stapletons came in afterwards, and the good doctor took us all to the yew alley at Sir Henry's request to show us exactly how everything occurred upon that fatal night. It is a long, dismal walk, the yew alley, between two high walls of clipped hedge, with a narrow band of grass upon either side. At the far end is an old tumble-down summer house. Halfway down is the moor-gate, where the old gentleman left his cigar-ash. It is a white wooden gate with a latch. Beyond it lies the wide moor. I remembered your theory of the affair and tried to picture all that had occurred. As the old man stood there he saw something coming across the moor, something which terrified him so that he lost his wits and ran an ran until he died of sheer horror and exhaustion. There was the long, gloomy tunnel down which he fled. And from what? A sheep-dog of the moor? Or a spectral hound, black, silent, and monstrous? Was there a human agency in the matter? Did the pale, watchful Barrymore know more than he cared to say? It was all dim and vague, but always there is the dark shadow of crime behind it.

One other neighbour I have met since I wrote last. This is Mr. Frankland, of Lafter Hall, who lives some four miles to the south of us. He is an elderly man, red-faced, white-haired, and choleric. His passion is for the British law, and he has spent a large fortune in litigation. He fights for the mere pleasure of fighting and is equally ready to take up either side of a question, so that it is no wonder that he has found it a costly amusement. Sometimes he will shut up a right of way and defy the parish to make him open it. At others he will with his own hands tear down some other man's gate and declare that a path has existed there form time immemorial, defying the owner to prosecute him for trespass. He is learned in old manorial and communal rights, and he applies his knowledge sometimes in favour of the villagers of Fernworthy and sometimes against them, so that he is periodically either carried in triumph down the village street or else burned in effigy, according to his latest exploit. He is said to have about seven lawsuits upon his hands at present, which will probably swallow up the remainder of his fortune and so draw his sting and leave him harmless for the future. Apart from the law he seems a kindly, good-natured person, and I only mention him because you were particular that I should send some description of the people who surround us. He is curi ously employed at present, for, being an amateur astronomer, he has an excellent telescope, with which he lies upon the roof of his own house and sweeps the moor all day in the hope of catching a glimpse of the escaped convict. If he would confine his energies to this all would be well, but there are rumours that he intends to prosecute Dr. Mortimer for opening a grave without the consent of the next of kin because he dug up the neolithic skull in the barrow on Long Down. He helps to keep our lives from being monotonous and gives a little comic relief where it is badly needed.

"And now, having brought you up to date in the escaped convict, the Stapletons, Dr. Mortimer, and Frankland, of Lafter Hall, let me end on that which is most important and tell you more about the Barrymores, and especially about the surprising development of last night.

First of all about the test telegram, which you sent from London in order to make sure that Barrymore was really here. I have al ready explained that the testimony of the postmaster shows that the test was worthless and that we have no proof one way or the other. I told Sir Henry how the matter stood, and he at once, in his downright fashion, had Barrymore up and asked him whether he had received the telegram himself Barrymore said that he had.

"Did the boy deliver it into your own hands?" asked Sir Henry.

Barrymore looked surprised, and considered for a little time.

"No," said he, "I was in the box-room at the time, and my wife brought it up to me."

"Did you answer it yourself?"

"No; I told my wife what to answer and she went down to write it."

In the evening he recurred to the subject of his own accord.

"I could not quite understand the object of your questions this morning, Sir Henry," said he. "I trust that they do not mean that I have done anything to forfeit your confidence?"

Sir Henry had to assure him that it was not so and pacify him by giving him a considerable part of his old wardrobe, the London outfit having now all arrived.

Mrs. Barrymore is of interest to me. She is a heavy, solid person very limited, intensely respectable, and inclined to be puritanical. You could hardly conceive a less emotional subject. Yet I have told you how, on the first night here, I heard her sobbing bitterly, and since then I have more than once observed traces of tears upon her face. Some deep sorrow gnaws ever at her heart. Sometimes I wonder if she has a guilty memory which haunts her, and sometimes I suspect Barrymore of being a domestic tyrant. I have always felt that there was something singular and questionable in this man's character, but the adventure of last night brings all my suspicions to a head.

"And yet it may seem a small matter in itself You are aware that I am not a very sound sleeper, and since I have been on guard in this house my slumbers have been lighter than ever. Last night, about two in the morning, I was aroused by a stealthy step passing my room. I rose, opened my door, and peeped out. A long black shadow was trailing down the corridor. It was thrown by a man who walked softly down the passage with a candle held in his hand. He was in shirt and trousers, with no covering to his feet. I could merely see the outline, but his height told me that it was Barry more. He walked very slowly and circumspectly, and there was something indescribably guilty and furtive in his whole appear ance.

I have told you that the corridor is broken by the balcony which runs round the hall, but that it is resumed upon the farther side. I waited until he had passed out of sight and then I followed him. When I came round the balcony he had reached the end of the far ther corridor, and I could see from the glimmer of light through an open door that he had entered one of the rooms. Now, all these rooms are unfurnished and unoccupied, so that his expedition be came more mysterious than ever. The light shone steadily as if he were standing motionless. I crept down the passage as noiselessly as I could and peeped round the corner of the door.

Barrymore was crouching at the window with the candle held against the glass. His profile was half turned towards me, and his face seemed to be rigid with expectation as he stared out into the blackness of the moor. For some minutes he stood watching intently. Then he gave a deep groan and with an impatient gesture he put out the light. Instantly I made my way back to my room, and very shortly came the stealthy steps passing once more upon their return journey. Long afterwards when I h.ad fallen into a light sleep I heard a key turn somewhere in a lock, but I could not tell whence the sound came. What it all means I cannot guess, but there is some secret business going on in this house of gloom which sooner or later we shall get to the bottom of I do not trouble you with my theories, for you asked me to furnish you only with facts. I have had a long talk with sir Henry this morning, and we have made a plan of campaign founded upon my observations of last night. I will not speak about it just now, but it should make my next report interesting reading.

## CHAPTER 9

# SECOND REPORT OF DR. WATSON

### THE LIGHT UPON THE MOOR

*Baskerville Hall, Oct. 15th.*

MY DEAR HOLMES:

If I was compelled to leave you without much news during the early days of my mission you must acknowledge that I am making up for lost time, and that events are now crowding thick and fast upon us. In my last report I ended upon my top note with Barry more at the window, and now I have quite a budget already which will, unless I am much mistaken, considerably surprise you. Things have taken a turn which I could not have anticipated. In some ways they have within the last forty-eight hours become much clearer and in some ways they have become more complicated. But I will tell you all and you shall judge for yourself

Before breakfast on the morning following my adventure I went down the corridor and examined the room in which Barrymore ha been on the night before. The western window through which he had stared so intently has, I noticed, one peculiarity above all other windows in the house—it commands the nearest outlook on to the moor. There is an opening between two trees which enables one from this point of view to look right down upon it, while from all the other windows it is only a distant glimpse which can be obtained. It follows, therefore, that Barrymore, since only this window would serve the purpose, must have been looking out for some thing or somebody upon the moor. The night was very dark, so that I can hardly imagine how he could have hoped to see anyone. It had struck me that it was possible that some love intrigue was on foot. That would have accounted for his stealthy movements and also for the uneasiness of his wife. The man is a striking-looking fellow, very well equipped to steal the heart of a country girl, so that this theory seemed to have something to support it. That opening of the door which I had heard after I had returned to my room might mean that he had gone out to keep some clandestine appointment. So I reasoned with myself in the morning, and I tell you the direction of my suspicions, however much the result may have shown that they were unfounded.

But whatever the true explanation of Barrymore's movements might be, I felt that the responsibility of keeping them to myself until I could explain them was more than I could bear. I had an interview with the baronet in his study after breakfast, and I told him all that I had seen. He was less surprised than I had expected.

"I knew that Barrymore walked about nights, and I had a mind to speak to him about it," said he. "Two or three times I have heard his steps in the passage, coming and going, just about the hour you name."

"Perhaps then he pays a visit every night to that particular win dow," I suggested.

"Perhaps he does. If so, we should be able to shadow him and see what it is that he is after. I wonder what your friend Holmes would do if he were here."

"I believe that he would do exactly what you now suggest," said I. "I would follow Barrymore and see what he did."

"Then we shall do it together."

"But surely he would hear us."

"The man is rather deaf, and in any case we must take our chance of that. We'll sit up in my room to-night and wait until he passes." Sir Henry rubbed his hands with pleasure, and it was evi dent that he hailed the adventure as a relief to his somewhat quiet life upon the moor.

The baronet has been in communication with the architect who prepared the plans for Sir Charles, and with a contractor from London, so that we may expect great changes to begin here soon. There have been decorators and furnishers up from Plymouth, and it is evident that our-friend has large ideas and means to spare no pains or expense to restore the grandeur of his family. When the house is renovated and refurnished, all that he will need will be a wife to make it complete. Between ourselves there are pretty clear signs that this will not be wanting if the lady is willing, for I have seldom seen a man more infatuated with a woman than he is with our beautiful neighbour, Miss Stapleton. And yet the course of true love does not run quite as smoothly as one would under the circumstances expect. To-day, for example, its surface was broken by a very unexpected ripple, which has caused our friend considerable perplexity and annoyance.

"After the conversation which I have quoted about Barrymore, Sir Henry put on his hat and prepared to go out. As a matter of course I did the same.

"What, are *you* coming, Watson?" he asked, looking at me in a curious way.

"That depends on whether you are going on the moor," said I.

"Yes, I am."

"Well, you know what my instructions are. I am sorry to intrude, but you heard how earnestly Holmes insisted that I should not leave you, and especially that you should not go alone upon the moor."

Sir Henry put his hand upon my shoulder with a pleasant smile.

"My dear fellow," said he, "Holmes, with all his wisdom, did not foresee some things which have happened since I have been on the moor. You understand me? I am sure that you are the last man in the world who would wish to be a spoil-sport. I must go out alone."

It put me in a most awkward position. I was at a loss what to say or what to do, and before I had made up my mind he picked up his cane and was gone.

But when I came to think the matter over my conscience reproached me bitterly for having on any pretext allowed him to go out of my sight. I imagined what my feelings would be if I had to return to you and to confess that some misfortune had occurred through my disregard for your instructions. I assure you my cheeks flushed at the very thought. It might not even now be too late to overtake him, so I set off at once in the direction of Merripit House.

I hurried along the road at the top of my speed without seeing anything of Sir Henry, until I came to the point where the moor path branches off. There, fearing that perhaps I had come in the wrong direction after all, I mounted a hill from which I could com mand a view—the same hill which is cut into the dark quarry. Thence I saw him at once. He was on the moor path, about a quarter of a mile off, and a lady was by his side who could only be Miss Stapleton. It was clear that there was already an understanding between them and that they had met by appointment. They were walking slowly along in deep conversation, and I saw her making quick little movements of her hands as if she were very earnest in what she was saying, while he listened intently, and once or twice shook his head in strong dissent. I stood among the rocks watching them, very much puzzled as to what I should do next. To follow them and break into their intimate conversation seemed to be an outrage, and yet my clear duty was never for an instant to let him out of my sight. To act the spy upon a friend was a hateful task. Still, I could see no better course than to observe him from the hill, and to clear my conscience by confessing to him afterwards what I had done. It is true that if any sudden danger had threatened him I was too far away to be of use, and yet I am sure that you will agree with me that the position was very difficult, and that there was nothing more which I could do.

Our friend, Sir Henry, and the lady had halted on the path and were standing deeply absorbed in their conversation, when I was suddenly aware that I was not the only witness of their interview. A wisp of green floating in the air caught my eye, and another glance showed me that it was carried on a stick by a man who was moving among the broken ground. It was Stapleton with his butterfly-net. He was very much closer to the pair than I was, and he appeared to be moving in their direction. At this instant Sir Henry suddenly drew Miss Stapleton to his side. His arm was round her, but it seemed to me that she was straining away from him with her face averted. He stooped his head to hers, and she raised one hand as if in protest. Next moment I saw them spring apart and turn hurriedly round. Stapleton was the cause of the interruption. He was running wildly towards them, his absurd net dangling behind him. He gesticulated and almost danced with excitement in front of the lovers. What the scene meant I could not imagine, but it seemed to me that Stapleton was abusing Sir Henry, who offered explana- tions, which became more angry as the other refused to accept them. The lady stood by in haughty silence. Finally Stapleton turned upon his heel and beckoned in a peremptory way to his sister, who, after an irresolute glance at Sir Henry, walked off by the side of her brother. The naturalist's angry gestures showed that the lady was included in his displeasure. The baronet stood for a minute looking after them, and then he walked slowly back the way that he had come, his head hanging, the very picture of dejection.

What all this meant r could not imagine, but I was deeply ashamed to have witnessed so intimate a scene without my friend's knowledge. I ran down the hill therefore and met the baronet at the bottom. His face was flushed with anger and his brows were wrinkled, like one who is at his wit's ends what to do.

"Hello, Watson! Where have you dropped from?" said he. "You don't mean to say that you came after me in spite of all?"

I explained everything to him: how I had found it impossible to remain behind, how I had followed him, and how I had witnessed all that had occurred. For an instant his eyes blazed at me, but my frankness disarmed his anger, and he broke at last into a rather rueful laugh.

"You would have thought the middle of that prairie a fairly safe place for a man to be private," said he, "but, by thunder, the whole countryside seems to have been out to see me do my wooing—and a mighty poor wooing at that! Where had you engaged a seat?"

"I was on that hill."

"Quite in the back row, eh? But her brother was well up to the front. Did you see him come out on us?"

"Yes, I did."

"Did he ever strike you as being crazy—this brother of hers?"

"I can't say that he ever did."

"I dare say not. I always thought him sane enough until to-day, but you can take it from me that either he or I ought to be in a straitjacket. What's the matter with me, anyhow? You've lived near me for some weeks, Watson. Tell me straight, now! Is there anything that would prevent me from making a good husband to a woman that I loved?"

"I should say not."

"He can't object to my worldly position, so it must be myself that he has this down on. What has he against me? I never hurt man or woman in my life that I know of And yet he would not so much as let me touch the tips of her fingers."

"Did he say so?"

"That, and a deal more. I tell you, Watson, I've only known her these few weeks, but from the first I just felt that she was made For me, and she, too—she was happy when she was with me, and that I'll swear. There's light in a woman's eyes that speaks louder than words. But he has never let us get together, and it was only to-day for the first time that I saw a chance of having a few words with her alone. She was glad to meet me, but when she did it was not love that she would talk about, and she wouldn't have let me talk about it either if she could have stopped it. She kept coming back to it that this was a place of danger, and that she would never be happy until I had left it. I told her that since I had seen her I was in no hurry to leave it, and that if she really wanted me to go, the only way to work it was for her to arrange to go with me. With that I offered in as many words to marry her, but before she could answer, down came this brother of hers, running at us with a face on him like a madman. He was just white with rage, and those light eyes of his were blazing with fury. What was I doing with the lady? How dared I offer her attentions which were distasteful to her? Did I think that because I was a baronet I could do what I liked? If he had not been her brother I should have known better how to answer him. As it was I told him that my feelings towards his sister were such as I was not ashamed of, and that I hoped that she might honour me by becoming my wife. That seemed to make the matter no better, so then I lost my temper too, and I answered him rather more hotly than I should perhaps, considering that she was stand ing by. So it ended by his going off with her, as you saw, and here am I as badly puzzled a man as any in this county.Just tell me what it all means, Watson, and I'll owe you more than ever I can hope to pay."

I tried one or two explanations, but, indeed, I was completely puzzled myself Our friend's title, his fortune, his age, his character, and his appearance are all in his favour, and I know nothing against him unless it be this dark fate which runs in his family. That his advances should be rejected so brusquely without any reference to the lady's own wishes and that the lady should accept the situation without protest is very amazing. However, our conjectures were set a rest by a visit from Stapleton himself that very afternoon. He had come to offer apologies for his rudeness of the morning, and after a long private interview with Sir Henry in his study the upshot of their conversation was that the breach is quite healed, and that we are to dine at Merripit House next Friday as a sign of it.

"I don't say now that he isn't a crazy man," said Sir Henry; "I can't forget the look in his eyes when he ran at me this morning, but I must allow that no man could make a more handsome apology than he has done."

"Did he give any explanation of his conduct?"

"His sister is everything in his life, he says. That is natural enough, and I am glad that he should understand her value. They have always been together, and according to his account he has been a very lonely man with only her as a companion, so that the thought of losing her was really terrible to him. He had not under stood, he said, that I was becoming attached to her, but when he saw with his own eyes that it was really so, and that she might be taken away from him, it gave him such a shock that for a time he was not responsible for what he said or did. He was very sorry for all that had passed, and he recognized how foolish and how selfish it was that he should imagine that he could hold a beautiful woman like his sister to himself for her whole life. If she had to leave him he had rather it was to a neighbour like myself than to anyone else. But in any case it was a blow to him, and it would take him some time before he could prepare himself to meet it. He would withdraw all opposition upon his part if I would promise for three months to let the matter rest and to be content with cultivating the lady's friendship during that time without claiming her love. This I promised, and so the matter rests."

So there is one of our small mysteries cleared up. It is something to have touched bottom anywhere in this bog in which we are floundering. We know now why Stapleton looked with disfavour upon his sister's suitor—even when that suitor was so eligible a one as Sir Henry. And now I pass on to another thread which I have extricated out of the tangled skein, the mystery of the sobs in the night, of the tear-stained face of Mrs. Barrymore, of the secret journey of the butler to the western lattice window. Congratulate me, my dear Holmes, and tell me that I have not disappointed you as an agent—that you do not regret the confidence which you showed in me when you sent me down. All these things have by one night's work been thoroughly cleared.

I have said "by one night's work," but, in truth, it was by two nights' work, for on the first we drew entirely blank. I sat up with Sir Henry in his rooms until nearly three o'clock in the morning, but no sound of any sort did we hear except the chiming clock upon the stairs. It was a most melancholy vigil and ended by each of us falling asleep in our chairs. Fortunately we were not discouraged, and we determined to try again. The next night we lowered the lamp and sat smoking cigarettes without making the least sound. It was incredible how slowly the hours crawled by, and yet we were helped through it by the same sort of patient interest which the hunter must feel as he watches the trap into which he hopes the game may wander. One struck, and two, and we had almost for the second time given it up in despair when in an instant we both sat bolt upright in our chairs, with all our weary senses keenly on the alert once more. We had heard the creak of a step in the passage.

Very stealthily we heard it pass along until it died away in the distance. Then the baronet gently opened his door and we set out in pursuit. Already our man had gone round the gallery, and the corridor was all in darkness. Softly we stole along until we had come into the other wing. We were just in time to catch a glimpse of the tall, black-bearded figure, his shoulders rounded, as he tip toed down the passage. Then he passed through the same door as before, and the light of the candle framed it in the darkness and shot one single yellow beam across the gloom of the corridor. We shuffled cautiously towards it, trying every plank before we dared to put our whole weight upon it. We had taken the precaution of leaving our boots behind us, but, even so, the old boards snapped and creaked beneath our tread. Sometimes it seemed impossible that he should fail to hear our approach. However, the man is fortunately rather deaf, and he was entirely preoccupied in that which he was doing. When at last we reached the door and peeped through we found him crouching at the window, candle in hand, his white, intent face pressed against the pane, exactly as I had seen him two nights before.

We had arranged no plan of campaign, but the baronet is a man to whom the most direct way is always the most natural. He walked into the room, and as he did so Barrymore sprang up from the win dow with a sharp hiss of his breath and stood, livid and trembling, before us. His dark eyes, glaring out of the white mask of his face, were full of horror and astonishment as he gazed from Sir Henry to me.

"What are you doing here, Barrymore?"

"Nothing, sir." His agitation was so great that he could hardly speak, and the shadows sprang up and down from the shaking of his candle. "It was the window, sir. I go round at night to see that they are fastened."

"On the second floor?"

"Yes, sir, all the windows."

"Look here, Barrymore," said Sir Henry sternly, awe have made up our minds to have the truth out of you, so it will save you trouble to tell it sooner rather than later. Come, now! No lies! What were you doing at that window.?"

The fellow looked at us in a helpless way, and he wrung his hands together like one who is in the last extremity of doubt and misery.

"I was doing no harm, sir. I was holding a candle to the window."

"And why were you holding a candle to the window.?"

"Don't ask me, Sir Henry—don't ask me! I give you my word, sir, that it is not my secret, and that I cannot tell it. If it concerned no one but myself I would not try to keep it from you."

" sudden idea occurred to me, and I took the candle from the trembling hand of the butler.

"He must have been holding it as a signal," said I. "Let us see if there is any answer." I held it as he had done, and stared out into the darkness of the night. Vaguely I could discern the black bank of the trees and the lighter expanse of the moor, for the moon was be hind the clouds. And then I gave a cry of exultation, for a tiny pin point of yellow light had suddenly transfixed the dark veil, and glowed steadily in the centre of the black square framed by the window.

"There it is!" I cried.

"No, no, sir, it is nothing—nothing at all!" the butler broke in; "I assure you, sir—"

"Move your light across the window, Watson!" cried the baronet. "See, the other moves also! Now, you rascal, do you deny that it is a signal? Come, speak up! Who is your confederate out yonder, and what is this conspiracy that is going on?"

The man's face became openly defiant.

"It is my business, and not yours. I will not tell."

"Then you leave my employment right away."

"Very good, sir. If I must I must."

"And you go in disgrace. By thunder, you may well be ashamed of yourself Your family has lived with mine for over a hundred years under this roof, and here I find you deep in some dark plot against me."

"No, no, sir; no, not against you!" It was a woman's voice, and Mrs. Barrymore, paler and more horror-struck than her husband, was standing at the door. Her bulky figure in a shawl and skirt might have been comic were it not for the intensity of feeling upon her face.

"We have to go, Eliza. This is the end of it. You can pack our things," said the butler.

"Oh, John, John, have I brought you to this? It is my doing, Sir Henry—all mine. He has done nothing except for my sake, and be cause I asked him."

"Speak out, then! What does it mean?"

"My unhappy brother is starving on the moor. We cannot let him perish at our very gates. The light is a signal to him that food is ready for him, and his light out yonder is to show the spot to which to bring it."

"Then your brother is

"The escaped convict, sir—Selden, the criminal."

"That's the truth, sir," said Barrymore. "I said that it was not my secret and that I could not tell it to you. But now you have heard it, and you will see that if there was a plot it was not against you."

This, then, was the explanation of the stealthy expeditions at night and the light at the window. Sir Henry and

I both stared at the woman in amazement. Was it possible that this stolidly respect able person was of the same blood as one of the most notorious criminals in the country?

"Yes, sir, my name was Selden, and he is my younger brother. We humoured him too much when he was a lad and gave him his own way in everything until he came to think that the world was made for his pleasure, and that he could do what he liked in it. Then as he grew older he met wicked companions, and the devil entered into him until he broke my mother's heart and dragged our name in the dirt. From crime to crime he sank lower and lower until it is only the mercy of God which has snatched him from the scaffold; but to me, sir, he was always the little curly-headed boy that I had nursed and played with as an elder sister would. That was why he broke prison, sir. He knew that I was here and that we could not refuse to help him. When he dragged himself here one night, weary and starving, with the warders hard at his heels, what could we do? We took him in and fed him and cared for him. Then you returned, sir, and my brother thought he would be safer on the moor than anywhere else until the hue and cry was over, so he lay in hiding there. But every second night we made sure if he was still there by putting a light in the window, and if there was an answer my husband took out some bread and meat to him. Every day we hoped that he was gone, but as long as he was there we could not desert him. That is the whole truth, as I am an honest Christian woman, and you will see that if there is blame in the matter it does not lie with my husband but with me, for whose sake he has done all that he has."

The woman's words came with an intense earnestness which car ried conviction with them.

"Is this true, Barrymore?"

"Yes, Sir Henry. Every word of it."

"Well, I cannot blame you for standing by your own wife. Forget what I have said. Go to your room, you two, and we shall talk further about this matter in the morning."

When they were gone we looked out of the window again. Sir Henry had flung it open, and the cold night wind beat in upon our faces. Far away in the black distance there still glowed that one tiny point of yellow light.

"I wonder he dares," said Sir Henry.

"It may be so placed as to be only visible from here."

'Very likely. How far do you think it is?"

"Out by the Cleft Tor, I think."

"Not more than a mile or two off."

"Hardly that."

"Well, it cannot be far if Barrymore had to carry out the food to it. And he is waiting, this villain, beside that candle. By thunder, Watson, I am going out to take that man!"

The same thought had crossed my own mind. It was not as if the Barrymores had taken us into their confidence. Their secret had been forced from them. The man was a danger to the community, an unmitigated scoundrel for whom there was neither pity nor excuse. We were only doing our duty in taking this chance of putting him back where he could do no harm. With his brutal and violent nature, others would have to pay the price if we held our hands. Any night, for example, our neighbours the Stapletons might be at tacked by him, and it may have been the thought of this which made Sir Henry so keen upon the adventure.

"I will come," said I.

"Then get your revolver and put on your boots. The sooner we start the better, as the fellow may put out his light and be off."

In five minutes we were outside the door, starting upon our expedition. We hurried through the dark shrubbery, amid the dull moaning of the autumn wind and the rustle of the falling leaves. The night air was heavy with the smell of damp and decay. Now and again the moon peeped out for an instant, but clouds were driving over the face of the sky, and just as we came out on the moor a thin rain began to fall. The light still burned steadily in front.

"Are you armed?" I asked.

"I have a hunting-crop."

"We must close in on him rapidly, for he is said to be a desperate fellow. We shall take him by surprise and have him at our mercy before he can resist."

"I say, Watson," said the baronet, "what would Holmes say to this? How about that hour of darkness in which the power of evil is exalted?"

As if in answer to his words there rose suddenly out of the vast gloom of the moor that strange cry which I had already heard upon the borders of the great Grimpen Mire. It came with the wind through the silence of the night, a long, deep mutter, then a rising howl, and then the sad moan in which it died away. Again and again it sounded, the whole air throbbing with it, strident, wild, and menacing. The baronet caught my sleeve and his face glimmered white through the darkness.

"My God, what's that, Watson?"

"I don't know. It's a sound they have on the moor. I heard it once before."

It died away, and an absolute silence closed in upon us. We stood straining our ears, but nothing came.

"Watson," said the baronet, "it was the cry of a hound."

My blood ran cold in my veins, for there was a break in his voice which told of the sudden horror which had seized him.

"What do they call this sound?" he asked.

"Who?"

"The folk on the countryside?"

"Oh, they are ignorant people. Why should you mind what they call it?"

"Tell me, Watson. What do they say of it?"

I hesitated but could not escape the question.

"They say it is the cry of the Hound of the Baskervilles."

He groaned and was silent for a few moments.

"A hound it was," he said at last, "but it seemed to come from miles away, over yonder, I think."

"It was hard to say whence it came."

"It rose and fell with the wind. Isn't that the direction of the great Grimpen Mire?"

"Yes, it is."

"Well, it was up there. Come now, Watson, didn't you think yourself that it was the cry of a hound? I am not a child. You need not fear to speak the truth."

"Stapleton was with me when I heard it last. He said that it might be the calling of a strange bird."

"No, no, it was a hound. My God, can there be some truth in all these stories? Is it possible that I am really in danger from so dark a cause? You don't believe it, do you, Watson?"

"No, no."

"And yet it was one thing to laugh about it in London, and it is another to stand out here in the darkness of the moor and to hear such a cry as that. And my uncle! There was the footprint of the hound beside him as he lay. It all fits together. I don't think that I am a coward, Watson, but that sound seemed to freeze my very blood. Feel my hand!"

It was as cold as a block of marble.

"You'll be all right to-morrow."

"I don't think I'll get that cry out of my head. What do you advise that we do now?"

"Shall we turn back?"

"No, by thunder; we have come out to get our man, and we will do it. We after the convict, and a hell-hound, as likely as not, after us. Come on! We'll see it through if all the fiends of the pit were loose upon the moor."

We stumbled slowly along in the darkness, with the black loom of the craggy hills around us, and the yellow speck of light burning steadily in front. There is nothing so deceptive as the distance of a light upon a pitch-dark night, and sometimes the glimmer seemed to be far away upon the horizon and sometimes it might have been within a few yards of us. But at last we could see whence it came, and then we knew that we were indeed very close. A fluttering candle was stuck in a crevice of the rocks which flanked it on each side so as to keep the wind from it and also to prevent it from being visible, save in the direction of Baskerville Hall. A boulder of granite concealed our approach, and crouching behind it we gazed over it at the signal light. It was strange to see this single candle burning there in the middle of the moor, with no sign of life near it—just the one straight yellow flame and the gleam of the rock on each side of it.

"What shall we do now?" whispered Sir Henry.

'Wait here. He must be near his light. Let us see if we can get a glimpse of him."

The words were hardly out of my mouth when we both saw him. Over the rocks, in the crevice of which the candle burned, there was thrust out an evil yellow face, a terrible animal face, all seamed and scored with vile passions. Foul with mire, with a bristling beard, and hung with matted hair, it might well have belonged to one of those old savages who dwelt in the burrows on the hillsides. The light beneath him was reflected in his small, cunning eyes which peered fiercely to right and left through the darkness like a crafty and savage animal who has heard the steps of the hunters.

Something had evidently aroused his suspicions. It may have been that Barrymore had some private signal which we had neglected to give, or the fellow may have had some other reason for thinking that all was not well, but I could read his fears upon his wicked face. Any instant he might dash out the light and vanish in the darkness. I sprang forward therefore, and Sir Henry did the same. At the same moment the convict screamed out a curse at us and hurled a rock which splintered up against the boulder which had sheltered us. I caught one glimpse of his short, squat, strongly built figure as he sprang to his feet and turned to run. At the same moment by a lucky chance the moon broke through the clouds. We rushed over the brow of the hill, and there was our man running with great speed down the other side, springing over the stones in his way with the activity of a mountain goat. A lucky long shot of my revolver might have crippled him, but I had brought it only to defend myself if attacked and not to shoot an unarmed man who was running away.

We were both swift runners and in fairly good training, but we soon found that we had no chance of overtaking him. We saw him for a long time in the moonlight until he was only a small speck moving swiftly among the boulders upon the side of a distant hill. We ran and ran until we were completely blown, but the space be tween us grew ever wider. Finally we stopped and sat panting on two rocks, while we watched him disappearing in the distance.

"And it was at this moment that there occurred a most strange and unexpected thing. We had risen from our rocks and were turning to go home, having abandoned the hopeless chase. The moon was low upon the right, and the jagged pinnacle of a granite tor stood up against the lower curve of its silver disc. There, outlined as black as an ebony statue on that shining background, I saw the figure of a man upon the tor. Do not think that it was a delusion, Holmes. I assure you that I have never in my life seen anything more clearly. As far as I could judge, the figure was that of a tall, thin man. He stood with his legs a little separated, his arms folded, his head bowed, as if he were brooding over that enormous wilder ness of peat and granite which lay before him. He might have been the very spirit of that terrible place. It was not the convict. This man was far from the place where the latter had disappeared. Be sides, he was a much taller man. With a cry of surprise

I pointed him out to the baronet, but in the instant during which I had turned to grasp his arm the man was gone. There was the sharp pinnacle of granite still cutting the lower edge of the moon, but its peak bore no trace of that silent and motionless figure.

I wished to go in that direction and to search the tor, but it was some distance away. The baronet's nerves were still quivering from that cry, which recalled the dark story of his family, and he was not in the mood for fresh adventures. He had not seen this lonely man upon the tor and could not feel the thrill which his strange pres ence and his commanding attitude had given to me. "A warder, no doubt," said he. "The moor has been thick with them since this fellow escaped." Well, perhaps his explanation may be the right one, but I should like to have some further proof of it. To-day we mean to communicate to the Princetown people where they should look for their missing man, but it is hard lines that we have not actually had the triumph of bringing him back as our own prisoner. Such are the adventures of last night, and you must acknowledge, my dear Holmes, that I have done you very well in the matter of a re port. Much of what I tell you is no doubt quite irrelevant, but still I feel that it is best that I should let you have all the facts and leave you to select for yourself those which will be of most service to you in helping you to your conclusions. We are certainly making some progress. So far as the Barrymores go we have found the motive of their actions, and that has cleared up the situation very much. But the moor with its mysteries and its strange inhabitants remains as inscrutable as ever. Perhaps in my next I may be able to throw some light upon this also. Best of all would it be if you could come down to us. In any case you will hear from me again in the course of the next few days.

CHAPTER 10

# EXTRACT FROM THE DIARY OF DR.WATSON

So far I have been able to quote from the reports which I have for warded during these early days to Sherlock Holmes. Now, how ever, I have arrived at a point in my narrative where I am compelled to abandon this method and to trust once more to my recollections, aided by the diary which I kept at the time. A few extracts from the latter will carry me on to those scenes which are indelibly fixed in every detail upon my memory. I proceed, then, from the morning which followed our abortive chase of the convict and our other strange experiences upon the moor.

October 16th. A dull and foggy day with a drizzle of rain. The house is banked in with rolling clouds, which rise now and then to show the dreary curves of the moor, with thin, silver veins upon the sides of the hills, and the distant boulders gleaming where the light strikes upon their wet faces. It is melancholy outside and in. The baronet is in a black reaction after the excitements of the night. I am conscious myself of a weight at my heart and a feeling of impending danger—ever present danger, which is the more terrible because I am unable to define it.

"And have I not cause for such a feeling? Consider the long sequence of incidents which have all pointed to some sinister influence which is at work around us. There is the death of the last occupant of the Hall, fulfilling so exactly the conditions of the family legend, and there are the repeated reports from peasants of the appearance of a strange creature upon the moor. Twice I have with my own ears heard the sound which resembled the distant baying of a hound. It is incredible, impossible, that it should really be outside the ordinary laws of nature. A spectral hound which leaves material footmarks and fills the air with its howling is surely not to be thought of Stapleton may fall in with such a superstition, and Mortimer also; but if I have one quality upon earth it is common sense, and nothing will persuade me to believe in such a thing. To do so would be to descend to the level of these poor peasants,who are not content with a mere fiend dog but must needs describe him with hell-fire shooting from his mouth and eyes. Holmes would not listen to such fancies, and I am his agent. But facts are facts, and I have twice heard this cry ing upon the moor. Suppose that there were really some huge hound loose upon it; that would go far to explain everything. But where could such a hound lie concealed, where did it get its food, where did it come from, how was it that no one saw it by day? It must be confessed that the natural explanation offers almost as many difficulties as the other. And always, apart from the hound, there is the fact of the human agency in London, the man in the cab, and the letter which warned sir Henry against the moor. This at least was real, but it might have been the work of a protecting friend as easily as of an enemy. Where is that friend or enemy now? Has he remained in London, or has he followed us down here? Could he—could he be the stranger whom I saw upon the tor?

It is true that I have had only the one glance at him, and yet there are some things to which I am ready to swear. He is no one whom I have seen down here, and I have now met all the neighbours. The figure was far taller than that of Stapleton, far thinner than that of Frankland. Barrymore it might possibly have been, but we had left him behind us, and I am certain that he could not have followed us. A stranger then is still dogging us, just as a stranger dogged us in London. We have never shaken him off. If I could lay my hands upon that man, then at last we might find ourselves at the end of all our difficulties. To this one purpose I must now de vote all my energies.

My first impulse was to tell sir Henry all my plans. My second and wisest one is to play my own game and speak as little as possible to anyone. He is silent and distrait. His nerves have been strangely shaken by that sound upon the moor. I will say nothing to add to his anxieties, but I will take my own steps to attain my own end.

We had a small scene this morning after breakfast. Barrymore asked leave to speak with sir Henry, and they were closeted in his study some little time. Sitting in the billiard-room I more than once heard the sound of voices raised, and I had a pretty good idea what the point was which was under discussion. After a time the baronet opened his door and called for me.

" Barrymore considers that he has a grievance," he said. "He thinks that it was unfair on our part to hunt his brother-in-law down when he, of his own free will, had told us the secret."

The butler was standing very pale but very collected before us.

"I may have spoken too warmly, sir," said he, "and if I have, I am sure that I beg your pardon. At the same time, I was very much surprised when I heard you two gentlemen come back this morning and learned that you had been chasing Selden. The poor fellow has enough to fight against without my putting more upon his track"

"If you had told us of your own free will it would have been a different thing," said the baronet, "you only told us, or rather your wife only told us, when it was forced from you and you could not help yourself"

"I didn't think you would have taken advantage of it, Sir Henry—indeed I didn't."

"The man is a public danger. There are lonely houses scattered over the moor, and he is a fellow who would stick at nothing. You only want to get a glimpse of his face to see that. Look at Mr. Stapleton's house, for example, with no one but himself to defend it. There's no safety for anyone until he is under lock and key."

"He'll break into no house, sir. I give you my solemn word upon that. But he will never trouble anyone in this country again. I as sure you, Sir Henry, that in a very few days the necessary arrangements will have been made and he will be on his way to South America. For God's sake, sir, I beg of you not to let the police know that he is still on the moor. They have given up the chase there, and he can lie quiet until the ship is ready for him. You can't tell on him without getting my wife and me into trouble. I beg you, sir, to say nothing to the police."

"What do you say, Watson?"

I shrugged my shoulders. "If he were safely out of the country it would relieve the tax-payer of a burden."

"But how about the chance of his holding someone up before he goes?"

"He would not do anything so mad, sir. We have provided him with all that he can want. To commit a crime would be to show where he was hiding."

"That is true," said Sir Henry. "Well, Barrymore—"

"God bless you, sir, and thank you from my heart! It would have killed my poor wife had he been taken again."

"I guess we are aiding and abetting a felony, Watson? But, after what we have heard, I don't feel as if I could give the man up, so there is an end of it. All right, Barrymore, you can go."

With a few broken words of gratitude the man turned, but he hesitated and then came back

"You've been so kind to us, sir, that I should like to do the best I can for you in return. I know something, Sir Henry, and perhaps I should have said it before, but it was long after the inquest that I found it out. I've never breathed a word about it yet to mortal man. It's about poor Sir Charles's death."

The baronet and I were both upon our feet. "Do you know how he died?"

"No, sir, I don't know that."

"What then?"

"I know why he was at the gate at that hour. It was to meet a woman."

"To meet a woman! He?"

"Yes, sir."

"And the woman's name?"

"I can't give you the name, sir, but I can give you the initials. Her initials were L. L."

"How do you know this, Barrymore?"

"Well, Sir Henry, your uncle had a letter that morning. He had usually a great many letters, for he was a public man and well known for his kind heart, so that everyone who was in trouble was glad to turn to him. But that morning, as it chanced, there was only this one letter, so I took the more notice of it It was from Coombe Tracey, and it was addressed in a woman's hand."

"Well?"

"Well, sir, I thought no more of the matter, and never would have done had it not been for my wife. Only a few weeks ago she was cleaning out Sir Charles's study—it had never been touched since his death—and she found the ashes of a burned letter in the back of the grate. The greater part of it was charred to pieces, but one little slip, the end of a page, hung together, and the writing could still be read, though it was gray on a black ground. It seemed to us to be a postscript at the end of the letter, and it said: 'Please, please, as you are a gentleman, burn this letter, and be at the gate by ten o'clock.' Beneath it were signed the initials L. L."

"Have you got that slip?"

"No, sir, it crumbled all to bits after we moved it."

"Had Sir Charles received any other letters in the same writing?"

"Well, sir, I took no particular notice of his letters. I should not have noticed this one, only it happened to come alone."

"And you have no idea who L. L. is?"

"No, sir. No more than you have. But I expect if we could lay our hands upon that lady we should know more about Sir Charles's death."

"I cannot understand, Barrymore, how you came to conceal this important information."

"Well, sir, it was immediately after that our own trouble came to us. And then again, sir, we were both of us very fond of Sir Charles, as we well might be considering all that he has done for us. To rake this up couldn't help our poor master, and it's well to go carefully when there's a lady in the case. Even the best of us—"

"You thought it might injure his reputation?"

"Well, sir, I thought no good could come of it. But now you have been kind to us, and I feel as if it would be treating you unfairly not to tell you all that I know about the matter."

"Very good, Barrymore; you can go." When the butler had left us Sir Henry turned to me. "Well, Watson, what do you think of this new light?"

"It seems to leave the darkness rather blacker than before."

"So I think. But if we can only trace L. L. it should clear up the whole business. We have gained that much. We know that there is someone who has the facts if we can only find her. What do you think we should do?"

"Let Holmes know all about it at once. It will give him the clue for which he has been seeking. I am much mistaken if it does not bring him down."

I went at once to my room and drew up my report of the morning's conversation for Holmes. It was evident to me that he had been very busy of late, for the notes which I had from Baker Street were few and short, with no comments upon the information which I had supplied and hardly any reference to my mission. No doubt his blackmailing case is absorbing all his faculties. And yet this new factor must surely arrest his attention and renew his interest I wish that he were here.

October 17th. All day to-day the rain poured down, rustling on the ivy and dripping from the eaves. I thought of the convict out upon the bleak, cold, shelterless moor. Poor devil! Whatever his crimes, he has suffered something to atone for them. And then I thought of that other one—the face in the cab, the figure against the moon. Was he also out in that deluge—the unseen watcher, the man of darkness? In the evening I put on my waterproof and I walked far upon the sodden moor, full of dark imaginings, the rain beating upon my face and the wind whistling about my ears. God help those who wander into the great mire now, for even the firm uplands are becoming a morass. I found the black tor upon which I had seen the solitary watcher, and from its craggy summit I looked out myself across the melancholy downs. Rain squalls drifted across their russet face, and the heavy, slate coloured clouds hung low over the landscape, trailing in gray wreaths down the sides of the fantastic hills. In the distant hollow on the left, half hidden by the mist, the two thin towers of Baskerville Hall rose above the trees. They were the only signs of human life which I could see, save only those prehistoric huts which lay thickly upon the slopes of the hills. Nowhere was there any trace of that lonely man whom I had seen on the same spot two nights before.

As I walked back I was overtaken by Dr. Mortimer driving in his dog-cart over a rough Moreland track which led from the outlying farmhouse of Foulmire. He has been very attentive to us, and hardly a day has passed that he has not called at the Hall to see how we were getting on. He insisted upon my climbing into his dog-cart, and he gave me a lift homeward. I found him much troubled over the disappearance of his little spaniel. It had wandered on to the moor and had never come back. I gave him such consolation as I might, but I thought of the pony on the Grimpen Mire, and I do not fancy that he will see his little dog again.

"By the way, Mortimer," said I as we jolted along the rough road, "I suppose there are few people living within driving distance of this whom you do not know?"

"Hardly any, I think."

"Can you, then, tell me the name of any woman whose initials are L. L.?"

He thought for a few minutes.

"No," said he. "There are a few gypsies and labouring folk for whom I can't answer, but among the farmers or gentry there is no one whose initials are those. Wait a bit though," he added after a pause. "There is Laura Lyons—her initials are L. L.—but she lives in Coombe Tracey."

"Who is she?" I asked.

"She is Frankland's daughter."

"What! Old Frankland the crank?"

"Exactly. She married an artist named Lyons, who came sketch ing on the moor. He proved to be a blackguard and deserted her. The fault from what I hear may not have been entirely on one side. Her father refused to have anything to do. with her because she had married without his consent and perhaps for one or two other reasons as well. So, between the old sinner and the young one the girl has had a pretty bad time."

"How does she live?"

"I fancy old Frankland allows her a pittance, but it cannot be more, for his own affairs are considerably involved. Whatever she may have deserved one could not allow her to go hopelessly to the bad. Her story got about, and several of the people here did some thing to enable her to earn an honest living. Stapleton did for one, and Sir Charles for another. I gave a trifle myself It was to set her up in a typewriting business."

He wanted to know the object of my inquiries, but I managed to satisfy his curiosity without telling him too much, for there is no reason why we should take anyone into our confidence. To morrow morning I shall find my way to Coombe Tracey, and if I can see this Mrs. Laura Lyons, of equivocal reputation, a long step will have been made towards clearing one incident in this chain of mysteries. I am certainly developing the wisdom of the serpent, for when Mortimer pressed his questions to an inconvenient extent I asked him casually to what type Frankland's skull belonged, and so heard nothing but craniology for the rest of our drive. I have not lived for years with Sherlock Holmes for nothing.

I have only one other incident to record upon this tempestuous and melancholy day. This was my conversation with Barrymore just now, which gives me one more strong card which I can play in due time.

Mortimer had stayed to dinner, and he and the baronet played écarté afterwards. The butler brought me my coffee into the library, and I took the chance to ask him a few questions.

"Well," said I, "has this precious relation of yours departed, or is he still lurking out yonder.?"

"I don't know, sir. I hope to heaven that he has gone, for he has brought nothing but trouble here! I've not heard of him since I left out food for him last, and that was three days ago."

"Did you see him then?"

"No, sir, but the food was gone when next I went that way."

"Then he was certainly there.?"

"So you would think, sir, unless it was the other man who took it."

I sat with my coffee-cup halfway to my lips and stared at Barry more.

"You know that there is another man then?"

"Yes, sir; there is another man upon the moor."

"Have you seen him?"

"No, sir."

"How do you know of him then?"

"Selden told me of him, sir, a week ago or. more. He's in hiding, too, but he's not a convict as far as I can make out. I don't like it, Dr. Watson—I tell you straight, sir, that I don't like it." He spoke with a sudden passion of earnestness.

"Now, listen to me, Barrymore! I have no interest in this matter but that of your master. I have come here with no object except to help him. Tell me, frankly, what it is that you don't like."

Barrymore hesitated for a moment, as if he regretted his out burst or found it difficult to express his own feelings in words.

"It's all these goings-on, sir," he cried at last, waving his hand towards the rain lashed window which faced the moor. "There's foul play somewhere, and there's black villainy brewing, to that I'll swear! Very glad I should be, sir, to see Sir Henry on his way back to London again!"

"But what is it that alarms you?"

"Look at Sir Charles's death! That was bad enough, for all that the coroner said. Look at the noises on the moor at night. There's not a man would cross it after sundown if he was paid for it. Look at this stranger hiding out yonder, and watching and waiting! What's he waiting for? What does it mean? It means no good to anyone of the name of Baskerville, and very glad I shall be to be quit of it all on the day that Sir Henry's new servants are ready to take over the Hall."

"But about this stranger," said I. "Can you tell me anything about him? What did Selden say? Did he find out where he hid, or what he was doing?"

"He saw him once or twice, but he is a deep one and gives nothing away. At first he thought that he was the police, but soon he found that he had some lay of his own. A kind of gentleman he was, as far as he could see, but what he was doing he could not make out."

"And where did he say that he lived?"

"Among the old houses on the hillside—the stone huts where the old folk used to live."

"But how about his food?"

"Selden found out that he has got a lad who works for him and brings all he needs. I dare say he goes to Coombe Tracey for what he wants."

"Very good, Barrymore. We may talk further of this some other time." When the butler had gone I walked over to the black win dow, and I looked through a blurred pane at the driving clouds and at the tossing outline of the wind-swept trees. It is a wild night indoors, and what must it be in a stone hut upon the moor. What passion of hatred can it be which leads a man to lurk in such a place at such a time! And what deep and earnest purpose can he have which calls for such a trial! There, in that hut upon the moor, seems to lie the very centre of that problem which has vexed me so sorely. I swear that another day shall not have passed before I have done all that man can do to reach the heart of the mystery.

## CHAPTER 11

# THE MAN ON THE TOR

The extract from my private diary which forms the last chapter has brought my narrative up to the eighteenth of October, a time when these strange events began to move swiftly towards their terrible conclusion. The incidents of the next few days are indelibly graven upon my recollection, and I can tell them without reference to the notes made at the time. I start them from the day which succeeded that upon which I had established two facts of great importance, the one that Mrs. Laura Lyons of Coombe Tracey had written to Sir Charles Baskerville and made an appointment with him at the very place and hour that he met his death, the other that the lurk ing man upon the moor was to be found among the stone huts upon the hillside. With these two facts in my possession I felt that either my intelligence or my courage must be deficient if I could not throw some further light upon these dark places

I had no opportunity to tell the baronet what I had learned about Mrs. Lyons upon the evening before, for Dr. Mortimer remained with him at cards until it was very late. At breakfast, how ever, I informed him about my discovery and asked him whether he would care to accompany me to Coombe Tracey. At first he was very eager to come, but on second thoughts it seemed to both of us that if I went alone the results might be better. The more formal we made the visit the less information we might obtain. I left Sir Henry behind, therefore, not without some pricking of conscience, and drove off upon my new quest.

When I reached Coombe Tracey I told Perkins to put up the horses, and I made inquiries for the lady whom I had come to interrogate. I had no difficulty in finding her rooms, which were central and well appointed. A maid showed me in without ceremony, and as 1 entered the sitting-room a lady, who was sitting before a Remington typewriter, sprang up with a pleasant smile of welcome. Her face fell, however, when she saw that I was a stranger, and she sat down again and asked me the object of my visit.

The first impression left by Mrs. Lyons was one of extreme beauty. Her eyes and hair were of the same rich hazel colour, and her cheeks, though considerably freckled, were flushed with the exquisite bloom of the brunette, the dainty pink which lurks at the heart of the sulphur rose. Admiration was, I repeat, the first im pression. But the second was criticism. There was something subtly wrong with the face, some coarseness of expression, some hardness, perhaps, of eye, some looseness of lip which marred its perfect beauty. But these, of course, are afterthoughts. At the moment I was simply conscious that I was in the presence of a very handsome woman, and that she was asking me the reasons for my visit. I had not quite understood until that instant how delicate my mission was.

I have the pleasure, said I, "of knowing your father."

"It was a clumsy introduction, and the lady made me feel it.

"There is nothing in common between my father and me," she said. "I owe him nothing, and his friends are not mine. If it were not for the late Sir Charles Baskerville and some other kind hearts I might have starved for all that my father cared."

"It was about the late Sir Charles Baskerville that I have come here to see you."

The freckles started out on the lady's face.

"What can I tell you about him?n she asked, and her fingers played nervously over the stops of her typewriter.

"You knew him, did you not?"

"I have already said that I owe a great deal to his kindness. If I am able to support myself it is largely due to the interest which he took in my unhappy situation."

"Did you correspond with him?"

The lady looked quickly up with an angry gleam in her hazel eyes.

"What is the object of these questions?" she asked sharply.

"The object is to avoid a public scandal. It is better that I should ask them here than that the matter should pass outside our control."

She was silent and her face was still very pale. At last she looked up with something reckless and defiant in her manner.

"Well, I'll answer," she said. "What are your questions?"

"Did you correspond with Sir Charles?"

"I certainly wrote to him once or twice to acknowledge his delicacy and his generosity."

"Have you the dates of those letters?"

"No."

"Have you ever met him?"

"Yes, once or twice, when he came into Coombe Tracey. He was a very retiring man, and he preferred to do good by stealth."

"But if you saw him so seldom and wrote so seldom, how did he know enough about your affairs to be able to help you, as you say that he has done?"

She met my difficulty with the utmost readiness.

"There were several gentlemen who knew my sad history and united to help me. One was Mr. Stapleton, a neighbour and intimate friend of sir Charles's. He was exceedingly kind, and it was through him that sir Charles learned about my affairs."

I knew already that sir Charles Baskerville had made Stapleton his almoner upon several occasions, so the lady's statement bore the impress of truth upon it.

"Did you ever write to sir Charles asking him to meet you?" I continued.

Mrs. Lyon flushed with anger again.

"Really, sir, this is a very extraordinary question."

"I am sorry, madam, but I must repeat it."

"Then I answer, certainly not."

"Not on the very day of sir Charles's death.?"

The flush had faded in an instant, and a deathly face was before me. Her dry lips could not speak the "No" which I saw rather than heard.

"Surely your memory deceives you," said I. "I could even quote a passage of your letter. It ran 'Please, please, as you are a gentleman, burn this letter, and be at the gate by ten o'clock."

I thought that she had fainted, but she recovered herself by a supreme effort.

"Is there no such thing as a gentleman?" she gasped.

"You do sir Charles an injustice. He did burn the letter. But sometimes a letter may be legible even when burned. You acknowledge now that you wrote it?"

"Yes, I did write it," she cried, pouring out her soul in a torrent of words. "I did write it. Why should I deny it? I have no reason to be ashamed of it. I wished him to help me. I believed that if I had an interview I could gain his help, so I asked him to meet me."

"But why at such an hour?"

"Because I had only just learned that he was going to London next day and might be away for months. There were reasons why I could not get there earlier."

"But why a rendezvous in the garden instead of a visit to the house?"

"Do you think a woman could go alone at that hour to a bachelor's house?"

"Well, what happened when you did get there?"

"I never went."

"Mrs. Lyons!"

"No, I swear it to you on all I hold sacred. I never went. Some thing intervened to prevent my going."

"What was that?"

"That is a private matter. I cannot tell it."

"You acknowledge then that you made an appointment with Sir Charles at the very hour and place at which he met his death, but you deny that you kept the appointment."

"That is the truth."

Again and again I cross-questioned her, but I could never get past that point.

"Mrs. Lyons," said I as I rose from this long and inconclusive interview, "you are taking a very great responsibility and putting yourself in a very false position by not making an absolutely clean breast of all that you know. If I have to call in the aid of the police you will find how seriously you are compromised. If your position is innocent, why did you in the first instance deny having written to Sir Charles upon that date?"

"Because I feared that some false conclusion might be drawn from it and that I might find myself involved in a scandal."

"And why were you so pressing that Sir Charles should destroy your letter?"

"If you have read the letter you will know."

"I did not say that I had read all the letter."

"You quoted some of it."

"I quoted the postscript. The letter had, as I said, been burned and it was not all legible. I ask you once again why it was that you were so pressing that Sir Charles should destroy this letter which he received on the day of his death."

"The matter is a very private one."

"The more reason why you should avoid a public investigation."

"I will tell you, then. If you have heard anything of my unhappy history you will know that I made a rash marriage and had reason to regret it."

"I have heard so much."

"My life has been one incessant persecution from a husband whom I abhor. The law is upon his side, and every day I am faced by the possibility that he may force me to live with him. At the time that I wrote this letter to Sir Charles I had learned that there was a prospect of my regaining my freedom if certain expenses could be met. It meant everything to me—peace of mind, happiness, seif respect—everything. I knew Sir Charles's generosity, and I thought that if he heard the story from my own lips he would help me."

"Then how is it that you did not go?"

"Because I received help in the interval from another source."

"Why, then, did you not write to Sir Charles and explain this.?"

"So I should have done had I not seen his death in the paper next morning."

The woman's story hung coherently together, and all my ques tions were unable to shake it. I could only check it by finding if she had, indeed, instituted divorce proceedings against her husband at or about the time of the tragedy.

It was unlikely that she would dare to say that she had not been to Baskerville Hall if she really had been, for a trap would be necessary to take her there, and could not have returned to Coombe Tracey until the early hours of the morning. Such an excusion could not be kept secret. The probability was, therefore, that she was tell ing the truth, or, at least, a part of the truth. I came away baffled and disheartened. Once again I had reached that dead wall which seemed to be built across every path by which I tried to get at the object of my mission. And yet the more I thought of the lady's face and of her manner the more I felt that something was being held back from me. Why should she turn so pale? Why should she fight against every admission until it was forced from her? Why should she have been so reticent at the time of the tragedy? Surely the explanation of all this could not be as innocent as she would have me believe. For the moment I could proceed no farther in that direc tion, but must turn back to that other clue which was to be sought for among the stone huts upon the moor.

"And that was a most vague direction. I realized it as I drove back and noted how hill after hill showed traces of the ancient people. Barrymore's only indication had been that the stranger lived in one of these abandoned huts, and many hundreds of them are scat tered throughout the length and breadth of the moor. But I had my own experience for a guide since it had shown me the man himself standing upon the summit of the Black Tor. That, then, should be the centre of my search. From there I should explore every hut upon the moor until I lighted upon the right one. If this man were inside it I should find out from his own lips, at the point of my revolver if necessary, who he was and why he had dogged us so long He might slip away from us in the crowd of Regent Street, but it would puzzle him to do so upon the lonely moor. On the other hand, if I should find the hut and its tenant should not be within it I must remain there, however long the vigil, until he returned. Holmes had missed him in London. It would indeed be a triumph for me if I could run him to earth where my master had failed.

Luck had been against us again and again in this inquiry, but now at last it came to my aid. And the messenger of good fortune was none other than Mr. Frankland, who was standing, gray whiskered and red-faced, outside the gate of his garden, which opened on to the highroad along which I travelled.

"Good-day, Dr. Watson," cried he with unwonted good humour, "you must really give your horses a rest and come in to have a glass of wine and to congratulate me."

My feelings towards him were very far from being friendly after what I had heard of his treatment of his daughter, but I was axhious to send Perkins and the wagonette home, and the opportunity was a good one. I alighted and sent a message to Sir Henry that I should walk over in time for dinner. Then I followed Frankland into his dining-room.

"It is a great day for me, sir—one of the red-letter days of my life," he cried with many chuckles. "I have brought off a double event. I mean to teach them in these parts that law is law, and that there is a man here who does not fear to invoke it. I have established a right of way through the centre of old Middleton's park, slap across it, sir, within a hundred yards of his own front door. What do you think of that? We'll teach these magnates that they cannot ride roughshod over the rights of the commoners, confound them! And I've closed the wood where the Fernworthy folk used to picnic. These infernal people seem to think that there are no rights of property, and that they can swarm where they like with their papers and their bottles. Both cases decided, Dr. Watson, and both in my favour. I haven't had such a day since I had Sir John Moreland for trespass because he shot in his own warren."

"How on earth did you do that?"

"Look it up in the books, sir. It will repay reading—Frankland v. Moreland, Court of Queen's Bench. It cost me £200, but I got my verdict."

"Did it do you any good?"

"None, sir, none. I am proud to say that I had no interest in the matter. I act entirely from a sense of public duty. I have no doubt, for example, that the Fernworthy people will burn me in effigy to night. I told the police last time they did it that they should stop these disgraceful exhibitions. The County Constabulary is in a scandalous state, sir, and it has not afforded me the protection to which I am entitled. The case of Frankland v. Regina will bring the matter before the attention of the public. I told them that they would have occasion to regret their treatment of me, and already my words have come true."

"How so?" I asked.

The old man put on a very knowing expression.

"Because I could tell them what they are dying to know; but nothing would induce me to help the rascals in any way."

I had been casting round for some excuse by which I could get away from his gossip, but now I began to wish to hear more of it. I had seen enough of the contrary nature of the old sinner to under stand that any strong sign of interest would be the surest way to stop his confidences.

"Some poaching case, no doubt?" said I with an indifferent manner.

"Ha, ha, my boy, a very much more important matter than that! What about the convict on the moor?"

I started. "You don't mean that you know where he is?" said I.

"I may not know exactly where he is, but I am quite sure that I could help the police to lay their hands on him. Has it never struck you that the way to catch that man was to find out where he got his food and so trace it to him?"

He certainly seemed to be getting uncomfortably near the truth. "No doubt," said I; "but how do you know that he is anywhere upon the moor?"

"I know it because I have seen with my own eyes the messenger who takes him his food."

My heart sank for Barrymore. It was a serious thing to be in the power of this spiteful old busybody. But his next remark took a weight from my mind.

"You'll be surprised to hear that his food is taken to him by a child. I see him every day through my telescope upon the roof He passes along the same path at the same hour, and to whom should he be going except to the convict?"

Here was luck indeed! And yet I suppressed all appearance of interest. A child! Barrymore had said that our unknown was sup plied by a boy. It was on his track, and not upon the convict's, that Frankland had stumbled. If I could get his knowledge it might save me a long and weary hunt. But incredulity and indifference were evidently my strongest cards.

"I should say that it was much more likely that it was the son of one of the Moreland shepherds taking out his father's dinner."

The least appearance of opposition struck fire out of the old autocrat. His eyes looked malignantly at me, and his gray whiskers bristled like those of an angry cat.

"Indeed, sir!" said he, pointing out over the wide-stretching moor. "Do you see that Black Tor over yonder? Well, do you see the low hill beyond with the thorn bush upon it? It is the stoniest part of the whole moor. Is that a place where a shepherd would be likely to take his station? Your suggestion, sir, is a most absurd one."

I meekly answered that had spoken without knowing all the facts. My submission pleased him and led him to further confidences.

"You may be sure, sir, that I have very good grounds before I come to an opinion. I have seen the boy again and again with his bundle. Every day, and sometimes twice a day, I have been able— but wait a moment, Dr. Watson. Do my eyes deceive me, or is there at the present moment something moving upon that hillside?"

It was several miles off, but I could distinctly see a small dark dot against the dull green and gray.

"Come, sir, come!" cried Frankland, rushing upstairs. "You will see with your own eyes and judge for yourself"

The telescope, a formidable instrument mounted upon a tripod, stood upon the flat leads of the house. Frankland clapped his eye to it and gave a cry of satisfaction.

"Quick, Dr. Watson, quick, before he passes over the hill!"

There he was, sure enough, a small urchin with a little bundle upon his shoulder, toiling slowly up the hill. When he reached the crest I saw the ragged uncouth figure outlined for an instant against the cold blue sky. He looked round him with a furtive and stealthy air, as one who dreads pursuit. Then he vanished over the hill.

'Well! Am I right?"

"Certainly, there is a boy who seems to have some secret errand."

"And what the errand is even a county constable could guess. But not one word shall they have from me, and I bind you to secrecy also, Dr. Watson. Not a word! You understand!"

'Just as you wish."

"They have treated me shamefully—shamefully. When the facts come out in Frankland v. Regina I venture to think that a thrill of indignation will run through the country. Nothing would induce me to help the police in any way. For all they cared it might have been me, instead of my effigy, which these rascals burned at the stake. Surely you are not going! You will help me to empty the de canter in honour of this great occasion!"

But I resisted all his solicitations and succeeded in dissuading him from his announced intention of walking home with me. I kept the road as long as his eye was on me, and then I struck off across the moor and made for the stony hill over which the boy had disap peared. Everything was working in my favour, and I swore that it should not be through lack of energy or perseverance that I should miss the chance which fortune had thrown in my way.

The sun was already sinking when I reached the summit of the hill, and the long slopes beneath me were all golden-green on one side and gray shadow on the other. A haze lay low upon the farthest sky-line, out of which jutted the fantastic shapes of Belliver and Vixen Tor. Over the wide expanse there was no sound and no movement. One great gray bird, a gull or curlew, soared aloft in the blue heaven. He and I seemed to be the only living things between the huge arch of the sky and the desert beneath it. The barren scene, the sense of loneliness, and the mystery and urgency of my task all struck a chill into my heart. The boy was nowhere to be seen. But down beneath me in a cleft of the hills there was a circle of the old stone huts, and in the middle of them there was one which retained sufficient roof to act as a screen against the weather. My heart leaped within me as I saw it. This must be the burrow where the stranger lurked. At last my foot was on the threshold of his hiding place—his secret was within my grasp.

"As I approached the hut, walking as warily as Stapleton would do when with poised net he drew near the settled butterfly, I satisfied myself that the place had indeed been used as a habitation. A vague pathway among the boulders led to the dilapidated opening which served as a door. All was silent within. The unknown might be lurking there, or he might be prowling on the moor. My nerves tingled with the sense of adventure. Throwing aside my cigarette, I closed my hand upon the butt of my revolver and, walking swiftly up to the door, I looked in. The place was empty.

But there were ample signs that I had not come upon a false scent. This was certainly where the man lived. Some blankets rolled in a waterproof lay upon that very stone slab upon which neolithic man had once slumbered. The ashes of a fire were heaped in a rude grate. Beside it lay some cooking utensils and a bucket half-full of water. A litter of empty tins showed that the place had been occupied for some time, and I saw, as my eyes became accustomed to the chequered light, a pannikin and a half-full bottle of spirits standing in the corner. In the middle of the hut a flat stone served the purpose of a table, and upon this stood a small cloth bundle—the same, no doubt, which I had seen through the telescope upon the shoulder of the boy. It contained a loaf of bread, a tinned tongue, and two tins of preserved peaches. As I set it down again, after having examined it, my heart leaped to see that beneath it there lay a sheet of paper with writing upon it. I raised it, and this was what I read, roughly scrawled in pencil: "Dr. Watson has gone to Coombe Tracey."

For a minute I stood there with the paper in my hands thinking out the meaning of this curt message. It was I, then, and not Sir Henry, who was being dogged by this secret man. He had not fol lowed me himself, but he had set an agent—the boy, perhaps—upon my track, and this was his report. Possibly I had taken no step since I had been upon the moor which had not been observed and reported. Always there was this feeling of an unseen force, a fine net drawn round us with infinite skill and delicacy, holding us so lightly that it was only at some supreme moment that one realized that one was indeed entangled in its meshes.

If there was one report there might be others, so I looked round the hut in search of them. There was no trace, however, of anything of the kind, nor could I discover any sign which might indicate the character or intentions of the man who lived in this singular place, save that he must be of Spartan habits and cared little for the com forts of life. When I thought of the heavy rains and looked at the gaping roof I understood how strong and immutable must be the purpose which had kept him in that inhospitable abode. Was he our malignant enemy, or was he by chance our guardian angel? I swore that I would not leave the hut until I knew.

Outside the sun was sinking low and the west was blazing with scarlet and gold. Its reflection was shot back in ruddy patches by the distant pools which lay amid the great Grimpen Mire. There were the two towers of Baskerville Hall, and there a distant blur of smoke which marked the village of Grimpen. Between the two, be hind the hill, was the house of the Stapletons. All was sweet and mellow and peaceful in the golden evening light, and yet as I looked at them my soul shared none of the peace of Nature but quivered at the vagueness and the terror of that interview which every instant was bringing nearer. With tingling nerves but a fixed purpose, I sat in the dark recess of the hut and waited with sombre patience for the coming of its tenant.

"And then at last I heard him. Far away came the sharp clink of a boot striking upon a stone. Then another and yet another, coming nearer and nearer. I shrank back into the darkest corner and cocked the pistol in my pocket, determined not to discover myself until I had on opportunity of seeing something of the stranger. There was a long pause which showed that he had stopped. Then once more the footsteps approached and a shadow fell across the opening of the hut.

"It is a lovely evening, my dear Watson," said a well-known voice. al really think that you will be more comfortable outside than in."

## Chapter 12

# DEATH ON THE MOOR

For a moment or two I sat breathless, hardly able to believe my ears. Then my senses and my voice came back to me, while a crush ing weight of responsibility seemed in an instant to be lifted from my soul. That cold, incisive, ironical voice could belong to but one man in all the world.

"Holmes!" I cried—"Holmes!"

"Come out," said he, "and please be careful with the revolver."

I stooped under the rude lintel, and there he sat upon a stone outside, his gray eyes dancing with amusement as they fell upon my astonished features. He was thin and worn, but clear and alert, his keen face bronzed by the sun and roughened by the wind. In his tweed suit and cloth cap he looked like any other tourist upon the moor, and he had contrived, with that catlike love of personal cleanliness which was one of his characteristics, that his chin should be as smooth and his linen as perfect as if he were in Baker Street.

"I never was more glad to see anyone in my life," said I as I wrung him by the hand.

"Or more astonished, eh?"

"Well, I must confess to it."

"The surprise was not all on one side, I assure you. I had no idea that you had found my occasional retreat, still less that you were in side it, until I was within twenty paces of the door."

"My footprint, I presume?"

"No, Watson; I fear that I could not undertake to recognize your footprint amid all the footprints of the world. If you seriously desire to deceive me you must change your tobacconist; for when I see the stub of a cigarette marked Bradley, Oxford Street, I know that my friend Watson is in the neighbourhood. You will see it there beside the path. You threw it down, no doubt, at that supreme moment when you charged into the empty hut."

"Exactly."

"I thought as much—and knowing your admirable tenacity I was convinced that you were sitting in ambush, a weapon within reach, waiting for the tenant to return. So you actually thought that I was the criminal.?"

"I did not know who you were, but I was determined to find out."

"Excellent, Watson! And how did you localize me? You saw me, perhaps, on the night of the convict hunt, when I was so imprudent as to allow the moon to rise behind me?"

"Yes, I saw you then."

"And have no doubt searched all the huts until you came to this one?"

"No, your boy had been observed, and that gave me a guide where to loo"

"The old gentleman with the telescope, no doubt. I could not make it out when first I saw the light flashing upon the lens." He rose and peeped into the hut. "Ha, I see that

Cartwright has brought up some supplies. What's this paper? So you have been to Coombe Tracey, have you?"

'Yes."

"To see Mrs. Laura Lyons?"

"Exactly."

"Well done! Our researches have evidently been running on parallel lines, and when we unite our results I expect we shall have a fairly full knowledge of the case."

"Well, I am glad from my heart that you are here, for indeed the responsibility and the mystery were both becoming too much for my nerves. But how in the name of wonder did you come here, and what have you been doing? I thought that you were in Baker Street working out that case of blackmailing."

"That was what I wished you to think."

"Then you use me, and yet do not trust me!" I cried with some bitterness. "I think that I have deserved better at your hands, Holmes."

"My dear fellow, you have been invaluable to me in this as in many other cases, and I beg that you will forgive me if I have seemed to play a trick upon you. In truth, it was partly for your own sake that I did it, and it was my appreciation of the danger which you ran which led me to come down and examine the matter for myself Had I been with Sir Henry and you it is confident that my point of view would have been the same as yours, and my presence would have warned our very formidable opponents to be on their guard. As it is, I have been able to get about as I could not possibly have done had I been living in the Hall, and I remain an unknown factor in the business, ready to throw in all my weight at a critical moment."

"But why keep me in the dark?"

"For)r you to know could not have helped us and might possibly have led to my discovery. You would have wished to tell me some thing, or in your kindness you would have brought me out some comfort or other, and so an unnecessary risk would be run. I brought Cartwright down with me—you remember the little chap at the express office—and he has seen after my simple wants: a loaf of bread and a clean collar. What does man want more? He has given me an extra pair of eyes upon a very active pair of feet, and both have been invaluable."

"Then my reports have all been wasted!"—My voice trembled as I recalled the pains and the pride with which I had composed them.

Holmes took a bundle of papers from his pocket.

"Here are your reports, my dear fellow, and very well thumbed, I assure you. I made excellent arrangements, and they are only delayed one day upon their way. I must compliment you exceedingly upon the zeal and the intelligence which you have shown over an extraordinarily difficult case."

I was still rather raw over the deception which had been practised upon me, but the warmth of Holmes' praise drove my anger from my mind. I felt also in my heart that he was right in what he said and that it was really best for our purpose that I should not have known that he was upon the moor.

"That's better," said he, seeing the shadow rise from my face. "And now tell me the result of your visit to Mrs. Laura Lyons—it was not difficult for me to guess that it was to see her that you had gone, for I am already aware that she is the one person in Coombe Tracey who might be of service to us in the matter. In fact, if you had not gone to-day it is exceedingly probable that I should have gone to-morrow."

The sun had set and dusk was settling over the moor. The air had turned chill and we withdrew into the hut for warmth. There, sitting together in the twilight, I told Holmes of my conversation with the lady. So interested was he that I had to repeat some of it twice before he was satisfied.

"This is most important," said he when I had concluded. "It fills up a gap which I had been unable to bridge in this most complex affair. You are aware, perhaps, that a close intimacy exists between this lady and the man Stapleton?"

"I did not know of a close intimacy."

"There can be no doubt about the matter. They meet, they write, there is a complete understanding between them. Now, this puts a very powerful weapon into our hands. If I could only use it to detach his wife—"

"His wife?"

"I am giving you some information now, in return for all that you have given me. The lady who has passed here as Miss Stapleton is in reality his wife."

"Good heavens, Holmes! Are you sure of what you say? How could he have permitted Sir Henry to fall in love with her?"

"Sir Henry's falling in love could do no harm to anyone except Sir Henry. He took particular care that Sir Henry did not make love to her, as you have yourself observed. I repeat that the lady is his wife and not his sister."

"But why this elaborate deception?"

"Because he foresaw that she would be very much more useful to him in the character of a free woman."

"All my unspoken instincts, my vague suspicions, suddenly took shape and centred upon the naturalist. In that impassive, colour less man, with his straw hat and his butterfly-net, I seemed to see something terrible—a creature of infinite patience and craft, with a smiling face and a murderous heart.

"It is he, then, who is our enemy—it is he who dogged us in Lon don?"

"So I read the riddle."

"And the warning—it must have come from her!"

"Exactly "

The shape of some monstrous villainy, half seen, half guessed, loomed through the darkness which had girt me so long.

"But are you sure of this, Holmes? How do you know that the woman is his wife?"

"Because he so far forgot himself as to tell you a true piece of autobiography upon the occasion when he first met you, and I dare say he has many a time regretted it since. He was once a school master in the north of England. Now, there is no one more easy to trace than a schoolmaster. There are scholastic agencies by which one may identify any man who has been in the profession. A little investigation showed me that a school had come to grief under atrocious circumstances, and that the man who had owned it—the name was different—had disappeared with his wife. The descriptions agreed. When I learned that the missing man was devoted to entomology the identification was complete."

The darkness was rising, but much was still hidden by the shadows.

"If this woman is in truth his wife, where does Mrs. Laura Lyons come in?" I asked.

"That is one of the points upon which your own researches have shed a light. Your interview with the lady has cleared the situation very much. I did not know about a projected divorce between herself and her husband. In that case, regarding Stapleton as an unmarried man, she counted no doubt upon becoming his wife."

"And when she is undeceived?"

"Why, then we may find the lady of service. It must be our first duty to see her—both of us—tomorrow. Don't you think, Watson, that you are away from your charge rather long? Your place should be at Baskerville Hall."

The last red streaks had faded away in the west and night had settled upon the moor. A few faint stars were gleaming in a violet sky.

"One last question, Holmes," I said as I rose. "Surely there is no need of secrecy between you and me. What is the meaning of it all? What is he after?"

Holmes's voice sank as he answered:

"It is murder, Watson—refined, cold-blooded, deliberate murder. Do not ask me for particulars. My nets are closing upon him, even as his are upon Sir Henry, and with your help he is already al most at my mercy. There is but one danger which can threaten us. It is that he should strike before we are ready to do so. Another day—two at the most—And I have my case complete, but until then guard your charge as closely as ever a fond mother watched her ail ing child. Your mission to-day has justified itself, and yet I could almost wish that you had not left his side. Hark!"

A terrible scream—a prolonged yell of horror and anguish burst out of the silence of the moor. That frightful cry turned the blood to ice in my veins.

"Oh, my God!" I gasped. "What is it? What does it mean?"

Holmes had sprung to his feet, and I saw his dark, athletic out line at the door of the hut, his shoulders stooping, his head thrust forward, his face peering into the darkness.

"Hush!" he whispered. "Hush!"

The cry had been loud on account of its vehemence, but it had pealed out from somewhere far off on the shadowy plain. Now it burst upon our ears, nearer, louder, more urgent than before.

"Where is it?" Holmes whispered; and I knew from the thrill of his voice that he, the man of iron, was shaken to the soul. "Where is it, Watson?"

"There, I think." I pointed into the darkness.

'"No, there!"

Again the agonised cry swept through the silent night, louder and much nearer than ever. And a new sound mingled with it, a deep, muttered rumble, musical and yet menacing, rising and fall ing like the low, constant murmur of the sea.

"The hound" cried Holmes. "Come, Watson, come! Great heavens, if we are too late!"

He had started running swiftly over the moor, and I had fol lowed at his heels. But now from somewhere among the broken ground immediately in front of us there came one last despairing yell, and then a dull, heavy thud. We halted and listened. Not an other sound broke the heavy silence of the windless night.

I saw Holmes put his hand to his forehead like a man distracted. He stamped his feet upon the ground.

"He has beaten us, Watson. We are too late."

"No, no, surely not!"

"Fool that I was to hold my hand. And you, Watson, see what comes of abandoning your charge! But, by Heaven, if the worst has happened we'll avenge him!"

Blindly we ran through the gloom, blundering against boulders, forcing our way through gorse bushes, panting up hills and rush ing down slopes, heading always in the direction whence those dreadful sounds had come. At every rise Holmes looked eagerly round him, but the shadows were thick upon the moor, and noth ing moved upon its dreary face.

"Can you see anything?"

"Nothing."

"But, hark, what is that?"

A low moan had fallen upon our ears. There it was again upon our left! On that side a ridge of rocks ended in a sheer cliff which overlooked a stone-strewn slope. On its jagged face was spread eagled some dark, irregular object. As we ran towards it the vague outline hardened into a definite shape. It was a prostrate man face downward upon the ground, the head doubled under him at a horrible angle, the shoulders rounded and the body hunched together as if in the act of throwing a somersault. So grotesque was the attitude that I could not for the instant realise that that moan had been the passing of his soul. Not a whisper, not a rustle, rose now from the dark figure over which we stooped. Holmes laid his hand upon him and held it up again with an exclamation of horror. The gleam of the match which he struck shone upon his clotted fingers and upon the ghastly pool which widened slowly from the crushed skull of the victim. And it shone upon something else which turned our hearts sick and faint within us—the body of Sir Henry Baskerville!

There was no chance of either of us forgetting that peculiar ruddy tweed suit—the very one which he had worn on the first morning that we had seen him in Baker Street. We caught the one clear glimpse of it, and then the match flickered and went out, even as the hope had gone out of our souls. Holmes groaned, and his face glimmered white through the darkness.

"The brute! the brute!" I cried with clenched hands. "Oh, Holmes, I shall never forgive myself for having left him to his fate."

"I am more to blame than you, Watson. In order to have my case well rounded and complete, I have thrown away the life of my client. It is the greatest blow which has befallen me in my career. But how could I know—how could I know—that he would risk his life alone upon the moor in the face of all my warnings?"

"That we should have heard his screams—my God, those screams!—and yet have been unable to save him! Where is this brute of a hound which drove him to his death? It may be lurking among these rocks at this instant. And Stapleton, where is he? He shall answer for this deed."

"He shall. I will see to that. Uncle and nephew have been murdered—the one frightened to death by the very sight of a beast which he thought to be supernatural, the other driven to his end in his wild flight to escape from it. But now we have to prove the connection between the man and the beast. Save from what we heard, we cannot even swear to the existence of the latter, since Sir Henry has evidently died from the fall. But, by heavens, cunning as he is, the fellow shall be in my power before another day is past!"

We stood with bitter hearts on either side of the mangled body, overwhelmed by this sudden and irrevocable disaster which had brought all our long and weary labours to so piteous an end. Then as the moon rose we climbed to the top of the rocks over which our poor friend had fallen, and from the summit we gazed out over the shadowy moor, half silver and half gloom. Far away, miles off, in the direction of Grimpen, a single steady yellow light was shining. It could only come from the lonely abode of the Stapletons. With a bitter curse I shook my fist at it as I gazed.

"Why should we not seize him at once?"

"Our case is not complete. The fellow is wary and cunning to the last degree. It is not what we know, but what we can prove. If we make one false move the villain may escape us yet."

"What can we do?"

"There will be plenty for us to do to-morrow. To-night we can only perform the last offices to our poor friend."

Together we made our way down the precipitous slope and ap proached the body, black and clear against the silvered stones. The agony of those contorted limbs struck me with a spasm of pain and blurred my eyes with tears.

"We must send for help, Holmes! We cannot carry him all the way to the Hall. Good heavens, are you mad?"

He had uttered a cry and bent over the body. Now he was dancing and laughing and wringing my hand. Could this be my stern, self-contained friend? These were hidden fires, indeed!

"A beard! A beard! The man has a beard!"

"A beard?"

"It is not the baronet—it is—why, it is my neighbour, the convict!"

With feverish haste we had turned the body over, and that dripping beard was pointing up to the cold, clear moon. There could be no doubt about the beetling forehead, the sunken animal eyes. It was indeed the same face which had glared upon me in the light of the candle from over the rock—the face of Selden, the crimi nal.

Then in an instant it was all clear to me. I remembered how the baronet had told me that he had handed his old wardrobe to Barrymore. Barrymore had passed it on in order to help Selden in his es cape. Boots, shirt, cap—it was all Sir Henry's. The tragedy was still black enough, but this man had at least deserved death by the laws of his country. I told Holmes how the matter stood, my heart bubbling over with thankfulness and joy.

"Then the clothes have been the poor devil's death," said he. "It is clear enough that the hound has been laid on from some article of Sir Henry's—the boot which was abstracted in the hotel, in all probability—and so ran this man down. There is one very singular thing, however: How came Selden, in the darkness, to know that the hound was on his trail?"

"He heard him."

"To hear a hound upon the moor would not work a hard man like this convict into such a paroxysm of terror that he would risk recapture by screaming wildly for help. By his cries he must have run a long way after he knew the animal was on his track. How did he know?"

"A greater mystery to me is why this hound, presuming that all our conjectures are correct—"

"I presume nothing."

"Well, then, why this hound should be loose to-night. I suppose that it does not always run loose upon the moor. Stapleton would not let it go unless he had reason to think that Sir Henry would be there."

"My difficulty is the more formidable of the two, for I think that we shall very shortly get an explanation of yours, while mine may remain forever a mystery. The question now is, what shall we do with this poor wretch's body? We cannot leave it here to the foxes and the ravens."

"I suggest that we put it in one of the huts until we can communicate with the police."

"Exactly. I have no doubt that you and I could carry it so far. Hello, Watson, what's this? It's the man himself, by all that's wonderful and audacious! Not a word to show your suspicions—not a word, or my plans crumble to the ground."

"A figure was approaching us over the moor, and I saw the dull red glow of a cigar. The moon shone upon him, and I could distinguish the dapper shape and jaunty walk of the naturalist. He stopped when he saw us, and then came on again.

"Why, Dr. Watson, that's not you, is it? You are the last man that I should have expected to see out on the moor at this time of night. But, dear me, what's this? Somebody hurt? Not—don't tell me that it is our friend Sir Henry!" He hurried past me and stooped over the dead man. I heard a sharp intake of his breath and the cigar fell from his fingers.

"Who—who's this?" he stammered.

"It is Selden, the man who escaped from Princetown."

Stapleton turned a ghastly face upon us, but by a supreme effort he had overcome his amazement and his disappointment. He looked sharply from Holmes to me.

"Dear me! What a very shocking affair! How did he die?"

"He appears to have broken his neck by falling over these rocks. My friend and I were strolling on the moor when we heard a cry."

"I heard a cry also. That was what brought me out. I was uneasy about Sir Henry."

"Why about Sir Henry in particular?" I could not help asking.

"Because I had suggested that he should come over. When he did not come I was surprised, and I naturally became alarmed for his safety when I heard cries upon the moor. By the way"—his eyes darted again from my face to Holmes'—"did you hear anything else besides a cry?"

"No," said Holmes; "did you?"

"No."

"What do you mean, then?"

"Oh, you know the stories that the peasants tell about a phantom hound, and so on. It is said to be heard at night upon the moor. I was wondering if there were any evidence of such a sound to night."

"We heard nothing of the kind," said I.

"And what is your theory of this poor fellow's death?"

"I have no doubt that anxiety and exposure have driven him o his head. He has rushed about the moor in a crazy state and eventually fallen over here and broken his neck."

"That seems the most reasonable theory," said Stapleton, and he gave a sigh which I took to indicate his relief. "What do you think about it, Mr. Sherlock Holmes?"

My friend bowed his compliments.

"You are quick at identification," said he.

"We have been expecting you in these parts since Dr. Watson came down. You are in time to see a tragedy."

"Yes, indeed. I have no doubt that my friend's explanation will cover the facts. I will take an unpleasant remembrance back to London with me to-morrow."

"Oh, you return to-morrow"

"That is my intention."

"I hope your visit has cast some light upon those occurrences which have puzzled us?"

Holmes shrugged his shoulders.

"One cannot always have the success for which one hopes. An investigator need facts and not legends or rumours. It has not been a satisfactory case."

My friend spoke in his frankest and most unconcerned manner. Stapleton still looked hard at him. Then he turned to me.

"I would suggest carrying this poor fellow tö my house, but it would give my sister such a fright that I do not feel justified in do ing it. I think that if we put something over his face he will be safe until morning."

"And so it was arranged. Resisting Stapleton's offer of hospitality, Holmes and I set off to Baskerville Hall, leaving the naturalist to return alone. Looking back we saw the figure moving slowly away over the broad moor, and behind him that one black smudge on the silvered slope which showed where the man was Iying who had come so horribly to his end.

## CHAPTER 13

# FIXING THE NETS

"Were at close grips at last," said Holmes as we walked together across the moor. "What a nerve the fellow has! How he pulled himself together in the face of what must have been a paralysing shock when he found that the wrong man had fallen a victim to his plot. I told you in London, Watson; and I tell you now again, that we have never had a foe more worthy of our steel."

"I am sorry that he has seen you."

"And so was I at first. But there was no getting out of it."

"What effect do you think it will have upon his plans now that he knows you are here?"

"It may cause him to be more cautious, or it may drive him to desperate measures at once. Like most clever criminals, he may be too confident in his own cleverness and imagine that he has completely deceived us."

"Why should we not arrest him at once?"

"My dear Watson, you were born to be a man of action. Your instinct is always to do something energetic. But supposing, for argument's sake, that we had him arrested to-night, what on earth the better off should we be for that? We could prove nothing against him.There's the devilish cunning of it! If he were acting through a human agent we could get some evidence, but if we were to drag this great dog to the light of day it would not help us in putting a rope round the neck of its master."

"Surely we have a case."

"Not a shadow of one—only surmise and conjecture. We should be laughed out of court if we came with such a story and such evi dence."

"There is Sir Charles's death."

"Found dead without a mark upon him. You and I know that he died of sheer fright, and we know also what frightened him; but how are we to get twelve stolid jurymen to know it? What signs are there of a hound? Where are the marks of its fangs? Of course we know that a hound does not bite a dead body and that Sir Charles was dead before ever the brute overtook him. But we have to prove all this, and we are not in a position to do it."

"Well, then, to-night?"

"We are not much better off to-night. Again, there was no direct connection between the hound and the man's death. We never saw the hound. We heard it, but we could not prove that it was running upon this man's trail. There is a complete absence of motive. No, my dear fellow; we must reconcile ourselves to the fact that we have no case at present, and that it is worth our while to run any risk in order to establish one."

"And how do you propose to do so?"

"I have great hopes of what Mrs. Laura Lyons may do for us when the position of affairs is made clear to her. And I have my own plan as well. Sufficient for to-morrow is the evil thereof; but I hope before the day is past to have the upper hand at last."

"I could draw nothing further from him, and he walked, lost in thought, as far as the Baskerville gates.

"Are you coming up?"

"Yes; I see no reason for further concealment. But one last word, Watson. Say nothing of the hound to Sir Henry. Let him think that Selden's death was as Stapleton would have us believe. He will have a better nerve for the ordeal which he will have to undergo to-morrow, when he is engaged, if I remember your report aright, to dine with these people."

"And so am I."

"Then you must excuse yourself and he must go alone. That will be easily arranged. And now, if we are too late for dinner, I think that we are both ready for our suppers."

Sir Henry was more pleased than surprised to see Sherlock Holmes, for he had for some days been expecting that recent events would bring him down from London. He did raise his eye brows, however, when he found that my friend had neither any luggage nor any explanations for its absence. Between us we soon sup plied his wants, and then over a belated supper we explained to the baronet as much of our experience as it seemed desirable that he should know. But first I had the unpleasant duty of breaking the news to Barrymore and his wife. To him it may have been an unmitigated relief, but she wept bitterly in her apron. To all the world he was the man of violence, half animal and half demon; but to her he always remained the little wilful boy of her own girlhood, the child who had clung to her hand. Evil indeed is the man who has not one woman to mourn him.

"I've been moping in the house all day since Watson went off in the morning," said the baronet. "I guess I should have some credit, for I have kept my promise. If I hadn't sworn not to go about alone I might have had a more lively evening, for I had a message from Stapleton asking me over there."

"I have no doubt that you would have had a more lively evening," said Holmes dryly. "By the way, I don't suppose you appreciate that we have been mourning over you as having broken your neck?"

Sir Henry opened his eyes. "How was that?"

"This poor wretch was dressed in your clothes. I fear your servant who gave them to him may get into trouble with the police."

"That is unlikely. There was no mark on any of them, as far as I know."

"That's lucky for him—in fact, it's lucky for all of you, since you are all on the wrong side of the law in this matter. I am not sure that as a conscientious detective my first duty is not to arrest the whole household. Watson's reports are most incriminating documents."

"But how about the case?" asked the baronet. "Have you made anything out of the tangle? I don't know that Watson and I are much the wiser since we came down."

"I think that I shall be in a position to make the situation rather more clear to you before long. It has been an exceedingly difficult and most complicated business. There are several points upon which we still want light—but it is coming all the same."

"We've had one experience, as Watson has no doubt told you. We heard the hound on the moor, so I can swear that it is not all empty superstition. I had something to do with dogs when I was out West, and I know one when I hear one. If you can muzzle that one and put him on a chain I'll be ready to swear you are the greatest detective of all time."

"I think I will muzzle him and chain him all right if you will give me your help."

"Whatever you tell me to do I will do."

"Very good; and I will ask you also to do it blindly, without al ways asking the reason."

"Just as you like."

"If you will do this I think the chances are that our little problem will soon be solved. I have no doubt—"

He stopped suddenly and stared fixedly up over my head into the air. The lamp beat upon his face, and so intent was it and so still that it might have been that of a clear-cut classical statue, a personification of alertness and expectation.

"What is it?" we both cried.

I could see as he looked down that he was repressing some internal emotion. His features were still composed, but his eyes shone with amused exultation.

"Excuse the admiration of a connoisseur," said he as he waved his hand towards the line of portraits which covered the opposite wall. "Watson won't allow that I know anything of art, but that is mere jealousy because our views upon the subject differ. Now, these are a really very fine series of portraits."

"Well, I'm glad to hear you say so," said Sir Henry, glancing with some surprise at my friend. "I don't pretend to know much about these things, and I'd be a better judge of a horse or a steer than of a picture. I didn't know that you found time for such things."

"I know what is good when I see it, and I see it now. That's a Kneller, I'll swear, that lady in the blue silk over yonder, and the stout gentleman with the wig ought to be a Reynolds. They are all family portraits, I presume?"

"Every one."

"Do you know the names?"

"Barrymore has been coaching me in them, and I think I can say my lessons fairly well."

"Who is the gentleman with the telescope?"

"That is Rear-Admiral Baskerville, who served under Rodney in the West Indies. The man with the blue coat and the roll of paper is Sir William Baskerville, who was Chairman of Committees of the House of Commons under Pitt."

"And this Cavalier opposite to me—the one with the black velvet and the lace.?"

"Ah, you have a right to know about him. That is the cause of all the mischief, the wicked Hugo, who started the Hound of the Bas kervilles. We're not likely to forget him."

I gazed with interest and some surprise upon the portrait.

"Dear me!" said Holmes, "he seems a quiet, meek-mannered man enough, but I dare say that there was a lurking devil in his eyes. I had pictured him as a more robust and ruffianly person."

"There's no doubt about the authenticity, for the name and the date, 1647, are on the back of the canvas."

Holmes said little more, but the picture of the old roisterer seemed to have a fascination for him, and his eyes were continually fixed upon it during supper. It was not until later, when Sir Henry had gone to his room, that I was able to follow the trend of his thoughts. He led me back into the banqueting-hall, his bedroom candle in his hand, and he held it up against the time-stained portrait on the wall.

"Do you see anything there?"

I looked at the broad plumed hat, the curling love-locks, the white lace collar, and the straight, severe face which was framed be tween them. It was not a brutal countenance, but it was prim, hard, and stern, with a firm-set, thin-lipped mouth, and a coldly intolerant eye.

"Is it like anyone you know?"

"There is something of Sir Henry about the jaw."

"Just a suggestion, perhaps. But wait an instant!" He stood upon a chair, and, holding up the light in his left hand, he curved his right arm over the broad hat and round the long ringlets.

"Good heavens!" I cried in amazement.

The face of Stapleton had sprung out of the canvas.

"Ha, you see it now. My eyes have been trained to examine faces and not their trimmings. It is the first quality of a criminal investigator that he should see through a disguise."

"But this is marvellous. It might be his portrait."

"Yes, it is an interesting instance of a throwback, which appears to be both physical and spiritual. A study of family portraits is enough to convert a man to the doctrine of reincarnation. The fel low is a Baskerville—that is evident."

"With designs upon the succession."

"Exactly. This chance of the picture has supplied us with one of our most obvious missing links. We have him, Watson, we have him, and I dare swear that before to-morrow night he will be fluttering in our net as helpless as one of his own butterflies. A pin, a cork, and a card, and we add him to the Baker Street collection!" He burst into one of his rare fits of laughter as he turned away from the picture. I have not heard him laugh often, and it has always boded ill to somebody.

I was up betimes in the morning, but Holmes was afoot earlier still, for I saw him as I dressed, coming up the drive.

"Yes, we should have a full day to-day," he remarked, and he rubbed his hands with the joy of action. "The nets are all in place, and the drag is about to begin. We'll know before the day is out whether we have caught our big, lean-jawed pike, or whether he has got through the meshes."

"Have you been on the moor already?"

"I have sent a report from Grimpen to Princetown as to the death of Selden. I think I can promise that none of you will be troubled in the matter. And I have also communicated with my faithful Cartwright, who would certainly have pined away at the door of my hut, as a dog does at his master's grave, if I had not set his mind at rest about my safety."

"What is the next move?"

"To see sir Henry. Ah, here he is!"

"Good-morning, Holmes," said the baronet. "You look like a general who is planning a battle with his chief of the staff."

That is the exact situation. Watson was asking for orders."

"And so do I."

"Very good. You are engaged, as I understand, to dine with our friends the Stapletons to-night."

"I hope that you will come also. They are very hospitable people, and I am sure that they would be very glad to see you."

"I fear that Watson and I must go to London."

"To London?"

"Yes, I think that we should be more useful there at the present juncture."

The baronet's face perceptibly lengthened.

"I hoped that you were going to see me through this business. The Hall and the moor are not very pleasant places when one is alone."

"My dear fellow, you must trust me implicitly and do exactly what I tell you. You can tell your friends that we should have been happy to have come with you, but that urgent business required us to be in town. We hope very soon to return to Devonshire. Will you remember to give them that message?"

"If you insist upon it."

"There is no alternative, I assure you."

I saw by the baronet's clouded brow that he was deeply hurt by what he regarded as our desertion.

"When do you desire to go?" he asked coldly.

"Immediately after breakfast. We will drive in to Coombe Tracey, but Watson will leave his things as a pledge that he will come back to you. Watson, you will send a note to Stapleton to tell him that you regret that you cannot come."

"I have a good mind to go to London with you," said the baronet. "Why should I stay here alone?"

"Because it is your post of duty. Because you gave me your word that you would do as you were told, and I tell you to stay."

"All right, then, I'll stay."

"One more direction! I wish you to drive to Merripit House. Send back your trap, however, and let them know that you intend to walk home."

"To walk across the moor?"

"Yes."

"But that is the very thing which you have so often cautioned me not to do."

"This time you may do it with safety. If I had not every confidence in your nerve and courage I would not suggest it, but it is essential that you should do it."

"Then I will do it."

"And as you value your life do not go across the moor in any direction save along the straight path which leads from Merripit House to the Grimpen Road, and is your natural way home."

"I will do just what you say."

"Very good. I should be glad to get away as soon after breakfast as possible, so as to reach London in the afternoon."

I was much astounded by this programme, though I remembered that Holmes had said to Stapleton on the night before that his visit would terminate next day. It had not crossed my mind, however, that he would wish me to go with him, nor could I under stand how we could both be absent at a moment which he himself declared to be critical. There was nothing for it, however, but implicit obedience; so we bade good-bye to our rueful friend, and a couple of hours afterwards we were at the station of Coombe Tra cey and had dispatched the trap upon its return journey. A small boy was waiting upon the platform.

"Any orders, sir?"

"You will take this train to town, Cartwright. The moment you arrive you will send a wire to Sir Henry Baskerville, in my name, to say that if he finds the pocketbook which I have dropped he is to send it by registered post to Baker Street."

"Yes, sir."

"And ask at the station office if there is a message for me."

The boy returned with a telegram, which Holmes handed to me. It ran:

> Wire received. Coming down with unsigned warrant. Arrive five-forty.
>
> LESTRADE.

"That is in answer to mine of this morning. He is the best of the professionals, I think and we may need his assistance. Now, Wat son, I think that we cannot employ our time better than by calling upon your acquaintance, Mrs. Laura Lyons."

His plan of campaign was beginning to be evident. He would use the baronet in order to convince the Stapletons that we were really gone, while we should actually return at the instant when we were likely to be needed. That telegram from London, if mentioned by Sir Henry to the Stapletons, must remove the last suspicions from their minds. Already I seemed to see our nets drawing closer around that lean-jawed pike.

Mrs. Laura Lyons was in her office, and Sherlock Holmes opened his interview with a frankness and directness which considerably amazed her.

"I am investigating the circumstances which attended the death of the late Sir Charles Baskerville," said he. "My friend here, Dr. Watson, has informed me of what you have communicated, and also of what you have withheld in connection with that matter."

"What have I withheld?" she asked defiantly.

"You have confessed that you asked Sir Charles to be at the gate at ten o'clock. We know that that was the place and hour of his death. You have withheld what the connection is between these events."

"There is no connection."

"In that case the coincidence must indeed be an extraordinary one. But I think that we shall succeed in establishing a connection, after all. I wish to be perfectly frank with you, Mrs. Lyons. We regard this case as one of murder, and the evidence may implicate not only your friend Mr. Stapleton but his wife as well."

The lady sprang from her chair.

"His wife!" she cried.

"The fact is no longer a secret. The person who has passed for his sister is really his wife."

Mrs. Lyons had resumed her seat. Her hands were grasping the arms of her chair, and I saw that the pink nails had turned white with the pressure of her grip.

"His wife!" she said again. "His wife! He is not a married man."

Sherlock Holmes shrugged his shoulders.

"Prove it to me! Prove it to me! And if you can do so—!" The fierce flash of her eyes said more than any words.

"I have come prepared to do so," said Holmes, drawing several papers from his pocket. "Here is a photograph of the couple taken in York four years ago. It is endorsed 'Mr. and Mrs. Vandeleur,' but you will have no difficulty in recognising him, and her also, if you know her by sight. Here are three written descriptions by trustworthy witnesses of Mr. and Mrs. Vandeleur, who at that time kept St. Oliver's private school. Read them and see if you can doubt the identity of these people."

She glanced at them and then looked up at us with the set, rigid face of a desperate woman.

"Mr. Holmes," she said, "this man had offered me marriage on condition that I could get a divorce from my husband. He has lied to me, the villain, in every conceivable way. Not one word of truth has he ever told me. And why—why? I imagined that all was for my own sake. But now I see that I was never anything but a tool in his hands.

Why should I preserve faith with him who never kept any with me? Why should I try to shield him from the consequences of his own wicked acts? Ask me what you like, and there is nothing which I shall hold back. One thing I swear to you, and that is that when I wrote the letter I never dreamed of any harm to the old gentleman, who had been my kindest friend."

"I entirely believe you, madam," said Sherlock Holmes. "The recital of these events must be very painful to you, and perhaps it will make it easier if I tell you what occurred, and you can check me if I make any material mistake. The sending of this letter was suggested to you by Stapleton?"

"He dictated it."

"I presume that the reason he gave was that you would receive help from Sir Charles for the legal expenses connected with your divorce?"

"Exactly."

"And then after you had sent the letter he dissuaded you from keeping the appointment?"

"He told me that it would hurt his self-respect that any other man should find the money for such an object, and that though he was a poor man himself he would devote his last penny to removing the obstacles which divided us."

"He appears to be a very consistent character. And then you heard nothing until you read the reports of the death in the paper?"

"No."

"And he made you swear to say nothing about your appointment with Sir Charles?"

"He did. He said that the death was a very mysterious one, and that I should certainly be suspected if the facts came out. He fright ened me into remaining silent."

"Quite so. But you had your suspicions?"

She hesitated and looked down.

"I knew him," she said. "But if he had kept faith with me I should always have done so with him."

"I think that on the whole you have had a fortunate escape," said Sherlock Holmes. "You have had him in your power and he knew it, and yet you are alive. You have been walking for some months very near to the edge of a precipice. We must wish you good-morn ing now, Mrs. Lyons, and it is probable that you will very shortly hear from us again."

"Our case becomes rounded off, and difficulty after difficulty thins away in front of us," said Holmes as we stood waiting for the arrival of the express from town. "I shall soon be in the position of being able to put into a single connected narrative one of the most singular and sensational crimes of modern times. Students of criminology will remember the analogous incidents in Godno, in Little Russia, in the year '66, and of course there are the Anderson murders in North Carolina, but this case possesses some features which are entirely its own. Even now we have no clear case against this very wily man. But I shall be very much surprised if it is not clear enough before we go to bed this night."

The London express came roaring into the station, and a small, wiry bulldog of a man had sprung from a first-class carriage. We all three shook hands, and I saw at once from the reverential way in which Lestrade gazed at my companion that he had learned a good deal since the days when they had first worked together. I could well remember the scorn which the theories of the reasoner used then to excite in the practical man.

"Anything good?" he asked.

"The biggest thing for years," said Holmes. awe have two hours before we need think of starting. I think we might employ it in getting some dinner and then, Lestrade, we will take the London fog out of your throat by giving you a breath of the pure night air of Dartmoor. Never been there? Ah, well, I don't suppose you will forget your first visit"

## CHAPTER 14

# THE HOUND OF THE BASKERVILLES

One of Sherlock Holmes's defects—if, indeed, one may call it a defect—was that he was exceedingly loath to communicate his full plans to any other person until the instant of their fulfilment. Partly it came no doubt from his own masterful nature, which loved to dominate and surprise those who were around him. Partly also from his professional caution, which urged him never to take any chances. The result, however, was very trying for those who were acting as his agents and assistants. I had often suffered under it, but never more so than during that long drive in the darkness. The great ordeal was in front of us; at last we were about to make our final effort, and yet Holmes had said nothing, and I could only surmise what his course of action would be. My nerves thrilled with anticipation when at last the cold wind upon our faces and the dark, void spaces on either side of the narrow road told me that we were back upon the moor once again. Every stride of the horses and every turn of the wheels was taking us nearer to our supreme adventure.

Our conversation was hampered by the presence of the driver of the hired wagonette, so that we were forced to talk of trivial mat ters when our nerves were tense with emotion and anticipation. It was a relief to me, after that unnatural restraint, when we at last passed Frankland's house and knew that we were drawing near to the Hall and to the scene of action. We did not drive up to the door but got down near the gate of the avenue. The wagonette was paid off and ordered to return to Coombe Tracey forthwith, while we started to walk to Merripit House.

"Are you armed, Lestrade?"

The little detective smiled.

"As long as I have my trousers I have a hip-pocket, and as long as I have my hip-pocket I have something in it."

"Good! My friend and I are also ready for emergencies."

"You're mighty close about this affair, Mr. Holmes. What's the game now?"

"A waiting game."

"My word, it does not seem a very cheerful place," said the detective with a shiver, glancing round him at the gloomy slopes of the hill and at the huge lake of fog which lay over the Grimpen Mire. "I see the lights of a house ahead of us."

"That is Merripit House and the end of our journey. I must re quest you to walk on tiptoe and not to talk above a whisper.

We moved cautiously along the track as if we were bound for the house, but Holmes halted us when we were about two hundred yards from it.

"This will do," said he. "These rocks upon the right make an admirable screen."

"We are to wait here?"

"Yes, we shall make our little ambush here. Get into this hollow, Lestrade. You have been inside the house, have you not, Watson? Can y you tell the position of the rooms? What are those latticed windows at this end?"

"I think they are the kitchen windows."

"And the one beyond, which shines so brightly.?"

"That is certainly the dining-room."

"The blinds are up. You know the lie of the land best. Creep for ward quietly and see what they are doing—but for heaven's sake don't let them know that they are watched!"

I tiptoed down the path and stooped behind the low wall which surrounded the stunted orchard. Creeping in its shadow I reached a point whence I could look straight through the uncurtained win dow.

There were only two men in the room, Sir Henry and Stapleton. They sat with their profiles towards me on either side of the round table. Both of them were smoking cigars, and coffee and wine were in front of them. Stapleton was talking with animation, but the baronet looked pale and distrait. Perhaps the thought of that lonely walk across the ill-omened moor was weighing heavily upon his mind.

As I watched them Stapleton rose and left the room, while Sir Henry filled his glass again and leaned back in his chair, puffing at his cigar. I heard the creak of a door and the crisp sound of boots upon gravel. The steps passed along the path on the other side of the wall under which I crouched. Looking over, I saw the naturalist pause at the door of an out-house in the corner of the orchard. A key turned in a lock, and as he passed in there was a curious scuffling noise from within. He was only a minute or so inside, and then I heard the key turn once more and he passed me and reëntered the house. I saw him rejoin his guest, and I crept quietly back to where my companions were waiting to tell them what I had seen.

"You say, Watson, that the lady is not there?" Holmes asked when I had finished my report.

"No."

"Where can she be, then, since there is no light in any other room except the kitchen.?"

"I cannot think where she is."

I have said that over the great Grimpen Mire there hung a dense, white fog. It was drifting slowly in our direction and banked itself up like a wall on that side of us, low but thick and well de fined. The moon shone on it, and it looked like a great shimmering ice-field, with the heads of the distant tors as rocks borne upon its surface. Holmes's face was turned towards it, and he muttered impatiently as he watched its sluggish drift.

"It's moving towards us, Watson."

"Is that serious?"

"Very serious, indeed—the one thing upon earth which could have disarranged my plans. He can't be very long, now. It is al ready ten o'clock. Our success and even his life may depend upon his coming out before the fog is over the path."

The night was clear and fine above us. The stars shone cold and bright, while a half-moon bathed the whole scene in a soft, uncertain light. Before us lay the dark bulk of the house, its serrated roof and bristling chimneys hard outlined against the silver-spangled sky. Broad bars of golden light from the lower windows stretched across the orchard and the moor. One of them was suddenly shut off. The servants had left the kitchen. There only remained the lamp in the dining-room where the two men, the murderous host and the unconscious guest, still chatted over their cigars.

Every minute that white woolly plain which covered one-half of the moor was drifting closer and closer to the house. Already the first thin wisps of it were curling across the golden square of the lighted window. The farther wall of the orchard was already invisible, and the trees were standing out of a swirl of white vapour. As we watched it the fog-wreaths came crawling round both corners of the house and rolled slowly into one dense bank, on which the upper floor and the roof floated like a strange ship upon a shadowy sea. Holmes struck his hand passionately upon the rock in front of us and stamped his feet in his impatience.

"If he isn't out in a quarter of an hour the path will be covered. In half an hour we won't be able to see our hands in front of us."

"Shall we move farther back upon higher ground?"

"Yes, I think it would be as well."

So as the fog-bank flowed onward we fell back before it until we were half a mile from the house, and still that dense white sea, with the moon silvering its upper edge, swept slowly and inexorably on.

"We are going too far," said Holmes. "We dare not take the chance of his being overtaken before he can reach us. At all costs we must hold our ground where we are." He dropped on his knees and clapped his ear to the ground. "Thank God, I think that I hear him coming."

A sound of quick steps broke the silence of the moor. Crouching among the stones we stared intently at the silver-tipped bank in front of us. The steps grew louder, and through the fog, as through a curtain, there stepped the man whom we were awaiting. He looked round him in surprise as he emerged into the clear, starlight night. Then he came swiftly along the path, passed close to where we lay, and went on up the long slope behind us. As he walked he glanced continually over either shoulder, like a man who is ill at ease.

"Hist?" cried Holmes, and I heard the sharp click of a cocking pistol. "Look out! It's coming!"

There was a thin, crisp, continuous patter from somewhere in the heart of that crawling bank. The cloud was within fifty yards of where we lay, and we glared at it, all three, uncertain what horror was about to break from the heart of it. I was at Holmes's elbow, and I glanced for an instant at his face. It was pale and exultant, his eyes shining brightly in the moonlight. But suddenly they started forward in a rigid, fixed stare, and his lips parted in amazement. At the same instant Lestrade gave a yell of terror and threw himself face downward upon the ground.

I sprang to my feet, my inert hand grasping my pistol, my mind paralysed by the dreadful shape which had sprung out upon us from the shadows of the fog. A hound it was, an enormous coal-black hound, but not such a hound as mortal eyes have ever seen. Fire burst from its open mouth, its eyes glowed with a smouldering glare, its muzzle and hackles and dewlap were outlined in flickering flame. Never in the delirious dream of a disordered brain could anything more savage, more appalling, more hellish be conceived than that dark form and savage face which broke upon us out of the wall of fog.

With long bounds the huge black creature was leaping down the track, following hard upon the footsteps of our friend. So paralysed were we by the apparition that we allowed him to pass before we had recovered our nerve. Then Holmes and I both fired together, and the creature gave a hideous howl, which showed that one at least had hit him. He did not pause, however, but bounded onward. Far away on the path we saw Sir Henry looking back, his face white in the moonlight, his hands raised in horror, glaring helplessly at the frightful thing which was hunting him down.

But that cry of pain from the hound had blown all our fears to the winds. If he was vulnerable he was mortal, and if we could wound him we could kill him. Never have I seen a man run as Holmes ran that night. I am reckoned fleet of foot, but he outpaced me as much as I outpaced the little professional. In front of us as we flew up the track we heard scream after scream from Sir Henry and the deep roar of the hound. I was in time to see the beast spring upon its victim, hurl him to the ground, and worry at his throat.

But the next instant Holmes had emptied five barrels of his revolver into the creature's flank. With a last howl of agony and a vicious snap in the air, it rolled upon its back, four feet pawing furiously, and then fell limp upon its side.

I stooped, panting, and pressed my pistol to the dreadful, shimmering head, but it was useless to press the trigger. The giant hound was dead.

Sir Henry lay insensible where he had fallen. We tore away his collar, and Holmes breathed a prayer of gratitude when we saw that there was no sign of a wound and that the rescue had been in time. Already our friend's eyelids shivered and he made a feeble effort to move. Lestrade thrust his brandy-flask between the baronet's teeth, and two frightened eyes were looking up at us.

"My God!" he whispered. "What was it? What, in heaven's name, was it?"

"It's dead, whatever it is" said Holmes. "We've laid the family ghost once and forever."

In mere size and strength it was a terrible creature which was lying stretched before us. It was not a pure bloodhound and it was not a pure mastiff; but it appeared to be a combination of the two—gaunt, savage, and as large as a small lioness. Even now, in the still ness of death, the huge jaws seemed to be dripping with a bluish flame and the small, deep-set, cruel eyes were ringed with fire. I placed my hand upon the glowing muzzle, and as I held them up my own fingers smouldered and gleamed in the darkness.

"Phosphorus," I said.

"A cunning preparation of it," said Holmes, sniffing at the dead animal. "There is no smell which might have interfered with his power of scent. We owe you a deep apology, Sir Henry, for having exposed you to this fright. I was prepared for a hound, but not for such a creature as this. And the fog gave us little time to receive him."

"You have saved my life."

"Having first endangered it. Are you strong enough to stand?"

"Give me another mouthful of that brandy and I shall be ready for anything. So ! Now, if you will help me up. What do you propose to do?"

"To leave you here. You are not fit for further adventures to night. If you will wait, one or other of us will go back with you to the Hall."

He tried to stagger to his feet; but he was still ghastly pale and trembling in every limb. We helped him to a rock, where he sat shivering with his face buried in his hands.

"We must leave you now," said Holmes. "The rest of our work must be done, and every moment is of importance. We have our case, and now we only want our man.

"It's a thousand to one against our finding him at the house," he continued as we retraced our steps swiftly down the path. "Those shots must have told him that the game was up."

"We were some distance off, and this fog may have deadened them."

"He followed the hound to call him off—of that you may be cer tain. No, no, he's gone by this time! But we'll search the house and make sure."

The front door was open, so we rushed in and hurried from room to room to the amazement of a doddering old manservant, who met us in the passage. There was no light save in the dining room, but Holmes caught up the lamp and left no corner of the house unexplored. No sign could we see of the man whom we were chasing. On the upper floor, however, one of the bedroom doors was locked.

"There's someone in here," cried Lestrade. "I can hear a move ment Open this door!"

A faint moaning and rustling came from within. Holmes struck the door just over the lock with the flat of his foot and it flew open. Pistol in hand, we all three rushed into the room.

But there was no sign within it of that desperate and defiant villain whom we expected to see. Instead we were faced by an object so strange and so unexpected that we stood for a moment staring at it in amazement.

The room had been fashioned into a small museum, and the walls were lined by a number of glass-topped cases full of that collection of butterflies and moths the formation of which had been the relaxation of this complex and dangerous man. In the centre of this room there was an upright beam, which had been placed at some period as a support for the old worm-eaten baulk of timber which spanned the roof To this post a figure was tied, so swathed and muffled in the sheets which had been used to secure it that one could not for the moment tell whether it was that of a man or a woman. One towel passed round the throat and was secured at the back of the pillar. Another covered the lower part of the face, and over it two dark eyes—eyes full of grief and shame and a dreadful questioning—stared back at us. In a minute we had torn off the gag, unswathed the bonds, and Mrs. Stapleton sank upon the floor in front of us. As her beautiful head fell upon her chest I saw the clear red weal of a whiplash across her neck.

"The brute!" cried Holmes. "Here, Lestrade, your brandy-bottle! Put her in the chair! She has fainted from ill-usage and exhaus tion."

She opened her eyes again.

"Is he safe?" she asked. "Has he escaped?"

"He cannot escape us, madam."

"No, no, I did not mean my husband. Sir Henry? Is he safe?"

"Yes."

"And the hound?"

"It is dead."

She gave a long sigh of satisfaction.

"Thank God! Thank God! Oh, this villain! See how he has treated me!" She shot her arms out from her sleeves, and we saw with horror that they were all mottled with bruises. "But this is nothing—nothing! It is my mind and soul that he has tortured and defiled. I could endure it all, ill-usage, solitude, a life of deception, everything, as long as I could still cling to the hope that I had his love, but now I know that in this also I have been his dupe and his tool." She broke into passionate sobbing as she spoke.

"Your bear him no good will, madam," said Holmes. "Tell us then where we shall find him. If you have ever aided him in evil, help us now and so atone."

"There is but one place where he can have fled," she answered. "There is an old tin mine on an island in the heart of the mire. It was there that he kept his hound and there also he had made preparations so that he might have a refuge. That is where he would fly."

The fog-bank lay like white wool against the window. Holmes held the lamp towards it.

"See," said he. "No one could find his way into the Grimpen Mire to-night."

She laughed and clapped her hands. Her eyes and teeth gleamed with fierce merriment.

"He may find his way in, but never out," she cried. "How can he see the guiding wands to-night? We planted them together, he and I, to mark the pathway through the mire. Oh, if I could only have plucked them out to-day. Then indeed you would have had him at your mercy!"

It was evident to us that all pursuit was in vain until the fog had lifted. Meanwhile we left Lestrade in possession of the house while Holmes and I went back with the baronet to Baskerville Hall. The story of the Stapletons could no longer be withheld from him, but he took the blow bravely when he learned the truth about the woman whom he had loved. But the shock of the night's adventures had shattered his nerves, and before morning he lay delirious in a high fever under the care of Dr. Mortimer. The two of them were destined to travel together round the world before Sir Henry had become once more the hale, hearty man that he had been before he became master of that ill-omened estate.

And now I come rapidly to the conclusion of this singular narrative, in which have tried to make the reader share those dark fears and vague surmises which clouded our lives so long and ended in so tragic a manner. On the morning after the death of the hound the fog had lifted and we were guided by Mrs. Stapleton to the point where they had found a pathway through the bog. It helped us to realise the horror of this woman's life when we saw the eager ness and joy with which she laid us on her husband's track. We left her standing upon the thin peninsula of firm, peat soil which tapered out into the widespread bog. From the end of it a small wand planted here and there showed where the path zigzagged from tuft to tuft of rushes among those green-scummed pits and foul quagmires which barred the way to the stranger. Rank reeds and lush, slimy water-plants sent an odour of decay and a heavy miasmatic vapour onto our faces, while a false step plunged us more than once thigh-deep into the dark, quivering mire, which shook for yards in soft undulations around our feet. Its tenacious grip plucked at our heels as we walked, and when we sank into it it was as if some malignant hand was tugging us down into those obscene depths, so grim and purposeful was the clutch in which it held us. Once only we saw a trace that someone had passed that perilous way before us. From amid a tuft of cotton grass which bore it up out of the slime some dark thing was projecting. Holmes sank to his waist as he stepped from the path to seize it, and had we not been there to drag him out he could never have set his foot upon firm land again. He held an old black boot in the air. "Meyers, Toronto," was printed on the leather inside.

"It is worth a mud bath," said he. "It is our friend Sir Henry's missing boot."

"Thrown there by Stapleton in his flight."

"Exactly. He retained it in his hand after using it to set the hound upon the track. He fled when he knew the game was up, still clutching it. And he hurled it away at this point of his flight. We know at least that he came so far in safety."

But more than that we were never destined to know, though there was much which we might surmise. There was no chance of finding footsteps in the mire, for the rising mud oozed swiftly in upon them, but as we at last reached firmer ground beyond the morass we all looked eagerly for them. But no slightest sign of them ever met our eyes. If the earth told a true story, then Stapleton never reached that island of refuge towards which he struggled through the fog upon that last night. Somewhere in the heart of the great Grimpen Mire, down in the foul slime of the huge morass which had sucked him in, this cold and cruel-hearted man is for ever buried.

Many traces we found of him in the bog-girt island where he had hid his savage ally. A huge driving-wheel and a shaft half-filled with rubbish showed the position of an abandoned mine. Beside it were the crumbling remains of the cottages of the miners, driven away no doubt by the foul reek of the surrounding swamp. In one of these a staple and chain with a quantity of gnawed bones showed where the animal had been confined. A skeleton with a tangle of brown hair adhering to it lay among the debris.

"A dog!" said Holmes. "By Jove, a curly-haired spaniel. Poor Mortimer will never see his pet again. Well, I do not know that this place contains any secret which we have not already fathomed. He could hide his hound, but he could not hush its voice, and hence came those cries which even in daylight were not pleasant to hear. On an emergency he could keep the hound in the out-house at Merripit, but it was always a risk, and it was only on the supreme day, which he regarded as the end of all his efforts, that he dared do it. This paste in the tin is no doubt the luminous mixture with which the creature was daubed. It was suggested, of course, by the story of the family hell-hound, and by the desire to frighten old Sir Charles to death. No wonder the poor devil of a convict ran and screamed, even as our friend did, and as we ourselves might have done, when he saw such a creature bounding through the darkness of the moor upon his track. It was a cunning device, for, apart from the chance of driving your victim to his death, what peasant would venture to inquire too closely into such a creature should he get sight of it, as many have done, upon the moor? I said it in London, Watson, and I say it again now, that never yet have we helped to hunt down a more dangerous man than he who is lying yonder"—he swept his long arm towards the huge mottled expanse of green-splotched bog which stretched away until it merged into the russet slopes of the moor.

## CHAPTER 15

# A RETROSPECTION

It was the end of November, and Holmes and I sat, upon a raw and foggy night, on either side of a blazing fire in our sitting-room in Baker Street. Since the tragic upshot of our visit to Devonshire he had been engaged in two affairs of the utmost importance, in the first of which he had exposed the atrocious conduct of Colonel Upwood in connection with the famous card scandal of the Nonpareil Club, while in the second he had defended the unfortunate Mme. Montpensier from the charge of murder which hung over her in connection with the death of her step-daughter, Mlle. Carère, the young lady who, as it will be remembered, was found six months later alive and married in New York.

My friend was in excellent spirits over the success which had attended a succession of difficult and important cases, so that I was able to induce him to discuss the details of the Baskerville mystery. I had waited patiently for the opportunity, for I was aware that he would never permit cases to overlap, and that his clear and logical mind would not be drawn from its present work to dwell upon memories of the past. Sir Henry and Dr. Mortimer were, however, in London, on their way to that log voyage which had been recommended for the restoration of his shattered nerves. They had called upon us that very afternoon, so that it was natural that the subject should come up for discussion.

"The whole course of events," said Holmes, "from the point of view of the man who called himself Stapleton was simple and direct, although to us, who had no means in the beginning of know ing the motives of his actions and could only learn part of the facts, it all appeared exceedingly complex. I have had the advantage of two conversations with Mrs. Stapleton, and the case has now been so entirely cleared up that I am not aware that there is anything which has remained a secret to us. You will find a few notes upon the matter under the heading B in my indexed list of cases."

"Perhaps you would kindly give me a sketch of the course of events from memory."

"Certainly, though I cannot guarantee that I carry all the facts in my mind. Intense mental concentration has a curious way of blotting out what has passed. The barrister who has his case at his fingers' ends and is able to argue with an expert upon his own subject finds that a week or two of the courts will drive it all out of his head once more. So each of my cases displaces the last, and Mlle. Carère has blurred my recollection of Baskerville Hall. To-morrow some other little problem may be submitted to my notice which will in turn dispossess the fair French lady and the infamous Upwood. So far as the case of the hound goes, however, I will give you the course of events as nearly as I can, and you will suggest anything which I may have forgotten.

"My inquiries show beyond all question that the family portrait did not lie, and that this fellow was indeed a Baskerville. He was a son of that Rodger Baskerville, the younger brother of Sir Charles, who fled with a sinister reputation to South America, where he was said to have died unmarried. He did, as a matter of fact, marry, and had one child, this fellow, whose real name is the same as his father's. He married Beryl Garcia, one of the beauties of Costa Rica, and, having purloined a considerable sum of public money, he changed his name to Vandeleur and fled to England, where he established a school in the east of Yorkshire. His reasons for attempting this special line of business was that he had struck up an acquaintance with a consumptive tutor upon the voyage home, and that he had used this man's ability to make the undertaking a success. Fraser, the tutor, died, however, and the school which had begun well sank from disrepute into infamy. The Vandeleurs found it convenient to change their name to Stapleton, and he brought the remains of his fortune, his schemes for the future, and his taste for entomology to the south of England. I learn at the British Museum that he was a recognized authority upon the subject, and that the name of Vandeleur has been permanently attached to a certain moth which he had, in his Yorkshire days, been the first to describe.

"We now come to that portion of his life which has proved to be of such intense interest to us. The fellow had evidently made inquiry and found that only two lives intervened between him and a valuable estate. When he went to Devonshire his plans were, I believe, exceedingly hazy, but that he meant mischief from the first is evident from the way in which he took his wife with him in the character of his sister. The idea of using her as a decoy was clearly already in his mind, though he may not have been certain how the details of his plot were to be arranged. He meant in the end to have the estate, and he was ready to use any tool or run any risk for that end. His first act was to establish himself as near to his ancestral home as he could, and his second was to cultivate a friendship with Sir Charles Baskerville and with the neighbours.

"The baronet himself told him about the family hound, and so prepared the way for his own death. Stapleton, as I will continue to call him, knew that the old man's heart was weak and that a shock would kill him. So much he had learned from Dr. Mortimer. He had heard also that Sir Charles was superstitious and had taken this grim legend very seriously. His ingenious mind instantly sug gested a way by which the baronet could be done to death, and yet it would be hardly possible to bring home the guilt to the real murderer.

"Having conceived the idea he proceeded to carry it out with considerable finesse. An ordinary schemer would have been content to work with a savage hound. The use of artificial means to make the creature diabolical was a flash of genius upon his part. The dog he bought in London from Ross and Mangles, the dealers in Fulham Road. It was the strongest and most savage in their possession. He brought it down by the North Devon line and walked a great distance over the moor so as to get it home without exciting any remarks. He had already on his insect hunts learned to penetrate the Grimpen Mire, and so had found a safe hiding-place for the creature. Here he kennelled it and waited his chance.

"But it was some time coming. The old gentleman could not be decoyed outside of his grounds at night. Several times Stapleton lurked about with his hound, but without avail. It was during these fruitless quests that he, or rather his ally, was seen by peasants, and that the legend of the demon dog received a new confirmation. He had hoped that his wife might lure Sir Charles to his ruin, but here she proved unexpectedly independent. She would not endeavour to entangle the old gentleman in a sentimental attachment which might deliver him over to his enemy. Threats and even, I am sorry to say, blows refused to move her. She would have nothing to do with it, and for a time Stapleton was at a deadlock.

"He found a way out of his difficulties through the chance that Sir Charles, who had conceived a friendship for him, made him the minister of his charity in the case of this unfortunate woman, Mrs. Laura Lyons. By representing himself as a single man he acquired complete influence over her, and he gave her to under stand that in the event of her obtaining a divorce from her husband he would marry her. His plans were suddenly brought to a head by his knowledge that Sir Charles was about to leave the Hall on the advice of Dr. Mortimer, with whose opinion he himself pretended to coincide. He must act at once, or his victim might get beyond his power. He therefore put pressure upon Mrs. Lyons to write this letter, imploring the old man to give her an interview on the evening before his departure for London. He then, by a specious argument, prevented her from going, and so had the chance for which he had waited.

"Driving back in the evening from Coombe Tracey he was in time to get his hound, to treat it with his infernal paint, and to bring the beast round to the gate at which he had reason to expect that he would find the old gentleman waiting. The dog, incited by its master, sprang over the wicket-gate and pursued the unfortunate baronet, who fled screaming down the yew alley. In that gloomy tunnel it must indeed have been a dreadful sight to see that huge black creature, with its flaming jaws and blazing eyes, bounding after its victim. He fell dead at the end of the alley from heart disease and terror. The hound had kept upon the grassy border while the baronet had run down the path, so that no track but the man's was visible. On seeing him lying still the creature had probably approached to sniff at him, but finding him dead had turned away again. It was then that it left the print which was actually observed by Dr. Mortimer. The hound was called off and hurried away to its lair in the Grimpen Mire, and a mystery was left which puzzled the authorities, alarmed the countryside, and finally brought the case within the scope of our observation.

"So much for the death of Sir Charles Baskerville. You perceive the devilish cunning of it, for really it would be almost impossible to make a case against the real murderer. His only accomplice was one who could never give him away, and the grotesque, inconceivable nature of the device only served to make it more effective. Both of the women concerned in the case, Mrs. Stapleton and Mrs. Laura Lyons, were left with a strong suspicion against Stap leton. Mrs. Stapleton knew that he had designs upon the old man, and also of the existence of the hound. Mrs. Lyons knew neither of these things, but had been impressed by the death occurring at the time of an uncancelled appointment which was only known to him. However, both of them were under his influence, and he had noth ing to fear from them. The first half of his task was successfully accomplished, but the more difficult still remained.

"It is possible that Stapleton did not know of the existence of an heir in Canada. In any case he would very soon learn it from his friend Dr. Mortimer, and he was told by the latter all details about the arrival of Henry Baskerville. Stapleton's first idea was that this young stranger from Canada might possibly be done to death in London without coming down to Devonshire at all. He distrusted his wife ever since she had refused to help him in laying a trap for the old man, and he dared not leave her long out of his sight for fear he should lose his influence over her. It was for this reason that he took her to London with him. They lodged, I find, at the Mexborough Private Hotel, in Craven Street, which was actually one of those called upon by my agent in search of evidence. Here he kept his wife imprisoned in her room while he, disguised in a beard, fol lowed Dr. Mortimer to Baker Street and afterwards to the station and to the Northumberland Hotel. His wife had some inkling of his plans; but she had such a fear of her husband—a fear founded upon brutal ill-treatment—that she dare not write to warn the man whom she knew to be in danger. If the letter should fall into Stap leton's hands her own life would not be safe. Eventually, as we know, she adopted the expedient of cutting out the words which would form the message, and addressing the letter in a disguised hand. It reached the baronet, and gave him the first warning of his danger.

"It was very essential for Stapleton to get some article of Sir Henry's attire so that, in case he was driven to use the dog, he might always have the means of setting him upon his track. With characteristic promptness and audacity he set about this at once, and we cannot doubt that the boots or chamber-maid of the hotel was well bribed to help him in his design. By chance, however, the first boot which was procured for him was a new one and, there fore, useless for his purpose. He then had it returned and obtained another—a most instructive incident, since it proved conclusively to my mind that we were dealing with a real hound, as no other supposition could explain this anxiety to obtain an old boot and this indifference to a new one. The more *outré* and grotesque an incident is the more carefully it deserves to be examined, and the very point which appears to complicate a case is, when duly consid ered and scientifically handled, the one which is most likely to elucidate it.

"Then we had the visit from our friends next morning, shadowed always by Stapleton in the cab. From his knowledge of our rooms and of my appearance, as well as from his general conduct, I am inclined to think that Stapleton's career of crime has been by no means limited to this single Baskerville affair. It is suggestive that during the last three years there have been four considerable burglaries in the west country, for none of which was any criminal ever arrested. The last of these, at Folkestone Court, in May, was remarkable for the cold-blooded pistolling of the page, who sur prised the masked and solitary burglar. I cannot doubt that Stap leton recruited his waning resources in this fashion, and that for years he has been a desperate and dangerous man.

"We had an example of his readiness of resource that morning when he got away from us so successfully, and also of his audacity in sending back my own name to me through the cabman. From that moment he understood that I had taken over the case in London, and that therefore there was no chance for him there. He returned to Dartmoor and awaited the arrival of the baronet."

"One moment!" said I. "You have, no doubt, described the sequence of events correctly, but there is one point which you have left unexplained. What became of the hound when its master was in London?"

"I have given some attention to this matter and it is undoubtedly of importance. There can be no question that Stapleton had a confidant, though it is unlikely that he ever placed himself in his power by sharing all his plans with him. There was an old manservant at Merripit House, whose name was Anthony. His connection with the Stapletons can be traced for several years, as far back as the schoolmastering days, so that he must have been aware that his master and mistress were really husband and wife. This man has disappeared and has escaped from the country. It is suggestive that Anthony is not a common name in England, while Antonio is so in all Spanish or Spanish-American countries. The man, like Mrs. Stapleton herself, spoke good English, but with a curious lisping accent. I have myself seen this old man cross the Grimpen Mire by the path which Stapleton had marked out. It is very probable, therefore, that in the absence of his master it was he who cared for the hound, though he may never known the purpose for which the beast was used.

"The Stapletons then went down to Devonshire, whither they were soon followed by Sir Henry and you. One word now as to how I stood myself at that time. It may possibly recur to your memory that when I examined the paper upon which the printed words were fastened I made a close inspection for the water-mark. In do ing so I held it within a few inches of my eyes, and was conscious of a faint smell of the scent known as white jessamine. There are seventy-five perfumes, which it is very necessary that a criminal expert should be able to distinguish from each other, and cases have more than once within my own experience depended upon their prompt recognition. The scent suggested the presence of a lady, and already my thoughts began to turn towards the Stapletons. Thus I had made certain of the hound, and had guessed at the criminal before ever we went to the west country.

"It was my game to watch Stapleton. It was evident, however, that I could not do this if I were with you, since he would be keenly on his guard. I deceived everybody, therefore, yourself included, and I came down secretly when I was supposed to be in London. My hardships were not so great as you imagined, though such trifling details must never interfere with the investigation of a case. I stayed for the most part at Coombe Tracey, and only used the hut upon the moor when it was necessary to be near the scene of action. Cartwright had come down with me, and in his disguise as a coun try boy he was of great assistance to me. I was dependent upon him for food and clean linen. When I was watching Stapleton, Cartwright was frequently watching you, so that I was able to keep my hand upon all the strings.

"I have already told you that your reports reached me rapidly, being forwarded instantly from Baker Street to Coombe Tracey. They were of great service to me, and especially that one incident tally truthful piece of biography of Stapleton's. I was able to establish the identity of the man and the woman and knew at last exactly how I stood. The case had been considerably complicated through the incident of the escaped convict and the relations be tween him and the Barrymores. This also you cleared up in a very effective way, though I had already come to the same conclusions from my own observations.

"By the time that you discovered me upon the moor I had a complete knowledge of the whole business, but I had not a case which could go to a jury. Even Stapleton's attempt upon Sir Henry that night which ended in the death of the unfortunate convict did not help us much in proving murder against our man. There seemed to be no alternative but to catch him red-handed, and to do so we had to use Sir Henry, alone and apparently unprotected, as a bait. We did so, and at the cost of a severe shock to our client we succeeded in completing our case and driving Stapleton to his destruction. That Sir Henry should have been exposed to this is, I must confess, a reproach to my management of the case, but we had no means of foreseeing the terrible and paralysing spectacle which the beast presented, nor could we predict the fog which enabled him to burst upon us at such short notice. We succeeded in our object at a cost which both the specialist and Dr. Mortimer assure me will be a temporary one. A long journey may enable our friend to recover not only from his shattered nerves but also from his wounded feelings. His love for the lady was deep and sincere, and to him the saddest part of all this black business was that he should have been deceived by her.

"It only remains to indicate the part which she had played throughout. There can be no doubt that Stapleton exercised an in luence over her which may have been love or may have been fear, or very possibly both, since they are by no means incompatible emotions. It was, at least, absolutely effective. At his command she consented to pass as his sister, though he found the limits of his power over her when he endeavoured to make her the direct acces sory to murder. She was ready to warn Sir Henry so far as she could without implicating her husband, and again and again she tried to do so. Stapleton himself seems to have been capable of jealousy, and when he saw the baronet paying court to the lady, even though it was part of his own plan, still he could not help interrupt ing with a passionate outburst which revealed the fiery soul which his self-contained manner so cleverly concealed. By encouraging the intimacy he made it certain that Sir Henry would frequently come to Merripit House and that he would sooner or later get the opportunity which he desired. On the day of the crisis, however, his wife turned suddenly against him. She had learned something of the death of the convict, and she knew that the hound was being kept in the out-house on the evening that Sir Henry was coming to dinner. She taxed her husband with his intended crime, and a furious scene followed in which he showed her for the first time that she had a rival in his love. Her fidelity turned in an instant to bitter hatred, and he saw that she would betray him. He tied her up, therefore, that she might have no chance of warning Sir Henry, and he hoped, no doubt, that when the whole countryside put down the baronet's death to the curse of his family, as they certainly would do, he could win his wife back to accept an accomplished fact and to keep silent upon what she knew. In this I fancy that in any case he made a miscalculation, and that, if we had not been there, his doom would none the less have been sealed. A woman of Spanish blood does not condone such an injury so lightly. And now, my dear Watson, without referring to my notes, I cannot give you a more detailed account of this curious case. I do not know that any thing essential has been left unexplained."

"He could not hope to frighten Sir Henry to death as he had done the old uncle with his bogie hound."

"The beast was savage and half-starved. If its appearance did not frighten its victim to death, at least it would paralyse the resistance which might be offered."

"No doubt. There only remains one difficulty. If Stapleton came into the succession, how could he explain the fact that he, the heir, had been living unannounced under another name so close to the property? How could he claim it without causing suspicion and inquiry?"

"It is a formidable difficulty, and I fear that you ask too much when you expect me to solve it. The past and the present are within the field of my inquiry, but what a man may do in the future is a hard question to answer. Mrs. Stapleton has heard her husband discuss the problem on several occasions. There were three possible courses. He might claim the property from South America, establish his identity before the British authorities there, and so obtain the fortune without ever coming to England at all; or he might adopt an elaborate disguise during the short time that he need be in London; or, again, he might furnish an accomplice with the proofs and papers, putting him in as heir, and retaining a claim upon some proportion of his income. We cannot doubt from what we know of him that he would have found some way out of the difficulty. And now, my dear Watson, we have had some weeks of severe work, and for one evening, I think, we may turn our thoughts into more pleasant channels. I have a box for 'Les Huguenots.' Have you heard the De Reszkes? Might I trouble you then to be ready in half an hour, and we can stop at Marcini's for a little dinner on the way?"

CHILDREN'S CLASSICS

# White Fang

JACK LONDON

# White Fang

PARRAGON

White Fang
A Parragon Classic

This is a Siena Book
Siena is an imprint of Parragon

First published in 1906

This edition published in 1999 by
Parragon
13 Whiteladies Road
Clifton
Bristol BS8 1PB



Printed and bound in the UK

# PART ONE

# THE WILD

## CHAPTER 1

## THE TRAIL OF THE MEAT

Dark spruce forest frowned on either side the frozen waterway. The trees had been stripped by a recent wind of their white covering of frost, and they seemed to lean toward each other, black and ominous, in the fading light. A vast silence reigned over the land. The land itself was a desolation, lifeless, without movement, so lone and cold that the spirit of it was not even that of sadness. There was a hint in it of laughter, but of a laughter more terrible than any sadness laughter that was mirthless as the smile of the Sphinx, a laughter cold as the frost and partaking of the grimness of infallibility. It was the masterful and incommunicable wisdom of eternity laughing at the futility of life and the effort of life. It was the Wild, the savage, frozen-hearted Northland Wild.

But there *was life*, abroad in the land and defiant. Down the frozen waterway toiled a string of wolfish dogs. Their bristly fur was rimed with frost. Their breath froze in the air as it left their mouths, spouting forth in spumes of vapour that settled upon the hair of their bodies and formed into crystals of frost. Leather harness was on the dogs, and leather traces attached them to a sled which dragged along behind. The sled was without runners. It was made of stout birch-bark, and its full surface rested on the snow. The front end of the sled was turned up, like a scroll, in order to force down and under the bore of soft snow that surged like a wave before it. On the sled, securely lashed, was a long and narrow oblong box. There were other things on the sled—blankets, an axe, and a coffee-pot and frying-pan; but prominent, occupying most of the space, was the long and narrow oblong box.

In advance of the dogs, on wide snowshoes, toiled a man. At the rear of the sled toiled a second man. On the sled, in the box, lay a third man whose toil was over,—a man whom the Wild had conquered and beaten down until he would never move nor struggle again. It is not the way of the Wild to like movement. Life is an offence to it, for life is movement; and the Wild aims always to destroy movement. It freezes the water to prevent it running to the sea; it drives the sap out of the trees till they are frozen to their mighty hearts; and most ferociously and terribly of all does the Wild harry and crush into submission man—man, who is the most restless of life, ever in revolt against the dictum that all movement must in the end come to the cessation of movement.

But at front and rear, unawed and indomitable, toiled the two men who were not yet dead. Their bodies were covered with fur and soft-tanned leather. Eyelashes and cheeks and lips were so coated with the crystals from their frozen breath that their faces were not discernible. This gave them the seeming of ghostly masques, undertakers in a spectral world at the funeral of some ghost. But under it all they were men, penetrating the land of desolation and mockery and silence, puny adventurers bent on colossal adventure, pitting themselves against the might of a world as remote and alien and pulseless as the abysses of space.

They travelled on without speech, saving their breath for the work of their bodies. On every side was the silence, pressing upon them with a tangible presence. It affected their minds as the many atmospheres of deep water affect the body of the diver. It crushed them with the weight of unending vastness and unalterable decree. It crushed them into the remotest recesses of their own minds, pressing out of them, like juices from the grape, all the false ardours and exaltations and undue self-values of the human soul, until they perceived themselves finite and small, specks and motes, moving with weak cunning and little wisdom amidst the play and interplay of the great blind elements and forces.

An hour went by, and a second hour. The pale light of the short sunless day was beginning to fade, when a faint far cry arose on the still air. It soared upward with a swift rush, till it reached its topmost note, where it persisted, palpitant and tense, and then slowly died away. It might have been a lost soul wailing, had it not been invested with a certain sad fierceness and hungry eagerness. The front man turned his head until his eyes met the eyes of the man behind. And then, across the narrow oblong box, each nodded to the other.

A second cry arose, piercing the silence with needle-like shrillness. Both men located the sound. It was to the rear, somewhere in the snow expanse they had just traversed. A third and answering cry arose, also to the rear and to the left of the second cry.

"They're after us, Bill," said the man at the front.

His voice sounded hoarse and unreal, and he had spoken with apparent effort.

"Meat is scarce," answered his comrade. "I ain't seen a rabbit sign for days."

Thereafter they spoke no more, though their ears were keen for the hunting-cries that continued to rise behind them.

At the fall of darkness they swung the dogs into a cluster of spruce trees on the edge of the waterway and made a camp. The coffin, at the side of the fire, served for seat and table. The wolf-dogs, clustered on the far side of the fire, snarled and bickered among themselves, but evinced no inclination to stray off into the darkness.

"Seems to me, Henry, they're stayin' remarkable close to camp," Bill commented.

Henry, squatting over the fire and settling the pot of coffee with a piece of ice, nodded. Nor did he speak till he had taken his seat on the coffin and begun to eat.

"They know where their hides is safe," he said. "They'd sooner eat grub than be grub. They're pretty wise, them dogs."

Bill shook his head. "Oh, I don't know."

His comrade looked at him curiously. "First time I ever heard you say anythin' about their not bein' wise."

"Henry," said the other, munching with deliberation the beans he was eating, "did you happen to notice the way them dogs kicked up when I was a-feedin' 'em?"

"They did cut up more'n usual," Henry acknowledged.

"How many dogs've we got, Henry?"

"Six."

"Well, Henry . . ." Bill stopped for a moment, in order that his words might gain greater significance. "As I was sayin', Henry, we've got six dogs. I took six fish out of the bag. I gave one fish to each dog, an', Henry, I was one fish short."

"You counted wrong."

"We've got six dogs," the other reiterated dispassionately. "I took out six fish. One Ear didn't get no fish. I come back to the bag afterward an' got 'm his fish."

"We've only got six dogs," Henry said.

"Henry," Bill went on, "I won't say they was all dogs, but there was seven of 'm that got fish."

Henry stopped eating to glance across the fire and count the dogs.

"There's only six now," he said.

"I saw the other one run off across the snow," Bill announced with cool positiveness. "I saw seven."

His comrade looked at him commiseratingly, and said, "I'll be almighty glad when this trip's over."

"What d'ye mean by that?" Bill demanded.

"I mean that this load of ourn is gettin' on your nerves, an' that you're beginnin' to see things."

"I thought of that," Bill answered gravely. "An' so, when I saw it run off across the snow, I looked in the snow an' saw its tracks. Then I counted the dogs an' there was still six of 'em. The tracks is there in the snow now. D'ye want to look at 'em? I'll show 'm to you."

Henry did not reply, but munched on in silence, until, the meal finished, he topped it with a final cup of coffee. He wiped his mouth with the back of his hand and said:

"Then you're thinkin' as it was—"

A long wailing cry, fiercely sad, from somewhere in the darkness, had interrupted him. He stopped to listen to it, then he finished his sentence with a wave of his hand toward the sound of the cry, "—one of them?"

Bill nodded. "I'd a blame sight sooner think that than anything else. You noticed yourself the row the dogs made."

Cry after cry, and answering cries, were turning the silence into a bedlam. From every side the cries arose, and the dogs betrayed their fear by huddling together and so close to the fire that their hair was scorched by the heat. Bill threw on more wood, before lighting his pipe.

"I'm thinkin' you're down in the mouth some," Henry said.

"Henry . . ." He sucked meditatively at his pipe for some time before he went on. "Henry, I was a-thinkin' what a blame sight luckier he is than you an' me'll ever be."

He indicated the third person by a downward thrust of the thumb to the box on which they sat.

"You an' me, Henry, when we die, we'll be lucky if we get enough stones over our carcasses to keep the dogs off of us."

"But we ain't got people an' money an' all the rest, like him," Henry rejoined. "Long-distance funerals is somethin' you an' me can't exactly afford."

"What gets me, Henry, is what a chap like this, that's a lord or something in his own country, and that's never had to bother about grub nor blankets, why he comes a-buttin' round the God-forsaken ends of the earth—that's what I can't exactly see."

"He might have lived to a ripe old age if he'd stayed to home," Henry agreed.

Bill opened his mouth to speak, but changed his mind. Instead, he pointed toward the wall of darkness that pressed about them from every side. There was no suggestion of form in the utter blackness; only could be seen a pair of eyes gleaming like live coals. Henry indicated with his head a second pair, and a third. A circle of the gleaming eyes had drawn about their camp. Now and again a pair of eyes moved, or disappeared to appear again a moment later.

The unrest of the dogs had been increasing, and they stampeded, in a surge of sudden fear, to the near side of the fire, cringing and crawling about the legs of the men. In the scramble one of the dogs had been overturned on the edge of the fire, and it had yelped with pain and fright as the smell of its singed coat possessed the air. The commotion caused the circle of eyes to shift restlessly for a moment and even to withdraw a bit, but it settled down again as the dogs became quiet.

"Henry, it's a blame misfortune to be out of ammunition."

Bill had finished his pipe and was helping his companion spread the bed of fur and blanket upon the spruce boughs which he had laid over the snow before supper. Henry grunted, and began unlacing his moccasins.

"How many cartridges did you say you had left?" he asked.

"Three," came the answer. "An' I wish 'twas three hundred. Then I'd shown 'em what for, damn 'em!"

He shook his fist angrily at the gleaming eyes, and began securely to prop his moccasins before the fire.

"An' I wisht this cold snap'd break," he went on. "It's been fifty below for two weeks now. An' I wish I'd never started on this trip, Henry. I don't like the looks of it. It don't feel right, somehow. An' while I'm wishin', I wish the trip was over an' done with, an' you an' me a-sittin' by the fire in Fort McGurry* just about now an' playin' cribbage—that's what I wish."

Henry grunted and crawled into bed. As he dozed off he was aroused by his comrade's voice.

"Say, Henry, that other one that come in an' got a fish— why didn't the dogs pitch into it? That's what's botherin' me."

"You're botherin' too much, Bill," came the sleepy response. "You was never like this before. You jes' shut up now, an' go to sleep, an' you'll be all hunky-dory in the mornin'. Your stomach's sour, that's what's botherin' you."

The men slept, breathing heavily, side by side, under the one covering. The fire died down, and the gleaming eyes drew closer the circle they had flung about the camp. The dogs clustered together in fear, now and again snarling menacingly as a pair of eyes drew close. Once their uproar became so loud that Bill woke up. He got out of bed carefully, so as not to disturb the sleep of his comrade, and threw more wood on the fire. As it began to flame up, the circle of eyes drew farther back. He glanced casually at the huddling dogs. He rubbed his eyes and looked at them more sharply. Then he crawled back into the blankets.

"Henry," he said. "Oh, Henry."

Henry groaned as he passed from sleep to waking, and demanded, "What's wrong now?"

"Nothin'," came the answer; "only there's seven of 'em again. I just counted."

Henry acknowledged receipt of the information with a grunt that slid into a snore as he drifted back into sleep.

In the morning it was Henry who awoke first and routed his companion out of bed. Daylight was yet three hours away, though it was already six o'clock; and in the darkness Henry went about preparing breakfast, while Bill rolled the blankets and made the sled ready for lashing.

"Say, Henry," he asked suddenly, "how many dogs did you say we had?"

"Six."

"Wrong," Bill proclaimed triumphantly.

"Seven again?" Henry queried.

"No, five; one's gone."

"The hell!" Henry cried in wrath, leaving the cooking to come and count the dogs.

"You're right, Bill," he concluded. "Fatty's gone."

"An' he went like greased lightnin' once he got started. Couldn't 've seen 'm for smoke."

"No chance at all," Henry concluded. "They jes' swallowed 'm alive. I bet he was yelpin' as he went down their throats, damn 'em!'

"He always was a fool dog," said Bill.

"But no fool dog ought to be fool enough to go off an' commit suicide that way." He looked over the remainder of the team with a speculative eye that summed up instantly the salient traits of each animal. "I bet none of the others would do it."

"Couldn't drive 'em away from the fire with a club," Bill agreed. "I always did think there was somethin' wrong with Fatty, anyway."

And this was the epitaph of a dead dog on the Northland trail—less scant than the epitaph of many another dog, of many a man.

## Chapter 2

# THE SHE-WOLF

Breakfast eaten and the slim camp-outfit lashed to the sled, the men turned their backs on the cheery fire and launched out into the darkness. At once began to rise the cries that were fiercely sad—cries that called through the darkness and cold to one another and answered back. Conversation ceased. Daylight came at nine o'clock. At midday the sky to the south warmed to rose-color, and marked where the bulge of the earth intervened between the meridian sun and the northern world. But the rose-color swiftly faded. The gray light of day that remained lasted until three o'clock, when it, too, faded, and the pall of the Arctic night descended upon the lone and silent land.

As darkness came on, the hunting-cries to right and left and rear drew closer—so close that more than once they sent surges of fear through the toiling dogs, throwing them into short-lived panics.

At the conclusion of one such panic, when he and Henry had got the dogs back in the traces, Bill said:

"I wisht they'd strike game somewheres, an' go away an' leave us alone."

"They do get on the nerves horrible," Henry sympathized.

They spoke no more until camp was made.

Henry was bending over and adding ice to the bubbling pot of beans when he was startled by the sound of a blow, an exclamation from Bill, and a sharp snarling cry of pain from among the dogs. He straightened up in time to see a dim form disappearing across the snow into the shelter of the dark. Then he saw Bill, standing amid the dogs, half triumphant, half crest-fallen, in one hand a stout club, in the other the tail and part of the body of a sun-cured salmon.

"It got half of it," he announced; "but I got a whack at it jes' the same. D'ye hear it squeal?"

"What'd it look like?" Henry asked.

"Couldn't see. But it had four legs an' a mouth an' hair an' looked like any dog."

"Must be a tame wolf, I reckon."

"It's damned tame, whatever it is, comin' in here at feedin' time an' gettin' its whack of fish."

That night, when supper was finished and they sat on the oblong box and pulled at their pipes, the circle of gleaming eyes drew in even closer than before.

"I wish they'd spring up a bunch of moose or somethin', an' go away an' leave us alone," Bill said.

Henry grunted with an intonation that was not all sympathy, and for a quarter of an hour they sat on in silence, Henry staring at the fire, and Bill at the circle of eyes that burned in the darkness just beyond the firelight.

"I wish we was pullin' into McGurry right now," he began again.

"Shut up your wishin' an' your croakin'," Henry burst out angrily. "Your stomach's sour. That's what's ailin' you. Swallow a spoonful of sody, an' you'll sweeten up wonderful an' be more pleasant company."

In the morning, Henry was aroused by fervid blasphemy that proceeded from the mouth of Bill. Henry propped himself up on an elbow and looked to see his comrade standing among the dogs beside the replenished fire, his arms raised in objurgation, his face distorted with passion.

"Hello!" Henry called. "What's up now?"

"Frog's gone," came the answer.

"No."

"I tell you yes."

Henry leaped out of the blankets and to the dogs. He counted them with care, and then joined his partner in cursing the powers of the Wild that had robbed them of another dog.

"Frog was the strongest dog of the bunch," Bill pronounced finally.

"An' he was no fool dog neither," Henry added.

And so was recorded the second epitaph in two days.

A gloomy breakfast was eaten, and the four remaining dogs were harnessed to the sled. The day was a repetition of the days that had gone before. The men toiled without speech across the face of the frozen world. The silence was unbroken save by the cries of their pursuers, that, unseen, hung upon their rear. With the coming of night in the mid-afternoon, the cries sounded closer as the pursuers drew in according to their custom; and the dogs grew excited and frightened, and were guilty of panics that tangled the traces and further depressed the two men.

"There, that'll fix you fool critters," Bill said with satisfaction that night, standing erect at completion of his task.

Henry left his cooking to come and see. Not only had his partner tied the dogs up, but he had tied them, after the Indian fashion, with sticks. About the neck of each dog he had fastened a leather thong. To this, and so close to the neck that the dog could not get his teeth to it, he had tied a stout stick four or five feet in length. The other end of the stick, in turn, was made fast to a stake in the ground by means of a leather thong. The dog was unable to gnaw through the leather at his own end of the stick. The stick prevented him from getting at the leather that fastened the other end.

Henry nodded his head approvingly.

"It's the only contraption that'll ever hold One Ear," he said. "He can gnaw through leather as clean as a knife an' jes' about half as quick. They all '11 be here in the mornin' hunkydory."

"You jes' bet they will," Bill affirmed. "If one of 'em turns up missin', I'll go without my coffee."

"They jes' know we ain't loaded to kill," Henry remarked at bedtime, indicating the gleaming circle that hemmed them in. "If we could put a couple of shots into 'em, they'd be more respectful. They come closer every night. Get the firelight out of your eyes an' look hard—there! Did you see that one?"

For some time the two men amused themselves with watching the movement of vague forms on the edge of the firelight. By looking closely and steadily at where a pair of eyes burned in the darkness, the form of the animal would slowly take shape. They could even see these forms move at times.

A sound among the dogs attracted the men's attention. One Ear was uttering quick, eager whines, lunging at the length of his stick toward the darkness, and desisting now and again in order to make frantic attacks on the stick with his teeth.

"Look at that, Bill," Henry whispered.

Full into the firelight, with a stealthy, sidelong movement, glided a doglike animal. It moved with commingled mistrust and daring, cautiously observing the men, its attention fixed on the dogs. One Ear strained the full length of the stick toward the intruder and whined with eagerness.

"That fool One Ear don't seem scairt much," Bill said in a low tone.

"It's a she-wolf," Henry whispered back, "an' that accounts for Fatty an' Frog. She's the decoy for the pack. She draws out the dog an' then all the rest pitches in an' eats 'm up."

The fire crackled. A log fell apart with a loud spluttering noise. At the sound of it the strange animal leaped back into the darkness.

"Henry, I'm a-thinkin'," Bill announced.

"Thinkin' what?"

"I'm a-thinkin' that was the one I lambasted with the club."

"Ain't the slightest doubt in the world," was Henry's response.

"An' right here I want to remark," Bill went on, "that that animal's familiarity with campfires is suspicious an' immoral."

"It knows for certain more'n a self-respectin' wolf ought to know," Henry agreed. "A wolf that knows enough to come in with the dogs at feedin' time has had experiences."

"Ol' Villan had a dog once that run away with the wolves," Bill cogitated aloud. "I ought to know. I shot it out of the pack in a moose pasture over on Little Stick. An' Ol' Villan cried like a baby. Hadn't seen it for three years, he said. Ben with the wolves all that time."

"I reckon you've called the turn, Bill. That wolf's a dog, an' it's eaten fish many's the time from the hand of man."

"An' if I get a chance at it, that wolf that's a dog'll be jes' meat," Bill declared. "We can't afford to lose no more animals."

"But you've only got three cartridges," Henry objected.

"I'll wait for a dead sure shot," was the reply.

In the morning Henry renewed the fire and cooked breakfast to the accompaniment of his partner's snoring.

"You was sleepin' jes' too comfortable for anythin'," Henry told him, as he routed him out for breakfast. "I hadn't the heart to rouse you."

Bill began to eat sleepily. He noticed that his cup was empty and started to reach for the pot. But the pot was beyond arm's length and beside Henry.

"Say, Henry," he chided gently, "ain't you forgot somethin'?"

Henry looked about with great carefulness and shook his head. Bill held up the empty cup.

"You don't get no coffee," Henry announced.

"Ain't run out?" Bill asked anxiously.

"Nope."

"Ain't thinkin' it'll hurt my digestion?"

"Nope."

A flush of angry blood pervaded Bill's face.

"Then it's jes' warm an' anxious I am to be hearin' you explain yourself," he said.

"Spanker's gone," Henry answered.

Without haste, with the air of one resigned to misfortune, Bill turned his head, and from where he sat counted the dogs.

"How'd it happen?" he asked apathetically.

Henry shrugged his shoulders. "Don't know. Unless One Ear gnawed 'm loose. He couldn't a-done it himself, that's sure."

"The darned cuss." Bill spoke gravely and slowly, with no hint of the anger that was raging within. "Jes' because he couldn't chew himself loose, he chews Spanker loose."

"Well, Spanker's troubles is over, anyway; I guess he's digested by this time an' cavortin' over the landscape in the bellies of twenty different wolves," was Henry's epitaph on this, the latest lost dog. "Have some coffee, Bill."

But Bill shook his head.

"Go on," Henry pleaded, elevating the pot.

Bill shoved his cup aside. "I'll be ding-dong-danged if I do. I said I wouldn't if ary dog turned up missin', an' I won't."

"It's darn good coffee," Henry said enticingly.

But Bill was stubborn, and he ate a dry breakfast, washed down with mumbled curses at One Ear for the trick he had played.

"I'll tie 'em up out of reach of each other tonight," Bill said, as they took the trail.

They had travelled little more than a hundred yards, when Henry, who was in front, bent down and picked up something with which his snowshoe had collided. It was dark, and he could not see it, but he recognized it by the touch. He flung it back. so that it struck the sled and bounced along until it fetched up on Bill's snowshoes.

"Mebbe you'll need that in your business," Henry said.

Bill uttered an exclamation. It was all that was left of Spanker — the stick with which he had been tied.

"They ate 'm hide an' all," Bill announced. 'The stick's as clean as a whistle. They've ate the leather offen both ends. They're damn hungry, Henry, an' they'll have you an' me guessin' before this trip's over."

Henry laughed defiantly. "I ain't been trailed this way by wolves before, but I've gone through a whole lot worse an' kept my health. Takes more'n a handful of them pesky critters to do for yours truly, Bill, my son."

"I don't know I don't know," Bill muttered ominously.

"Well, you'll know all right when we pull into McGurry."

"I ain't feelin' special enthusiastic," Bill persisted.

"You're off color, that's what's the matter with you," Henry dogmatized. "What you need is quinine, an' I'm goin' to dose you up stiff as soon as we make McGurry."

Bill grunted his disagreement with the diagnosis, and lapsed into silence. The day was like all the days. Light came at nine o'clock. At twelve o'clock the southern horizon was warmed by the unseen sun; and then began the cold gray of afternoon that would merge, three hours later, into night.

It was just after the sun's futile effort to appear, that Bill slipped the rifle from under the sled-lashings and said:

"You keep right on, Henry, I'm goin' to see what I can see."

"You'd better stick by the sled," his partner protested. "You've only got three cartridges, an' there's no tellin' what might happen."

"Who's croakin' now?" Bill demanded triumphantly.

Henry made no reply, and plodded on alone, though often he cast anxious glances back into the gray solitude where his partner had disappeared. An hour later, taking advantage of the cut-offs around which the sled had to go, Bill arrived.

"They're scattered an' rangin' along wide," he said; "keepin' up with us an' lookin' for game at the same time. You see, they're sure of us, only they know they've got to wait to get us. In the meantime they're willin' to pick up anythin' eatable that comes handy."

"You mean they think they're sure of us," Henry objected pointedly.

But Bill ignored him. "I seen some of them. They're pretty thin. They ain't had a bite in weeks, I reckon, outside of Fatty an' Frog an' Spanker; an' there's so many of 'em that didn't go far. They're remarkable thin. Their ribs is like washboards, an' their stomachs is right up against their backbones. They're pretty desperate, I can tell you. They'll be goin' mad, yet, an' then watch out."

A few minutes later, Henry, who was now travelling behind the sled, emitted a low, warning whistle. Bill turned and looked, then quietly stopped the dogs. To the rear, from around the last bend and plainly into view, on the very trail they had just covered, trotted a furry, slinking form. Its nose was to the trail, and it trotted with a peculiar, sliding, effortless gait. When they halted, it halted, throwing up its head and regarding them steadily with nostrils that twitched as it caught and studied the scent of them.

"It's the she-wolf," Bill whispered.

The dogs had lain down in the snow, and he walked past them to join his partner at the sled. Together they watched the strange animal that had pursued them for days and that had already accomplished the destruction of half their dog-team.

After a searching scrutiny, the animal trotted forward a few steps. This it repeated several times, till it was a short hundred yards away. It paused, head up, close by a clump of spruce trees, and with sight and scent studied the outfit of the watching men. It looked at them in a strangely wistful way, after the manner of a dog; but in its wistfulness there was none of the dog affection. It was a wistfulness bred of hunger, as cruel as its own fangs, as merciless as the frost itself.

It was large for a wolf, its gaunt frame advertising the lines of an animal that was among the largest of its kind.

"Stands pretty close to two feet an' a half at the shoulders," Henry commented. "An' I'll bet it ain't far from five feet long."

"Kind of strange color for a wolf," was Bill's criticism. "I never seen a red wolf before. Looks almost cinnamon to me."

The animal was certainly not cinnamon-colored. Its coat was the true wolf-coat. The dominant color was gray, and yet there was to it a faint reddish hue—a hue that was baffling, that appeared and disappeared, that was more like an illusion of the vision, now gray, distinctly gray, and again giving hints and glints of a vague redness of color not classifiable in terms of ordinary experience.

"Looks for all the world like a big husky sled-dog," Bill said. "I wouldn't be s'prised to see it wag its tail.

"Hello, you husky!" he called. "Come here, you, whatever-your-name-is."

"Ain't a bit scairt of you," Henry laughed.

Bill waved his hand at it threateningly and shouted loudly; but the animal betrayed no fear. The only change in it that they could notice was an accession of alertness. It still regarded them with the merciless wistfulness of hunger. They were meat, and it was hungry; and it would like to go in and eat them if it dared.

"Look here, Henry," Bill said, unconsciously lowering his voice to a whisper because of what he meditated. "We've got three cartridges. But it's a dead shot. Couldn't miss it. It's got away with three of our dogs, an' we oughter put a stop to it. What d'ye say?"

Henry nodded his consent. Bill cautiously slipped the gun from under the sled-lashing. The gun was on the way to his shoulder, but it never got there. For in that instant the she-wolf leaped sidewise from the trail into the clump of spruce trees and disappeared.

The two men looked at each other. Henry whistled long and comprehendingly.

"I might have knowed it," Bill chided himself aloud, as he replaced the gun. "Of course a wolf that knows enough to come in with the dogs at feedin' time, 'd know all about shooting-irons. I tell you right now, Henry, that critter's the cause of all our trouble. We'd have six dogs at the present time, 'stead of three, if it wasn't for her. An' I tell you right now, Henry, I'm goin' to get her. She's too smart to be shot in the open. But I'm goin' to lay for her. I'll bushwhack her as sure as my name is Bill."

"You needn't stray off too far in doin' it," his partner admonished. 'If that pack ever starts to jump you, them three cartridges'd be wuth no more'n three whoops in hell. Them animals is damn hungry, an' once they start in, they'll sure get you, Bill."

They camped early that night. Three dogs could not drag the sled so fast nor for so long hours as could six, and they were showing unmistakable signs of playing out. And the men went early to bed, Bill first seeing to it that the dogs were tied out of gnawing-reach of one another.

But the wolves were growing bolder, and the men were aroused more than once from their sleep. So near did the wolves approach, that the dogs became frantic with terror, and it was necessary to replenish the fire from time to time in order to keep the adventurous marauders at safer distance.

"I've hearn sailors talk of sharks followin' a ship," Bill remarked, as he crawled back into the blankets after one such replenishing of the fire. "Well, them wolves is land sharks. They know their business better'n we do, an' they ain't a-holdin' our trail this way for their health. They're goin' to get us. They're sure goin' to get us, Henry."

"They've half got you a'ready, a-talkin' like that," Henry retorted sharply. "A man's half licked when he says he is. An' you're half eaten from the way you're goin' on about it."

"They've got away with better men than you an' me," Bill answered.

"Oh, shet up your croakin'. You make me all-fired tired."

Henry rolled over angrily on his side, but was surprised that Bill made no similar display of temper. This was not Bill's way, for he was easily angered by sharp words. Henry thought long over it before he went to sleep, and as his eyelids fluttered down and he dozed off, the thought in his mind was: "There's no mistakin' it, Bill's almighty blue. I'll have to cheer him up to-morrow."

## CHAPTER 3

# THE HUNGER CRY

The day began auspiciously. They had lost no dogs during the night, and they swung out upon the trail and into the silence, the darkness, and the cold with spirits that were fairly light. Bill seemed to have forgotten his forebodings of the previous night, and even waxed facetious with the dogs when, at midday, they overturned the sled on a bad piece of trail.

It was an awkward mix-up. The sled was upside down and jammed between a tree-trunk and a huge rock, and they were forced to unharness the dogs in order to straighten out the tangle. The two men were bent over the sled and trying to right it, when Henry observed One Ear sidling away.

"Here, you, One Ear!" he cried, straightening up and turning around on the dog.

But One Ear broke into a run across the snow, his traces trailing behind him. And there, out in the snow of their back-track, was the she-wolf waiting for him. As he neared her, he became suddenly cautious. He slowed down to an alert and mincing walk and then stopped. He regarded her carefully and dubiously, yet desirefully. She seemed to smile at him, showing her teeth in an ingratiating rather than a menacing way. She moved toward him a few steps, playfully, and then halted. One Ear drew near to her, still alert and cautious, his tail and ears in the air, his head held high.

He tried to sniff noses with her, but she retreated playfully and coyly. Every advance on his part was accompanied by a corresponding retreat on her part. Step by step she was luring him away from the security of his human companionship. Once, as though a warning had in vague ways flitted through his intelligence, he turned his head and looked back at the overturned sled, at his team-mates, and at the two men who were calling to him.

But whatever idea was forming in his mind, was dissipated by the she-wolf, who advanced upon him, sniffed noses with him for a fleeting instant, and then resumed her coy retreat before his renewed advances.

In the meantime, Bill had bethought himself of the rifle. But it was jammed beneath the overturned sled, and by the time Henry had helped him to right the load, One Ear and the she-wolf were too close together and the distance too great to risk a shot.

Too late, One Ear learned his mistake. Before they saw the cause, the two men saw him turn and start to run back toward them. Then, approaching at right angles to the trail and cutting off his retreat, they saw a dozen wolves, lean and gray, bounding across the snow. On the instant, the she-wolf's coyness and playfulness disappeared. With a snarl she sprang upon One Ear. He thrust her off with his shoulder, and, his retreat cut off and still intent on regaining the sled, he altered his course in an attempt to circle around to it. More wolves were appearing every moment and joining in the chase. The she-wolf was one leap behind One Ear and holding her own.

"Where are you goin'?" Henry suddenly demanded, laying his hand on his partner's arm.

Bill shook it off. "I won't stand it," he said. "They ain't a-goin' to get any more of our dogs if I can help it."

Gun in hand, he plunged into the underbrush that lined the side of the trail. His intention was apparent enough. Taking the sled as the centre of the circle that One Ear was making, Bill planned to tap that circle at a point in advance of the pursuit. With his rifle, in the broad daylight, it might be possible for him to awe the wolves and save the dog.

"Say, Bill!" Henry called after him. "Be careful! Don't take no chances!"

Henry sat down on the sled and watched. There was nothing else for him to do. Bill had already gone from sight; but now and again, appearing and disappearing amongst the underbrush and the scattered clumps of spruce, could be seen One Ear. Henry judged his case to be hopeless. The dog was thoroughly alive to its danger, but it was running on the outer circle while the wolf-pack was running on the inner and shorter circle. It was vain to think of One Ear so outdistancing his pursuers as to be able to cut across their circle in advance of them and to regain the sled.

The different lines were rapidly approaching a point. Somewhere out there in the snow, screened from his sight by trees and thickets,

Henry knew that the wolf-pack, One Ear, and Bill were coming together. All too quickly, far more quickly than he had expected, it happened. He heard a shot, then two shots in rapid succession, and he knew that Bill's ammunition was gone. Then he heard a great outcry of snarls and yelps. He recognized One Ear's yell of pain and terror, and he heard a wolf-cry that bespoke a stricken animal. And that was all. The snarls ceased. The yelping died away. Silence settled down again over the lonely land.

He sat for a long while upon the sled. There was no need for him to go and see what had happened. He knew it as though it had taken place before his eyes. Once, he roused with a start and hastily got the axe out from underneath the lashings. But for some time longer he sat and brooded, the two remaining dogs crouching and trembling at his feet.

At last he arose in a weary manner, as though all the resilience had gone out of his body, and proceeded to fasten the dogs to the sled. He passed a rope over his shoulder, a man-trace, and pulled with the dogs. He did not go far. At the first hint of darkness he hastened to make a camp, and he saw to it that he had a generous supply of firewood. He fed the dogs, cooked and ate his supper, and made his bed close to the fire.

But he was not destined to enjoy that bed. Before his eyes closed the wolves had drawn too near for safety. It no longer required an effort of the vision to see them. They were all about him and the fire, in a narrow circle, and he could see them plainly in the firelight, lying down, sitting up, crawling forward on their bellies, or slinking back and forth. They even slept. Here and there he could see one curled up in the snow like a dog, taking the sleep that was now denied himself.

He kept the fire brightly blazing, for he knew that it alone intervened between the flesh of his body and their hungry fangs. His two dogs stayed close by him, one on either side, leaning against him for protection, crying and whimpering, and at times snarling desperately when a wolf approached a little closer than usual. At such moments, when his dogs snarled, the whole circle would be agitated, the wolves coming to their feet and pressing tentatively forward, a chorus of snarls and eager yelps rising about him. Then the circle would lie down again and here and there a wolf would resume its broken nap.

But this circle had a continuous tendency to draw in upon him. Bit by bit, an inch at a time, with here a wolf bellying forward, and there a wolf bellying forward, the circle would narrow until the brutes were almost within springing distance. Then he would seize brands from the fire and hurl them into the pack. A hasty drawing back always resulted, accompanied by angry yelps and frightened snarls when a well-aimed brand struck and scorched a too daring animal.

Morning found the man haggard and worn, wide-eyed from want of sleep. He cooked breakfast in the darkness, and at nine o'clock, when, with the coming of daylight, the wolf-pack drew back, he set about the task he had planned through the long hours of the night. Chopping down young saplings, he made them cross-bars of a scaffold by lashing them high up to the trunks of standing trees. Using the sled-lashings for a heaving rope, and with the aid of the dogs, he hoisted the coffin to the top of the scaffold.

"They got Bill, an' they may get me, but they'll sure never get you, young man," he said, addressing the dead body in its tree-sepulchre.

Then he took the trail, the lightened sled bounding along behind the willing dogs; for they, too, knew that safety lay only in the gaining of Fort McGurry. The wolves were now more open in their pursuit, trotting sedately behind and ranging along on either side, their red tongues lolling out, their lean sides showing the undulating ribs with every movement. They were very lean, mere skin-bags stretched over bony frames, with strings for muscles—so lean that Henry found it in his mind to marvel that they still kept their feet and did not collapse forthright in the snow.

He did not dare travel until dark. At midday, not only did the sun warm the southern horizon, but it even thrust its upper rim, pale and golden, above the sky-line. He received it as a sign. The days were growing longer. The sun was returning. But scarcely had the cheer of its light departed, than he went into camp. There were still several hours of gray daylight and sombre twilight, and he utilized them in chopping an enormous supply of firewood.

With night came horror. Not only were the starving wolves growing bolder, but lack of sleep was telling upon Henry. He dozed despite himself, crouching by the fire, the blankets about his shoulders, the axe between his knees, and on either side a dog pressing close against him. He awoke once and saw in front of him, not a dozen feet away, a big gray wolf, one of the largest of the pack. And even as he looked, the brute deliberately stretched himself after the manner of a lazy dog, yawning full in his face and looking upon him with a possessive eye, as if, in truth, he were merely a delayed meal that was soon to be eaten.

This certitude was shown by the whole pack. Fully a score he could count, staring hungrily at him or calmly sleeping in the snow. They reminded him of children gathered about a spread table and awaiting permission to begin to eat. And he was the food they were to eat! He wondered how and when the meal would begin.

As he piled wood on the fire he discovered an appreciation of his own body which he had never felt before. He watched his moving muscles and was interested in the cunning mechanism of his fingers. By the light of the fire he crooked his fingers slowly and repeatedly, now one at a time, now all together, spreading them wide or making quick gripping movements. He studied the nail-formation, and prodded the fingertips, now sharply, and again softly, gauging the while the nerve-sensations produced. It fascinated him, and he grew suddenly fond of this subtle flesh of his that worked so beautifully and smoothly and delicately. Then he would cast a glance of fear at the wolf-circle drawn expectantly about him, and like a blow the realization would strike him that this wonderful body of his, this living flesh, was no more than so much meat, a quest of ravenous animals, to be torn and slashed by their hungry fangs, to be sustenance to them as the moose and the rabbit had often been sustenance to him.

He came out of a doze that was half nightmare, to see the red-hued she-wolf before him. She was not more than half a dozen feet away, sitting in the snow and wistfully regarding him. The two dogs were whimpering and snarling at his feet, but she took no notice of them. She was looking at the man, and for some time he returned her look. There was nothing threatening about her. She looked at him merely with a great wistfulness, but he knew it to be the wistfulness of an equally great hunger. He was the food, and the sight of him excited in her the gustatory sensations. Her mouth opened, the saliva drooled forth, and she licked her chops with the pleasure of anticipation.

A spasm of fear went through him. He reached hastily for a brand to throw at her. But even as he reached, and before his fingers had closed on the missile, she sprang back into safety; and he knew that she was used to having things thrown at her. She had snarled as she sprang away, baring her white fangs to their roots, all her wistfulness vanishing, being replaced by a carnivorous malignity that made him shudder. He glanced at the hand that held the brand, noticing the cunning delicacy of the fingers that gripped it, how they adjusted themselves to all the inequalities of the surface, curling over and under and about the rough wood, and one little finger, too close to the burning portion of the brand, sensitively and automatically writhing back from the hurtful heat to a cooler gripping-place; and in the same instant he seemed to see a vision of those same sensitive and delicate fingers being crushed and torn by the white teeth of the she-wolf. Never had he been so fond of this body of his as now when his tenure of it was so precarious.

All night, with burning brands, he fought off the hungry pack. When he dozed despite himself, the whimpering and snarling of the dogs aroused him. Morning came, but for the first time the light of day failed to scatter the wolves. The man waited in vain for them to go. They remained in a circle about him and his fire, displaying an arrogance of possession that shook his courage born of the morning light.

He made one desperate attempt to pull out on the trail. But the moment he left the protection of the fire, the boldest wolf leaped for him, but leaped short. He saved himself by springing back, the jaws snapping together a scant six inches from his thigh. The rest of the pack was now up and surging upon him, and a throwing of firebrands right and left was necessary to drive them back to a respectful distance.

Even in the daylight he did not dare leave the fire to chop fresh wood. Twenty feet away towered a huge dead spruce. He spent half the day extending his campfire to the tree, at any moment a half dozen burning faggots ready at hand to fling at his enemies. Once at the tree, he studied the surrounding forest in order to fell the tree in the direction of the most firewood.

The night was a repetition of the night before, save that the need for sleep was becoming overpowering. The snarling of his dogs was losing its efficacy. Besides, they were snarling all the time, and his benumbed and drowsy senses no longer took note of changing pitch and intensity. He awoke with a start. The she-wolf was less than a yard from him. Mechanically, at short range, without letting go of it, he thrust a brand full into her open and snarling mouth. She sprang away, yelling with pain, and while he took delight in the smell of burning flesh and hair, he watched her shaking her head and growling wrathfully a score of feet away.

But this time, before he dozed again, he tied a burning pine-knot to his right hand. His eyes were closed but a few minutes when the burn of the flame on his flesh awakened him. For several hours he adhered to this programme. Every time he was thus awakened he drove back the wolves with flying brands, replenished the fire, and rearranged the pine-knot on his hand. All worked well, but there came a time when he fastened the pine knot insecurely. As his eyes closed it fell away from his hand.

He dreamed. It seemed to him that he was in Fort McGurry. It was warm and comfortable, and he was playing cribbage with the Factor.* Also, it seemed to him that the fort was besieged by wolves. They were howling at the very gates, and sometimes he and the Factor paused from the game to listen and laugh at the futile efforts of the wolves to get in. And then, so strange was the dream, there was a crash. The door was burst open. He could see the wolves flooding into the big living-room of the fort. They were leaping straight for him and the Factor. With the bursting open of the door, the noise of their howling had increased tremendously. This howling now bothered him. His dream was merging into something else—he knew not what; but through it all, following him, persisted the howling.

And then he awoke to find the howling real. There was a great snarling and yelping. The wolves were rushing him. They were all about him and upon him. The teeth of one had closed upon his arm. Instinctively he leaped into the fire, and as he leaped, he felt the sharp slash of teeth that tore through the flesh of his leg. Then began a fire fight. His stout mittens temporarily protected his hands, and he scooped live coals into the air in all directions, until the camp-fire took on the semblance of a volcano.

But it could not last long. His face was blistering in the heat, his eyebrows and lashes were singed off, and the heat was becoming unbearable to his feet. With a flaming brand in each hand, he sprang to the edge of the fire. The wolves had been driven back. On every side, wherever the live coals had fallen, the snow was sizzling, and every little while a retiring wolf, with wild leap and snort and snarl, announced that one such live coal had been stepped upon.

Flinging his brands at the nearest of his enemies, the man thrust his smouldering mittens into the snow and stamped about to cool his feet. His two dogs were missing, and he well knew that they had served as a course in the protracted meal which had begun days before with Fatty, the last course of which would likely be himself in the days to follow.

"You ain't got me yet!" he cried, savagely shaking his fist at the hungry beasts; and at the sound of his voice the whole circle was agitated, there was a general snarl, and the she-wolf slid up close to him across the snow and watched him with hungry wistfulness.

He set to work to carry out a new idea that had come to him. He extended the fire into a large circle. Inside this circle he crouched, his sleeping outfit under him as a protection against the melting snow. When he had thus disappeared within his shelter of flame, the whole pack came curiously to the rim of the fire to see what had become of him. Hitherto they had been denied access to the fire, and they now settled down in a close-drawn circle, like so many dogs, blinking and yawning and stretching their lean bodies in the unaccustomed warmth. Then the she-wolf sat down, pointed her nose at a star, and began to howl. One by one the wolves joined her, till the whole pack, on haunches, with noses pointed skyward, was howling its hungry cry.

Dawn came, and daylight. The fire was burning low. The fuel had run out, and there was need to get more. The man attempted to step out of his circle of flame, but the wolves surged to meet him. Burning brands made them spring aside, but they no longer sprang back. In vain he strove to drive them back. As he gave up and stumbled inside his circle, a wolf leaped for him, missed, and landed with all four feet in the coals. It cried out with terror, at the same time snarling, and scrambled back to cool its paws in the snow.

The man sat down on his blankets in a crouching position. His body leaned forward from the hips. His shoulders, relaxed and drooping, and his head on his knees advertised that he had given up the struggle. Now and again he raised his head to note the dying down of the fire. The circle of flame and coals was breaking into segments with openings in between. These openings grew in size, the segments diminished.

"I guess you can come an' get me any time," he mumbled. "Anyway, I'm goin' to sleep."

Once he wakened, and in an opening in the circle, directly in front of him, he saw the she-wolf gazing at him.

Again he awakened, a little later, though it seemed hours to him. A mysterious change had taken place-so mysterious a change that he was shocked wider awake. Something had happened. He could not understand at first. Then he discovered it. The wolves were gone. Remained only the trampled snow to show how closely they had pressed him. Sleep was welling up and gripping him again, his head was sinking down upon his knees, when he roused with a sudden start.

There were cries of men, the churn of sleds, the creaking of harnesses, and the eager whimpering of straining dogs. Four sleds pulled in from the river bed to the camp among the trees. Half a dozen men were about the man who crouched in the centre of the dying fire. They were shaking and prodding him into consciousness. He looked at them like a drunken man and maundered in strange, sleepy speech:

"Red she-wolf.... Come in with the dogs at feedin' time.... First she ate the dogfood.... Then she ate the dogs.... An' after that she ate Bill...."

"Where's Lord Alfred?" one of the men bellowed in his ear, shaking him roughly.

He shook his head slowly. "No, she didn't eat him.... He's roostin' in a tree at the last camp."

"Dead?" the man shouted.

"An' in a box," Henry answered. He jerked his shoulder petulantly away from the grip of his questioner. "Say, you lemme alone.... I'm jes' plumb tuckered out.... Goo' night, everybody."

His eyes fluttered and went shut. His chin fell forward on his chest. And even as they eased him down upon the blankets his snores were rising on the frosty air.

But there was another sound. Far and faint it was, in the remote distance, the cry of the hungry wolf-pack as it took the trail of other meat than the man it had just missed.

# PART TWO

# BORN OF THE WILD

## CHAPTER 1

## THE BATTLE OF THE FANGS

It was the she-wolf who had first caught the sound of men's voices and he whining of the sled-dogs; and it was the she-wolf who was first to spring away from the cornered man in his circle of dying flame. The pack had been loath to forego the kill it had hunted down, and it lingered for several minutes, making sure of the sounds; and then it, too, sprang away on the trail made by the she-wolf.

Running at the forefront of the pack was a large gray wolf —one of its several leaders. It was he who directed the pack's course on the heels of the she-wolf. It was he who snarled warningly at the younger members of the pack or slashed at them with his fangs when they ambitiously tried to pass him. And it was he who increased the pace when he sighted the she-wolf, now trotting slowly across the snow.

She dropped in alongside by him, as though it were her appointed position, and took the pace of the pack. He did not snarl at her, nor show his teeth, when any leap of hers chanced to put her in advance of him. On the contrary, he seemed kindly disposed toward her—too kindly to suit her, for he was prone to run near to her, and when he ran too near it was she who snarled and showed her teeth. Nor was she above slashing his shoulder sharply on occasion. At such times he betrayed no anger. He merely sprang to the side and ran stiffly ahead for several awkward leaps, in carriage and conduct resembling an abashed country swain.

This was his one trouble in the running of the pack; but she had other troubles. On her other side ran a gaunt old wolf, grizzled and marked with the scars of many battles. He ran always on her right side. The fact that he had but one eye, and that the left eye, might account for this. He, also, was addicted to crowding her, to veering toward her till his scarred muzzle touched her body, or shoulder, or neck. As with the running mate on the left, she repelled these attentions with her teeth; but when both bestowed their attentions at the same time she was roughly jostled, being compelled, with quick snaps to either side, to drive both lovers away and at the same time to maintain her forward leap with the pack and see the way of her feet before her. At such times her running mates flashed their teeth and growled threateningly across at each other. They might have fought, but even wooing and its rivalry waited upon the more pressing hunger-need of the pack.

After each repulse, when the old wolf sheered abruptly away from the sharp-toothed object of his desire, he shouldered against a young three-year-old that ran on his blind right side. This young wolf had attained his full size; and, considering the weak and famished condition of the pack, he possessed more than the average vigour and spirit. Nevertheless, he ran with his head even with the shoulder of his one-eyed elder. When he ventured to run abreast of the older wolf, (which was seldom), a snarl and a snap sent him back even with the shoulder again. Sometimes, however, he dropped cautiously and slowly behind and edged in between the old leader and the she-wolf. This was doubly resented, even triply resented. When she snarled her displeasure, the old leader would whirl on the three-year-old. Sometimes she whirled with him. And sometimes the young leader on the left whirled, too.

At such times, confronted by three sets of savage teeth, the young wolf stopped precipitately, throwing himself back on his haunches, with forelegs stiff, mouth menacing, and mane bristling. This confusion in the front of the moving pack always caused confusion in the rear. The wolves behind collided with the young wolf and expressed their displeasure by administering sharp nips on his hindlegs and flanks. He was laying up trouble for himself, for lack of food and short tempers went together; but with the boundless faith of youth he persisted in repeating the manoeuvre every little while, though it never succeeded in gaining anything for him but discomfiture.

Had there been food, love-making and fighting would have gone on apace, and the pack-formation would have been broken up. But the situation of the pack was desperate. It was lean with long-standing hunger. It ran below its ordinary speed. At the rear limped the weak members, the very young and the very old. At the front were the strongest. Yet all were more like skeletons than full-bodied wolves. Nevertheless, with the exception of the ones that limped, the movements of the animals were effortless and tireless. Their stringy muscles seemed founts of inexhaustible energy. Behind every steel-like contraction of a muscle, lay another steel-like contraction, and another, and another, apparently without end.

They ran many miles that day. They ran through the night. And the next day found them still running. They were running over the surface of a world frozen and dead. No life stirred. They alone moved through the vast inertness. They alone were alive, and they sought for other things that were alive in order that they might devour them and continue to live.

They crossed low divides and ranged a dozen small streams in a lowerlying country before their quest was rewarded. Then they came upon moose. It was a big bull they first found. Here was meat and life, and it was guarded by no mysterious fires nor flying missiles of flame. Splay hoofs and palmated antlers they knew, and they flung their customary patience and caution to the wind. It was a brief fight and fierce. The big bull was beset on every side. He ripped them open or split their skulls with shrewdly driven blows of his great hoofs. He crushed them and broke them on his large horns. He stamped them into the snow under him in the wallowing struggle. But he was foredoomed, and he went down with the she-wolf tearing savagely at his throat, and with other teeth fixed everywhere upon him, devouring him alive, before ever his last struggles ceased or his last damage had been wrought.

There was food in plenty. The bull weighed over eight hundred pounds—fully twenty pounds of meat per mouth for the forty-odd wolves of the pack. But if they could fast prodigiously, they could feed prodigiously, and soon a few scattered bones were all that remained of the splendid live brute that had faced the pack a few hours before.

There was now much resting and sleeping. With full stomachs, bickering and quarrelling began among the younger males, and this continued through the few days that followed before the breaking-up of the pack. The famine was over. The wolves were now in the country of game, and though they still hunted in pack, they hunted more cautiously, cutting out heavy cows or crippled old bulls from the small moose-herds they ran across.

There came a day, in this land of plenty, when the wolf-pack split in half and went in different directions. The she-wolf, the young leader on her left, and the one-eyed elder on her right, led their half of the pack down to the Mackenzie River and across into the lake country to the east. Each day this remnant of the pack dwindled. Two by two, male and female, the wolves were deserting. Occasionally a solitary male was driven out by the sharp teeth of his rivals. In the end there remained only four: the she-wolf, the young leader, the one-eyed one, and the ambitious three-year-old.

The she-wolf had by now developed a ferocious temper. Her three suitors all bore the marks of her teeth. Yet they never replied in kind, never defended themselves against her. They turned their shoulders to her most savage slashes, and with wagging tails and mincing steps strove to placate her wrath. But if they were all mildness toward her, they were all fierceness toward one another. The three-year-old grew too ambitious in his fierceness. He caught the one-eyed elder on his blind side and ripped his ear into ribbons. Though the grizzled old fellow could see only on one side, against the youth and vigour of the other he brought into play the wisdom of long years of experience. His lost eye and his scarred muzzle bore evidence to the nature of his experience. He had survived too many battles to be in doubt for a moment about what to do.

The battle began fairly, but it did not end fairly. There was no telling what the outcome would have been, for the third wolf joined the elder, and together, old leader and young leader, they attacked the ambitious three-year-old and proceeded to destroy him. He was beset on either side by the merciless fangs of his erstwhile comrades. Forgotten were the days they had hunted together, the game they had pulled down, the famine they had suffered. That business was a thing of the past. The business of love was at hand—ever a sterner and crueler business than that of food-getting.

And in the meanwhile, the she-wolf, the cause of it all, sat down contentedly on her haunches and watched. She was even pleased. This was her day,—and it came not often,— when manes bristled, and fang smote fang or ripped and tore the yielding flesh, all for the possession of her.

And in the business of love the three-year-old, who had made this his first adventure upon it, yielded up his life. On either side of his body stood his two rivals. They were gazing at the she-wolf, who sat smiling in the snow. But the elder leader was wise, very wise, in love even as in battle. The younger leader turned his head to lick a wound on his shoulder. The curve of his neck was turned toward his rival. With his one eye the elder saw the opportunity. He darted in low and closed with his fangs. It was a long, ripping slash, and deep as well. His teeth, in passing, burst the wall of the great vein of the throat. Then he leaped clear.

The young leader snarled terribly, but his snarl broke mid-most into a tickling cough. Bleeding and coughing, already stricken, he sprang at the elder and fought while life faded from him, his legs going weak beneath him, the light of day dulling on his eyes, his blows and springs falling shorter and shorter.

And all the while the she-wolf sat on her haunches and smiled. She was made glad in vague ways by the battle, for this was the love-making of the Wild, the sex-tragedy of the natural world that was tragedy only to those that died. To those that survived it was not tragedy, but realization and achievement.

When the young leader lay in the snow and moved no more, One Eye stalked over to the she-wolf. His carriage was one of mingled triumph and caution. He was plainly expectant of a rebuff, and he was just as plainly surprised when her teeth did not flash out at him in anger. For the first time she met him with a kindly manner. She sniffed noses with him, and even condescended to leap about and frisk and play with him in quite puppyish fashion. And he, for all his gray years and sage experience, behaved quite as puppyishly and even a little more foolishly.

Forgotten already were the vanquished rivals and the lovetale red-written on the snow. Forgotten, save once, when old One Eye stopped for a moment to lick his stiffening wounds. Then it was that his lips half writhed into a snarl, and the hair of his neck and shoulders involuntarily bristled, while he half crouched for a spring, his claws spasmodically clutching into the snowsurface for firmer footing. But it was all forgotten the next moment, as he sprang after the she-wolf, who was coyly leading him a chase through the woods.

After that they ran side by side, like good friends who have come to an understanding. The days passed by, and they kept together, hunting their meat and killing and eating it in common. After a time the she-wolf began to grow restless. She seemed to be searching for something that she could not find. The hollows under fallen trees seemed to attract her, and she spent much time nosing about among the larger snow-piled crevices in the rocks and in the caves of overhanging banks. Old One Eye was not interested at all, but he followed her good-naturedly in her quest, and when her investigations in particular places were unusually protracted, he would lie down and wait until she was ready to go on.

They did not remain in one place, but travelled across country until they regained the Mackenzie River, down which they slowly went, leaving it often to hunt game along the small streams that entered it, but always returning to it again. Sometimes they chanced upon other wolves, usually in pairs; but there was no friendliness of intercourse displayed on either side, no gladness at meeting, no desire to return to the pack-formation. Several times they encountered solitary wolves. These were always males, and they were pressingly insistent on joining with One Eye and his mate. This he resented, and when she stood shoulder to shoulder with him, bristling and showing her teeth, the aspiring solitary ones would back off, turn tail, and continue on their lonely way.

One moonlight night, running through the quiet forest, One Eye suddenly halted. His muzzle went up, his tail stiffened, and his nostrils dilated as he scented the air. One foot also he held up, after the manner of a dog. He was not satisfied, and he continued to smell the air, striving to understand the message borne upon it to him. One careless sniff had satisfied his mate, and she trotted on to reassure him. Though he followed her, he was still dubious, and he could not forbear an occasional halt in order more carefully to study the warning.

She crept out cautiously on the edge of a large open space in the midst of the trees. For some time she stood alone. Then One Eye, creeping and crawling, every sense on the alert, every hair radiating infinite suspicion, joined her. They stood side by side, watching and listening and smelling.

To their ears came the sounds of dogs wrangling and scuffling, the guttural cries of men, the sharper voices of scolding women, and once the shrill and plaintive cry of a child. With the exception of the huge bulks of the skin lodges, little could be seen save the flames of the fire, broken by the movements of intervening bodies, and the smoke rising slowly on the quiet air. But to their nostrils came the myriad smells of an Indian camp, carrying a story that was largely incomprehensible to One Eye, but every detail of which the she-wolf knew.

She was strangely stirred, and sniffed and sniffed with an increasing delight. But old One Eye was doubtful. He betrayed his apprehension, and started tentatively to go. She turned and touched his neck with her muzzle in a reassuring way, then regarded the camp again. A new wistfulness was in her face, but it was not the wistfulness of hunger. She was thrilling to a desire that urged her to go forward, to be in closer to that fire, to be squabbling with the dogs, and to be avoiding and dodging the stumbling feet of men.

One Eye moved impatiently beside her; her unrest came back upon her, and she knew again her pressing need to find the thing for which she searched. She turned and trotted back into the forest, to the great relief of One Eye, who trotted a little to the fore until they were well within the shelter of the trees.

As they slid along, noiseless as shadows, in the moonlight, they came upon a runway. Both noses went down to the footprints in the snow. These footprints were very fresh. One Eye ran ahead cautiously, his mate at his heels. The broad pads of their feet were spread wide and in contact with the snow were like velvet. One Eye caught sight of a dim movement of white in the midst of the white. His sliding gait had been deceptively swift, but it was as nothing to the speed at which he now ran. Before him was bounding the faint patch of white he had discovered.

They were running along a narrow alley flanked on either side by a growth of young spruce. Through the trees the mouth of the alley could be seen, opening out on a moonlit glade. Old One Eye was rapidly overhauling the fleeing shape of white. Bound by bound he gained. Now he was upon it. One leap more and his teeth would be sinking into it. But that leap was never made. High in the air, and straight up, soared the shape of white, now a struggling snowshoe rabbit that leaped and bounded, executing a fantastic dance there above him in the air and never once returning to earth.

One Eye sprang back with a snort of sudden fright, then shrank down to the snow and crouched, snarling threats at this thing of fear he did not understand. But the she-wolf coolly thrust past him. She poised for a moment, then sprang for the dancing rabbit. She, too, soared high, but not so high as the quarry, and her teeth clipped emptily together with a metallic snap. She made another leap, and another.

Her mate had slowly relaxed from his crouch and was watching her. He now evinced displeasure at her repeated failures, and himself made a mighty spring upward. His teeth closed upon the rabbit, and he bore it back to earth with him. But at the same time there was a suspicious crackling movement beside him, and his astonished eye saw a young spruce sapling bending down above him to strike him. His jaws let go their grip, and he leaped backward to escape this strange danger, his lips drawn back from his fangs, his throat snarling, every hair bristling with rage and fright. And in that moment the sapling reared its slender length upright and the rabbit soared dancing in the air again.

The she-wolf was angry. She sank her fangs into her mate's shoulder in reproof; and he, frightened, unaware of what constituted this new onslaught, struck back ferociously and in still greater fright, ripping down the side of the she-wolf's muzzle. For him to resent such reproof was equally unexpected to her, and she sprang upon him in snarling indignation. Then he discovered his mistake and tried to placate her. But she proceeded to punish him roundly, until he gave over all attempts at placation, and whirled in a circle, his head away from her, his shoulders receiving the punishment of her teeth.

In the meantime the rabbit danced above them in the air. The she-wolf sat down in the snow, and old One Eye, now more in fear of his mate than of the mysterious sapling, again sprang for the rabbit. As he sank back with it between his teeth, he kept his eye on the sapling. As before, it followed him back to earth. He crouched down under the impending blow, his hair bristling, but his teeth still keeping tight hold of the rabbit. But the blow did not fall. The sapling remained bent above him. When he moved it moved, and he growled at it through his clenched jaws; when he remained still, it remained still, and he concluded it was safer to continue remaining still. Yet the warm blood of the rabbit tasted good in his mouth.

It was his mate who relieved him from the quandary in which he found himself. She took the rabbit from him, and while the sapling swayed and teetered threateningly above her she calmly gnawed off the rabbit's head. At once the sapling shot up, and after that gave no more trouble, remaining in the decorous and perpendicular position in which nature had intended it to grow. Then, between them, the she-wolf and One Eye devoured the game which the mysterious sapling had caught for them.

There were other runways and alleys where rabbits were hanging in the air, and the wolf-pair prospected them all, the she-wolf leading the way, old One Eye following and observant, learning the method of robbing snares—a knowledge destined to stand him in good stead in the days to come.

# CHAPTER 2

# THE LAIR

For two days the she-wolf and One Eye hung about the Indian camp. He was worried and apprehensive, yet the camp lured his mate and she was loath to depart. But when, one morning, the air was rent with the report of a rifle close at hand, and a bullet smashed against a tree trunk several inches from One Eye's head, they hesitated no more, but went off on a long, swinging lope that put quick miles between them and the danger.

They did not go far—a couple of days' journey. The she-wolf's need to find the thing for which she searched had now become imperative. She was getting very heavy, and could run but slowly. Once, in the pursuit of a rabbit, which she ordinarily would have caught with ease, she gave over and lay down and rested. One Eye came to her; but when he touched her neck gently with his muzzle she snapped at him with such quick fierceness that he tumbled over backward and cut a ridiculous figure in his effort to escape her teeth. Her temper was now shorter than ever; but he had become more patient than ever and more solicitous.

And then she found the thing for which she sought. It was a few miles up a small stream that in the summer time flowed into the Mackenzie, but that then was frozen over and frozen down to its rocky bottom—a dead stream of solid white from source to mouth. The she-wolf was trotting wearily along, her mate well in advance, when she came upon the overhanging, high clay-bank. She turned aside and trotted over to it. The wear and tear of spring storms and melting snows had under-washed the bank and in one place had made a small cave out of a narrow fissure.

She paused at the mouth of the cave and looked the wall over carefully. Then, on one side and the other, she ran along the base of the wall to where its abrupt bulk merged from the softer-lined landscape. Returning to the cave, she entered its narrow mouth. For a short three feet she was compelled to crouch, then the walls widened and rose higher in a little round chamber nearly six feet in diameter. The roof barely cleared her head. It was dry and cosy. She inspected it with painstaking care, while One Eye, who had returned, stood in the entrance and patiently watched her. She dropped her head, with her nose to the ground and directed toward a point near to her closely bunched feet, and around this point she circled several times; then, with a tired sigh that was almost a grunt, she curled her body in, relaxed her legs, and dropped down, her head toward the entrance. One Eye, with pointed, interested ears, laughed at her, and beyond, outlined against the white light, she could see the brush of his tail waving good-naturedly. Her own ears, with a snuggling movement, laid their sharp points backward and down against the head for a moment, while her mouth opened and her tongue lolled peaceably out, and in this way she expressed that she was pleased and satisfied.

One Eye was hungry. Though he lay down in the entrance and slept, his sleep was fitful. He kept awaking and cocking his ears at the bright world without, where the April sun was blazing across the snow. When he dozed, upon his ears would steal the faint whispers of hidden trickles of running water, and he would rouse and listen intently. The sun had come back, and all the awakening Northland world was calling to him. Life was stirring. The feel of spring was in the air, the feel of growing life under the snow, of sap ascending in the trees, of buds bursting the shackles of the frost.

He cast anxious glances at his mate, but she showed no desire to get up. He looked outside, and half a dozen snow-birds fluttered across his field of vision. He started to get up, then looked back to his mate again, and settled down and dozed. A shrill and minute singing stole upon his hearing. Once, and twice, he sleepily brushed his nose with his paw. Then he woke up. There, buzzing in the air at the tip of his nose, was a lone mosquito. It was a full-grown mosquito, one that had lain frozen in a dry log all winter and that had now been thawed out by the sun. He could resist the call of the world no longer. Besides, he was hungry

He crawled over to his mate and tried to persuade her to get up. But she only snarled at him, and he walked out alone into the bright sunshine to find the snow-surface soft underfoot and the travelling difficult. He went up the frozen bed of the stream, where the snow, shaded by the trees, was yet hard and crystalline. He was gone eight hours, and he came back through the darkness hungrier than when he had started. He had found game, but he had not caught it. He had broken through the melting snow-crust, and wallowed, while the snowshoe rabbits had skimmed along on top lightly as ever.

He paused at the mouth of the cave with a sudden shock of suspicion. Faint, strange sounds came from within. They were sounds not made by his mate, and yet they were remotely familiar. He bellied cautiously inside and was met by a warning snarl from the she-wolf. This he received without perturbation, though he obeyed it by keeping his distance; but he remained interested in the other sounds—faint, muffled sobbing and slubbering.

His mate warned him irritably away, and he curled up and slept in the entrance. When morning came and a dim light pervaded the lair, he again sought after the source of the remotely familiar sounds. There was a new note in his mate's warning snarl. It was a jealous note, and he was very careful in keeping a respectful distance. Nevertheless, he made out, sheltering between her legs against the length of her body, five strange little bundles of life, very feeble, very helpless, making tiny whimpering noises, with eyes that did not open to the light. He was surprised. It was not the first time in his long and successful life that this thing had happened. It had happened many times, yet each time it was as fresh a surprise as ever to him.

His mate looked at him anxiously. Every little while she emitted a low growl, and at times, when it seemed to her he approached too near, the growl shot up in her throat to a sharp snarl. Of her own experience she had no memory of the thing happening; but in her instinct, which was the experience of all the mothers of wolves, there lurked a memory of fathers that had eaten their newborn and helpless progeny. It manifested itself as a fear strong within her, that made her prevent One Eye from more closely inspecting the cubs he had fathered.

But there was no danger. Old One Eye was feeling the urge of an impulse, that was, in turn, an instinct that had come down to him from all the fathers of wolves. He did not question it, nor puzzle over it. It was there, in the fibre of his being; and it was the most natural thing in the world that he should obey it by turning his back on his newborn family and by trotting out and away on the meat-trail whereby he lived.

Five or six miles from the lair, the stream divided, its forks going off among the mountains at a right angle. Here, leading up the left fork, he came upon a fresh track. He smelled it and found it so recent that he crouched swiftly, and looked in the direction in which it disappeared. Then he turned deliberately and took the right fork. The footprint was much larger than the one his own feet made, and he knew that in the wake of such a trail there was little meat for him.

Half a mile up the right fork, his quick ears caught the sound of gnawing teeth. He stalked the quarry and found it to be a porcupine, standing upright against a tree and trying his teeth on the bark. One Eye approached carefully but hopelessly. He knew the breed, though he had never met it so far north before; and never in his long life had porcupine served him for a meal. But he had long since learned that there was such a thing as Chance, or Opportunity, and he continued to draw near. There was never any telling what might happen, for with live things events were somehow always happening differently.

The porcupine rolled itself into a ball, radiating long, sharp needles in all directions that defied attack. In his youth One Eye had once sniffed too near a similar, apparently inert ball of quills, and had the tail flick out suddenly in his face. One quill he had carried away in his muzzle, where it had remained for weeks, a rankling flame, until it finally worked out. So he lay down, in a comfortable crouching position, his nose fully a foot away, and out of the line of the tail. Thus he waited, keeping perfectly quiet. There was no telling. Something might happen. The porcupine might unroll. There might be opportunity for a deft and ripping thrust of paw into the tender, unguarded belly.

But at the end of half an hour he arose, growled wrathfully at the motionless ball, and trotted on. He had waited too often and futilely in the past for porcupines to unroll, to waste any more time. He continued up the right fork. The day wore along, and nothing rewarded his hunt.

The urge of his awakened instinct of fatherhood was strong upon him. He must find meat. In the afternoon he blundered upon a ptarmigan. He came out of a thicket and found himself face to face with the slow-witted bird. It was sitting on a log, not a foot beyond the end of his nose. Each saw the other. The bird made a startled rise, but he struck it with his paw, and smashed it down to earth, then pounced upon it, and caught it in his teeth as it scuttled across the snow trying to rise in the air again. As his teeth crunched through the tender flesh and fragile bones, he began naturally to eat. Then he remembered, and, turning on the backtrack, started for home, carrying the ptarmigan in his mouth.

A mile above the forks, running velvet-footed as was his custom, a gliding shadow that cautiously prospected each new vista of the trail, he came upon later imprints of the large tracks he had discovered in the early morning. As the track led his way, he followed, prepared to meet the maker of it at every turn of the stream.

He slid his head around a corner of rock, where began an unusually large bend in the stream, and his quick eyes made out something that sent him crouching swiftly down. It was the maker of the track, a large female lynx. She was crouching as he had crouched once that day, in front of her the tight-rolled ball of quills. If he had been a gliding shadow before, he now became the ghost of such a shadow, as he crept and circled around, and came up well to leeward of the silent, motionless pair.

He lay down in the snow, depositing the ptarmigan beside him, and with eyes peering through the needles of a low-growing spruce he watched the play of life before him—the waiting lynx and the waiting porcupine, each intent on life; and, such was the curiousness of the game, the way of life for one lay in the eating of the other, and the way of life for the other lay in being not eaten. While old One Eye, the wolf, crouching in the covert, played his part, too, in the game, waiting for some strange freak of Chance, that might help him on the meat-trail which was his way of life.

Half an hour passed, an hour; and nothing happened. The ball of quills might have been a stone for all it moved; the lynx might have been frozen to marble; and old One Eye might have been dead. Yet all three animals were keyed to a tenseness of living that was almost painful, and scarcely ever would it come to them to be more alive than they were then in their seeming petrifaction.

One Eye moved slightly and peered forth with increased eagerness. Something was happening. The porcupine had at last decided that its enemy had gone away. Slowly, cautiously, it was unrolling its ball of impregnable armour. It was agitated by no tremor of anticipation. Slowly, slowly, the bristling ball straightened out and lengthened. One Eye, watching, felt a sudden moistness in his mouth and a drooling of saliva, involuntary, excited by the living meat that was spreading itself like a repast before him.

Not quite entirely had the porcupine unrolled when it discovered its enemy. In that instant the lynx struck. The blow was like a flash of light. The paw, with rigid claws curving like talons, shot under the tender belly and came back with a swift ripping movement. Had the porcupine been entirely unrolled, or had it not discovered its enemy a fraction of a second before the blow was struck, the paw would have escaped unscathed; but a side-flick of the tail sank sharp quills into it as it was withdrawn.

Everything had happened at once,—the blow, the counterblow, the squeal of agony from the porcupine, the big cat's squall of sudden hurt and astonishment. One Eye half arose in his excitement, his ears up, his tail straight out and quivering behind him. The lynx's bad temper got the best of her. She sprang savagely at the thing that had hurt her. But the porcupine, squealing and grunting, with disrupted anatomy trying feebly to roll up into its ball-protection, flicked out its tail again, and again the big cat squalled with hurt and astonishment. Then she fell to backing away and sneezing, her nose bristling with quills like a monstrous pincushion. She brushed her nose with her paws, trying to dislodge the fiery darts, thrust it into the snow, and rubbed it against twigs and branches, all the time leaping about, ahead, sidewise, up and down, in a frenzy of pain and fright.

She sneezed continually, and her stub of a tail was doing its best toward lashing about by giving quick, violent jerks. She quit her antics, and quieted down for a long minute. One Eye watched. And even he could not repress a start and an involuntary bristling of hair along his back when she suddenly leaped, without warning, straight up in the air, at the same time emitting a long and most terrible squall. Then she sprang away, up the trail, squalling with every leap she made.

It was not until her racket had faded away in the distance and died out that One Eye ventured forth. He walked as delicately as though all the snow were carpeted with porcupine quills, erect and ready to pierce the soft pads of his feet. The porcupine met his approach with a furious squealing and a clashing of its long teeth. It had managed to roll up in a ball again, but it was not quite the old compact ball; its muscles were too much torn for that. It had been ripped almost in half, and was still bleeding profusely.

One Eye scooped out mouthfuls of the blood-soaked snow, and chewed and tasted and swallowed. This served as a relish, and his hunger increased mightily; but he was too old in the world to forget his caution. He waited. He lay down and waited, while the porcupine grated its teeth and uttered grunts and sobs and occasional sharp little squeals. In a little while, One Eye noticed that the quills were drooping and that a great quivering had set up. The quivering came to an end suddenly. There was a final defiant clash of the long teeth. Then all the quills drooped quite down, and the body relaxed and moved no more.

With a nervous, shrinking paw, One Eye stretched out the porcupine to its full length and turned it over on its back. Nothing had happened. It was surely dead. He studied it intently for a moment, then took a careful grip with his teeth and started off down the stream, partly carrying, partly dragging the porcupine, with head turned to the side so as to avoid stepping on the prickly mass. He recollected something, dropped the burden, and trotted back to where he had left the ptarmigan. He did not hesitate a moment. He knew clearly what was to be done, and this he did by promptly eating the ptarmigan. Then he returned and took up his burden.

When he dragged the result of his day's hunt into the cave, the she-wolf inspected it, turned her muzzle to him, and lightly licked him on the neck. But the next instant she was warning him away from the cubs with a snarl that was less harsh than usual and that was more apologetic than menacing. Her instinctive fear of the father of her progeny was toning down. He was behaving as a wolf father should, and manifesting no unholy desire to devour the young lives she had brought into the world.

## Chapter 3

# THE GRAY CUB

He was different from his brothers and sisters. Their hair already betrayed the reddish hue inherited from their mother, the she-wolf; while he alone, in this particular, took after his father. He was the one little gray cub of the litter. He had bred true to the straight wolf-stock—in fact, he had bred true, physically, to old One Eye himself, with but a single exception, and that was that he had two eyes to his father's one.

The gray cub's eyes had not been open long, yet already he could see with steady clearness. And while his eyes were still closed, he had felt, tasted, and smelled. He knew his two brothers and his two sisters very well. He had begun to romp with them in a feeble, awkward way, and even to squabble, his little throat vibrating with a queer rasping noise, (the forerunner of the growl), as he worked himself into a passion. And long before his eyes had opened, he had learned by touch, taste, and smell to know his mother—a fount of warmth and liquid food and tenderness. She possessed a gentle, caressing tongue that soothed him when it passed over his soft little body, and that impelled him to snuggle close against her and to doze off to sleep.

Most of the first month of his life had been passed thus in sleeping; but now he could see quite well, and he stayed awake for longer periods of time, and he was coming to learn his world quite well. His world was gloomy; but he did not know that, for he knew no other world. It was dimlighted; but his eyes had never had to adjust themselves to any other light. His world was very small. Its limits were the walls of the lair; but as he had no knowledge of the wide world outside, he was never oppressed by the narrow confines of his existence.

But he had early discovered that one wall of his world was different from the rest. This was the mouth of the cave and the source of light. He had discovered that it was different from the other walls long before he had any thoughts of his own, any conscious volitions. It had been an irresistible attraction before ever his eyes opened and looked upon it. The light from it had beat upon his sealed lids, and the eyes and the optic nerves had pulsated to little, sparklike flashes, warm-colored and strangely pleasing. The life of his body, and of every fibre of his body, the life that was the very substance of his body and that was apart from his own personal life, had yearned toward this light and urged his body toward it in the same way that the cunning chemistry of a plant urges it toward the sun.

Always, in the beginning, before his conscious life dawned, he had crawled toward the mouth of the cave. And in this his brothers and sisters were one with him. Never, in that period, did any of them crawl toward the dark corners of the backwall. The light drew them as if they were plants; the chemistry of the life that composed them demanded the light as a necessity of being; and their little puppet-bodies crawled blindly and chemically, like the tendrils of a vine. Later on, when each developed individuality and became personally conscious of impulsions and desires, the attraction of the light increased. They were always crawling and sprawling toward it, and being driven back from it by their mother.

It was in this way that the gray cub learned other attributes of his mother than the soft, soothing tongue. In his insistent crawling toward the light, he discovered in her a nose that with a sharp nudge administered rebuke, and later, a paw, that crushed him down or rolled him over and over with swift, calculating stroke. Thus he learned hurt; and on top of it he learned to avoid hurt, first, by not incurring the risk of it; and second, when he had incurred the risk, by dodging and by retreating. These were conscious actions, and were the results of his first generalizations upon the world. Before that he had recoiled automatically from hurt, as he had crawled automatically toward the light. After that he recoiled from hurt because he *knew* that it was hurt.

He was a fierce little cub. So were his brothers and sisters. It was to be expected. He was a carnivorous animal. He came of a breed of meat-killers and meat-eaters. His father and mother lived wholly upon meat. The milk he had sucked with his first flickering life was milk transformed directly from meat, and now, at a month old, when his eyes had been open for but a week, he was beginning himself to eat meat—meat half-digested by the she-wolf and disgorged for the five growing cubs that already made too great demand upon her breast.

But he was, further, the fiercest of the litter. He could make a louder rasping growl than any of them. His tiny rages were much more terrible than theirs. It was he that first learned the trick of rolling a fellow-cub over with a cunning paw-stroke. And it was he that first gripped another cub by the ear and pulled and tugged and growled through jaws tight-clenched. And certainly it was he that caused the mother the most trouble in keeping her litter from the mouth of the cave.

The fascination of the light for the gray cub increased from day to day. He was perpetually departing on yard-long adventures toward the cave's entrance, and as perpetually being driven back. Only he did not know it for an entrance. He did not know anything about entrances—passages whereby one goes from one place to another place. He did not know any other place, much less of a way to get there. So to him the entrance of the cave was a wall—a wall of light. As the sun was to the outside dweller, this wall was to him the sun of his world. It attracted him as a candle attracts a moth. He was always striving to attain it. The life that was so swiftly expanding within him, urged him continually toward the wall of light. The life that was within him knew that it was the one way out, the way he was predestined to tread. But he himself did not know anything about it. He did not know there was any outside at all.

There was one strange thing about this wall of light. His father (he had already come to recognize his father as the one other dweller in the world, a creature like his mother, who slept near the light and was a bringer of meat)-his father had a way of walking right into the white far wall and disappearing. The gray cub could not understand this. Though never permitted by his mother to approach that wall, he had approached the other walls, and encountered hard obstruction on the end of his tender nose. This hurt. And after several such adventures, he left the walls alone. Without thinking about it, he accepted this disappearing into the wall as a peculiarity of his father, as milk and halfdigested meat were peculiarities of his mother.

In fact, the gray cub was not given to thinking—at least, to the kind of thinking customary of men. His brain worked in dim ways. Yet his conclusions were as sharp and distinct as those achieved by men. He had a method of accepting things, without questioning the why and wherefore. In reality, this was the act of classification. He was never disturbed over *why* a thing happened. *How* it happened was sufficient for him. Thus, when he had bumped his nose on the backwall a few times, he accepted that he would not disappear into walls. In the same way he accepted that his father could disappear into walls. But he was not in the least disturbed by desire to find out the reason for the difference between his father and himself. Logic and physics were no part of his mental make-up.

Like most creatures of the Wild, he early experienced famine. There came a time when not only did the meat-supply cease, but the milk no longer came from his mother's breast. At first, the cubs whimpered and cried, but for the most part they slept. It was not long before they were reduced to a coma of hunger. There were no more spats and squabbles, no more tiny rages nor attempts at growling; while the adventures toward the far white wall ceased altogether. The cubs slept, while the life that was in them flickered and died down.

One Eye was desperate. He ranged far and wide, and slept but little in the lair that had now become cheerless and miserable. The she-wolf, too, left her litter and went out in search of meat. In the first days after the birth of the cubs, One Eye had journeyed several times back to the Indian camp and robbed the rabbit snares; but, with the melting of the snow and the opening of the streams, the Indian camp had moved away, and that source of supply was closed to him.

When the gray cub came back to life and again took interest in the far white wall, he found that the population of his world had been reduced. Only one sister remained to him. The rest were gone. As he grew stronger, he found himself compelled to play alone, for the sister no longer lifted her head nor moved about. His little body rounded out with the meat he now ate; but the food had come too late for her. She slept continuously, a tiny skeleton flung round with skin in which the flame flickered lower and lower and at last went out.

Then there came a time when the gray cub no longer saw his father appearing and disappearing in the wall nor lying down asleep in the entrance. This had happened at the end of a second and less severe famine. The she-wolf knew why One Eye never came back, but there was no way by which she could tell what she had seen to the gray cub. Hunting herself for meat, up the left fork of the stream where lived the lynx, she had followed a day-old trail of One Eye. And she had found him, or what remained of him, at the end of the trail. There were many signs of the battle that had been fought, and of the lynx's withdrawal to her lair after having won the victory. Before she went away, the she-wolf had found this lair, but the signs told her that the lynx was inside, and she had not dared to venture in.

After that, the she-wolf in her hunting avoided the left fork. For she knew that in the lynx's lair was a litter of kittens, and she knew the lynx for a fierce, bad-tempered creature and a terrible fighter. It was all very well for half a dozen wolves to drive a lynx, spitting and bristling, up a tree; but it was quite a different matter for a lone wolf to encounter a lynx—especially when the lynx was known to have a litter of hungry kittens at her back.

But the Wild is the Wild, and motherhood is motherhood, at all times fiercely protective whether in the Wild or out of it; and the time was to come when the she-wolf, for her gray cub's sake, would venture the left fork, and the lair in the rocks, and the lynx's wrath.

## CHAPTER 4

# THE WALL OF THE WORLD

BY the time his mother began leaving the cave on hunting expeditions, the cub had learned well the law that forbade his approaching the entrance. Not only had this law been forcibly and many times impressed on him by his mother's nose and paw, but in him the instinct of fear was developing. Never, in his brief cave-life, had he encountered anything of which to be afraid. Yet fear was in him. It had come down to him from a remote ancestry through a thousand thousand lives. It was a heritage he had received directly from One Eye and the she-wolf; but to them, in turn, it had been passed down through all the generations of wolves that had gone before. Fear!—that legacy of the Wild which no animal may escape nor exchange for pottage.

So the gray cub knew fear, though he knew not the stuff of which fear was made. Possibly he accepted it as one of the restrictions of life. For he had already learned that there were such restrictions. Hunger he had known; and when he could not appease his hunger he had felt restriction. The hard obstruction of the cave-wall, the sharp nudge of his mother's nose, the smashing stroke of her paw, the hunger unappeased of several famines, had borne in upon him that all was not freedom in the world, that to life there were limitations and restraints. These limitations and restraints were laws. To be obedient to them was to escape hurt and make for happiness.

He did not reason the question out in this man-fashion. He merely classified the things that hurt and the things that did not hurt. And after such classification he avoided the things that hurt, the restrictions and restraints, in order to enjoy the satisfactions and the remunerations of life.

Thus it was that in obedience to the law laid down by his mother, and in obedience to the law of that unknown and nameless thing, fear, he kept away from the mouth of the cave. It remained to him a white wall of light. When his mother was absent, he slept most of the time, while during the intervals that he was awake he kept very quiet, suppressing the whimpering cries that tickled in his throat and strove for noise.

Once, lying awake, he heard a strange sound in the white wall. He did not know that it was a wolverine, standing outside, all a-tremble with its own daring, and cautiously scenting out the contents of the cave. The cub knew only that the sniff was strange, a something unclassified, therefore unknown and terrible—for the unknown was one of the chief elements that went into the making of fear.

The hair bristled up on the gray cub's back, but it bristled silently. How was he to know that this thing that sniffed was a thing at which to bristle? It was not born of any knowledge of his, yet it was the visible expression of the fear that was in him, and for which, in his own life, there was no accounting. But fear was accompanied by another instinct—that of concealment. The cub was in a frenzy of terror, yet he lay without movement or sound, frozen, petrified into immobility, to all appearances dead. His mother, coming home, growled as she smelt the wolverine's track, and bounded into the cave and licked and nuzzled him with undue vehemence of affection. And the cub felt that somehow he had escaped a great hurt.

But there were other forces at work in the cub, the greatest of which was growth. Instinct and law demanded of him obedience. But growth demanded disobedience. His mother and fear impelled him to keep away from the white wall. Growth is life, and life is forever destined to make for light. So there was no damming up the tide of life that was rising within him—rising with every mouthful of meat he swallowed, with every breath he drew. In the end, one day, fear and obedience were swept away by the rush of life, and the cub straddled and sprawled toward the entrance.

Unlike any other wall with which he had had experience, this wall seemed to recede from him as he approached. No hard surface collided with the tender little nose he thrust out tentatively before him. The substance of the wall seemed as permeable and yielding as light. And as condition, in his eyes, had the seeming of form, so he entered into what had been wall to him and bathed in the substance that composed it.

It was bewildering. He was sprawling through solidity. And ever the light grew brighter. Fear urged him to go back, but growth drove him on. Suddenly he found himself at the mouth of the cave. The wall, inside which he had thought himself, as suddenly leaped back before him to an immeasurable distance. The light had become painfully bright. He was dazzled by it. Likewise he was made dizzy by this abrupt and tremendous extension of space. Automatically, his eyes were adjusting themselves to the brightness, focussing themselves to meet the increased distance of objects. At first, the wall had leaped beyond his vision. He now saw it again; but it had taken upon itself a remarkable remoteness. Also, its appearance had changed. It was now a variegated wall, composed of the trees that fringed the stream, the opposing mountain that towered above the trees, and the sky that out-towered the mountain.

A great fear came upon him. This was more of the terrible unknown. He crouched down on the lip of the cave and gazed out on the world. He was very much afraid. Because it was unknown, it was hostile to him. Therefore the hair stood up on end along his back and his lips wrinkled weakly in an attempt at a ferocious and intimidating snarl. Out of his puniness and fright he challenged and menaced the whole wide world.

Nothing happened. He continued to gaze, and in his interest he forgot to snarl. Also, he forgot to be afraid. For the time, fear had been routed by growth, while growth had assumed the guise of curiosity. He began to notice near objects—an open portion of the stream that flashed in the sun, the blasted pine tree that stood at the base of the slope, and the slope itself, that ran right up to him and ceased two feet beneath the lip of the cave on which he crouched.

Now the gray cub had lived all his days on a level floor. He had never experienced the hurt of a fall. He did not know what a fall was. So he stepped boldly out upon the air. His hindlegs still rested on the cave-lip, so he fell forward head downward. The earth struck him a harsh blow on the nose that made him yelp. Then he began rolling down the slope, over and over. He was in a panic of terror. The unknown had caught him at last. It had gripped savagely hold of him and was about to wreak upon him some terrific hurt. Growth was now routed by fear, and he ki-yi'd like any frightened puppy.

The unknown bore him on he knew not to what frightful hurt, and he yelped and ki-yi'd unceasingly. This was a different proposition from crouching in frozen fear while the unknown lurked just alongside. Now the unknown had caught tight hold of him. Silence would do no good. Besides, it was not fear, but terror, that convulsed him.

But the slope grew more gradual, and its base was grass-covered. Here the cub lost momentum. When at last he came to a stop, he gave one last agonized yelp and then a long, whimpering wail. Also, and quite as a matter of course, as though in his life he had already made a thousand toilets, he proceeded to lick away the dry clay that soiled him.

After that he sat up and gazed about him, as might the first man of the earth who landed upon Mars. The cub had broken through the wall of the world, the unknown had let go its hold of him, and here he was without hurt. But the first man on Mars would have experienced less unfamiliarity than did he. Without any antecedent knowledge, without any warning whatever that such existed, he found himself an explorer in a totally new world.

Now that the terrible unknown had let go of him, he forgot that the unknown had any terrors. He was aware only of curiosity in all the things about him. He inspected the grass beneath him, the moss-berry plant just beyond, and the dead trunk of the blasted pine that stood on the edge of an open space among the trees. A squirrel, running around the base of the trunk, came full upon him, and gave him a great fright. He cowered down and snarled. But the squirrel was as badly scared. It ran up the tree, and from a point of safety chattered back savagely.

This helped the cub's courage, and though the woodpecker he next encountered gave him a start, he proceeded confidently on his way. Such was his confidence, that when a moose-bird impudently hopped up to him, he reached out at it with a playful paw. The result was a sharp peck on the end of his nose that made him cower down and ki-yi. The noise he made was too much for the moose-bird, who sought safety in flight.

But the cub was learning. His misty little mind had already made an unconscious classification. There were live things and things not alive. Also, he must watch out for the live things. The things not alive remained always in one place; but the live things moved about, and there was no telling what they might do. The thing to expect of them was the unexpected, and for this he must be prepared.

He travelled very clumsily. He ran into sticks and things. A twig that he thought a long way off, would the next instant hit him on the nose or rake along his ribs. There were inequalities of surface. Sometimes he overstepped and stubbed his nose. Quite as often he understepped and stubbed his feet. Then there were the pebbles and stones that turned under him when he trod upon them; and from them he came to know that the things not alive were not all in the same state of stable equilibrium as was his cave; also, that small things not alive were more liable than large things to fall down or turn over. But with every mishap he was learning. The longer he walked, the better he walked. He was adjusting himself. He was learning to calculate his own muscular movements, to know his physical limitations, to measure distances between objects, and between objects and himself.

His was the luck of the beginner. Born to be a hunter of meat, (though he did not know it), he blundered upon meat just outside his own cavedoor on his first foray into the world. It was by sheer blundering that he chanced upon the shrewdly hidden ptarmigan nest. He fell into it. He had essayed to walk along the trunk of a fallen pine. The rotten bark gave way under his feet, and with a despairing yelp he pitched down the rounded descent, smashed through the leafage and stalks of a small bush, and in the heart of the bush, on the ground, fetched up amongst seven ptarmigan chicks.

They made noises, and at first he was frightened at them. Then he perceived that they were very little, and he became bolder. They moved. He placed his paw on one, and its movements were accelerated. This was a source of enjoyment to him. He smelled it. He picked it up in his mouth. It struggled and tickled his tongue. At the same time he was made aware of a sensation of hunger. His jaws closed together. There was a crunching of fragile bones, and warm blood ran in his mouth. The taste of it was good. This was meat, the same as his mother gave him, only it was alive between his teeth and therefore better. So he ate the ptarmigan. Nor did he stop till he had devoured the whole brood. Then he licked his chops in quite the same way his mother did, and began to crawl out of the bush.

He encountered a feathered whirlwind. He was confused and blinded by the rush of it and the beat of angry wings. He hid his head between his paws and yelped. The blows increased. The mother-ptarmigan was in a fury. Then he became angry. He rose up, snarling, striking out with his paws. He sank his tiny teeth into one of the wings and pulled and tugged sturdily. The ptarmigan struggled against him, showering blows upon him with her free wing. It was his first battle. He was elated. He forgot all about the unknown. He no longer was afraid of anything. He was fighting, tearing at a live thing that was striking at him. Also, this live thing was meat. The lust to kill was on him. He had just destroyed little live things. He would now destroy a big live thing. He was too busy and happy to know that he was happy. He was thrilling and exulting in ways new to him and greater to him than any he had known before.

He held on to the wing and growled between his tight-clenched teeth. The ptarmigan dragged him out of the bush. When she turned and tried to drag him back into the bush's shelter, he pulled her away from it and on into the open. And all the time she was making outcry and striking with her wing, while feathers were flying like a snowfall. The pitch to which he was aroused was tremendous. All the fighting blood of his breed was up in him and surging through him. This was living, though he did not know it. He was realizing his own meaning in the world; he was doing that for which he was made—killing meat and battling to kill it. He was justifying his existence, than which life can do no greater; for life achieves its summit when it does to the uttermost that which it was equipped to do.

After a time, the ptarmigan ceased her struggling. He still held her by the wing, and they lay on the ground and looked at each other. He tried to growl threateningly, ferociously. She pecked on his nose, which by now, what of previous adventures, was sore. He winced but held on. She pecked him again and again. From wincing he went to whimpering. He tried to back away from her, oblivious of the fact that by his hold on her he dragged her after him. A rain of pecks fell on his illused nose. The flood of fight ebbed down in him, and, releasing his prey, he turned tail and scampered off across the open in inglorious retreat.

He lay down to rest on the other side of the open, near the edge of the bushes, his tongue lolling out, his chest heaving and panting, his nose still hurting him and causing him to continue his whimper. But as he lay there, suddenly there came to him a feeling as of something terrible impending. The unknown with all its terrors rushed upon him, and he shrank back instinctively into the shelter of the bush. As he did so, a draught of air fanned him, and a large, winged body swept ominously and silently past. A hawk, driving down out of the blue, had barely missed him.

While he lay in the bush, recovering from this fright and peering fearfully out, the mother-ptarmigan on the other side of the open space fluttered out of the ravaged nest. It was because of her loss that she paid no attention to the winged bolt of the sky. But the cub saw, and it was a warning and a lesson to him—the swift downward swoop of the hawk, the short skim of its body just above the ground, the strike of its talons in the body of the ptarmigan, the ptarmigan's squawk of agony and fright, and the hawk's rush upward into the blue, carrying the ptarmigan away with it.

It was a long time before the cub left his shelter. He had learned much. Live things were meat. They were good to eat. Also, live things when they were large enough, could give hurt. It was better to eat small live things like ptarmigan chicks, and to let alone large live things like ptarmigan hens. Nevertheless he felt a little prick of ambition, a sneaking desire to have another battle with that ptarmigan hen—only the hawk had carried her away. Maybe there were other ptarmigan hens. He would go and see.

He came down a shelving bank to the stream. He had never seen water before. The footing looked good. There were no inequalities of surface. He stepped boldly out on it; and went down, crying with fear, into the embrace of the unknown. It was cold, and he gasped, breathing quickly. The water rushed into his lungs instead of the air that had always accompanied his act of breathing. The suffocation he experienced was like the pang of death. To him it signified death. He had no conscious knowledge of death, but like every animal of the Wild, he possessed the instinct of death. To him it stood as the greatest of hurts. It was the very essence of the unknown; it was the sum of the terrors of the unknown, the one culminating and unthinkable catastrophe that could happen to him, about which he knew nothing and about which he feared everything.

He came to the surface, and the sweet air rushed into his open mouth. He did not go down again. Quite as though it had been a long-established custom of his, he struck out with all his legs and began to swim. The near bank was a yard away; but he had come up with his back to it, and the first thing his eyes rested upon was the opposite bank, toward which he immediately began to swim. The stream was a small one, but in the pool it widened out to a score of feet.

Midway in the passage, the current picked up the cub and swept him downstream. He was caught in the miniature rapid at the bottom of the pool. Here was little chance for swimming. The quiet water had become suddenly angry. Sometimes he was under, sometimes on top.

At all times he was in violent motion, now being turned over or around, and again, being smashed against a rock. And with every rock he struck, he yelped. His progress was a series of yelps, from which might have been adduced the number of rocks he encountered.

Below the rapid was a second pool, and here, captured by the eddy, he was gently borne to the bank and as gently deposited on a bed of gravel. He crawled frantically clear of the water and lay down. He had learned some more about the world. Water was not alive. Yet it moved. Also, it looked as solid as the earth, but was without any solidity at all. His conclusion was that things were not always what they appeared to be. The cub's fear of the unknown was an inherited distrust, and it had now been strengthened by experience. Thenceforth, in the nature of things, he would possess an abiding distrust of appearances. He would have to learn the reality of a thing before he could put his faith into it.

One other adventure was destined for him that day. He had recollected that there was such a thing in the world as his mother. And then there came to him a feeling that he wanted her more than all the rest of the things in the world. Not only was his body tired with the adventures it had undergone, but his little brain was equally tired. In all the days he had lived it had not worked so hard as on this one day. Furthermore, he was sleepy. So he started out to look for the cave and his mother, feeling at the same time an overwhelming rush of loneliness and helplessness.

He was sprawling along between some bushes, when he heard a sharp, intimidating cry. There was a flash of yellow before his eyes. He saw a weasel leaping swiftly away from him. It was a small live thing, and he had no fear. Then, before him, at his feet, he saw an extremely small live thing, only several inches long—a young weasel, that, like himself, had disobediently gone out adventuring. It tried to retreat before him. He turned it over with his paw. It made a queer, grating noise. The next moment the flash of yellow reappeared before his eyes. He heard again the intimidating cry, and at the same instant received a severe blow on the side of the neck and felt the sharp teeth of the mother-weasel cut into his flesh.

While he yelped and ki-yi'd and scrambled backward, he saw the mother-weasel leap upon her young one and disappear with it into the neighbouring thicket. The cut of her teeth in his neck still hurt, but his feelings were hurt more grievously, and he sat down and weakly whimpered. This mother-weasel was so small and so savage! He was yet to learn that for size and weight the weasel was the most ferocious, vindictive, and terrible of all the killers of the Wild. But a portion of this knowledge was quickly to be his.

He was still whimpering when the mother-weasel reappeared. She did not rush him, now that her young one was safe. She approached more cautiously, and the cub had full opportunity to obscene her lean, snakelike body, and her head, erect, eager, and snakelike itself. Her sharp, menacing cry sent the hair bristling along his back, and he snarled warningly at her. She came closer and closer. There was a leap, swifter than his unpractised sight, and the lean, yellow body disappeared for a moment out of the field of his vision. The next moment she was at his throat, her teeth buried in his hair and flesh.

At first he snarled and tried to fight; but he was very young, and this was only his first day in the world, and his snarl became a whimper, his fight a struggle to escape. The weasel never relaxed her hold. She hung on, striving to press down with her teeth to the great vein where his life-blood bubbled. The weasel was a drinker of blood, and it was ever her preference to drink from the throat of life itself.

The gray cub would have died, and there would have been no story to write about him, had not the she-wolf come bounding through the bushes. The weasel let go the cub and flashed at the she-wolf's throat, missing, but getting a hold on the jaw instead. The she-wolf flirted her head like the snap of a whip, breaking the weasel's hold and flinging it high in the air. And, still in the air, the she-wolf's jaws closed on the lean, yellow body, and the weasel knew death between the crunching teeth.

The cub experienced another access of affection on the part of his mother. Her joy at finding him seemed greater even than his joy at being found. She nuzzled him and caressed him and licked the cuts made in him by the weasel's teeth. Then, between them, mother and cub, they ate the blood-drinker, and after that went back to the cave and slept.

## CHAPTER 5

# THE LAW OF MEAT

The cub's development was rapid. He rested for two days, and then ventured forth from the cave again. It was on this adventure that he found the young weasel whose mother he had helped eat, and he saw to it that the young weasel went the way of its mother. But on this trip he did not get lost. When he grew tired, he found his way back to the cave and slept. And every day thereafter found him out and ranging a wider area.

He began to get an accurate measurement of his strength and his weakness, and to know when to be bold and when to be cautious. He found it expedient to be cautious all the time, except for the rare moments, when, assured of his own intrepidity, he abandoned himself to petty rages and lusts.

He was always a little demon of fury when he chanced upon a stray ptarmigan. Never did he fail to respond savagely to the chatter of the squirrel he had first met on the blasted pine. While the sight of a moose-bird almost invariably put him into the wildest of rages; for he never forgot the peck on the nose he had received from the first of that ilk he encountered.

But there were times when even a moose-bird failed to affect him, and those were times when he felt himself to be in danger from some other prowling meat-hunter. He never forgot the hawk, and its moving shadow always sent him crouching into the nearest thicket. He no longer sprawled and straddled, and already he was developing the gait of his mother, slinking and furtive, apparently without exertion, yet sliding along with a swiftness that was as deceptive as it was imperceptible.

In the matter of meat, his luck had been all in the beginning. The seven ptarmigan chicks and the baby weasel represented the sum of his killings. His desire to kill strengthened with the days, and he cherished hungry ambitions for the squirrel that chattered so volubly and always informed all wild creatures that the wolf-cub was approaching. But as birds flew in the air, squirrels could climb trees, and the cub could only try to crawl unobserved upon the squirrel when it was on the ground.

The cub entertained a great respect for his mother. She could get meat, and she never failed to bring him his share. Further, she was unafraid of things. It did not occur to him that this fearlessness was founded upon experience and knowledge. Its effect on him was that of an impression of power. His mother represented power; and as he grew older he felt this power in the sharper admonition of her paw; while the reproving nudge of her nose gave place to the slash of her fangs. For this, likewise, he respected his mother. She compelled obedience from him, and the older he grew the shorter grew her temper.

Famine came again, and the cub with clearer consciousness knew once more the bite of hunger. The she-wolf ran herself thin in the quest for meat. She rarely slept any more in the cave, spending most of her time on the meat-trail and spending it vainly. This famine was not a long one, but it was severe while it lasted. The cub found no more milk in his mother's breast, nor did he get one mouthful of meat for himself.

Before, he had hunted in play, for the sheer joyousness of it; now he hunted in deadly earnestness, and found nothing. Yet the failure of it accelerated his development. He studied the habits of the squirrel with greater carefulness, and strove with greater craft to steal upon it and surprise it. He studied the woodmice and tried to dig them out of their burrows; and he learned much about the ways of moose-birds and wood-peckers. And there came a day when the hawk's shadow did not drive him crouching into the bushes. He had grown stronger, and wiser, and more confident. Also, he was desperate. So he sat on his haunches, conspicuously, in an open space, and challenged the hawk down out of the sky. For he knew that there, floating in the blue above him, was meat, the meat his stomach yearned after so insistently. But the hawk refused to come down and give battle, and the cub crawled away into a thicket and whimpered his disappoint-ment and hunger.

The famine broke. The she-wolf brought home meat. It was strange meat, different from any she had ever brought before. It was a lynx kitten, partly grown, like the cub, but not so large. And it was all for him. His mother had satisfied her hunger elsewhere; though he did not know that it was the rest of the lynx litter that had gone to satisfy her. Nor did he know the desperateness of her deed. He knew only that the velvet-furred kitten was meat, and he ate and waxed happier with every mouthful.

A full stomach conduces to inaction, and the cub lay in the cave, sleeping against his mother's side. He was aroused by her snarling. Never had he heard her snarl so terribly. Possibly in her whole life it was the most terrible snarl she ever gave. There was reason for it, and none knew it better than she. A lynx's lair is not despoiled with impunity. In the full glare of the afternoon light, crouching in the entrance of the cave, the cub saw the lynx-mother. The hair rippled up all along his back at the sight. Here was fear, and it did not require his instinct to tell him of it. And if sight alone were not sufficient, the cry of rage the intruder gave, beginning with a snarl and rushing abruptly upward into a hoarse screech, was convincing enough in itself.

The cub felt the prod of the life that was in him, and stood up and snarled valiantly by his mother's side. But she thrust him ignominiously away and behind her. Because of the low-roofed entrance the lynx could not leap in, and when she made a crawling rush of it the she-wolf sprang upon her and pinned her down. The cub saw little of the battle. There was a tremendous snarling and spitting and screeching. The two animals threshed about, the lynx ripping and tearing with her claws and using her teeth as well, while the she-wolf used her teeth alone.

Once, the cub sprang in and sank his teeth into the hind leg of the lynx. He clung on, growling savagely. Though he did not know it, by the weight of his body he clogged the action of the leg and thereby saved his mother much damage. A change in the battle crushed him under both their bodies and wrenched loose his hold. The next moment the two mothers separated, and, before they rushed together again, the lynx lashed out at the cub with a huge fore-paw that ripped his shoulder open to the bone and sent him hurtling sidewise against the wall. Then was added to the uproar the cub's shrill yelp of pain and fright. But the fight lasted so long that he had time to cry himself out and to experience a second burst of courage; and the end of the battle found him again clinging to a hindleg and furiously growling between his teeth.

The lynx was dead. But the she-wolf was very weak and sick. At first she caressed the cub and licked his wounded shoulder; but the blood she had lost had taken with it her strength, and for all of a day and a night she lay by her dead foe's side, without movement, scarcely breathing. For a week she never left the cave, except for water, and then her movements were slow and painful. At the end of that time the lynx was devoured, while the she-wolf's wounds had healed sufficiently to permit her to take the meat-trail again.

The cub's shoulder was stiff and sore, and for some time he limped from the terrible slash he had received. But the world now seemed changed. He went about in it with greater confidence, with a feeling of prowess that had not been his in the days before the battle with the lynx. He had looked upon life in a more ferocious aspect; he had fought; he had buried his teeth in the flesh of a foe; and he had survived. And because of all this, he carried himself more boldly, with a touch of defiance that was new in him. He was no longer afraid of minor things, and much of his timidity had vanished, though the unknown never ceased to press upon him with its mysteries and terrors, intangible and ever-menacing.

He began to accompany his mother on the meat-trail, and he saw much of the killing of meat and began to play his part in it. And in his own dim way he learned the law of meat. There were two kinds of life,—his own kind and the other kind. His own kind included his mother and himself. The other kind included all live things that moved. But the other kind was divided. One portion was what his own kind killed and ate. This portion was composed of the non-killers and the small killers. The other portion killed and ate his own kind, or was killed and eaten by his own kind. And out of this classification arose the law. The aim of life was meat. Life itself was meat. Life lived on life. There were the eaters and the eaten. The law was: EAT OR BE EATEN. He did not formulate the law in clear, set terms and moralize about it. He did not even think the law; he merely lived the law without thinking about it at all.

He saw the law operating around him on every side. He had eaten the ptarmigan chicks. The hawk had eaten the ptarmigan-mother. The hawk would also have eaten him. Later, when he had grown more formidable, he wanted to eat the hawk. He had eaten the lynx kitten. The lynx-mother would have eaten him had she not herself been killed and eaten. And so it went. The law was being lived about him by all live things, and he himself was part and parcel of the law. He was a killer. His only food was meat, live meat, that ran away swiftly before him, or flew into the air, or climbed trees, or hid in the ground, or faced him and fought with him, or turned the tables and ran after him.

Had the cub thought in man-fashion, he might have epitomized life as a voracious appetite, and the world as a place wherein ranged a multitude of appetites, pursuing and being pursued, hunting and being hunted, eating and being eaten, all in blindness and confusion, with violence and disorder, a chaos of gluttony and slaughter, ruled over by chance, merciless, planless, endless.

But the cub did not think in man-fashion. He did not look at things with wide vision. He was single-purposed, and entertained but one thought or desire at a time. Besides the law of meat, there was a myriad other and lesser laws for him to learn and obey. The world was filled with surprise. The stir of the life that was in him, the play of his muscles, was an unending happiness. To run down meat was to experience thrills and elations. His rages and battles were pleasures. Terror itself, and the mystery of the unknown, lent to his living.

And there were easements and satisfactions. To have a full stomach, to doze lazily in the sunshine—such things were remuneration in full for his ardours and toils, while his ardours and toils were in themselves self-remunerative. They were expressions of life, and life is always happy when it is expressing itself. So the cub had no quarrel with his hostile environment. He was very much alive, very happy, and very proud of himself.

# PART THREE

# THE GODS OF THE WILD

## CHAPTER 1

## THE MAKERS OF FIRE

The cub came upon it suddenly. It was his own fault. He had been careless. He had left the cave and run down to the stream to drink. It might have been that he took no notice because he was heavy with sleep. (He had been out all night on the meat-trail, and had but just then awakened). And his carelessness might have been due to the familiarity of the trail to the pool. He had travelled it often, and nothing had ever happened on it.

He went down past the blasted pine, crossed the open space, and trotted in amongst the trees. Then, at the same instant, he saw and smelt. Before him, sitting silently on their haunches, were five live things, the like of which he had never seen before. It was his first glimpse of mankind. But at the sight of him the five men did not spring to their feet, nor show their teeth, nor snarl. They did not move, but sat there, silent and ominous.

Nor did the cub move. Every instinct of his nature would have impelled him to dash wildly away, had there not suddenly and for the first time arisen in him another and counter instinct. A great awe descended upon him. He was beaten down to movelessness by an overwhelming sense of his own weakness and littleness. Here was mastery and power, something far and away beyond him.

The cub had never seen man, yet the instinct concerning man was his. In dim ways he recognized in man the animal that had fought itself to primacy over the other animals of the Wild. Not alone out of his own eyes, but out of the eyes of all his ancestors was the cub now looking upon man—out of eyes that had circled in the darkness around countless winter campfires, that had peered from safe distances and from the hearts of thickets at the strange, two-legged animal that was lord over living things. The spell of the cub's heritage was upon him, the fear and the respect born of the centuries of struggle and the accumulated experience of the generations. The heritage was too compelling for a wolf that was only a cub. Had he been fullgrown, he would have run away. As it was, he cowered down in a paralysis of fear, already half proffering the submission that his kind had proffered from the first time a wolf came in to sit by man's fire and be made warm.

One of the Indians arose and walked over to him and stooped above him. The cub cowered closer to the ground. It was the unknown, objectified at last, in concrete flesh and blood, bending over him and reaching down to seize hold of him. His hair bristled involuntarily; his lips writhed back and his little fangs were bared. The hand, poised like doom above him, hesitated, and the man spoke, laughing, *"Wabam wabisca ip pit tah."* ("Look! The white fangs!")

The other Indians laughed loudly, and urged the man on to pick up the cub. As the hand descended closer and closer, there raged within the cub a battle of the instincts. He experienced two great impulsions,—to yield and to fight. The resulting action was a compromise. He did both. He yielded till the hand almost touched him. Then he fought, his teeth flashing in a snap that sank them into the hand. The next moment he received a clout alongside the head that knocked him over on his side. Then all fight fled out of him. His puppyhood and the instinct of submission took charge of him. He sat up on his haunches and ki-yi'd. But the man whose hand he had bitten was angry. The cub received a clout on the other side of his head. Whereupon he sat up and ki-yi'd louder than ever.

The four Indians laughed more loudly, while even the man who had been bitten began to laugh. They surrounded the cub and laughed at him, while he wailed out his terror and his hurt. In the midst of it, he heard something. The Indians heard it, too. But the cub knew what it was, and with a last, long wail that had in it more of triumph than grief, he ceased his noise and waited for the coming of his mother, of his ferocious and indomitable mother who fought and killed all things and was never afraid. She was snarling as she ran. She had heard the cry of her cub and was dashing to save him.

She bounded in amongst them, her anxious and militant motherhood making her anything but a pretty sight. But to the cub the spectacle of her protective rage was pleasing. He uttered a glad little cry and bounded to meet her, while the man-animals went back hastily several steps. The she-wolf stood over against her cub, facing the men, with bristling hair, a snarl rumbling deep in her throat. Her face was distorted and malignant with menace, even the bridge of the nose wrinkling from tip to eyes so prodigious was her snarl.

Then it was that a cry went up from one of the men. "Kiche!" was what he uttered. It was an exclamation of surprise. The cub felt his mother wilting at the sound.

"Kiche!" the man cried again, this time with sharpness and authority.

And then the cub saw his mother, the she-wolf, the fearless one, crouching down till her belly touched the ground, whimpering, wagging her tail, making peace signs. The cub could not understand. He was appalled. The awe of man rushed over him again. His instinct had been true. His mother verified it. She, too, rendered submission to the man-animals.

The man who had spoken came over to her. He put his hand upon her head, and she only crouched closer. She did not snap, nor threaten to snap. The other men came up, and surrounded her, and felt her, and pawed her, which actions she made no attempt to resent. They were greatly excited, and made many noises with their mouths. These noises were not indications of danger, the cub decided, as he crouched near his mother, still bristling from time to time but doing his best to submit.

"It is not strange," an Indian was saying. "Her father was a wolf. It is true, her mother was a dog; but did not my brother tie her out in the woods all of three nights in the mating season? Therefore was the father of Kiche a wolf."

"It is a year, Gray Beaver, since she ran away," spoke a second Indian.

"It is not strange, Salmon Tongue," Gray Beaver answered. "It was the time of the famine, and there was no meat for the dogs."

"She has lived with the wolves," said a third Indian.

"So it would seem, Three Eagles," Gray Beaver answered, laying his hand on the cub; "and this be the sign of it."

The cub snarled a little at the touch of the hand, and the hand flew back to administer a clout. Whereupon the cub covered its fangs and sank down submissively, while the hand, returning, rubbed behind his ears, and up and down his back.

"This be the sign of it," Gray Beaver went on. "It is plain that his mother is Kiche. But his father was a wolf. Wherefore is there in him little dog and much wolf. His fangs be white, and White Fang shall be his name. I have spoken. He is my dog. For was not Kiche my brother's dog? And is not my brother dead?"

The cub, who had thus received a name in the world, lay and watched. For a time the man-animals continued to make their mouth-noises. Then Gray Beaver took a knife from a sheath that hung around his neck, and went into the thicket and cut a stick. White Fang watched him. He notched the stick at each end and in the notches fastened strings of raw-hide. One string he tied around the throat of Kiche. Then he led her to a small pine, around which he tied the other string.

White Fang followed and lay down beside her. Salmon Tongue's hand reached out to him and rolled him over on his back. Kiche looked on anxiously. White Fang felt fear mounting in him again. He could not quite suppress a snarl, but he made no offer to snap. The hand, with fingers crooked and spread apart, rubbed his stomach in a playful way and rolled him from side to side. It was ridiculous and ungainly, lying there on his back with legs sprawling in the air. Besides, it was a position of such utter helplessness that White Fang's whole nature revolted against it. He could do nothing to defend himself. If this man-animal intended harm, White Fang knew that he could not escape it. How could he spring away with his four legs in the air above him? Yet submission made him master his fear, and he only growled softly. This growl he could not suppress; nor did the man-animal resent it by giving him a blow on the head. And furthermore, such was the strangeness of it, White Fang experienced an unaccountable sensation of pleasure as the hand rubbed back and forth. When he was rolled on his side he ceased the growl; when the fingers pressed and prodded at the base of his ears the pleasurable sensation increased; and when, with a final rub and scratch, the man left him alone and went away, all fear had died out of White Fang. He was to know fear many times in his dealings with man; yet it was a token of the fearless companionship with man that was ultimately to be his.

After a time, White Fang heard strange noises approaching. He was quick in his classification, for he knew them at once for man-animal noises. A few minutes later the remainder of the tribe, strung out as it was on the march, trailed in. There were more men and many women and children, forty souls of them, and all heavily burdened with camp equipage and outfit. Also there were many dogs; and these, with the exception of the part-grown puppies, were likewise burdened with camp outfit. On their backs, in bags that fastened tightly around underneath, the dogs carried from twenty to thirty pounds of weight.

White Fang had never seen dogs before, but at sight of them he felt that they were his own kind, only somehow different. But they displayed little difference from the wolf when they discovered the cub and his mother. There was a rush. White Fang bristled and snarled and snapped in the face of the openmouthed oncoming wave of dogs, and went down and under them, feeling the sharp slash of teeth in his body, himself biting and tearing at the legs and bellies above him. There was a great uproar. He could hear the snarl of Kiche as she fought for him; and he could hear the cries of the man-animals, the sound of clubs striking upon bodies, and the yelps of pain from the dogs so struck.

Only a few seconds elapsed before he was on his feet again. He could now see the man-animals driving back the dogs with clubs and stones, defending him, saving him from the savage teeth of his kind that somehow was not his kind. And though there was no reason in his brain for a clear conception of so abstract a thing as justice, nevertheless, in his own way, he felt the justice of the man-animals, and he knew them for what they were—makers of law and executors of law. Also, he appreciated the power with which they administered the law. Unlike any animals he had ever encountered, they did not bite nor claw. They enforced their live strength with the power of dead things. Dead things did their bidding. Thus, sticks and stones, directed by these strange creatures, leaped through the air like living things, inflicting grievous hurts upon the dogs.

To his mind this was power unusual, power inconceivable and beyond the natural, power that was god-like. White Fang, in the very nature of him, could never know anything about gods; at the best he could know only things that were beyond knowing; but the wonder and awe that he had of these man-animals in ways resembled what would be the wonder and awe of man at sight of some celestial creature, on a mountain top, hurling thunderbolts from either hand at an astonished world.

The last dog had been driven back. The hubbub died down. And White Fang licked his hurts and meditated upon this, his first taste of pack-cruelty and his introduction to the pack. He had never dreamed that his own kind consisted of more than One Eye, his mother, and himself. They had constituted a kind apart, and here, abruptly, he had discovered many more creatures apparently of his own kind. And there was a subconscious resentment that these, his kind, at first sight had pitched upon him and tried to destroy him. In the same way he resented his mother being tied with a stick, even though it was done by the superior man-animals. It savoured of the trap, of bondage. Yet of the trap and of bondage he knew nothing. Freedom to roam and run and lie down at will, had been his heritage; and here it was being infringed upon. His mother's movements were restricted to the length of a stick, and by the length of that same stick was he restricted, for he had not yet got beyond the need of his mother's side.

He did not like it. Nor did he like it when the man-animals arose and went on with their march; for a tiny man-animal took the other end of the stick and led Kiche captive behind him, and behind Kiche followed White Fang, greatly perturbed and worried by this new adventure he had entered upon.

They went down the valley of the stream, far beyond White Fang's widest ranging, until they came to the end of the valley, where the stream ran into the Mackenzie River. Here, where canoes were cached on poles high in the air and where stood fish-racks for the drying of fish, camp was made; and White Fang looked on with wondering eyes. The superiority of these man-animals increased with every moment. There was their mastery over all these sharp-fanged dogs. It breathed of power. But greater than that, to the wolf-cub, was their mastery over things not alive; their capacity to communicate motion to unmoving things; their capacity to change the very face of the world.

It was this last that especially affected him. The elevation of frames of poles caught his eye; yet this in itself was not so remarkable, being done by the same creatures that flung sticks and stones to great distances. But when the frames of poles were made into tepees by being covered with cloth and skins, White Fang was astounded. It was the colossal bulk of them that impressed him. They arose around him, on every side, like some monstrous quick-growing form of life. They occupied nearly the whole circumference of his field of vision. He was afraid of them. They loomed ominously above him; and when the breeze stirred them into huge movements, he cowered down in fear, keeping his eyes warily upon them, and prepared to spring away if they attempted to precipitate themselves upon him.

But in a short while his fear of the tepees passed away. He saw the women and children passing in and out of them without harm, and he saw the dogs trying often to get into them, and being driven away with sharp words and flying stones. After a time, he left Kiche's side and crawled cautiously toward the wall of the nearest tepee. It was the curiosity of growth that urged him on—the necessity of learning and living and doing that brings experience. The last few inches to the wall of the tepee were crawled with painful slowness and precaution. The day's events had prepared him for the unknown to manifest itself in most stupendous and unthinkable ways. At last his nose touched the canvas. He waited. Nothing happened. Then he smelled the strange fabric, saturated with the man-smell. He closed on the canvas with his teeth and gave a gentle tug. Nothing happened, though the adjacent portions of the tepee moved. He tugged harder. There was a greater movement. It was delightful. He tugged still harder, and repeatedly, until the whole tepee was in motion. Then the sharp cry of a squaw inside sent him scampering back to Kiche. But after that he was afraid no more of the looming bulks of the tepees.

A moment later he was straying away again from his mother. Her stick was tied to a peg in the ground and she could not follow him. A part-grown puppy, somewhat larger and older than he, came toward him slowly, with ostentatious and belligerent importance. The puppy's name, as White Fang was afterward to hear him called, was Lip-lip. He had had experience in puppy fights and was already something of a bully.

Lip-lip was White Fang's own kind, and, being only a puppy, did not seem dangerous; so White Fang prepared to meet him in friendly spirit. But when the stranger's walk became stiff-legged and his lips lifted clear of his teeth, White Fang stiffened, too, and answered with lifted lips. They half circled about each other, tentatively, snarling and bristling. This lasted several minutes, and White Fang was beginning to enjoy it, as a sort of game. But suddenly, with remarkable swiftness, Lip-lip leaped in, delivered a slashing snap, and leaped away again. The snap had taken effect on the shoulder that had been hurt by the Iynx and that was still sore deep down near the bone. The surprise and hurt of it brought a yelp out of White Fang; but the next moment, in a rush of anger, he was upon Lip-lip and snapping viciously.

But Lip-lip had lived his life in camp and had fought many puppy fights. Three times, four times, and half a dozen times, his sharp little teeth scored on the newcomer, until White Fang, yelping shamelessly, fled to the protection of his mother. It was the first of the many fights he was to have with Lip-lip, for they were enemies from the start, born so, with natures destined perpetually to clash.

Kiche licked White Fang soothingly with her tongue, and tried to prevail upon him to remain with her. But his curiosity was rampant, and several minutes later he was venturing forth on a new quest. He came upon one of the man-animals, Gray Beaver, who was squatting on his hams and doing something with sticks and dry moss spread before him on the ground. White Fang came near to him and watched. Gray Beaver made mouth-noises which White Fang interpreted as not hostile, so he came still nearer.

Women and children were carrying more sticks and branches to Gray Beaver. It was evidently an affair of moment. White Fang came in until he touched Gray Beaver's knee, so curious was he, and already forgetful that this was a terrible man-animal. Suddenly he saw a strange thing like mist beginning to arise from the sticks and moss beneath Gray Beaver's hands. Then, amongst the sticks themselves, appeared a live thing, twisting and turning, of a color like the color of the sun in the sky. White Fang knew nothing about fire. It drew him as the light in the mouth of the cave had drawn him in his early puppyhood. He crawled the several steps toward the flame. He heard Gray Beaver chuckle above him, and he knew the sound was not hostile. Then his nose touched the flame, and at the same instant his little tongue went out to it.

For a moment he was paralyzed. The unknown, lurking in the midst of the sticks and moss, was savagely clutching him by the nose. He scrambled backward, bursting out in an astonished explosion of ki-yi's. At the sound, Kiche leaped snarling to the end of her stick, and there raged terribly because she could not come to his aid. But Gray Beaver laughed loudly, and slapped his thighs, and told the happening to all the rest of the camp, till everybody was laughing uproariously. But White Fang sat on his haunches and ki-yi'd and ki-yi'd, a forlorn and pitiable little figure in the midst of the man-animals.

It was the worst hurt he had ever known. Both nose and tongue had been scorched by the live thing, sun-colored, that had grown up under Gray Beaver's hands. He cried and cried interminably, and every fresh wail was greeted by bursts of laughter on the part of the man-animals. He tried to soothe his nose with his tongue, but the tongue was burnt too, and the two hurts coming together produced greater hurt; where-upon he cried more hopelessly and helplessly than ever.

And then shame came to him. He knew laughter and the meaning of it. It is not given us to know how some animals know laughter, and know when they are being laughed at; but it was this same way that White Fang knew it. And he felt shame that the man-animals should be laughing at him. He turned and fled away, not from the hurt of the fire, but from the laughter that sank even deeper, and hurt in the spirit of him. And he fled to Kiche, raging at the end of her stick like an animal gone mad—to Kiche, the one creature in the world who was not laughing at him.

Twilight drew down and night came on, and White Fang lay by his mother's side. His nose and tongue still hurt, but he was perplexed by a greater trouble. He was homesick. He felt a vacancy in him, a need for the hush and quietude of the stream and the cave in the cliff. Life had become too populous. There were so many of the man-animals, men, women, and children, all making noises and irritations. And there were the dogs, ever squabbling and bickering, bursting into uproars and creating confusions. The restful loneliness of the only life he had known was gone. Here the very air was palpitant with life. It hummed and buzzed unceasingly. Continually changing its intensity and abruptly variant in pitch, it impinged on his nerves and senses, made him nervous and restless and worried him with a perpetual imminence of happening.

He watched the man-animals coming and going and moving about the camp. In fashion distantly resembling the way men look upon the gods they create, so looked White Fang upon the man-animals before him. They were superior creatures, of a verity, gods. To his dim comprehension they were as much wonder-workers as gods are to men. They were creatures of mastery, possessing all manner of unknown and impossible potencies, overlords of the alive and the not alive,—making obey that which moved, imparting movement to that which did not move, and making life, sun-colored and biting life, to grow out of dead moss and wood. They were fire-makers! They were gods!

## Chapter 2

# THE BONDAGE

The days were thronged with experience for White Fang. During the time that Kiche was tied by the stick, he ran about over all the camp, inquiring, investigating, learning. He quickly came to know much of the ways of the man-animals, but familiarity did not breed contempt. The more he came to know them, the more they vindicated their superiority, the more they displayed their mysterious powers, the greater loomed their god-likeness.

To man has been given the grief, often, of seeing his gods overthrown and his altars crumbling; but to the wolf and the wild dog that have come in to crouch at man's feet, this grief has never come. Unlike man, whose gods are of the unseen and the overguessed, vapours and mists of fancy eluding the garmenture of reality, wandering wraiths of desired goodness and power, intangible outcroppings of self into the realm of spirit—unlike man, the wolf and the wild dog that have come in to the fire find their gods in the living flesh, solid to the touch, occupying earthspace and requiring time for the accomplishment of their ends and their existence. No effort of faith is necessary to believe in such a god; no effort of will can possibly induce disbelief in such a god. There is no getting away from it. There it stands, on its two hindlegs, club in hand, immensely potential, passionate and wrathful and loving, god and mystery and power all wrapped up and around by flesh that bleeds when it is torn and that is good to eat like any flesh.

And so it was with White Fang. The man-animals were gods unmistakable and unescapable. As his mother, Kiche, had rendered her allegiance to them at the first cry of her name, so he was beginning to render his allegiance. He gave them the trail as a privilege indubitably theirs. When they walked, he got out of their way. When they called, he came. When they threatened, he cowered down. When they commanded him to go, he went away hurriedly. For behind any wish of theirs was power to enforce that wish, power that hurt, power that expressed itself in clouts and clubs, in flying stones and stinging lashes of whips.

He belonged to them as all dogs belonged to them. His actions were theirs to command. His body was theirs to maul, to stamp upon, to tolerate. Such was the lesson that was quickly borne in upon him. It came hard, going as it did, counter to much that was strong and dominant in his own nature; and, while he disliked it in the learning of it, unknown to himself he was learning to like it. It was a placing of his destiny in another's hands, a shifting of the responsibilities of existence. This in itself was compensation, for it is always easier to lean upon another than to stand alone.

But it did not all happen in a day, this giving over of himself, body and soul, to the man-animals. He could not immediately forego his wild heritage and his memories of the Wild. There were days when he crept to the edge of the forest and stood and listened to something calling him far and away. And always he returned, restless and uncomfortable, to whimper softly and wistfully at Kiche's side and to lick her face with eager, questioning tongue.

White Fang learned rapidly the ways of the camp. He knew the injustice and greediness of the older dogs when meat or fish was thrown out to be eaten. He came to know that men were more just, children more cruel, and women more kindly and more likely to toss him a bit of meat or bone. And after two or three painful adventures with the mothers of part-grown puppies, he came into the knowledge that it was always good policy to let such mothers alone, to keep away from them as far as possible, and to avoid them when he saw them coming.

But the bane of his life was Lip-lip. Larger, older, and stronger, Lip-lip had selected White Fang for his special object of persecution. White Fang fought willingly enough, but he was outclassed. His enemy was too big. Lip-lip became a nightmare to him. Whenever he ventured away from his mother, the bully was sure to appear, trailing at his heels, snarling at him, picking upon him, and watchful of an opportunity, when no man-animal was near, to spring upon him and force a fight. As Lip-lip invariably won, he enjoyed it hugely. It became his chief delight in life, as it became White Fang's chief torment.

But the effect upon White Fang was not to cow him. Though he suffered most of the damage and was always defeated, his spirit remained unsubdued. Yet a bad effect was produced. He became malignant and morose. His temper had been savage by birth, but it became more savage under this unending persecution. The genial, playful, puppyish side of him found little expression. He never played and gambolled about with the other puppies of the camp. Lip-lip would not permit it. The moment White Fang appeared near them, Lip-lip was upon him, bullying and hectoring him, or fighting with him until he had driven him away.

The effect of all this was to rob White Fang of much of his puppyhood and to make him in his comportment older than his age. Denied the outlet, through play, of his energies, he recoiled upon himself and developed his mental processes. He became cunning; he had idle time in which to devote himself to thoughts of trickery. Prevented from obtaining his share of meat and fish when a general feed was given to the camp-dogs, he became a clever thief. He had to forage for himself, and he foraged well, though he was ofttimes a plague to the squaws in consequence. He learned to sneak about camp, to be crafty, to know what was going on everywhere, to see and to hear everything and to reason accordingly, and successfully to devise ways and means of avoiding his implacable persecutor.

It was early in the days of his persecution that he played his first really big crafty game and got therefrom his first taste of revenge. As Kiche, when with the wolves, had lured out to destruction dogs from the camps of men, so White Fang, in manner somewhat similar, lured Lip-lip into Kiche's avenging jaws. Retreating before Lip-lip, White Fang made an indirect flight that led in and out and around the various tepees of the camp. He was a good runner, swifter than any other puppy of his size, and swifter than Lip-lip. But he did not run his best in this chase. He barely held his own, one leap ahead of his pursuer.

Lip-lip, excited by the chase and by the persistent nearness of his victim, forgot caution and locality. When he remembered locality, it was too late. Dashing at top speed around a tepee, he ran full tilt into Kiche lying at the end of her stick. He gave one yelp of consternation, and then her punishing jaws closed upon him. She was tied, but he could not get away from her easily. She rolled him off his legs so that he could not run, while she repeatedly ripped and slashed him with her fangs.

When at last he succeeded in rolling clear of her, he crawled to his feet, badly dishevelled, hurt both in body and in spirit. His hair was standing out all over him in tufts where her teeth had mauled. He stood where he has arisen, opened his mouth, and broke out the long, heartbroken puppy wail. But even this he was not allowed to complete. In the middle of it, White Fang, rushing in, sank his teeth into Lip-lip's hind leg. There was no fight left in Lip-lip, and he ran away shamelessly, his victim hot on his heels and worrying him all the way back to his own tepee. Here the squaws came to his aid, and White Fang, transformed into a raging demon, was finally driven off only by a fusillade of stones.

Came the day when Gray Beaver, deciding that the liability of her running away was past, released Kiche. White Fang was delighted with his mother's freedom. He accompanied her joyfully about the camp; and, so long as he remained close by her side, Lip-lip kept a respectful distance. White Fang even bristled up to him and walked stiff-legged, but Lip-lip ignored the challenge. He was no fool himself, and whatever vengeance he desired to wreak, he could wait until he caught White Fang alone.

Later on that day, Kiche and White Fang strayed into the edge of the woods next to the camp. He had led his mother there, step by step, and now, when she stopped, he tried to inveigle her farther. The stream, the lair, and the quiet woods were calling to him, and he wanted her to come. He ran on a few steps, stopped, and looked back. She had not moved. He whined pleadingly, and scurried playfully in and out of the underbrush. He ran back to her, licked her face, and ran on again. And still she did not move. He stopped and regarded her, all of an intentness and eagerness, physically expressed, that slowly faded out of him as she turned her head and gazed back at the camp.

There was something calling to him out there in the open. His mother heard it, too. But she heard also that other and louder call, the call of the fire and of man—the call which it has been given alone of all animals to the wolf to answer, to the wolf and the wild-dog, who are brothers.

Kiche turned and slowly trotted back toward camp. Stronger than the physical restraint of the stick was the clutch of the camp upon her. Unseen and occultly, the gods still gripped with their power and would not let her go. White Fang sat down in the shadow of a birch and whimpered softly. There was a strong smell of pine, and subtle woods fragrances filled the air, reminding him of his old life of freedom before the days of his bondage. But he was still only a part-grown puppy, and stronger than the call either of man or of the Wild was the call of his mother. All the hours of his short life he had depended upon her. The time was yet to come for independence. So he arose and trotted forlornly back to camp, pausing once, and twice, to sit down and whimper and to listen to the call that still sounded in the depths of the forest.

In the Wild the time of a mother with her young is short; but under the dominion of man it is sometimes even shorter. Thus it was with White Fang. Gray Beaver was in the debt of Three Eagles. Three Eagles was going away on a trip up the Mackenzie to the Great Slave Lake.* A strip of scarlet cloth, a bearskin, twenty cartridges, and Kiche, went to pay the debt. White Fang saw his mother taken aboard Three Eagles' canoe, and tried to follow her. A blow from Three Eagles knocked him backward to the land. The canoe shoved off. He sprang into the water and swam after it, deaf to the sharp cries of Gray Beaver to return. Even a man-animal, a god, White Fang ignored, such was the terror he was in of losing his mother.

But gods are accustomed to being obeyed, and Gray Beaver wrathfully launched a canoe in pursuit. When he overtook White Fang, he reached down and by the nape of the neck lifted him clear of the water. He did not deposit him at once in the bottom of the canoe. Holding him suspended with one hand, with the other hand he proceeded to give him a beating. And it was a beating. His hand was heavy. Every blow was shrewd to hurt; and he delivered a multitude of blows.

Impelled by the blows that rained upon him, now from this side, now from that, White Fang swung back and forth like an erratic and jerky pendulum. Varying were the emotions that surged through him. At first, he had known surprise. Then came a momentary fear, when he yelped several times to the impact of the hand. But this was quickly followed by anger. His free nature asserted itself, and he showed his teeth and snarled fearlessly in the face of the wrathful god. This but served to make the god more wrathful. The blows came faster, heavier, more shrewd to hurt.

Gray Beaver continued to beat, White Fang continued to snarl. But this could not last forever. One or the other must give over, and that one was White Fang. Fear surged through him again. For the first time he was being really man-handled. The occasional blows of sticks and stones he had previously experienced were as caresses compared with this. He broke down and began to cry and yelp. For a time each blow brought a yelp from him; but fear passed into terror, until finally his yelps were voiced in unbroken succession, unconnected with the rhythm of the punishment.

At last Gray Beaver withheld his hand. White Fang, hanging limply, continued to cry. This seemed to satisfy his master, who flung him down roughly in the bottom of the canoe. In the meantime the canoe had drifted down the stream. Gray Beaver picked up the paddle. White Fang was in his way. He spurned him savagely with his foot. In that moment White Fang's free nature flashed forth again, and he sank his teeth into the moccasined foot.

The beating that had gone before was as nothing compared with the beating he now received. Gray Beaver's wrath was terrible; likewise was White Fang's fright. Not only the hand, but the hard wooden paddle was used upon him; and he was bruised and sore in all his small body when he was again flung down in the canoe. Again, and this time with purpose, did Gray Beaver kick him. White Fang did not repeat his attack on the foot. He had learned another lesson of his bondage. Never, no matter what the circumstance, must he dare to bite the god who was lord and master over him; the body of the lord and master was sacred, not to be defiled by the teeth of such as he. That was evidently the crime of crimes, the one offence there was no condoning nor overlooking.

When the canoe touched the shore, White Fang lay whimpering and motionless, waiting the will of Gray Beaver. It was Gray Beaver's will that he should go ashore, for ashore he was flung, striking heavily on his side and hurting his bruises afresh. He crawled tremblingly to his feet and stood whimpering. Lip-lip, who had watched the whole proceeding from the bank, now rushed upon him, knocking him over and sinking his teeth into him. White Fang was too helpless to defend himself, and it would have gone hard with him had not Gray Beaver's foot shot out, lifting Lip-lip into the air with its violence so that he smashed down to earth a dozen feet away. This was the man-animal's justice; and even then, in his own pitiable plight, White Fang experienced a little grateful thrill. At Gray Beaver's heels he limped obediently through the village to the tepee. And so it came that White Fang learned that the right to punish was something the gods reserved for themselves and denied to the lesser creatures under them.

That night, when all was still, White Fang remembered his mother and sorrowed for her. He sorrowed too loudly and woke up Gray

Beaver, who beat him. After that he mourned gently when the gods were around. But sometimes, straying off to the edge of the woods by himself, he gave vent to his grief, and cried it out with loud whimperings and wailings.

It was during this period that he might have hearkened to the memories of the lair and the stream and run back to the Wild. But the memory of his mother held him. As the hunting man-animals went out and came back, so she would come back to the village sometime. So he remained in his bondage waiting for her.

But it was not altogether an unhappy bondage. There was much to interest him. Something was always happening. There was no end to the strange things these gods did, and he was always curious to see. Besides, he was learning how to get along with Gray Beaver. Obedience, rigid, undeviating obedience, was what was exacted of him; and in return he escaped beatings and his existence was tolerated.

Nay, Gray Beaver himself sometimes tossed him a piece of meat, and defended him against the other dogs in the eating of it. And such a piece of meat was of value. It was worth more, in some strange way, than a dozen pieces of meat from the hand of a squaw. Gray Beaver never petted nor caressed. Perhaps it was the weight of his hand, perhaps his justice, perhaps the sheer power of him, and perhaps it was all these things that influenced White Fang; for a certain tie of attachment was forming between him and his surly lord.

Insidiously, and by remote ways, as well as by the power of stick and stone and clout of hand, were the shackles of White Fang's bondage being riveted upon him. The qualities in his kind that in the beginning made it possible for them to come in to the fires of men, were qualities capable of development. They were developing in him, and the camplife, replete with misery as it was, was secretly endearing itself to him all the time. But White Fang was unaware of it. He knew only grief for the loss of Kiche, hope for her return, and a hungry yearning for the free life that had been his.

## CHAPTER 3

# THE OUTCAST

Lip-Lip continued so to darken his days that White Fang became wickeder and more ferocious than it was his natural right to be. Savageness was a part of his make-up, but the savageness thus developed exceeded his make-up. He acquired a reputation for wickedness amongst the man-animals themselves. Wherever there was trouble and uproar in camp, fighting and squabbling or the outcry of a squaw over a bit of stolen meat, they were sure to find White Fang mixed up in it and usually at the bottom of it. They did not bother to look after the causes of his conduct. They saw only the effects, and the effects were bad. He was a sneak and a thief, a mischief-maker, a fomenter of trouble; and irate squaws told him to his face, the while he eyed them alert and ready to dodge any quick-flung missile, that he was a wolf and worthless and bound to come to an evil end.

He found himself an outcast in the midst of the populous camp. All the young dogs followed Lip-lip's lead. There was a difference between White Fang and them. Perhaps they sensed his wild-wood breed, and instinctively felt for him the enmity that the domestic dog feels for the wolf. But be that as it may, they joined with Lip-lip in the persecution. And, once declared against him, they found good reason to continue declared against him. One and all, from time to time, they felt his teeth; and to his credit, he gave more than he received. Many of them he could whip in single fight; but single fight was denied him. The beginning of such a fight was a signal for all the young dogs in camp to come running and pitch upon him.

Out of this pack-persecution he learned two important things: how to take care of himself in a massfight against him; and how, on a single dog, to inflict the greatest amount of damage in the briefest space of time. To keep one's feet in the midst of the hostile mass meant life, and this he learned well. He became catlike in his ability to stay on his feet. Even grown dogs might hurtle him backward or sideways with the impact of their heavy bodies; and backward or sideways he would go, in the air or sliding on the ground, but always with his legs under him and his feet downward to the mother earth.

When dogs fight, there are usually preliminaries to the actual combat—snarlings and bristlings and stifflegged struttings. But White Fang learned to omit these preliminaries. Delay meant the coming against him of all the young dogs. He must do his work quickly and get away. So he learned to give no warning of his intention. He rushed in and snapped and slashed on the instant, without notice, before his foe could prepare to meet him. Thus he learned how to inflict quick and severe damage. Also he learned the value of surprise. A dog, taken off its guard, its shoulder slashed open or its ear ripped in ribbons before it knew what was happening, was a dog half whipped.

Furthermore, it was remarkably easy to overthrow a dog taken by surprise; while a dog, thus overthrown, invariably exposed for a moment the soft underside of its neck—the vulnerable point at which to strike for its life. White Fang knew this point. It was a knowledge bequeathed to him directly from the hunting generations of wolves. So it was that White Fang's method, when he took the offensive, was: first, to find a young dog alone; second, to surprise it and knock it off its feet; and third, to drive in with his teeth at the soft throat.

Being but partly grown, his jaws had not yet become large enough nor strong enough to make his throat-attack deadly; but many a young dog went around camp with a lacerated throat in token of White Fang's intention. And one day, catching one of his enemies alone on the edge of the woods, he managed, by repeatedly overthrowing him and attacking the throat, to cut the great vein and let out the life. There was a great row that night. He had been observed, the news had been carried to the dead dog's master, the squaws remembered all the instances of stolen meat, and Gray Beaver was beset by many angry voices. But he resolutely held the door of his tepee, inside which he had placed the culprit, and refused to permit the vengeance for which his tribes people clamoured.

White Fang became hated by man and dog. During this period of his development he never knew a moment's security. The tooth of every dog was against him, the hand of every man. He was greeted with snarls by his kind, with curses and stones by his gods. He lived tensely. He was always keyed up, alert for attack, wary of being attacked, with an eye for sudden and unexpected missiles, prepared to act precipitately and coolly, to leap in with a flash of teeth, or to leap away with a menacing snarl.

As for snarling, he could snarl more terribly than any dog, young or old, in camp. The intent of the snarl is to warn or frighten, and judgment is required to know when it should be used. White Fang knew how to make it and when to make it. Into his snarl he incorporated all that was vicious, malignant, and horrible. With nose serrulated by continuous spasms, hair bristling in recurrent waves, tongue whipping out like a red snake and whipping back again, ears flattened down, eyes gleaming hatred, lips wrinkled back, and fangs exposed and dripping, he could compel a pause on the part of almost any assailant. A temporary pause, when taken off his guard, gave him the vital moment in which to think and determine his action. But often a pause so gained lengthened out until it evolved into a complete cessation from the attack. And before more than one of the grown dogs White Fang's snarl enabled him to beat an honourable retreat.

An outcast himself from the pack of the part-grown dogs, his sanguinary methods and remarkable efficiency made the pack pay for its persecution of him. Not permitted himself to run with the pack, the curious state of affairs obtained that no member of the pack could run outside the pack. White Fang would not permit it. What of his bushwhacking and waylaying tactics, the young dogs were afraid to run by themselves. With the exception of Lip-lip, they were compelled to bunch together for mutual protection against the terrible enemy they had made. A puppy alone by the river bank meant a puppy dead or a puppy that aroused the camp with its shrill pain and terror as it fled back from the wolf-cub that had waylaid it.

But White Fang's reprisals did not cease, even when the young dogs had learned thoroughly that they must stay together. He attacked them when he caught them alone, and they attacked him when they were bunched. The sight of him was sufficient to start them rushing after him, at which times his swiftness usually carried him into safety. But woe to the dog that outran his fellows in such pursuit! White Fang had learned to turn suddenly upon the pursuer that was ahead of the pack and thoroughly to rip him up before the pack could arrive. This occurred with great frequency, for, once in full cry, the dogs were prone to forget themselves in the excitement of the chase, while White Fang never forgot himself. Stealing backward glances as he ran, he was always ready to whirl around and down the overzealous pursuer that outran his fellows.

Young dogs are bound to play, and out of the exigencies of the situation they realized their play in this mimic warfare. Thus it was that the hunt of White Fang became their chief game—a deadly game, withal, and at all times a serious game. He, on the other hand, being the fastest-footed, was unafraid to venture anywhere. During the period that he waited vainly for his mother to come back, he led the pack many a wild chase through the adjacent woods. But the pack invariably lost him. Its noise and outcry warned him of its presence, while he ran alone, velvet-footed, silently, a moving shadow among the trees after the manner of his father and mother before him. Further, he was more directly connected with the Wild than they; and he knew more of its secrets and stratagems. A favourite trick of his was to lose his trail in running water and then lie quietly in a nearby thicket while their baffled cries arose around him.

Hated by his kind and by mankind, indomitable, perpetually warred upon and himself waging perpetual war, his development was rapid and onesided. This was no soil for kindliness and affection to blossom in. Of such things he had not the faintest glimmering. The code he learned was to obey the strong and to oppress the weak. Gray Beaver was a god, and strong. Therefore White Fang obeyed him. But the dog younger or smaller than himself was weak, a thing to be destroyed. His development was in the direction of power. In order to face the constant danger of hurt and even of destruction, his predatory and protective faculties were unduly developed. He became quicker of movement than the other dogs, swifter of foot, craftier, deadlier, more lithe, more lean with ironlike muscle and sinew, more enduring, more cruel, more ferocious, and more intelligent. He had to become all these things, else he would not have held his own nor survived the hostile environment in which he found himself.

CHAPTER 4

# THE TRAIL OF THE GODS

I the fall of the year, when the days were shortening and the bite of the frost was coming into the air, White Fang got his chance for liberty. For several days there had been a great hubbub in the village. The summer camp was being dismantled, and the tribe, bag and baggage, was preparing to go off to the fall hunting. White Fang watched it all with eager eyes, and when the tepees began to come down and the canoes were loading at the bank, he understood. Already the canoes were departing, and some had disappeared down the river.

Quite deliberately he determined to stay behind. He waited his opportunity to slink out of camp to the woods. Here, in the running stream where ice was beginning to form, he hid his trail. Then he crawled into the heart of a dense thicket and waited. The time passed by, and he slept intermittently for hours. Then he was aroused by Gray Beaver's voice calling him by name. There were other voices. White Fang could hear Gray Beaver's squaw taking part in the search, and Mit-sah, who was Gray Beaver's son.

White Fang trembled with fear, and though the impulse came to crawl out of his hidingplace, he resisted it. After a time the voices died away, and some time after that he crept out to enjoy the success of his undertaking. Darkness was coming on, and for a while he played about among the trees, pleasuring in his freedom. Then, and quite suddenly, he became aware of loneliness. He sat down to consider, listening to the silence of the forest and perturbed by it. That nothing moved nor sounded, seemed ominous. He felt the lurking of danger, unseen and unguessed. He was suspicious of the looming bulks of the trees and of the dark shadows that might conceal all manner of perilous things.

Then it was cold. Here was no warm side of a tepee against which to snuggle. The frost was in his feet, and he kept lifting first one forefoot and then the other. He curved his bushy tail around to cover them, and at the same time he saw a vision. There was nothing strange about it. Upon his inward sight was impressed a succession of memory-pictures. He saw the camp again, the tepees, and the blaze of the fires. He heard the shrill voices of the women, the gruff basses of the men, and the snarling of the dogs. He was hungry, and he remembered pieces of meat and fish that had been thrown him. Here was no meat, nothing but a threatening and inedible silence.

His bondage had softened him. Irresponsibility had weakened him. He had forgotten how to shift for himself. The night yawned about him. His senses, accustomed to the hum and bustle of the camp, used to the continuous impact of sights and sounds, were now left idle. There was nothing to do, nothing to see nor hear. They strained to catch some interruption of the silence and immobility of nature. They were appalled by inaction and by the feel of something terrible impending.

He gave a great start of fright. A colossal and formless something was rushing across the field of his vision. It was a tree-shadow flung by the moon, from whose face the clouds had been brushed away. Reassured, he whimpered softly; then he suppressed the whimper for fear that it might attract the attention of the lurking dangers.

A tree, contracting in the cool of the night, made a loud noise. It was directly above him. He yelped in his fright. A panic seized him, and he ran madly toward the village. He knew an overpowering desire for the protection and companionship of man. In his nostrils was the smell of the camp-smoke. In his ears the camp sounds and cries were ringing loud. He passed out of the forest and into the moonlit open where were no shadows nor darknesses. But no village greeted his eyes. He had forgotten. The village had gone away.

His wild flight ceased abruptly. There was no place to which to flee. He slunk forlornly through the deserted camp, smelling the rubbish-heaps and the discarded rags and tags of the gods. He would have been glad for the rattle of stones about him, flung by an angry squaw, glad for the hand of Gray Beaver descending upon him in wrath; while he would have welcomed with delight Lip-lip and the whole snarling, cowardly pack.

He came to where Gray Beaver's tepee had stood. In the centre of the space it had occupied, he sat down. He pointed his nose at the moon. His throat was afflicted by rigid spasms, his mouth opened, and in a heartbroken cry bubbled up his loneliness and fear, his grief for Kiche, all his past sorrows and miseries as well as his apprehension of sufferings and dangers to come. It was the long wolf-howl, fullthroated and mournful, the first howl he had ever uttered.

The coming of daylight dispelled his fears, but increased his loneliness. The naked earth, which so shortly before had been so populous, thrust his loneliness more forcibly upon him. It did not take him long to make up his mind. He plunged into the forest and followed the river bank down the stream. All day he ran. He did not rest. He seemed made to run on forever. His iron-like body ignored fatigue. And even after fatigue came, his heritage of endurance braced him to endless endeavour and enabled him to drive his complaining body onward.

Where the river swung in against precipitous bluffs, he climbed the high mountains behind. Rivers and streams that entered the main river he forded or swam. Often he took to the rimice that was beginning to form, and more than once he crashed through and struggled for life in the icy current. Always he was on the lookout for the trail of the gods where it might leave the river and proceed inland.

White Fang was intelligent beyond the average of his kind; yet his mental vision was not wide enough to embrace the other bank of the Mackenzie. What if the trail of the gods led out on that side? It never entered his head. Later on, when he had travelled more and grown older and wiser and come to know more of trails and rivers, it might be that he could grasp and apprehend such a possibility. But that mental power was yet in the future. Just now he ran blindly, his own bank of the Mackenzie alone entering into his calculations.

All night he ran, blundering in the darkness into mishaps and obstacles that delayed but did not daunt. By the middle of the second day he had been running continuously for thirty hours, and the iron of his flesh was giving out. It was the endurance of his mind that kept him going. He had not eaten in forty hours, and he was weak with hunger. The repeated drenchings in the icy water had likewise had their effect on him. His handsome coat was draggled. The broad pads of his feet were bruised and bleeding. He had begun to limp, and this limp increased with the hours. To make it worse, the light of the sky was obscured and snow began to fall—a raw, moist, melting, clinging snow, slippery under foot, that hid from him the landscape he traversed, and that covered over the inequalities of the ground so that the way of his feet was more difficult and painful.

Gray Beaver had intended camping that night on the far bank of the Mackenzie, for it was in that direction that the hunting lay. But on the near bank, shortly before dark, a moose, coming down to drink, had been espied by Kloo-kooch, who was Gray Beaver's squaw. Now, had not the moose come down to drink, had not Mit-sah been steering out of the course because of the snow, had not Kloo-kooch sighted the moose, and had not Gray Beaver killed it with a lucky shot from his rifle, all subsequent things would have happened differently. Gray Beaver would not have camped on the near side of the Mackenzie, and White Fang would have passed by and gone on, either to die or to find his way to his wild brothers and become one of them,—a wolf to the end of his days.

Night had fallen. The snow was flying more thickly, and White Fang, whimpering softly to himself as he stumbled and limped along, came upon a fresh trail in the snow. So fresh was it that he knew it immediately for what it was. Whining with eagerness, he followed back from the river bank and in among the trees. The camp-sounds came to his ears. He saw the blaze of the fire, Kloo-kooch cooking, and Gray Beaver squatting on his hams and mumbling a chunk of raw tallow. There was fresh meat in camp!

White Fang expected a beating. He crouched and bristled a little at the thought of it. Then he went forward again. He feared and disliked the beating he knew to be waiting for him. But he knew, further, that the comfort of the fire would be his, the protection of the gods, the companionship of the dogs—the last, a companionship of enmity, but none the less a companionship and satisfying to his gregarious needs.

He came cringing and crawling into the firelight. Gray Beaver saw him, and stopped munching the tallow. White Fang crawled slowly, cringing and grovelling in the abjectness of his abasement and submission. He crawled straight toward Gray Beaver, every inch of his progress becoming slower and more painful. At last he lay at the master's feet, into whose possession he now surrendered himself, voluntarily, body and soul. Of his own choice, he came in to sit by man's fire and to be ruled by him. White Fang trembled, waiting for the punishment to fall upon him. There was a movement of the hand above him. He cringed involuntarily under the expected blow. It did not fall. He stole a glance upward. Gray Beaver was breaking the lump of tallow in half! Gray Beaver was offering him one piece of the tallow! Very gently and somewhat suspiciously, he first smelled the tallow and then proceeded to eat it. Gray Beaver ordered meat to be brought to him, and guarded him from the other dogs while he ate. After that, grateful and content, White Fang lay at Gray Beaver's feet, gazing at the fire that warmed him, blinking and dozing, secure in the knowledge that the morrow would find him, not wandering forlorn through bleak forest-stretches, but in the camp of the man-animals, with the gods to whom he had given himself and upon whom he was now dependent.

## CHAPTER 5

# THE COVENANT

When December was well along, Gray Beaver went on a journey up the Mackenzie. Mit-sah and Kloo-kooch went with him. One sled he drove himself, drawn by dogs he had traded for or borrowed. A second and smaller sled was driven by Mit-sah, and to this was harnessed a team of puppies. It was more of a toy affair than anything else, yet it was the delight of Mit-sah, who felt that he was beginning to do a man's work in the world. Also, he was learning to drive dogs and to train dogs; while the puppies themselves were being broken in to the harness. Furthermore, the sled was of some service, for it carried nearly two hundred pounds of outfit and food.

White Fang had seen the camp-dogs toiling in the harness, so that he did not resent overmuch the first placing of the harness upon himself. About his neck was put a moss-stuffed collar, which was connected by two pulling-traces to a strap that passed around his chest and over his back. It was to this that was fastened the long rope by which he pulled at the sled.

There were seven puppies in the team. The others had been born earlier in the year and were nine and ten months old, while White Fang was only eight months old. Each dog was fastened to the sled by a single rope. No two ropes were of the same length, while the difference in length between any two ropes was at least that of a dog's body. Every rope was brought to a ring at the front end of the sled. The sled itself was without runners, being a birch-bark toboggan, with upturned forward end to keep it from ploughing under the snow. This construction enabled the weight of the sled and load to be distributed over the largest snow-surface; for the snow was crystal-powder and very soft. Observing the same principle of widest distribution of weight, the dogs at the ends of their ropes radiated fan-fashion from the nose of the sled, so that no dog trod in another's footsteps.

There was, furthermore, another virtue in the fan-formation. The ropes of varying length prevented the dogs attacking from the rear those that ran in front of them. For a dog to attack another, it would have to turn upon one at a shorter rope. In which case it would find itself face to face with the dog attacked, and also it would find itself facing the whip of the driver. But the most peculiar virtue of all lay in the fact that the dog that strove to attack one in front of him must pull the sled faster, and that the faster the sled travelled, the faster could the dog attacked run away. Thus, the dog behind could never catch up with the one in front. The faster he ran, the faster ran the one he was after, and the faster ran all the dogs. Incidentally, the sled went faster, and thus, by cunning indirection, did man increase his mastery over the beasts.

Mit-sah resembled his father, much of whose gray wisdom he possessed. In the past he had observed Lip-lip's persecution of White Fang; but at that time Lip-lip was another man's dog, and Mit-sah had never dared more than to shy an occasional stone at him. But now Lip-lip was his dog, and he proceeded to wreak his vengeance on him by putting him at the end of the longest rope. This made Lip-lip the leader, and was apparently an honour; but in reality it took away from him all honour, and instead of being bully and master of the pack, he now found himself hated and persecuted by the pack.

Because he ran at the end of the longest rope, the dogs had always the view of him running away before them. All that they saw of him was his bushy tail and fleeing hind legs—a view far less ferocious and intimidating than his bristling mane and gleaming fangs. Also, dogs being so constituted in their mental ways, the sight of him running away gave desire to run after him and a feeling that he ran away from them.

The moment the sled started, the team took after Lip-lip in a chase that extended throughout the day. At first he had been prone to turn upon his pursuers, jealous of his dignity and wrathful; but at such times Mit-sah would throw the stinging lash of the thirtyfoot cariboo-gut whip into his face and compel him to turn tail and run on. Lip-lip might face the pack, but he could not face that whip, and all that was left him to do was to keep his long rope taut and his flanks ahead of the teeth of his mates.

But a still greater cunning lurked in the recesses of the Indian mind. To give point to unending pursuit of the leader, Mit-sah favoured him over the other dogs. These favours aroused in them jealousy and hatred. In their presence Mit-sah would give him meat and would give it to him only. This was maddening to them. They would rage around just outside the throwing-distance of the whip, while Lip-lip devoured the meat and Mit-sah protected him. And when there was no meat to give, Mit-sah would keep the team at a distance and make believe to give meat to Lip-lip.

White Fang took kindly to the work. He had travelled a greater distance than the other dogs in the yielding of himself to the rule of the gods, and he had learned more thoroughly the futility of opposing their will. In addition, the persecution he had suffered from the pack had made the pack less to him in the scheme of things, and man more. He had not learned to be dependent on his kind for companionship. Besides, Kiche was wellnigh forgotten; and the chief outlet of expression that remained to him was in the allegiance he tendered the gods he had accepted as masters. So he worked hard, learned discipline, and was obedient. Faithfulness and willingness characterized his toil. These are essential traits of the wolf and the wild-dog when they have become domesticated, and these traits White Fang possessed in unusual measure.

A companionship did exist between White Fang and the other dogs, but it was one of warfare and enmity. He had never learned to play with them. He knew only how to fight, and fight with them he did, returning to them a hundred-fold the snaps and slashes they had given him in the days when Lip-lip was leader of the pack. But Lip-lip was no longer leader—except when he fled away before his mates at the end of his rope, the sled bounding along behind. In camp he kept close to Mit-sah or Gray Beaver or Kloo-kooch. He did not dare venture away from the gods, for now the fangs of all dogs were against him, and he tasted to the dregs the persecution that had been White Fang's.

With the overthrow of Lip-lip, White Fang could have become leader of the pack. But he was too morose and solitary for that. He merely thrashed his team-mates. Otherwise he ignored them. They got out of his way when he came along; nor did the boldest of them ever dare to rob him of his meat. On the contrary, they devoured their own meat hurriedly, for fear that he would take it away from them. White Fang knew the law well: *to oppress the weak and obey the strong*. He ate his share of meat as rapidly as he could. And then woe the dog that had not yet finished! A snarl and a flash of fangs, and that dog would wail his indignation to the uncomforting stars while White Fang finished his portion for him.

Every little while, however, one dog or another would flame up in revolt and be promptly subdued. Thus White Fang was kept in training. He was jealous of the isolation in which he kept himself in the midst of the pack, and he fought often to maintain it. But such fights were of brief duration. He was too quick for the others. They were slashed open and bleeding before they knew what had happened, were whipped almost before they had begun to fight.

As rigid as the sled-discipline of the gods, was the discipline maintained by White Fang amongst his fellows. He never allowed them any latitude. He compelled them to an unremitting respect for him. They might do as they pleased amongst themselves. That was no concern of his. But it was his concern that they leave him alone in his isolation, get out of his way when he elected to walk among them, and at all times acknowledge his mastery over them. A hint of stiff-leggedness on their part, a lifted lip or a bristle of hair, and he would be upon them, merciless and cruel, swiftly convincing them of the error of their way.

He was a monstrous tyrant. His mastery was rigid as steel. He oppressed the weak with a vengeance. Not for nothing had he been exposed to the pitiless struggle for life in the days of his cubhood, when his mother and he, alone and unaided, held their own and survived in the ferocious environment of the Wild. And not for nothing had he learned to walk softly when superior strength went by. He oppressed the weak, but he respected the strong. And in the course of the long journey with Gray Beaver he walked softly indeed amongst the fullgrown dogs in the camps of the strange man-animals they encountered.

The months passed by. Still continued the journey of Gray Beaver. White Fang's strength was developed by the long hours on trail and the steady toil at the sled; and it would have seemed that his mental development was wellnigh complete. He had come to know quite thoroughly the world in which he lived. His outlook was bleak and materialistic. The world as he saw it was a fierce and brutal world, a world without warmth, a world in which caresses and affection and the bright sweetnesses of the spirit did not exist.

He had no affection for Gray Beaver. True, he was a god, but a most savage god. White Fang was glad to acknowledge his lordship, but it was a lordship based upon superior intelligence and brute strength. There was something in the fibre of White Fang's being that made this lordship a thing to be desired, else he would not have come back from the Wild when he did to tender his allegiance. There were deeps in his nature which had never been sounded. A kind word, a caressing touch of the hand, on the part of Gray Beaver, might have sounded these deeps; but Gray Beaver did not caress nor speak kind words. It was not his way. His primacy was savage, and savagely he ruled, administering justice with a club, punishing transgression with the pain of a blow, and rewarding merit, not by kindness, but by withholding a blow.

So White Fang knew nothing of the heaven a man's hand might contain for him. Besides, he did not like the hands of the man-animals. He was suspicious of them. It was true that they sometimes gave meat, but more often they gave hurt. Hands were things to keep away from. They hurled stones, wielded sticks and clubs and whips, administered slaps and clouts, and, when they touched him, were cunning to hurt with pinch and twist and wrench. In strange villages he had encountered the hands of the children and learned that they were cruel to hurt. Also, he had once nearly had an eye poked out by a toddling papoose. From these experiences he became suspicious of all children. He could not tolerate them. When they came near with their ominous hands, he got up.

It was in a village at the Great Slave Lake, that, in the course of resenting the evil of the hands of the man-animals, he came to modify the law that he had learned from Gray Beaver; namely, that the unpardonable crime was to bite one of the gods. In this village, after the custom of all dogs in all villages, White Fang went foraging for food. A boy was chopping frozen moose-meat with an axe, and the chips were flying in the snow. White Fang, sliding by in quest of meat, stopped and began to eat the chips. He observed the boy lay down the axe and take up a stout club. White Fang sprang clear, just in time to escape the descending blow. The boy pursued him, and he, a stranger in the village, fled between two tepees, to find himself cornered against a high earth bank.

There was no escape for White Fang. The only way out was between the two tepees, and this the boy guarded. Holding his club prepared to strike, he drew in on his cornered quarry. White Fang was furious. He faced the boy, bristling and snarling, his sense of justice outraged. He knew the law of forage. All the wastage of meat, such as the frozen chips, belonged to the dog that found it. He had done no wrong, broken no law, yet here was this boy preparing to give him a beating. White Fang scarcely knew what happened. He did it in a surge of rage. And he did it so quickly that the boy did not know, either. All the boy knew was that he had in some unaccountable way been overturned into the snow, and that his club-hand had been ripped wide open by White Fang's teeth.

But White Fang knew that he had broken the law of the gods. He had driven his teeth into the sacred flesh of one of them, and could expect nothing but a most terrible punishment. He fled away to Gray Beaver, behind whose protecting legs he crouched when the bitten boy and the boy's family came, demanding vengeance. But they went away with vengeance unsatisfied. Gray Beaver defended White Fang. So did Mit-sah and Kloo-kooch. White Fang, listening to the wordy war and watching the angry gestures, knew that his act was justified. And so it came that he learned there were gods and gods. There were his gods, and there were other gods, and between them there was a difference. Justice or injustice, it was all the same, he must take all things from the hands of his own gods. But he was not compelled to take injustice from the other gods. It was his privilege to resent it with his teeth. And this also was a law of the gods.

Before the day was out, White Fang was to learn more about this law. Mit-sah, alone, gathering firewood in the forest, encountered the boy that had been bitten. With him were other boys. Hot words passed. Then all the boys attacked Mit-sah. It was going hard with him. Blows were raining upon him from all sides. White Fang looked on at first. This was an affair of the gods, and no concern of his. Then he realized that this was Mit-sah, one of his own particular gods, who was being maltreated. It was no reasoned impulse that made White Fang do what he then did. A mad rush of anger sent him leaping in amongst the combatants. Five minutes later the landscape was covered with fleeing boys, many of whom dripped blood upon the snow in token that White Fang's teeth had not been idle. When Mit-sah told his story in camp, Gray Beaver ordered meat to be given to White Fang. He ordered much meat to be given, and White Fang, gorged and sleepy by the fire, knew that the law had received its verification.

It was in line with these experiences that White Fang came to learn the law of property and the duty of the defence of property. From the protection of his god's body to the protection of his god's possessions was a step, and this step he made. What was his god's was to be defended against all the world—even to the extent of biting other gods. Not only was such an act sacrilegious in its nature, but it was fraught with peril. The gods were all-powerful, and a dog was no match against them; yet White Fang learned to face them, fiercely belligerent and unafraid. Duty rose above fear, and thieving gods learned to leave Gray Beaver's property alone.

One thing, in this connection, White Fang quickly learned, and that was that a thieving god was usually a cowardly god and prone to run away at the sounding of the alarm. Also, he learned that but brief time elapsed between his sounding of the alarm and Gray Beaver's coming to his aid. He came to know that it was not fear of him that drove the thief away, but fear of Gray Beaver. White Fang did not give the alarm by barking. He never barked. His method was to drive straight at the intruder, and to sink his teeth in if he could. Because he was morose and solitary, having nothing to do with the other dogs, he was unusually fitted to guard his master's property; and in this he was encouraged and trained by Gray Beaver. One result of this was to make White Fang more ferocious and indomitable, and more solitary.

The months went by, binding stronger and stronger the covenant between dog and man. This was the ancient covenant that the first wolf that came in from the Wild entered into with man. And, like all succeeding wolves and wild dogs that had done likewise, White Fang worked the covenant out for himself. The terms were simple. For the possession of a flesh-and-blood god, he exchanged his own liberty. Food and fire, protection and companionship, were some of the things he received from the god. In return, he guarded the god's property, defended his body, worked for him, and obeyed him.

The possession of a god implies service. White Fang's was a service of duty and awe, but not of love. He did not know what love was. He had no experience of love. Kiche was a remote memory. Besides, not only had he abandoned the Wild and his kind when he gave himself up to man, but the terms of the covenant were such that if he ever met Kiche again he would not desert his god to go with her. His allegiance to man seemed somehow a law of his being greater than the love of liberty, of kind and kin.

## CHAPTER 6

# THE FAMINE

The spring of the year was at hand when Gray Beaver finished his long journey. It was April, and White Fang was a year old when he pulled into the home village and was loosed from the harness by Mit-sah. Though a long way from his full growth, White Fang, next to Lip-lip, was the largest yearling in the village. Both from his father, the wolf, and from Kiche, he had inherited stature and strength, and already he was measuring up alongside the fullgrown dogs. But he had not yet grown compact. His body was slender and rangy, and his strength more stringy than massive. His coat was the true wolf-gray, and to all appearances he was true wolf himself. The quarter-strain of dog he had inherited from Kiche had left no mark on him physically, though it played its part in his mental make-up.

He wandered through the village, recognizing with staid satisfaction the various gods he had known before the long journey. Then there were the dogs, puppies growing up like himself, and grown dogs that did not look so large and formidable as the memory-pictures he retained of them. Also, he stood less in fear of them than formerly, stalking among them with a certain careless ease that was as new to him as it was enjoyable.

There was Baseek, a grizzled old fellow that in his younger days had but to uncover his fangs to send White Fang cringing and crouching to the right-about. From him White Fang had learned much of his own insignificance; and from him he was now to learn much of the change and development that had taken place in himself. While Baseek had been growing weaker with age, White Fang had been growing stronger with youth.

It was at the cutting-up of a moose, fresh-killed, that White Fang learned of the changed relations in which he stood to the dog-world. He had got for himself a hoof and part of the shin-bone, to which quite a bit of meat was attached. Withdrawn from the immediate scramble of the other dogs,—in fact, out of sight behind a thicket,—he was devouring his prize, when Baseek rushed in upon him. Before he knew what he was doing, he had slashed the intruder twice and sprung clear. Baseek was surprised by the other's temerity and swiftness of attack. He stood, gazing stupidly across at White Fang, the raw, red shin-bone between them.

Baseek was old, and already he had come to know the increasing valour of the dogs it had been his wont to bully. Bitter experiences these, which, perforce, he swallowed, calling upon all his wisdom to cope with them. In the old days, he would have sprung upon White Fang in a fury of righteous wrath. But now his waning powers would not permit such a course. He bristled fiercely and looked ominously across the shin-bone at White Fang. And White Fang, resurrecting quite a deal of the old awe, seemed to wilt and to shrink in upon himself and grow small, as he cast about in his mind for a way to beat a retreat not too inglorious.

And right here Baseek erred. Had he contented himself with looking fierce and ominous, all would have been well. White Fang, on the verge of retreat, would have retreated, leaving the meat to him. But Baseek did not wait. He considered the victory already his and stepped forward to the meat. As he bent his head carelessly to smell it, White Fang bristled slightly. Even then it was not too late for Baseek to retrieve the situation. Had he merely stood over the meat, head up and glowering, White Fang would ultimately have slunk away. But the fresh meat was strong in Baseek's nostrils, and greed urged him to take a bite of it.

This was too much for White Fang. Fresh upon his months of mastery over his own team-mates, it was beyond his selfcontrol to stand idly by while another devoured the meat that belonged to him. He struck, after his custom, without warning. With the first slash, Baseek's right ear was ripped into ribbons. He was astounded at the suddenness of it. But more things, and most grievous ones, were happening with equal suddenness. He was knocked off his feet. His throat was bitten. While he was struggling to his feet the young dog sank teeth twice into his shoulder. The swiftness of it was bewildering. He made a futile rush at White Fang, clipping the empty air with an outraged snap. The next moment his nose was laid open and he was staggering backward away from the meat.

The situation was now reversed. White Fang stood over the shin-bone, bristling and menacing, while Baseek stood a little way off, preparing to retreat. He dared not risk a fight with this young lightning-flash, and again he knew, and more bitterly, the enfeeblement of oncoming age. His attempt to maintain his dignity was heroic. Calmly turning his back upon young dog and shin-bone, as though both were beneath his notice and unworthy of consideration, he stalked grandly away. Nor, until well out of sight, did he stop to lick his bleeding wounds.

The effect on White Fang was to give him a greater faith in himself, and a greater pride. He walked less softly among the grown dogs; his attitude toward them was less compromising. Not that he went out of his way looking for trouble. Far from it. But upon his way he demanded consideration. He stood upon his right to go his way unmolested and to give trail to no dog. He had to be taken into account, that was all. He was no longer to be disregarded and ignored, as was the lot of puppies and as continued to be the lot of the puppies that were his team-mates. They got out of the way, gave trail to the grown dogs, and gave up meat to them under compulsion. But White Fang, uncompanionable, solitary, morose, scarcely looking to right or left, redoubtable, forbidding of aspect, remote and alien, was accepted as an equal by his puzzled elders. They quickly learned to leave him alone, neither venturing hostile acts nor making overtures of friendliness. If they left him alone, he left them alone-state of affairs that they found, after a few encounters, to be preëminently desirable.

In midsummer White Fang had an experience. Trotting along in his silent way to investigate a new tepee which had been erected on the edge of the village while he was away with the hunters after moose, he came full upon Kiche. He paused and looked at her. He remembered her vaguely, but he *remembered* her, and that was more than could be said for her. She lifted her lip at him in the old snarl of menace, and his memory became clear. His forgotten cubhood, all that was associated with that familiar snarl, rushed back to him. Before he had known the gods, she had been to him the centre-pin of the universe. The old familiar feelings of that time came back upon him, surged up within him. He bounded toward her joyously, and she met him with shrewd fangs that laid his cheek open to the bone. He did not understand. He backed away, bewildered and puzzled.

But it was not Kiche's fault. A wolf-mother was not made to remember her cubs of a year or so before. So she did not remember

White Fang. He was a strange animal, an intruder; and her present litter of puppies gave her the right to resent such intrusion.

One of the puppies sprawled up to White Fang. They were half-brothers, only they did not know it. White Fang sniffed the puppy curiously, whereupon Kiche rushed upon him, gashing his face a second time. He backed farther away. All the old memories and associations died down again and passed into the grave from which they had been resurrected. He looked at Kiche licking her puppy and stopping now and then to snarl at him. She was without value to him. He had learned to get along without her. Her meaning was forgotten. There was no place for her in his scheme of things, as there was no place for him in hers.

He was still standing, stupid and bewildered, the memories forgotten, wondering what it was all about, when Kiche attacked him a third time, intent on driving him away altogether from the vicinity. And White Fang allowed himself to be driven away. This was a female of his kind, and it was a law of his kind that the males must not fight the females. He did not know anything about this law, for it was no generalization of the mind, not a something acquired by experience in the world. He knew it as a secret prompting, as an urge of instinct—of the same instinct that made him howl at the moon and stars of nights and that made him fear death and the unknown.

The months went by. White Fang grew stronger, heavier, and more compact, while his character was developing along the lines laid down by his heredity and his environment. His heredity was a life-stuff that may be likened to clay. It possessed many possibilities, was capable of being moulded into many different forms. Environment served to model the clay, to give it a particular form. Thus, had White Fang never come in to the fires of man, the Wild would have moulded him into a true wolf. But the gods had given him a different environment, and he was moulded into a dog that was rather wolfish, but that was a dog and not a wolf.

And so, according to the clay of his nature and the pressure of his surroundings, his character was being moulded into a certain particular shape. There was no escaping it. He was becoming more morose, more uncompanionable, more solitary, more ferocious; while the dogs were learning more and more that it was better to be at peace with him than at war, and Gray Beaver was coming to prize him more greatly with the passage of each day.

White Fang, seeming to sum up strength in all his qualities, nevertheless suffered from one besetting weakness. He could not stand being laughed at. The laughter of men was a hateful thing. They might laugh among themselves about anything they pleased except himself, and he did not mind. But the moment laughter was turned upon him he would fly into a most terrible rage. Grave, dignified, sombre, a laugh made him frantic to ridiculousness. It so outraged him and upset him that for hours he would behave like a demon. And woe to the dog that at such times ran foul of him. He knew the law too well to take it out on Gray Beaver; behind Gray Beaver were a club and god-head. But behind the dogs there was nothing but space, and into this space they fled when White Fang came on the scene, made mad by laughter.

In the third year of his life there came a great famine to the Mackenzie Indians. In the summer the fish failed. In the winter the cariboo forsook their accustomed track. Moose were scarce, the rabbits almost disappeared, hunting and preying animals perished. Denied their usual food-supply, weakened by hunger, they fell upon and devoured one another. Only the strong survived. White Fang's gods were also hunting animals. The old and the weak of them died of hunger. There was wailing in the village, where the women and children went without in order that what little they had might go into the bellies of the lean and hollow-eyed hunters who trod the forest in the vain pursuit of meat.

To such extremity were the gods driven that they ate the soft-tanned leather of their moccasins and mittens, while the dogs ate the harnesses off their backs and the very whip-lashes. Also, the dogs ate one another, and also the gods ate the dogs. The weakest and the more worthless were eaten first. The dogs that still lived, looked on and understood. A few of the boldest and wisest forsook the fires of the gods, which had now become a shambles, and fled into the forest, where, in the end, they starved to death or were eaten by wolves.

In this time of misery, White Fang, too, stole away into the woods. He was better fitted for the life than the other dogs, for he had the training of his cubhood to guide him. Especially adept did he become in stalking small living things. He would lie concealed for hours, following every movement of a cautious tree-squirrel, waiting, with a patience as huge as the hunger he suffered from, until the squirrel ventured out upon the ground. Even then, White Fang was not premature. He waited until he was sure of striking before the squirrel could gain a tree-refuge. Then, and not until then, would he flash from his hiding-place, a gray projectile, incredibly swift, never failing its mark—the fleeing squirrel that fled not fast enough.

Successful as he was with squirrels, there was one difficulty that prevented him from living and growing fat on them. There were not enough squirrels. So he was driven to hunt still smaller things. So acute did his hunger become at times that he was not above rooting out wood-mice from their burrows in the ground. Nor did he scorn to do battle with a weasel as hungry as himself and many times more ferocious.

In the worst pinches of the famine he stole back to the fires of the gods. But he did not go in to the fires. He lurked in the forest, avoiding discovery and robbing the snares at the rare intervals when game was caught. He even robbed Gray Beaver's snare of a rabbit at a time when Gray Beaver staggered and tottered through the forest, sitting down often to rest, what of weakness and of shortness of breath.

One day White Fang encountered a young wolf, gaunt and scrawny, loose-jointed with famine. Had he not been hungry himself, White Fang might have gone with him and eventually found his way into the pack amongst his wild brethren. As it was, he ran the young wolf down and killed and ate him.

Fortune seemed to favour him. Always, when hardest pressed for food, he found something to kill. Again, when he was weak, it was his luck that none of the larger preying animals chanced upon him. Thus, he was strong from the two days' eating a lynx had afforded him, when the hungry wolf-pack ran full tilt upon him. It was a long, cruel chase, but he was better nourished than they, and in the end outran them. And not only did he outrun them, but, circling widely back on his track, he gathered in one of his exhausted pursuers.

After that he left that part of the country and journeyed over to the valley wherein he had been born. Here, in the old lair, he encountered Kiche. Up to her old tricks, she, too, had fled the inhospitable fires of the gods and gone back to her old refuge to give birth to her young. Of this litter but one remained alive when White Fang came upon the scene, and this one was not destined to live long. Young life had little chance in such a famine.

Kiche's greeting of her grown son was anything but affectionate. But White Fang did not mind. He had outgrown his mother. So he turned tail philosophically and trotted on up the stream. At the forks he took the turning to the left, where he found the lair of the lynx with whom his mother and he had fought long before. Here, in the abandoned lair, he settled down and rested for a day.

During the early summer, in the last days of the famine, he met Lip-lip, who had likewise taken to the woods, where he had eked out a miserable existence. White Fang came upon him unexpectedly. Trotting in opposite directions along the base of a high bluff, they rounded a corner of rock and found themselves face to face. They paused with instant alarm, and looked at each other suspiciously.

White Fang was in splendid condition. His hunting had been good, and for a week he had eaten his fill. He was even gorged from his latest kill. But in the moment he looked at Lip-lip his hair rose on end all along his back. It was an involuntary bristling on his part, the physical state that in the past had always accompanied the mental state produced in him by Lip-lip's bullying and persecution. As in the past he had bristled and snarled at sight of Lip-lip, so now, and automatically, he bristled and snarled. He did not waste any time. The thing was done thoroughly and with dispatch. Lip-lip essayed to back away, but White Fang struck him hard, shoulder to shoulder. Lip-lip was overthrown and rolled upon his back. White Fang's teeth drove into the scrawny throat. There was a death-struggle, during which White Fang walked around, stiff-legged and observant. Then he resumed his course and trotted on along the base of the bluff.

One day, not long after, he came to the edge of the forest, where a narrow stretch of open land sloped down to the Mackenzie. He had been over this ground before, when it was bare, but now a village occupied it. Still hidden amongst the trees, he paused to study the situation. Sights and sounds and scents were familiar to him. It was the old village changed to a new place. But sights and sounds and smells were different from those he had last had when he fled away from it. There was no whimpering nor wailing. Contented sounds saluted his ear, and when he heard the angry voice of a woman he knew it to be the anger that proceeds from a full stomach. And there was a smell in the air of fish. There was food. The famine was gone. He came out boldly from the forest and trotted into camp straight to Gray Beaver's tepee. Gray Beaver was not there; but Kloo-kooch welcomed him with glad cries and the whole of a fresh-caught fish, and he lay down to wait Gray Beaver's coming.

# PART FOUR

# THE SUPERIOR GODS

## CHAPTER 1

## THE ENEMY OF HIS KIND

Had there been in White Fang's nature any possibility, no matter how remote, of his ever coming to fraternise with his kind, such possibility was irretrievably destroyed when he was made leader of the sled-team. For now the dogs hated him—hated him for the extra meat bestowed upon him by Mit-sah; hated him for all the real and fancied favours he received; hated him for that he fled always at the head of the team, his waving brush of a tail and his perpetually retreating hind-quarters forever maddening their eyes.

And White Fang just as bitterly hated them back. Being sled-leader was anything but gratifying to him. To be compelled to run away before the yelling pack, every dog of which, for three years, he had thrashed and mastered, was almost more than he could endure. But endure it he must, or perish, and the life that was in him had no desire to perish. The moment Mit-sah gave his order for the start, that moment the whole team, with eager, savage cries, sprang forward at White Fang.

There was no defence for him. If he turned upon them, Mit-sah would throw the stinging lash of the whip into his face. Only remained to him to run away. He could not encounter that howling horde with his tail and hind-quarters. These were scarcely fit weapons with which to meet the many merciless fangs. So run away he did, violating his own nature and pride with every leap he made, and leaping all day long.

One cannot violate the promptings of one's nature without having that nature recoil upon itself. Such a recoil is like that of a hair, made to grow out from the body, turning unnaturally upon the direction of its growth and growing into the body—a rankling, festering thing of hurt. And so with White Fang. Every urge of his being impelled him to spring upon the pack that cried at his heels, but it was the will of the gods that this should not be; and behind the will, to enforce it, was the whip of cariboo-gut with its biting thirty-foot lash. So White Fang could only eat his heart in bitterness and develop a hatred and malice commensurate with the ferocity and indomitability of his nature.

If ever a creature was the enemy of its kind, White Fang was that creature. He asked no quarter, gave none. He was continually marred and scarred by the teeth of the pack, and as continually he left his own marks upon the pack. Unlike most leaders, who, when camp was made and the dogs were unhitched, huddled near to the gods for protection, White Fang disdained such protection. He walked boldly about the camp, inflicting punishment in the night for what he had suffered in the day. In the time before he was made leader of the team, the pack had learned to get out of his way. But now it was different. Excited by the day-long pursuit of him, swayed subconsciously by the insistent iteration on their brains of the sight of him fleeing away, mastered by the feeling of mastery enjoyed all day, the dogs could not bring themselves to give way to him. When he appeared amongst them, there was always a squabble. His progress was marked by snarl and snap and growl. The very atmosphere he breathed was surcharged with hatred and malice, and this but served to increase the hatred and malice within him.

When Mit-sah cried out his command for the team to stop, White Fang obeyed. At first this caused trouble for the other dogs. All of them would spring upon the hated leader, only to find the tables turned. Behind him would be Mit-sah, the great whip singing in his hand. So the dogs came to understand that when the team stopped by order, White Fang was to be let alone. But when White Fang stopped without orders, then it was allowed them to spring upon him and destroy him if they could. After several experiences, White Fang never stopped without orders. He learned quickly. It was in the nature of things that he must learn quickly, if he were to survive the unusually severe conditions under which life was vouchsafed him.

But the dogs could never learn the lesson to leave him alone in camp. Each day, pursuing him and crying defiance at him, the lesson of the previous night was erased, and that night would have to be learned over again, to be as immediately forgotten. Besides, there was a greater consistence in their dislike of him. They sensed between themselves and him a difference of kind—cause sufficient in itself for hostility. Like him, they were domesticated wolves. But they had been domesticated for generations. Much of the Wild had been lost, so that to them the Wild was the unknown, the terrible, the ever menacing and ever warring. But to him, in appearance and action and impulse, still clung the Wild. He symbolized it, was its personification; so that when they showed their teeth to him they were defending themselves against the powers of destruction that lurked in the shadows of the forest and in the dark beyond the camp-fire.

But there was one lesson the dogs did learn, and that was to keep together. White Fang was too terrible for any of them to face single-handed. They met him with the mass-formation, otherwise he would have killed them, one by one, in a night. As it was, he never had a chance to kill them. He might roll a dog off its feet, but the pack would be upon him before he could follow up and deliver the deadly throat-stroke. At the first hint of conflict, the whole team drew together and faced him. The dogs had quarrels among themselves, but these were forgotten when trouble was brewing with White Fang.

On the other hand, try as they would, they could not kill White Fang. He was too quick for them, too formidable, too wise. He avoided tight places and always backed out of it when they bade fair to surround him. While, as for getting him off his feet, there was no dog among them capable of doing the trick. His feet clung to the earth with the same tenacity that he clung to life. For that matter, life and footing were synonymous in this unending warfare with the pack, and none knew it better than White Fang.

So he became the enemy of his kind, domesticated wolves that they were, softened by the fires of man, weakened in the sheltering shadow of man's strength. White Fang was bitter and implacable. The clay of him was so moulded. He declared a vendetta against all dogs. And so terribly did he live this vendetta that Gray Beaver, fierce savage himself, could not but marvel at White Fang's ferocity. Never, he swore, had there been the like of this animal; and the Indians in strange villages swore likewise when they considered the tale of his killings amongst their dogs.

When White Fang was nearly five years old, Gray Beaver took him on another great journey, and long remembered was the havoc he worked amongst the dogs of the many villages along the Mackenzie, across the Rockies, and down the Porcupine to the Yukon. He revelled in the vengeance he wreaked upon his kind. They were ordinary, unsuspecting dogs. They were not prepared for his swiftness and directness, for his attack without warning. They did not know him for what he was, a lightning-flash of slaughter. They bristled up to him, stiff-legged and challenging, while he, wasting no time on elaborate preliminaries, snapping into action like a steel spring, was at their throats and destroying them before they knew what was happening and while they were yet in the throes of surprise.

He became an adept at fighting. He economized. He never wasted his strength, never tussled. He was in too quickly for that, and, if he missed, was out again too quickly. The dislike of the wolf for close quarters was his to an unusual degree. He could not endure a prolonged contact with another body. It smacked of danger. It made him frantic. He must be away, free, on his own legs, touching no living thing. It was the Wild still clinging to him, asserting itself through him. This feeling had been accentuated by the Ishmaelite life he had led from his puppyhood. Danger lurked in contacts. It was the trap, ever the trap, the fear of it lurking deep in the life of him, woven into the fibre of him.

In consequence, the strange dogs he encountered had no chance against him. He eluded their fangs. He got them, or got away, himself untouched in either event. In the natural course of things there were exceptions to this. There were times when several dogs, pitching on to him, punished him before he could get away; and there were times when a single dog scored deeply on him. But these were accidents. In the main, so efficient a fighter had he become, he went his way unscathed.

Another advantage he possessed was that of correctly judging time and distance. Not that he did this consciously, however. He did not calculate such things. It was all automatic. His eyes saw correctly, and the nerves carried the vision correctly to his brain. The parts of him were better adjusted than those of the average dog. They worked together more smoothly and steadily. His was a better, far better, nervous, mental, and muscular coordination. When his eyes conveyed to his brain the moving image of an action, his brain, without conscious effort, knew the space that limited that action and the time required for its completion. Thus, he could avoid the leap of another dog, or the drive of its fangs, and at the same moment could seize the infinitesimal fraction of time in which to deliver his own attack. Body and brain, his was a more perfected mechanism. Not that he was to be praised for it. Nature had been more generous to him than to the average animal, that was all.

It was in the summer that White Fang arrived at Fort Yukon. * Gray Beaver had crossed the great water-shed between the Mackenzie and the Yukon in the later winter, and spent the spring in hunting among the western outlying spurs of the Rockies. Then, after the break-up of the ice on the Porcupine, he had built a canoe and paddled down that stream to where it effected its junction with the Yukon just under the Arctic Circle. Here stood the old Hudson's Bay Company fort; and here were many Indians, much food, and unprecedented excitement. It was the summer of 1898, and thousands of gold-hunters were going up the Yukon to Dawson and the Klondike. Still hundreds of miles from their goal, nevertheless many of them had been on the way for a year, and the least any of them had travelled to get that far was five thousand miles, while some had come from the other side of the world.

Here Gray Beaver stopped. A whisper of the gold-rush had reached his ears, and he had come with several bales of furs, and another of gut-sewn mittens and moccasins. He would not have ventured so long a trip had he not expected generous profits. But what he had expected was nothing to what he realized. His wildest dream had not exceeded a hundred per cent profit; he made a thousand per cent. And, like a true Indian, he settled down to trade carefully and slowly, even if it took all summer and the rest of the winter to dispose of his goods.

It was at Fort Yukon that White Fang saw his first white men. As compared with the Indians he had known, they were to him another race of beings, a race of superior gods. They impressed him as possessing superior power, and it is on power that god-head rests. White Fang did not reason it out, did not in his mind make the sharp generalization that the white gods were more powerful. It was a feeling, nothing more, and yet none the less potent. As, in his puppyhood, the looming bulks of the tepees, man-reared, had affected him as manifestations of power, so was he affected now by the houses and the huge fort all of massive logs. Here was power. Those white gods were strong. They possessed greater mastery over matter than the gods he had known, most powerful among which was Gray Beaver. And yet Gray Beaver was as a child-god among these white-skinned ones.

To be sure, White Fang only felt these things. He was not conscious of them. Yet it is upon feeling, more often than thinking, that animals act; and every act White Fang now performed was based upon the feeling that the white men were the superior gods. In the first place he was very suspicious of them. There was no telling what unknown terrors were theirs, what unknown hurts they could administer. He was curious to observe them, fearful of being noticed by them. For the first few hours he was content with slinking around and watching them from a safe distance. Then he saw that no harm befell the dogs that were near to them, and he came in closer.

In turn, he was an object of great curiosity to them. His wolfish appearance caught their eyes at once, and they pointed him out to one another. This act of pointing put White Fang on his guard, and when they tried to approach him he showed his teeth and backed away. Not one succeeded in laying a hand on him, and it was well that they did not.

White Fang soon learned that very few of these gods—not more than a dozen—lived at this place. Every two or three days a steamer (another and colossal manifestation of power) came in to the bank and stopped for several hours. The white men came from off these steamers and went away on them again. There seemed untold numbers of these white men. In the first day or so, he saw more of them than he had seen Indians in all his life; and as the days went by they continued to come up the river, stop, and then go on up the river and out of sight.

But if the white gods were all-powerful, their dogs did not amount to much. This White Fang quickly discovered by mixing with those that came ashore with their masters. They were of irregular shapes and sizes. Some were short-legged—too short; others were long-legged—too long. They had hair instead of fur, and a few had very little hair at that. And none of them knew how to fight.

As an enemy of his kind, it was in White Fang's province to fight with them. This he did, and he quickly achieved for them a mighty contempt. They were soft and helpless, made much noise, and floundered around clumsily, trying to accomplish by main strength what he accomplished by dexterity and cunning. They rushed bellowing at him. He sprang to the side. They did not know what had become of him; and in that moment he struck them on the shoulder, rolling them off their feet and delivering his stroke at the throat.

Sometimes this stroke was successful, and a stricken dog rolled in the dirt, to be pounced upon and torn to pieces by the pack of Indian dogs that waited. White Fang was wise. He had long since learned that the gods were made angry when their dogs were killed. The white men were no exception to this. So he was content, when he had overthrown and slashed wide the throat of one of their dogs, to drop back and let the pack go in and do the cruel finishing work. It was then that the white men rushed in, visiting their wrath heavily on the pack, while White Fang went free. He would stand off at little distance and look on, while stones, clubs, axes, and all sorts of weapons fell upon his fellows. White Fang was very wise.

But his fellows grew wise, in their own way; and in this White Fang grew wise with them. They learned that it was when a steamer first tied to the bank that they had their fun. After the first two or three strange dogs had been downed and destroyed, the white men hustled their own animals back on board and wreaked savage vengeance on the offenders. One white man, having seen his dog, a setter, torn to pieces before his eyes, drew a revolver. He fired rapidly, six times, and six of the pack lay dead or dying—another manifestation of power that sank deep into White Fang's consciousness.

White Fang enjoyed it all. He did not love his kind, and he was shrewd enough to escape hurt himself. At first, the killing of the white men's dogs had been a diversion. After a time it became his occupation. There was no work for him to do. Gray Beaver was busy trading and getting wealthy. So White Fang hung around the landing with the disreputable gang of Indian dogs, waiting for steamers. With the arrival of a steamer the fun began. After a few minutes, by the time the white men had got over their surprise, the gang scattered. The fun was over until the next steamer should arrive.

But it can scarcely be said that White Fang was a member of the gang. He did not mingle with it, but remained aloof, always himself, and was even feared by it. It is true, he worked with it. He picked the quarrel with the strange dog while the gang waited. And when he had overthrown the strange dog the gang went in to finish it. But it is equally true that he then withdrew, leaving the gang to receive the punishment of the outraged gods.

It did not require much exertion to pick these quarrels. All he had to do, when the strange dogs came ashore, was to show himself. When they saw him they rushed for him. It was their instinct. He was the Wild—the unknown, the terrible, the ever menacing, the thing that prowled in the darkness around the fires of the primeval world when they, cowering close to the fires, were reshaping their instincts, learning to fear the Wild out of which they had come, and which they had deserted and betrayed. Generation by generation, down all the generations, had this fear of the Wild been stamped into their natures. For centuries the Wild had stood for terror and destruction. And during all this time free license had been theirs, from their masters, to kill the things of the Wild. In doing this they had protected both themselves and the gods whose companionship they shared.

And so, fresh from the soft southern world, these dogs, trotting down the gangplank and out upon the Yukon shore, had but to see White Fang to experience the irresistible impulse to rush upon him and destroy him. They might be town-reared dogs, but the instinctive fear of the Wild was theirs just the same. Not alone with their own eyes did they see the wolfish creature in the clear light of day, standing before them. They saw him with the eyes of their ancestors, and by their inherited memory they knew White Fang for the wolf, and they remembered the ancient feud.

All of which served to make White Fang's days enjoyable. If the sight of him drove these strange dogs upon him, so much the better for him, so much the worse for them. They looked upon him as legitimate prey, and as legitimate prey he looked upon them.

Not for nothing had he first seen the light of day in a lonely lair and fought his first fights with the ptarmigan, the weasel, and the lynx. And not for nothing had his puppyhood been made bitter by the persecution of Lip-lip and the whole puppy-pack. It might have been otherwise, and he would then have been otherwise. Had Lip-lip not existed, he would have passed his puppyhood with the other puppies and grown up more doglike and with more liking for dogs. Had Gray Beaver possessed the plummet of affection and love, he might have sounded the deeps of White Fang's nature and brought up to the surface all manner of kindly qualities. But these things had not been so. The clay of White Fang had been moulded until he became what he was, morose and lonely, unloving and ferocious, the enemy of all his kind.

# CHAPTER 2

# THE MAD GOD

A small number of white men lived in Fort Yukon. These men had been long in the country. They called themselves Sour-doughs, and took great pride in so classifying themselves. For other men, new in the land, they felt nothing but disdain. The men who came ashore from the steamers were newcomers. They were known as *chechaquos*, and they always wilted at the application of the name. They made their bread with bakingpowder. This was the invidious distinction between them and the Sour-doughs, who, forsooth, made their bread from sour-dough because they had no bakingpowder.

All of which is neither here nor there. The men in the fort disdained the newcomers and enjoyed seeing them come to grief. Especially did they enjoy the havoc worked amongst the newcomers' dogs by White Fang and his disreputable gang. When a steamer arrived, the men of the fort made it a point always to come down to the bank and see the fun. They looked forward to it with as much anticipation as did the Indian dogs, while they were not slow to appreciate the savage and crafty part played by White Fang.

But there was one man amongst them who particularly enjoyed the sport. He would come running at the first sound of a steamboat's whistle; and when the last fight was over and White Fang and the pack had scattered, he would return slowly to the fort, his face heavy with regret. Sometimes, when a soft Southland dog went down, shrieking its deathcry under the fangs of the pack, this man would be unable to contain himself, and would leap into the air and cry out with delight. And always he had a sharp and covetous eye for White Fang.

This man was called "Beauty" by the other men of the fort. No one knew his first name, and in general he was known in the country as Beauty Smith. But he was anything save a beauty. To antithesis was due his naming. He was preëminently unbeautiful. Nature had been niggardly with him. He was a small man to begin with; and upon his meagre frame was deposited an even more strikingly meagre head.

Its apex might be likened to a point. In fact, in his boyhood, before he had been named Beauty by his fellows, he had been called "Pinhead."

Backward, from the apex, his head slanted down to his neck; and forward, it slanted uncompromisingly to meet a low and remarkably wide forehead. Beginning here, as though regretting her parsimony, Nature had spread his features with a lavish hand. His eyes were large, and between them was the distance of two eyes. His face, in relation to the rest of him, was prodigious. In order to discover the necessary area, Nature had given him an enormous prognathous jaw. It was wide and heavy, and protruded outward and down until it seemed to rest on his chest. Possibly this appearance was due to the weariness of the slender neck, unable properly to support so great a burden.

This jaw gave the impression of ferocious determination. But something lacked. Perhaps it was from excess. Perhaps the jaw was too large. At any rate, it was a lie. Beauty Smith was known far and wide as the weakest of weak-kneed and snivelling cowards. To complete his description, his teeth were large and yellow, while the two eye-teeth, larger than their fellows, showed under his lean lips like fangs. His eyes were yellow and muddy, as though Nature had run short on pigments and squeezed together the dregs of all her tubes. It was the same with his hair, sparse and irregular of growth, muddy-yellow and dirty-yellow, rising on his head and sprouting out of his face in unexpected tufts and bunches, in appearance like clumped and windblown grain.

In short, Beauty Smith was a monstrosity, and the blame of it lay elsewhere. He was not responsible. The day of him had been so moulded in the making. He did the cooking for the other men in the fort, the dishwashing and the drudgery. They did not despise him. Rather did they tolerate him in a broad human way, as one tolerates any creature evilly treated in the making. Also, they feared him. His cowardly rages made them dread a shot in the back or poison in their coffee. But somebody had to do the cooking, and whatever else his shortcomings, Beauty Smith could cook.

This was the man that looked at White Fang, delighted in his ferocious prowess, and desired to possess him. He made overtures to White Fang from the first. White Fang began by ignoring him. Later on, when the overtures became more insistent, White Fang bristled and bared his teeth and backed away. He did not like the man. The feel of him was bad. He sensed the evil in him, and feared the extended hand and the attempts at softspoken speech. Because of all this, he hated the man.

With the simpler creatures, good and bad are things simply understood. The good stands for all things that bring easement and satisfaction and surcease from pain. Therefore, the good is liked. The bad stands for all things that are fraught with discomfort, menace, and hurt, and is hated accordingly. White Fang's feel of Beauty Smith was bad. From the man's distorted body and twisted mind, in occult ways, like mists rising from malarial marshes, came emanations of the unhealth within. Not by reasoning, not by the five senses alone, but by other and remoter and uncharted senses, came the feeling to White Fang that the man was ominous with evil, pregnant with hurtfulness, and therefore a thing bad, and wisely to be hated.

White Fang was in Gray Beaver's camp when Beauty Smith first visited it. At the faint sound of his distant feet, before he came in sight, White Fang knew who was coming and began to bristle. He had been lying down in an abandon of comfort, but he arose quickly, and, as the man arrived, slid away in true wolf-fashion to the edge of the camp. He did not know what they said, but he could see the man and Gray Beaver talking together. Once, the man pointed at him, and White Fang snarled back as though the hand were just descending upon him instead of being, as it was, fifty feet away. The man laughed at this; and White Fang slunk away to the sheltering woods, his head turned to observe as he glided softly over the ground.

Gray Beaver refused to sell the dog. He had grown rich with his trading and stood in need of nothing. Besides, White Fang was a valuable animal, the strongest sled-dog he had ever owned, and the best leader. Furthermore, there was no dog like him on the Mackenzie nor the Yukon. He could fight. He killed other dogs as easily as men killed mosquitoes. (Beauty Smith's eyes lighted up at this, and he licked his thin lips with an eager tongue.) No, White Fang was not for sale at any price.

But Beauty Smith knew the ways of Indians. He visited Gray Beaver's camp often, and hidden under his coat was always a black bottle or so. One of the potencies of whiskey is the breeding of thirst. Gray Beaver got the thirst. His fevered membranes and burnt stomach began to clamour for more and more of the scorching fluid; while his brain, thrust all awry by the unwonted stimulant, permitted him to go any length to obtain it. The money he had received for his furs and mittens and moccasins began to go. It went faster and faster, and the shorter his money-sack grew, the shorter grew his temper.

In the end his money and goods and temper were all gone. Nothing remained to him but his thirst, a prodigious possession in itself that grew more prodigious with every sober breath he drew. Then it was that Beauty Smith had talk with him again about the sale of White Fang; but this time the price offered was in bottles, not dollars, and Gray Beaver's ears were more eager to hear.

"You ketch 'um dog you take 'um all right," was his last word.

The bottles were delivered, but after two days, "You ketch 'um dog," were Beauty Smith's words to Gray Beaver.

White Fang slunk into camp one evening and dropped down with a sigh of content. The dreaded white god was not there. For days his manifestations of desire to lay hands on him had been growing more insistent, and during that time White Fang had been compelled to avoid the camp. He did not know what evil was threatened by those insistent hands. He knew only that they did threaten evil of some sort, and that it was best for him to keep out of their reach.

But scarcely had he lain down when Gray Beaver staggered over to him and tied a leather thong around his neck. He sat down beside White Fang, holding the end of the thong in his hand. In the other hand he held a bottle, which, from time to time, was inverted above his head to the accompaniment of gurgling noises.

An hour of this passed, when the vibrations of feet in contact with the ground foreran the one who approached. White Fang heard it first, and he was bristling with recognition while Gray Beaver still nodded stupidly. White Fang tried to draw the thong softly out of his master's hand; but the relaxed fingers closed tightly and Gray Beaver roused himself.

Beauty Smith strode into camp and stood over White Fang. He snarled softly up at the thing of fear, watching keenly the deportment of the hands. One hand extended outward and began to descend upon his head. His soft snarl grew tense and harsh. The hand continued slowly to descend, while he crouched beneath it, eyeing it malignantly, his snarl growing shorter and shorter as, with quickening breath, it approached its culmination. Suddenly he snapped, striking with his fangs like a snake. The hand was jerked back, and the teeth came together emptily with a sharp click. Beauty Smith was frightened and angry. Gray Beaver clouted White Fang alongside the head, so that he cowered down close to the earth in respectful obedience.

White Fang's suspicious eyes followed every movement. He saw Beauty Smith go away and return with a stout club. Then the end of the thong was given over to him by Gray Beaver. Beauty Smith started to walk away. The thong grew taut. White Fang resisted it. Gray Beaver clouted him right and left to make him get up and follow. He obeyed, but with a rush, hurling himself upon the stranger who was dragging him away. Beauty Smith did not jump away. He had been waiting for this. He swung the club smartly, stopping the rush midway and smashing White Fang down upon the ground. Gray Beaver laughed and. nodded approval. Beauty Smith tightened the thong again, and White Fang crawled limply and dizzily to his feet.

He did not rush a second time. One smash from the club was sufficient to convince him that the white god knew how to handle it, and he was too wise to fight the inevitable. So he followed morosely at Beauty Smith's heels, his tail between his legs, yet snarling softly under his breath. But Beauty Smith kept a wary eye on him, and the club was held always ready to strike.

At the fort Beauty Smith left him securely tied and went in to bed. White Fang waited an hour. Then he applied his teeth to the thong, and in the space of ten seconds was free. He had wasted no time with his teeth. There had been no useless gnawing. The thong was cut across, diagonally, almost, as clean as though done by a knife. White Fang looked up at the fort, at the same time bristling and growling. Then he turned and trotted back to Gray Beaver's camp. He owed no allegiance to this strange and terrible god. He had given himself to Gray Beaver, and to Gray Beaver he considered he still belonged.

But what had occurred before was repeated—with a difference. Gray Beaver again made him fast with a thong, and in the morning turned him over to Beauty Smith. And here was where the difference came in. Beauty Smith gave him a beating. Tied securely, White Fang could only rage futilely and endure the punishment. Club and whip were both used upon him, and he experienced the worst beating he had ever received in his life. Even the big beating given him in his puppyhood by Gray Beaver was mild compared with this.

Beauty Smith enjoyed the task. He delighted in it. He gloated over his victim, and his eyes flamed dully, as he swung the whip or club and listened to White Fang's cries of pain and to his helpless bellows and snarls. For Beauty Smith was cruel in the way that cowards are cruel. Cringing and snivelling himself before the blows or angry speech of a man, he revenged himself, in turn, upon creatures weaker than he. All life likes power, and Beauty Smith was no exception. Denied the expression of power amongst his own kind, he fell back upon the lesser creatures and there vindicated the life that was in him. But Beauty Smith had not created himself, and no blame was to be attached to him. He had come into the world with a twisted body and a brute intelligence. This had constituted the clay of him, and it had not been kindly moulded by the world.

White Fang knew why he was being beaten. When Gray Beaver tied the thong around his neck, and passed the end of the thong into Beauty Smith's keeping, White Fang knew that it was his god's will for him to go with Beauty Smith. And when Beauty Smith left him tied outside the fort, he knew that it was Beauty Smith's will that he should remain there. Therefore, he had disobeyed the will of both the gods, and earned the consequent punishment. He had seen dogs change owners in the past, and he had seen the runaways beaten as he was being beaten. He was wise, and yet in the nature of him there were forces greater than wisdom. One of these was fidelity. He did not love Gray Beaver; yet, even in the face of his will and his anger, he was faithful to him. He could not help it. This faithfulness was a quality of the clay that composed him. It was the quality that was peculiarly the possession of his kind; the quality that set apart his species from all other species; the quality that had enabled the wolf and the. wild dog to come in from the open and be the companions of man.

After the beating, White Fang was dragged back to the fort. But this time Beauty Smith left him tied with a stick. One does not give up a god easily, and so with White Fang. Gray Beaver was his own particular god, and, in spite of Gray Beaver's will, White Fang still clung to him and would not give him up. Gray Beaver had betrayed and forsaken him, but that had no effect upon him. Not for nothing had he surrendered himself body and soul to Gray Beaver. There had been no reservation on White Fang's part, and the bond was not to be broken easily.

So, in the night, when the men in the fort were asleep, White Fang applied his teeth to the stick that held him. The wood was seasoned and dry, and it was tied so closely to his neck that he could scarcely get his teeth to it. It was only by the severest muscular exertion and neck-arching that he succeeded in getting the wood between his teeth, and barely between his teeth at that; and it was only by the exercise of an immense patience, extending through many hours, that he succeeded in gnawing through the stick. This was something that dogs were not supposed to do. It was unprecedented. But White Fang did it, trotting away from the fort in the early morning, with the end of the stick hanging to his neck.

He was wise. But had he been merely wise he would not have gone back to Gray Beaver, who had already twice betrayed him. But there was his faithfulness, and he went back to be betrayed yet a third time. Again he yielded to the tying of a thong around his neck by Gray Beaver, and again Beauty Smith came to claim him. And this time he was beaten even more severely than before.

Gray Beaver looked on stolidly while the white man wielded the whip. He gave no protection. It was no longer his dog. When the beating was over White Fang was sick. A soft Southland dog would have died under it, but not he. His school of life had been sterner, and he was himself of sterner stuff. He had too great vitality. His clutch on life was too strong. But he was very sick. At first he was unable to drag himself along, and Beauty Smith had to wait half an hour on him. And then, blind and reeling, he followed at Beauty Smith's heels back to the fort.

But now he was tied with a chain that defied his teeth, and he strove in vain, by lunging, to draw the staple from the timber into which it was driven. After a few days, sober and bankrupt, Gray Beaver departed up the Porcupine on his long journey to the Mackenzie. White Fang remained on the Yukon, the property of a man more than half mad and all brute. But what is a dog to know in its consciousness of madness? To White Fang, Beauty Smith was a veritable, if terrible, god. He was a mad god at best, but White Fang knew nothing of madness; he knew only that he must submit to the will of this new master, obey his every whim and fancy.

## CHAPTER 3

# THE REIGN OF HATE

Under the tutelage of the mad god, White Fang became 2 fiend. He was kept chained in a pen at the rear of the fort and here Beauty Smith teased and irritated and drove him wild with petty torments. The man early discovered White Fang's susceptibility to laughter, and made it a point, after painfully tricking him, to laugh at him. This laughter was uproarious and scornful, and at the same time the god pointed his finger derisively at White Fang. At such times reason fled from White Fang, and in his transports of rage he was even more mad than Beauty Smith.

Formerly, White Fang had been merely the enemy of his kind, withal a ferocious enemy. He now became the enemy of all things, and more ferocious than ever. To such an extent was he. tormented, that he hated blindly and without the faintest spark of reason. He hated the chain that bound him, the men who peered in at him through the slats of the pen, the dogs that accompanied the men and that snarled malignantly at him in his helplessness. He hated the very wood of the pen that confined him. And first, last, and most of all, he hated Beauty Smith.

But Beauty Smith had a purpose in all that he did to White Fang. One day a number of men gathered about the pen. Beauty Smith entered, club in hand, and took the chain from off White Fang's neck. When his master had gone out, White Fang turned loose and tore around the pen, trying to get at the men outside. He was magnificently terrible. Fully five feet in length, and standing two and one-half feet at the shoulder, he far outweighed a wolf of corresponding size. From his mother he had inherited the heavier proportions of the dog, so that he weighed, without any fat and without an ounce of superfluous flesh, over ninety pounds. It was all muscle, bone, and sinew—fighting flesh in the finest condition.

The door of the pen was being opened again. White Fang paused. Something unusual was happening. He waited. The door was opened wider. Then a huge dog was thrust inside, and the door was slammed shut behind him. White Fang had never seen such a dog (it was a mastiff); but the size and fierce aspect of the intruder did not deter him. Here was something, not wood nor iron, upon which to wreak his hate. He leaped in with a flash of fangs that ripped down the side of the mastiff's neck. The mastiff shook his head, growled hoarsely, and plunged at White Fang. But White Fang was here, there, and everywhere, always evading and eluding, and always leaping in and slashing with his fangs and leaping out again in time to escape punishment.

The men outside shouted and applauded, while Beauty Smith, in an ecstasy of delight, gloated over the ripping and mangling performed by White Fang. There was no hope for the mastiff from the first. He was too ponderous and slow. In the end, while Beauty Smith beat White Fang back with a club, the mastiff was dragged out by its owner. Then there was a payment of bets, and money clinked in Beauty Smith's hand.

White Fang came to look forward eagerly to the gathering of the men around his pen. It meant a fight; and this was the only way that was now vouchsafed him of expressing the life that was in him. Tormented, incited to hate, he was kept a prisoner so that there was no way of satisfying that hate except at the times his master saw fit to put another dog against him. Beauty Smith had estimated his powers well, for he was invariably the victor. One day, three dogs were turned in upon him in succession. Another day, a fullgrown wolf, fresh-caught from the Wild, was shoved in through the door of the pen. And on still another day two dogs were set against him at the same time. This was his severest fight, and although in the end he killed them both he was himself half killed in doing it.

In the fall of the year, when the first snows were falling and mush-ice was running in the river, Beauty Smith took passage for himself and White Fang on a steamboat bound up the Yukon to Dawson. White Fang had now achieved a reputation in the land. As "The Fighting Wolf" he was known far and wide, and the cage in which he was kept on the steamboat's deck was usually surrounded by curious men. He raged and snarled at them, or lay quietly and studied them with cold hatred. Why should he not hate them? He never asked himself the question. He knew only hate and lost himself in the passion of it. Life had become a hell to him. He had not been made for the close confinement wild beasts endure at the hands of men. And yet it was in precisely this way that he was treated. Men stared at him, poked sticks between the bars to make him snarl, and then laughed at him.

They were his environment, these men, and they were moulding the clay of him into a more ferocious thing than had been intended by Nature. Nevertheless, Nature had given him plasticity. Where many another animal would have died or had its spirit broken, he adjusted himself and lived, and at no expense of the spirit. Possibly Beauty Smith, arch-fiend and tormentor, was capable of breaking White Fang's spirit, but as yet there were no signs of his succeeding.

If Beauty Smith had in him a devil, White Fang had another; and the two of them raged against each other unceasingly. In the days before, White Fang had had the wisdom to cower down and submit to a man with a club in his hand; but this wisdom now left him. The mere sight of Beauty Smith was sufficient to send him into transports of fury. And when they came to close quarters, and he had been beaten back by the club, he went on growling and snarling and showing his fangs. The last growl could never be extracted from him. No matter how terribly he was beaten, he had always another growl; and when Beauty Smith gave up and withdrew, the defiant growl followed after him, or White Fang sprang at the bars of the cage bellowing his hatred.

When the steamboat arrived at Dawson, White Fang went ashore. But he still lived a public life, in a cage, surrounded by curious men. He was exhibited as "The Fighting Wolf," and men paid fifty cents in gold dust to see him. He was given no rest. Did he lie down to sleep, he was stirred up by a sharp stick—so that the audience might get its money's worth. In order to make the exhibition interesting, he was kept in a rage most of the time. But worse than all this, was the atmosphere in which he lived. He was regarded as the most fearful of wild beasts, and this was borne in to him through the bars of the cage. Every word, every cautious action, on the part of the men, impressed upon him his own terrible ferocity. It was so much added fuel to the flame of his fierceness. There could be but one result, and that was that his ferocity fed upon itself and increased. It was another instance of the plasticity of his clay, of his capacity for being moulded by the pressure of environment.

In addition to being exhibited, he was a professional fighting animal. At irregular intervals, whenever a fight could be arranged, he was taken out of his cage and led off into the woods a few miles from town. Usually this occurred at night, so as to avoid interference from the mounted police of the Territory. After a few hours of waiting, when daylight had come, the audience and the dog with which he was to fight arrived. In this manner it came about that he fought all sizes and breeds of dogs. It was a savage land, the men were savage, and the fights were usually to the death.

Since White Fang continued to fight, it is obvious that it was the other dogs that died. He never knew defeat. His early training, when he fought with Lip-lip and the whole puppy-pack, stood him in good stead. There was the tenacity with which he clung to the earth. No dog could make him lose his footing. This was the favourite trick of the wolf breeds—to rush in upon him, either directly or with an unexpected swerve, in the hope of striking his shoulder and overthrowing him. Mackenzie hounds, Eskimo and Labrador dogs, huskies and Malamutes—all tried it on him, and all failed. He was never known to lose his footing. Men told this to one another, and looked each time to see it happen; but White Fang always disappointed them.

Then there was his lightning quickness. It gave him a tremendous advantage over his antagonists. No matter what their fighting experience, they had never encountered a dog that moved so swiftly as he. Also to be reckoned with, was the immediateness of his attack. The average dog was accustomed to the preliminaries of snarling and bristling and growling, and the average dog was knocked off his feet and finished before he had begun to fight or recovered from his surprise. So often did this happen, that it became the custom to hold White Fang until the other dog went through its preliminaries, was good and ready, and even made the first attack.

But greatest of all the advantages in White Fang's favour, was his experience. He knew more about fighting than did any of the dogs that faced him. He had fought more fights, knew how to meet more tricks and methods, and had more tricks himself, while his own method was scarcely to be improved upon.

As the time went by, he had fewer and fewer fights. Men despaired of matching him with an equal, and Beauty Smith was compelled to pit wolves against him. These were trapped by the Indians for the purpose, and a fight between White Fang and a wolf was always sure to draw a crowd. Once, a fullgrown female lynx was secured, and this time White Fang fought for his life. Her quickness matched his; her ferocity equalled his; while he fought with his fangs alone, and she fought with her sharpclawed feet as well.

But after the lynx, all fighting ceased for White Fang. There were no more animals with which to fight—at least, there was none considered worthy of fighting with him. So he remained on exhibition until spring, when one Tim Keenan, a faro-dealer, arrived in the land. With him came the first bulldog that had ever entered the Klondike. That this dog and White Fang should come together was inevitable, and for a week the anticipated fight was the mainspring of conversation in certain quarters of the town.

## CHAPTER 4

# THE CLINGING DEATH

Beauty Smith slipped the chain from his neck and stepped back.

For once White Fang did not make an immediate attack. He stood still, ears pricked forward, alert and curious, surveying the strange animal that faced him. He had never seen such a dog before. Tim Keenan shoved the bulldog forward with a muttered "Go to it." The animal waddled toward the centre of the circle, short and squat and ungainly. He came to a stop and blinked across at White Fang.

There were cries from the crowd of "Go to him, Cherokee!" "Sick 'm, Cherokee!" "Eat 'm up!"

But Cherokee did not seem anxious to fight. He turned his head and blinked at the men who shouted, at the same time wagging his stump of a tail good-naturedly. He was not afraid, but merely lazy. Besides, it did not seem to him that it was intended he should fight with the dog he saw before him. He was not used to fighting with that kind of dog, and he was waiting for them to bring on the real dog.

Tim Keenan stepped in and bent over Cherokee, fondling him on both sides of the shoulders with hands that rubbed against the grain of the hair and that made slight, pushing-forward movements. These were so many suggestions. Also, their effect was irritating, for Cherokee began to growl, very softly, deep down in his throat. There was a correspondence in rhythm between the growls and the movements of the man's hands. The growl rose in the throat with the culmination of each forward-pushing movement, and ebbed down to start up afresh with the beginning of the next movement. The end of each movement was the accent of the rhythm, the movement ending abruptly and the growling rising with a jerk.

This was not without its effect on White Fang. The hair began to rise on his neck and across the shoulders. Tim Keenan gave a final shove forward and stepped back again. As the impetus that carried Cherokee forward died down, he continued to go forward of his own volition, in a swift, bow-legged run. Then White Fang struck. A cry of startled admiration went up. He had covered the distance and gone in more like a cat than a dog; and with the same cat-like swiftness he had slashed with his fangs and leaped clear.

The bulldog was bleeding back of one ear from a rip in his thick neck. He gave no sign, did not even snarl, but turned and followed after White Fang. The display on both sides, the quickness of the one and the steadiness of the other, had excited the partisan spirit of the crowd, and the men were making new bets and increasing original bets. Again, and yet again, White Fang sprang in, slashed, and got away untouched; and still his strange foe followed after him, without too great haste, not slowly, but deliberately and determinedly, in a businesslike sort of way. There was purpose in his method—something for him to do that he was intent upon doing and from which nothing could distract him.

His whole demeanour, every action, was stamped with this purpose. It puzzled White Fang. Never had he seen such a dog. It had no hair protection. It was soft, and bled easily. There was no thick mat of fur to baffle White Fang's teeth, as they were often baffled by dogs of his own breed. Each time that his teeth struck they sank easily into the yielding flesh, while the animal did not seem able to defend itself. Another disconcerting thing was that it made no outcry, such as he had been accustomed to with the other dogs he had fought. Beyond a growl or a grunt, the dog took its punishment silently. And never did it flag in its pursuit of him.

Not that Cherokee was slow. He could turn and whirl swiftly enough, but White Fang was never there. Cherokee was puzzled, too. He had never fought before with a dog with which he could not close. The desire to close had always been mutual. But here was a dog that kept at a distance, dancing and dodging here and there and all about. And when it did get its teeth into him, it did not hold on but let go instantly and darted away again.

But White Fang could not get at the soft underside of the throat. The bulldog stood too short, while its massive jaws were an added protection. White Fang darted in and out unscathed, while Cherokee's wounds increased. Both sides of his neck and head were ripped and slashed. He bled freely, but showed no signs of being disconcerted. He continued his plodding pursuit, though once, for the moment baffled, he came to a full stop and blinked at the men who looked on, at the same time wagging his stump of a tail as an expression of his willingness to fight.

In that moment White Fang was in upon him and out, in passing ripping his trimmed remnant of an ear. With a slight manifestation of anger, Cherokee took up the pursuit again, running on the inside of the circle White Fang was making, and striving to fasten his deadly grip on White Fang's throat. The bulldog missed by a hair'sbreadth, and cries of praise went up as White Fang doubled suddenly out of danger in the opposite direction.

The time went by. White Fang still danced on, dodging and doubling, leaping in and out, and ever inflicting damage. And still the bulldog, with grim certitude, toiled after him. Sooner or later he would accomplish his purpose, get the grip that would win the battle. In the meantime he accepted all the punishment the other could deal him. His tufts of ears had become tassels, his neck and shoulders were slashed in a score of places, and his very lips were cut and bleeding—all from those lightning snaps that were beyond his foreseeing and guarding.

Time and again White Fang had attempted to knock Cherokee off his feet; but the difference in their height was too great. Cherokee was too squat, too close to the ground. White Fang tried the trick once too often. The chance came in one of his quick doubling and counter-circlings. He caught Cherokee with head turned away as he whirled more slowly. His shoulder was exposed. White Fang drove in upon it; but his own shoulder was high above, while he struck with such force that his momentum carried him on across over the other's body. For the first time in his fighting history, men saw White Fang lose his footing. His body turned a half-somersault in the air, and he would have landed on his back had he not twisted, catlike, still in the air, in the effort to bring his feet to the earth. As it was, he struck heavily on his side. The next instant he was on his feet, but in that instant Cherokee's teeth closed on his throat.

It was not a good grip, being too low down toward the chest; but Cherokee held on. White Fang sprang to his feet and tore wildly around, trying to shake off the bulldog's body. It made him frantic, this clinging, dragging weight. It bound his movements, restricted his freedom. It was like the trap, and all his instinct resented it and revolted against it. It was a mad revolt. For several minutes he was to all intents insane. The basic life that was in him took charge of him. The will to exist of his body surged over him. He was dominated by this mere flesh-love of life. All intelligence was gone. It was as though he had no brain. His reason was unseated by the blind yearning of the flesh to exist and move, at all hazards to move, to continue to move, for movement was the expression of its existence.

Round and round he went, whirling and turning and reversing, trying to shake off the fifty-pound weight that dragged at his throat. The bulldog did little but keep his grip. Sometimes, and rarely, he managed to get his feet to the earth and for a moment to brace himself against White Fang. But the next moment his footing would be lost and he would be dragging around in the whirl of one of White Fang's mad gyrations. Cherokee identified himself with his instinct. He knew that he was doing the right thing by holding on, and there came to him certain blissful thrills of satisfaction. At such moments he even closed his eyes and allowed his body to be hurled hither and thither, willy-nilly, careless of any hurt that might thereby come to it. That did not count. The grip was the thing, and the grip he kept.

White Fang ceased only when he had tired himself out. He could do nothing, and he could not understand. Never, in all his fighting, had this thing happened. The dogs he had fought with did not fight that way. With them it was snap and slash and get away, snap and slash and get away. He lay partly on his side, panting for breath. Cherokee, still holding his grip, urged against him, trying to get him over entirely on his side. White Fang resisted, and he could feel the jaws shifting their grip, slightly relaxing and coming together again in a chewing movement. Each shift brought the grip closer in to his throat. The bulldog's method was to hold what he had, and when opportunity favoured to work in for more. Opportunity favoured when White Fang remained quiet. When White Fang struggled, Cherokee was content merely to hold on.

The bulging back of Cherokee's neck was the only portion of his body that White Fang's teeth could reach. He got hold toward the base where the neck comes out from the shoulders; but he did not know the chewing method of fighting, nor were his jaws adapted to it. He spasmodically ripped and tore with his fangs for a space. Then a change in their position diverted him. The bulldog had managed to roll him over on his back, and still hanging on to his throat, was on top of him. Like a cat, White Fang bowed his hind-quarters in, and, with the feet digging into his enemy's abdomen above him, he began to claw with long, tearing strokes. Cherokee might well have been disembowelled had he not quickly pivoted on his grip and got his body off of White Fang's and at right angles to it.

There was no escaping that grip. It was like Fate itself, and as inexorable. Slowly it shifted up along the jugular. All that saved White Fang from death was the loose skin of his neck and the thick fur that covered it. This served to form a large roll in Cherokee's mouth, the fur of which wellnigh defied his teeth. But bit by bit, whenever the chance offered, he was getting more of the loose skin and fur in his mouth. The result was that he was slowly throttling White Fang. The latter's breath was drawn with greater and greater difficulty as the moments went by.

It began to look as though the battle were over. The backers of Cherokee waxed jubilant and offered ridiculous odds. White Fang's backers were correspondingly depressed, and refused bets of ten to one and twenty to one, though one man was rash enough to close a wager of fifty to one. This man was Beauty Smith. He took a step into the ring and pointed his finger at White Fang. Then he began to laugh derisively and scornfully. This produced the desired effect. White Fang went wild with rage. He called up his reserves of strength and gained his feet. As he struggled around the ring, the fifty pounds of his foe ever dragging on his throat, his anger passed on into panic. The basic life of him dominated him again, and his intelligence fled before the will of his flesh to live. Round and round and back again, stumbling and falling and rising, even uprearing at times on his hind-legs and lifting his foe clear of the earth, he struggled vainly to shake off the clinging death.

At last he fell, toppling backward, exhausted; and the bulldog promptly shifted his grip, getting in closer, mangling more and more of the fur-folded flesh, throttling White Fang more severely than ever. Shouts of applause went up for the victor, and there were many cries of "Cherokee!" "Cherokee!" To this Cherokee responded by vigorous wagging of the stump of his tail. But the clamour of approval did not distract him. There was no sympathetic relation between his tail and his massive jaws. The one might wag, but the others held their terrible grip on White Fang's throat.

It was at this time that a diversion came to the spectators. There was a jingle of bells. Dog-mushers' cries were heard. Everybody, save Beauty Smith, looked apprehensively, the fear of the police strong upon them. But they saw, up the trail, and not down, two men running with sled and dogs. They were evidently coming down the creek from some prospecting trip. At sight of the crowd they stopped their dogs and came over and joined it, curious to see the cause of the excitement. The dog-musher wore a moustache, but the other, a taller and younger man, was smooth-shaven, his skin rosy from the pounding of his blood and the running in the frosty air.

White Fang had practically ceased struggling. Now and again he resisted spasmodically and to no purpose. He could get little air, and that little grew less and less under the merciless grip that ever tightened. In spite of his armour of fur, the great vein of his throat would have long since been torn open, had not the first grip of the bulldog been so low down as to be practically on the chest. It had taken Cherokee a long time to shift that grip upward, and this had also tended further to clog his jaws with fur and skin-fold.

In the meantime, the abysmal brute in Beauty Smith had been rising up into his brain and mastering the small bit of sanity that he possessed at best. When he saw White Fang's eyes beginning to glaze, he knew beyond doubt that the fight was lost. Then he broke loose. He sprang upon White Fang and began savagely to kick him. There were hisses from the crowd and cries of protest, but that was all. While this went on, and Beauty Smith continued to kick White Fang, there was a commotion in the crowd. The tall young newcomer was forcing his way through, shouldering men right and left without ceremony or gentleness. When he broke through into the ring, Beauty Smith was just in the act of delivering another kick. All his weight was on one foot, and he was in a state of unstable equilibrium. At that moment the newcomer's fist landed a smashing blow full in his face. Beauty Smith's remaining leg left the ground, and his whole body seemed to lift into the air as he turned over backward and struck the snow. The newcomer turned upon the crowd.

"You cowards!" he cried. "You beasts!"

He was in a rage himself—a sane rage. His gray eyes seemed metallic and steellike as they flashed upon the crowd. Beauty Smith regained his feet and came toward him, sniffling and cowardly. The newcomer did not understand. He did not know how abject a coward the other was, and thought he was coming back intent on fighting. So, with a "You beast!" he smashed Beauty Smith over backward with a second blow in the face. Beauty Smith decided that the snow was the safest place for him, and lay where he had fallen, making no effort to get up.

"Come on, Matt, lend a hand," the newcomer called to the dog-musher, who had followed him into the ring.

Both men bent over the dogs. Matt took hold of White Fang, ready to pull when Cherokee's jaws should be loosened. This the younger man endeavoured to accomplish by clutching the bulldog's jaws in his hands and trying to spread them. It was a vain undertaking. As he pulled and tugged and wrenched, he kept exclaiming with every expulsion of breath, "Beasts!"

The crowd began to grow unruly, and some of the men were protesting against the spoiling of the sport; but they were silenced when the newcomer lifted his head from his work for a moment and glared at them.

"You damn beasts!" he finally exploded, and went back to his task.

"It's no use, Mr. Scott, you can't break 'm apart that way," Matt said at last.

The pair paused and surveyed the locked dogs.

"Ain't bleedin' much," Matt announced. "Ain't got all the way in yet."

"But he's liable to any moment," Scott answered. "There, did you see that! He shifted his grip in a bit."

The younger man's excitement and apprehension for White Fang was growing. He struck Cherokee about the head savagely again and again. But that did not loosen the jaws. Cherokee wagged the stump of his tail in advertisement that he understood the meaning of the blows, but that he knew he was himself in the right and only doing his duty by keeping his grip.

"Won't some of you help?" Scott cried desperately at the crowd.

But no help was offered. Instead, the crowd began sarcastically to cheer him on and showered him with facetious advice.

"You'll have to get a pry," Matt counselled.

The other reached into the holster at his hip, drew his revolver, and tried to thrust its muzzle between the bulldog's jaws. He shoved, and shoved hard, till the grating of the steel against the locked teeth could be distinctly heard. Both men were on their knees, bending over the dogs. Tim Keenan strode into the ring. He paused beside Scott and touched him on the shoulder, saying ominously:

"Don't break them teeth, stranger."

"Then I'll break his neck," Scott retorted, continuing his shoving and wedging with the revolver muzzle.

"I said don't break them teeth," the faro-dealer repeated more ominously than before.

But if it was a bluff he intended, it did not work. Scott never desisted from his efforts, though he looked up coolly and asked:

"Your dog?"

The faro-dealer grunted.

"Then get in here and break this grip."

"Well, stranger," the other drawled irritatingly, "I don't mind telling you that's something I ain't worked out for myself. I don't know how to turn the trick."

"Then get out of the way," was the reply, "and don't bother me. I'm busy."

Tim Keenan continued standing over him, but Scott took no further notice of his presence. He had managed to get the muzzle in between the jaws on one side, and was trying to get it out between the jaws on the other side. This accomplished, he pried gently and carefully, loosening the jaws a bit at a time, while Matt, a bit at a time, extricated White Fang's mangled neck.

"Stand by to receive your dog," was Scott's peremptory order to Cherokee's owner.

The faro-dealer stooped down obediently and got a firm hold on Cherokee.

"Now!" Scott warned, giving the final pry.

The dogs were drawn apart, the bulldog struggling vigorously.

"Take him away," Scott commanded, and Tim Keenan dragged Cherokee back into the crowd.

White Fang made several ineffectual efforts to get up. Once he gained his feet, but his legs were too weak to sustain him, and he slowly wilted and sank back into the snow. His eyes were half closed, and the surface of them was glassy. His jaws were apart, and through them the tongue protruded, draggled and limp. To all appearances he looked like a dog that had been strangled to death. Matt examined him.

"Just about all in," he announced; "but he's breathin' all right."

Beauty Smith had regained his feet and come over to look at White Fang.

"Matt, how much is a good sled-dog worth?" Scott asked.

The dog-musher, still on his knees and stooped over White Fang, calculated for a moment.

"Three hundred dollars," he answered.

"And how much for one that's all chewed up like this one?" Scott asked, nudging White Fang with his foot.

"Half of that," was the dog-musher's judgment.

Scott turned upon Beauty Smith.

"Did you hear, Mr. Beast? I'm going to take your dog from you, and I'm going to give you a hundred and fifty for him."

He opened his pocket-book and counted out the bills.

Beauty Smith put his hands behind his back, refusing to touch the proffered money.

"I ain't a-sellin'," he said.

"Oh, yes you are," the other assured him. "Because I'm buying. Here's your money. The dog's mine."

Beauty Smith, his hands still behind him, began to back away.

Scott sprang toward him, drawing his fist back to strike. Beauty Smith cowered down in anticipation of the blow.

"I've got my rights," he whimpered.

"You've forfeited your rights to own that dog," was the rejoinder. "Are you going to take the money? or do I have to hit you again?"

"All right," Beauty Smith spoke up with the alacrity of fear. "But I take the money under protest," he added. "The dog's a mint. I ain't a-goin' to be robbed. A man's got his rights."

"Correct," Scott answered, passing the money over to him. "A man's got his rights. But you're not a man. You're a beast."

"Wait till I get back to Dawson," Beauty Smith threatened. "I'll have the law on you."

"If you open your mouth when you get back to Dawson, I'll have you run out of town. Understand?"

Beauty Smith replied with a grunt.

"Understand?" the other thundered with abrupt fierceness.

"Yes," Beauty Smith grunted, shrinking away.

"Yes what?"

"Yes, sir," Beauty Smith snarled.

"Look out! He'll bite!" some one shouted, and a guffaw of laughter went up.

Scott turned his back on him, and returned to help the dog-musher, who was working over White Fang.

Some of the men were already departing; others stood in groups, looking on and talking. Tim Keenan joined one of the groups.

"Who's that mug?" he asked.

"Weedon Scott," some one answered.

"And who in hell is Weedon Scott?" the faro-dealer demanded.

"Oh, one of them crack-a-jack minin' experts. He's in with all the big bugs. If you want to keep out of trouble, you'll steer clear of him, that's my talk. He's all hunky with the officials. The Gold Commissioner's' a special pal of his."

"I thought he must be somebody," was the faro-dealer's comment. "That's why I kept my hands offen him at the start."

## CHAPTER 5

# THE INDOMITABLE

"It's hopeless," Weedon Scott confessed.

He sat on the step of his cabin and stared at the dog-musher, who responded with a shrug that was equally hopeless.

Together they looked at White Fang at the end of his stretched chain, bristling, snarling, ferocious, straining to get at the sled-dogs. Having received sundry lessons from Matt, said lessons being imparted by means of a club, the sled-dogs had learned to leave White Fang alone; and even then they were lying down at a distance, apparently oblivious of his existence.

"It's a wolf and there's no taming it," Weedon Scott announced.

"Oh, I don't know about that," Matt objected. "Might be a lot of dog in 'm, for all you can tell. But there's one thing I know sure, an' that there's no gettin' away from."

The dog-musher paused and nodded his head confidentially at Moosehide Mountain.

"Well, don't be a miser with what you know," Scott said sharply, after waiting a suitable length of time. "Spit it out. What is it?"

The dog-musher indicated White Fang with a backward thrust of his thumb.

"Wolf or dog, it's all the same—he's been tamed a'ready."

"No!"

"I tell you yes, an' broke to harness. Look close there. D'ye see them marks across the chest?"

"You're right, Matt. He was a sled-dog before Beauty Smith got hold of him."

"An' there's not much reason against his bein' a sled-dog again."

"What d'ye think?" Scott queried eagerly. Then the hope died down as he added, shaking his head, "We've had him two weeks now, and if anything, he's wilder than ever at the present moment."

"Give 'm a chance," Matt counselled. "Turn 'm loose for a spell."

The other looked at him incredulously.

"Yes," Matt went on, "I know you've tried to, but you didn't take a club."

"You try it then."

The dog-musher secured a club and went over to the chained animal. White Fang watched the club after the manner of a caged lion watching the whip of its trainer.

"See 'm keep his eye on that club," Matt said. "That's a good sign. He's no fool. Don't dast tackle me so long as I got that dub handy. He's not clean crazy, sure."

As the man's hand approached his neck, White Fang bristled and snarled and crouched down. But while he eyed the approaching hand, he at the same time contrived to keep track of the club in the other hand, suspended threateningly above him. Matt unsnapped the chain from the collar and stepped back.

White Fang could scarcely realize that he was free. Many months had gone by since he passed into the possession of Beauty Smith, and in all that period he had never known a moment of freedom except at the times he had been loosed to fight with other dogs. Immediately after such fights he had always been imprisoned again.

He did not know what to make of it. Perhaps some new deviltry of the gods was about to be perpetrated on him. He walked slowly and cautiously, prepared to be assailed at any moment. He did not know what to do, it was all so unprecedented. He took the precaution to sheer off from the two watching gods, and walked carefully to the corner of the cabin. Nothing happened. He was plainly perplexed, and he came back again, pausing a dozen feet away and regarding the two men intently.

"Won't he run away?" his new owner asked.

Matt shrugged his shoulders. "Got to take a gamble. Only way to find out is to find out."

"Poor devil," Scott murmured pityingly. "What he needs is some show of human kindness," he added, turning and going into the cabin.

He came out with a piece of meat, which he tossed to White Fang. He sprang away from it, and from a distance studied it suspiciously.

"Hi-yu, Major!" Matt shouted warningly, but too late.

Major had made a spring for the meat. At the instant his jaws closed on it, White Fang struck him. He was overthrown. Matt rushed in, but quicker than he was White Fang. Major staggered to his feet, but the blood spouting from his throat reddened the snow in a widening path.

"It's too bad, but it served him right," Scott said hastily.

But Matt's foot had already started on its way to kick White Fang. There was a leap, a flash of teeth, a sharp exclamation. White Fang, snarling fiercely, scrambled backward for several yards, while Matt stooped and investigated his leg.

"He got me all right," he announced, pointing to the torn trousers and undercloths, and the growing stain of red.

"I told you it was hopeless, Matt," Scott said in a discouraged voice. "I've thought about it off and on, while not wanting to think of it. But we've come to it now. It's the only thing to do."

As he talked, with reluctant movements he drew his revolver, threw open the cylinder, and assured himself of its contents.

"Look here, Mr. Scott," Matt objected; "that dog's been through hell. You can't expect 'm to come out a white an' shinin' angel. Give 'm time."

"Look at Major," the other rejoined.

The dog-musher surveyed the stricken dog. He had sunk down on the snow in the circle of his blood, and was plainly in the last gasp.

"Served 'm right. You said so yourself, Mr. Scott. He tried to take White Fang's meat, an' he's dead-O. That was to be expected. I wouldn't give two whoops in hell for a dog that wouldn't fight for his own meat."

"But look at yourself, Matt. It's all right about the dogs, but we must draw the line somewhere."

"Served me right," Matt argued stubbornly. "What'd I want to kick 'm for? You said yourself he'd done right. Then I had no right to kick 'm."

"It would be a mercy to kill him," Scott insisted. "He's untamable."

"Now look here, Mr. Scott, give the poor devil a fightin' chance. He ain't had no chance yet. He's just come through hell, an' this is the first time he's been loose. Give 'm a fair chance, an' if he don't deliver the goods, I'll kill 'm myself. There!"

"God knows I don't want to kill him or have him killed," Scott answered, putting away the revolver. "We'll let him run loose and see what kindness can do for him. And here's a try at it."

He walked over to White Fang and began talking to him gent!.y and soothingly.

"Better have a club handy," Matt warned.

Scott shook his head and went on trying to win White Fang's confidence.

White Fang was suspicious. Something was impending. He had killed this god's dog, bitten his companion god, and what else was to be expected than some terrible punishment? But in the face of it he was indomitable. He bristled and showed his teeth, his eyes vigilant, his whole body wary and prepared for anything. The god had no club, so he suffered him to approach quite near. The god's hand had come out and was descending upon his head. White Fang shrank together and grew tense as he crouched under it. Here was danger, some treachery or something. He knew the hands of the gods, their proved mastery, their cunning to hurt. Besides, there was his old antipathy to being touched. He snarled more menacingly, crouched still lower, and still the hand descended. He did not want to bite the hand, and he endured the peril of it until his instinct surged up in him, mastering him with its insatiable yearning for life.

Weedon Scott had believed that he was quick enough to avoid any snap or slash. But he had yet to learn the remarkable quickness of White Fang, who struck with the certainty and swiftness of a coiled snake.

Scott cried out sharply with surprise, catching his torn hand and holding it tightly in his other hand. Matt uttered a great oath and sprang to his side. White Fang crouched down and backed away, bristling, showing his fangs, his eyes malignant with menace. Now he could expect a beating as fearful as any he had received from Beauty Smith.

"Here! What are you doing?" Scott cried suddenly.

Matt had dashed into the cabin and come out with a rifle.

"Nothin'," he said slowly, with a careless calmness that was assumed; "only goin' to keep that promise I made. I reckon it's up to me to kill 'm as I said I'd do."

"No, you don't!"

"Yes I do. Watch me."

As Matt had pleaded for White Fang when he had been bitten, it was now Weedon Scott's turn to plead.

"You said to give him a chance. Well, give it to him. We've only just started, and we can't quit at the beginning. It served me right, this time. And—look at him!"

White Fang, near the corner of the cabin and forty feet away, was snarling with blood-curdling viciousness, not at Scott, but at the dog-musher.

"Well, I'll be everlastin'ly gosh-swoggled!" was the dog-musher's expression of astonishment.

"Look at the intelligence of him," Scott went on hastily. "He knows the meaning of firearms as well as you do. He's got intelligence, and we've got to give that intelligence a chance. Put up the gun."

"All right, I'm willin'," Matt agreed, leaning the rifle against the woodpile.

"But will you look at that!" he exclaimed the next moment.

White Fang had quieted down and ceased snarlling.

"This is worth investigatin'. Watch."

Matt reached for the rifle, and at the same moment White Fang snarled. He stepped away from the rifle, and White Fang's lifted lips descended, covering his teeth.

"Now, just for fun."

Matt took the rifle and began slowly to raise it to his shoulder. White Fang's snarling began with the movement, and increased as the movement approached its culmination. But the moment before the rifle came to a level on him, he leaped sidewise behind the corner of the cabin. Matt stood staring along the sights at the empty space of snow which had been occupied by White Fang.

The dog-musher put the rifle down solemnly, then turned and looked at his employer.

"I agree with you, Mr. Scott. That dog's too intelligent to kill."

## Chapter 6

# THE LOVE-MASTER

As White Fang watched Weedon Scott approach, he bristled and snarled to advertise that he would not submit to punishment. Twenty-four hours had passed since he had slashed open the hand that was now bandaged and held up by a sling to keep the blood out of it. In the past White Fang had experienced delayed punishments, and he apprehended that such a one was about to befall him. How could it be otherwise? He had committed what was to him sacrilege, sunk his fangs into the holy flesh of a god, and of a white-skinned superior god at that. In the nature of things, and of intercourse with gods, something terrible awaited him.

The god sat down several feet away. White Fang could see nothing dangerous in that. When the gods administered punishment they stood on their legs. Besides, this god had no club, no whip, no firearm. And furthermore, he himself was free. No chain nor stick bound him. He could escape into safety while the god was scrambling to his feet. In the meantime he would wait and see.

The god remained quiet, made no movement; and White Fang's snarl slowly dwindled to a growl that ebbed down in his throat and ceased. Then the god spoke, and at the first sound of his voice, the hair rose on White Fang's neck and the growl rushed up in his throat. But the god made no hostile movement, and went on calmly talking. For a time White Fang growled in unison with him, a correspondence of rhythm being established between growl and voice. But the god talked on interminably. He talked to White Fang as White Fang had never been talked to before. He talked softly and soothingly, with a gentleness that somehow, somewhere, touched White Fang. In spite of himself and all the pricking warnings of his instinct, White Fang began to have confidence in this god. He had a feeling of security that was belied by all his experience with men.

After a long time, the god got up and went into the cabin. White Fang scanned him apprehensively when he came out. He had neither whip nor dub nor weapon. Nor was his uninjured hand behind his back hiding something. He sat down as before, in the same spot, several feet away. He held out a small piece of meat. White Fang pricked his ears and investigated it suspiciously, managing to look at the same time both at the meat and the god, alert for any overt act, his body tense and ready to spring away at the first sign of hostility.

Still the punishment delayed. The god merely held near to his nose a piece of meat. And about the meat there seemed nothing wrong. Still White Fang suspected; and though the meat was proffered to him with short inviting thrusts of the hand, he refused to touch it. The gods were all-wise, and there was no telling what masterful treachery lurked behind that apparently harmless piece of meat. In past experience, especially in dealing with squaws, meat and punishment had often been disastrously related.

In the end, the god tossed the meat on the snow at White Fang's feet. He smelled the meat carefully; but he did not look at it. While he smelled it he kept his eyes on the god. Nothing happened. He took the meat into his mouth and swallowed it. Still nothing happened. The god was actually offering him another piece of meat. Again he refused to take it from the hand, and again it was tossed to him. This was repeated a number of times. But there came a time when the god refused to toss it. He kept it in his hand and steadfastly proffered it.

The meat was good meat, and White Fang was hungry. Bit by bit, infinitely cautious, he approached the hand. At last the time came that he decided to eat the meat from the hand. He never took his eyes from the god, thrusting his head forward with ears flattened back and hair involuntarily rising and cresting on his neck. Also a low growl rumbled in his throat as warning that he was not to be trifled with. He ate the meat, and nothing happened. Piece by piece, he ate all the meat, and nothing happened. Still the punishment delayed.

He licked his chops and waited. The god went on talking. In his voice was kindness—something of which White Fang had no experience whatever. And within him it aroused feelings which he had likewise never experienced before. He was aware of a certain strange satisfaction, as though some need were being gratified, as though some void in his being were being filled. Then again came the prod of his instinct and the warning of past experience. The gods were ever crafty, and they had unguessed ways of attaining their ends.

Ah, he had thought so! There it came now, the god's hand, cunning to hurt, thrusting out at him, descending upon his head. But the god went on talking. His voice was soft and soothing. In spite of the menacing hand, the voice inspired confidence. And in spite of the assuring voice, the hand inspired distrust. White Fang was torn by conflicting feelings, impulses. It seemed he would fly to pieces, so terrible was the control he was exerting, holding together by an unwonted indecision the counter-forces that struggled within him for mastery.

He compromised. He snarled and bristled and flattened his ears. But he neither snapped nor sprang away. The hand descended. Nearer and nearer it came. It touched the ends of his upstanding hair. He shrank down under it. It followed down after him, pressing more closely against him. Shrinking, almost shivering, he still managed to hold himself together. It was a torment, this hand that touched him and violated his instinct. He could not forget in a day all the evil that had been wrought him at the hands of men. But it was the will of the god, and he strove to submit.

The hand lifted and descended again in a patting, caressing movement. This continued, but every time the hand lifted, the hair lifted under it. And every time the hand descended, the ears flattened down and a cavernous growl surged in his throat. White Fang growled and growled with insistent warning. By this means he announced that he was prepared to retaliate for any hurt he might receive. There was no telling when the god's ulterior motive might be disclosed. At any moment that soft, confidence-inspiring voice might break forth in a roar of wrath, that gentle and caressing hand transform itself into a viselike grip to hold him helpless and administer punishment.

But the god talked on softly, and ever the hand rose and fell with non-hostile pats. White Fang experienced dual feelings. It was distasteful to his instinct. It restrained him, opposed the will of him toward personal liberty. And yet it was not physically painful. On the contrary, it was even pleasant, in a physical way. The patting movement slowly and carefully changed to a rubbing of the ears about their bases, and the physical pleasure even increased a little. Yet he continued to fear, and he stood on guard, expectant of unguessed evil, alternately suffering and enjoying as one feeling or the other came uppermost and swayed him.

"Well, I'll be gosh-swoggled!"

So spoke Matt, coming out of the cabin, his sleeves rolled up, a pan of dirty dishwater in his hands, arrested in the act of emptying the pan by the sight of Weedon Scott patting White Fang.

At the instant his voice broke the silence, White Fang leaped back, snarling savagely at him.

Matt regarded his employer with grieved disapproval.

"If you don't mind my expressin' my feelin's, Mr. Scott, I'll make free to say you're seventeen kinds of a damn fool an' all of 'em different, and then some."

Weedon Scott smiled with a superior air, gained his feet, and walked over to White Fang. He talked soothingly to him, but not for long, then slowly put out his hand, rested it on White Fang's head, and resumed the interrupted patting. White Fang endured it, keeping his eyes fixed suspiciously, not upon the man that petted him, but upon the man that stood in the doorway.

"You may be a number one, tip-top minin' expert, all right all right," the dog-musher delivered himself oracularly, "but you missed the chance of your life when you was a boy an' didn't run off an' join a circus."

White Fang snarled at the sound of his voice, but this time did not leap away from under the hand that was caressing his head and the back of his neck with long, soothing strokes.

It was the beginning of the end for White Fang—the ending of the old life and the reign of hate. A new and incomprehensibly fairer life was dawning. It required much thinking and endless patience on the part of Weedon Scott to accomplish this. And on the part of White Fang it required nothing less than a revolution. He had to ignore the urges and promptings of instinct and reason, defy experience, give the lie to life itself.

Life, as he had known it, not only had had no place in it for much that he now did; but all the currents had gone counter to those to which he now abandoned himself. In short, when all things were considered, he had to achieve an orientation far vaster than the one he had achieved at the time he came voluntarily in from the Wild and accepted Gray Beaver as his lord. At that time he was a mere puppy, soft from the making, without form, ready for the thumb of circumstance to begin its work upon him. But now it was different. The thumb of circumstance had done its work only too well. By it he had been formed and hardened into the Fighting Wolf, fierce and implacable, unloving and unlovable. To accomplish the change was like a reflux of being, and this when the plasticity of youth was no longer his; when the fibre of him had become tough and knotty; when the warp and the woof of him had made of him an adamantine texture, harsh and unyielding; when the face of his spirit had become iron and all his instincts and axioms had crystallized into set rules, cautions, dislikes, and desires.

Yet again, in this new orientation, it was the thumb of circumstance that pressed and prodded him, softening that which had become hard and remolding it into fairer form. Weedon Scott was in truth this thumb. He had gone to the roots of White Fang's nature, and with kindness touched to life potencies that had languished and wellnigh perished. One such potency was love. It took the place of like, which latter had been the highest feeling that thrilled him in his intercourse with the gods.

But this love did not come in a day. It began with like and out of it slowly developed. White Fang did not run away, though he was allowed to remain loose, because he liked this new god. This was certainly better than the life he had lived in the cage of Beauty Smith, and it was necessary that he should have some god. The lordship of man was a need of his nature. The seal of his dependence on man had been set upon him in that early day when he turned his back on the Wild and crawled to Gray Beaver's feet to receive the expected beating. This seal had been stamped upon him again, and ineradicably, on his second return from the Wild, when the long famine was over and there was fish once more in the village of Gray Beaver.

And so, because he needed a god and because he preferred Weedon Scott to Beauty Smith, White Fang remained. In acknowledgment of fealty, he proceeded to take upon himself the guardianship of his master's property. He prowled about the cabin while the sled-dogs slept, and the first night-visitor to the cabin fought him off with a club until Weedon Scott came to the rescue. But White Fang soon learned to differentiate between thieves and honest men, to appraise the true value of step and carriage. The man who travelled, loud-stepping, the direct line to the cabin door, he let alone—though he watched him vigilantly until the door opened and he received the endorsement of the master. But the man who went softly, by circuitous ways, peering with caution, seeking after secrecy—that was the man who received no suspension of judgment from White Fang, and who went away abruptly, hurriedly, and without dignity.

Weedon Scott had set himself the task of redeeming White Fang—or rather, of redeeming mankind from the wrong it had done White Fang. It was a matter of principle and conscience. He felt that the ill done White Fang was a debt incurred by man and that it must be paid. So he went out of his way to be especially kind to the Fighting Wolf. Each day he made it a point to caress and pet White Fang, and to do it at length.

At first suspicious and hostile, White Fang grew to like this petting. But there was one thing that he never outgrew—his growling. Growl he would, from the moment the petting began until it ended. But it was a growl with a new note in it. A stranger could not hear this note, and to such a stranger the growling of White Fang was an exhibition of primordial savagery, nerve-racking and blood-curdling. But White Fang's throat had become harsh-fibred from the making of ferocious sounds through the many years since his first little rasp of anger in the lair of his cubhood, and he could not soften the sounds of that throat now to express the gentleness he felt. Nevertheless, Weedon Scott's ear and sympathy were fine enough to catch the new note all but drowned in the fierceness—the note that was the faintest hint of a croon of content and that none but he could hear.

As the days went by, the evolution of like into love was accelerated. White Fang himself began to grow aware of it, though in his consciousness he knew not what love was. It manifested itself to him as a void in his being—a hungry, aching, yearning void that clamoured to be filled. It was a pain and an unrest; and it received easement only by the touch of the new god's presence. At such times love was a joy to him, a wild, keen-thrilling satisfaction. But when away from his god, the pain and the unrest returned; the void in him sprang up and pressed against him with its emptiness, and the hunger gnawed and gnawed unceasingly.

White Fang was in the process of finding himself. In spite of the maturity of his years and of the savage rigidity of the mould that had formed him, his nature was undergoing an expansion. There was a burgeoning within him of strange feelings and unwonted impulses. His old code of conduct was changing. In the past he had liked comfort and surcease from pain, disliked discomfort and pain, and he had adjusted his actions accordingly. But now it was different. Because of this new feeling within him, he ofttimes elected discomfort and pain for the sake of his god. Thus, in the early morning, instead of roaming and foraging, or lying in a sheltered nook, he would wait for hours on the cheerless cabin-stoop for a sight of the god's face. At night, when the god returned home, White Fang would leave the warm sleeping-place he had burrowed in the snow in order to receive the friendly snap of fingers and the word of greeting. Meat, even meat itself, he would forego to be with his god, to receive a caress from him or to accompany him down into the town.

Like had been replaced by love. And love was the plummet dropped down into the deeps of him where like had never gone. And responsive, out of his deeps had come the new thing—love. That which was given unto him did he return. This was a god indeed, a love-god, a warm and radiant god, in whose light White Fang's nature expanded as a flower expands under the sun.

But White Fang was not demonstrative. He was too old, too firmly moulded, to become adept at expressing himself in new ways. He was too self-possessed, too strongly poised in his own isolation. Too long had he cultivated reticence, aloofness, and moroseness. He had never barked in his life, and he could not now learn to bark a welcome when his god approached. He was never in the way, never extravagant nor foolish in the expression of his love. He never ran to meet his god. He waited at a distance; but he always waited, was always there. His love partook of the nature of worship, dumb, inarticulate, a silent adoration. Only by the steady regard of his eyes did he express his love, and by the unceasing following with his eyes of his god's every movement. Also, at times, when his god looked at him and spoke to him, he betrayed an awkward self-consciousness, caused by the struggle of his love to express itself and his physical inability to express it.

He learned to adjust himself in many ways to his new mode of life. It was borne in upon him that he must let his master's dogs alone. Yet his dominant nature asserted itself, and he had first to thrash them into an acknowledgment of his superiority and leadership. This accomplished, he had little trouble with them. They gave trail to him when he came and went or walked among them, and when he asserted his will they obeyed.

In the same way, he came to tolerate Matt—as a possession of his master. His master rarely fed him. Matt did that, it was his business; yet White Fang divined that it was his master's food he ate and that it was his master who thus fed him vicariously. Matt it was who tried to put him into the harness and make him haul sled with the other dogs. But Matt failed. It was not until Weedon Scott put the harness on White Fang and worked him, that he understood. He took it as his master's will that Matt should drive him and work him just as he drove and worked his master's other dogs.

Different from the Mackenzie toboggans were the Klondike sleds with runners under them. And different was the method of driving the dogs. There was no fan-formation of the team. The dogs worked in single file, one behind another, hauling on double traces. And here, in the Klondike, the leader was indeed the leader. The wisest as well as strongest dog was the leader, and the team obeyed him and feared him. That White Fang should quickly gain this post was inevitable. He could not be satisfied with less, as Matt learned after much inconvenience and trouble. White Fang picked out the post for himself, and Matt backed his judgment with strong language after the experiment had been tried. But, though he worked in the sled in the day, White Fang did not forego the guarding of his master's property in the night. Thus he was on duty all the time, ever vigilant and faithful, the most valuable of all the dogs.

"Makin' free to spit out what's in me," Matt said, one day, "I beg to state that you was a wise guy all right when you paid the price you did for that dog. You clean swindled Beauty Smith on top of pushin' his face in with your fist."

A recrudescence of anger glinted in Weedon Scott's gray eyes, and he muttered savagely, "The beast!"

In the late spring a great trouble came to White Fang. Without warning, the love-master disappeared. There had been warning, but White Fang was unversed in such things and did not understand the packing of a grip. He remembered afterward that this packing had preceded the master's disappearance; but at the time he suspected nothing. That night he waited for the master to return. At midnight the chill wind that blew drove him to shelter at the rear of the cabin. There he drowsed, only half asleep, his ears keyed for the first sound of the familiar step. But, at two in the morning, his anxiety drove him out to the cold front stoop, where he crouched and waited.

But no master came. In the morning the door opened and Matt stepped outside. White Fang gazed at him wistfully. There was no common speech by which he might learn what he wanted to know. The days came and went, but never the master. White Fang, who had never known sickness in his life, became sick. He became very sick, so sick that Matt was finally compelled to bring him inside the cabin. Also, in writing to his employer, Matt devoted a postscript to White Fang.

Weedon Scott, reading the letter down in Circle City, came upon the following:

"That dam wolf wont work. Wont eat. ain't got no spunk left. All the dogs is licking him. Wants to know what has become of you, and I don't know how to tell him. Mebbe he is going to die."

It was as Matt had said. White Fang had ceased eating, lost heart, and allowed every dog of the team to thrash him. In the cabin he lay on the floor near the stove, without interest in food, in Matt, nor in life. Matt might talk gently to him or swear at him, it was all the same; he never did more than turn his dull eyes upon the man, then drop his head back to its customary position on his fore-paws.

And then, one night, Matt, reading to himself with moving lips and mumbled sounds, was startled by a low whine from White Fang. He had got upon his feet, his ears cocked toward the door, and he was listening intently. A moment later, Matt heard a footstep. The door opened, and Weedon Scott stepped in. The two men shook hands. Then Scott looked around the room.

"Where's the wolf?" he asked.

Then he discovered him, standing where he had been lying, near to the stove. He had not rushed forward after the manner of other dogs. He stood, watching and waiting.

"Holy smoke!" Matt exclaimed. "Look at 'm wag his tail!"

Weedon Scott strode half across the room toward him, at the same time calling him. White Fang came to him, not with a great bound, yet quickly. He was awkward from self-consciousness, but as he drew near, his eyes took on a strange expression. Something, an incommunicable vastness of feeling, rose up into his eyes as a light and shone forth.

"He never looked at me that way all the time you was gone," Matt commented.

Weedon Scott did not hear. He was squatting down on his heels, face to face with White Fang and petting him—rubbing at the roots of the ears, making long, caressing strokes down the neck to the shoulders, tapping the spine gently with the balls of his fingers. And White Fang was growling responsively, the crooning note of the growl more pronounced than ever.

But that was not all. What of his joy, the great love in him, ever surging and struggling to express itself, succeeded in finding a new mode of expression. He suddenly thrust his head forward and nudged his way in between the master's arm and body. And here, confined, hidden from view all except his ears, no longer growling, he continued to nudge and snuggle.

The two men looked at each other. Scott's eyes were shining.

"Gosh!" said Matt in an awe-stricken voice.

A moment later, when he had recovered himself, he said, "I always insisted that wolf was a dog. Look at 'm!"

With the return of the love-master, White Fang's recovery was rapid. Two nights and a day he spent in the cabin. Then he sallied forth. The sled-dogs had forgotten his prowess. They remembered only the latest, which was his weakness and sickness. At the sight of him as he came out of the cabin, they sprang upon him.

"Talk about your rough-houses," Matt murmured glee-fully, standing in the doorway and looking on. "Give 'm hell, you wolf! Give 'm hell!—and then some!"

White Fang did not need the encouragement. The return of the love-master was enough. Life was flowing through him again, splendid and indomitable. He fought from sheer joy, finding in it an expression of much that he felt and that other vise was without speech. There could be but one ending. The team dispersed in ignominious defeat, and it was not until after dark that the dogs came sneaking back, one by one, by meekness and humility signifying their fealty to White Fang.

Having learned to snuggle, White Fang was guilty of it often. It was the final word. He could not go beyond it. The one thing of which he had always been particularly jealous, was his head. He had always disliked to have it touched. It was the Wild in him, the fear of hurt and of the trap, that had given rise to the panicky impulses to avoid contacts. It was the mandate of his instinct that that head must be free. And now, with the love-master, his snuggling was the deliberate act of putting himself into a position of hopeless helplessness. It was an expression of perfect confidence, of absolute self-surrender, as though he said: "I put myself into thy hands. Work thou thy will with me."

One night, not long after the return, Scott and Matt sat at a game of cribbage preliminary to going to bed. "Fifteen-two, fifteen-four an' a pair makes six," Matt was pegging up, when there was an outcry and sound of snarling without. They looked at each other as they started to rise to their feet.

"The wolf's nailed somebody," Matt said.

A wild scream of fear and anguish hastened them.

"Bring a light!" Scott shouted, as he sprang outside.

Matt followed with the lamp, and by its light they saw a man lying on his back in the snow. His arms were folded, one above the other, across his face and throat. Thus he was trying to shield himself from White Fang's teeth. And there was need for it. White Fang was in a rage, wickedly making his attack on the most vulnerable spot. From shoulder to wrist of the crossed arms, the coat-sleeve, blue flannel shirt and undershirt were ripped in rags, while the arms themselves were terribly slashed and streaming blood.

All this the two men saw in the first instant. The next instant Weedon Scott had White Fang by the throat and was dragging him clear. White Fang struggled and snarled, but made no attempt to bite, while he quickly quieted down at a sharp word from the master.

Matt helped the man to his feet. As he arose he lowered his crossed arms, exposing the bestial face of Beauty Smith. The dog-musher let go of him precipitately, with action similar to that of a man who has picked up live fire. Beauty Smith blinked in the lamplight and looked about him. He caught sight of White Fang and terror rushed into his face.

At the same moment Matt noticed two objects lying in the snow. He held the lamp close to them, indicating them with his toe for his employer's benefit—a steel dog-chain and a stout club.

Weedon Scott saw and nodded. Not a word was spoken. The dog-musher laid his hand on Beauty Smith's shoulder and faced him to the right-about. No word needed to be spoken. Beauty Smith started.

In the meantime the love-master was patting White Fang and talking to him.

"Tried to steal you, eh? And you wouldn't have it! Well, well, he made a mistake, didn't he?"

"Must 'a' thought he had hold of seventeen devils," the dog-musher sniggered.

White Fang, still wrought up and bristling, growled and growled, the hair slowly lying down, the crooning note remote and dim, but growing in his throat.

# PART FIVE

# THE TAME

## CHAPTER 1

## THE LONG TRAIL

It was in the air. White Fang sensed the coming calamity, even before there was tangible evidence of it. In vague ways it was borne in upon him that a change was impending. He knew not how nor why, yet he got his feel of the oncoming event from the gods themselves. In ways subtler than they knew, they betrayed their intentions to the wolf-dog that haunted the cabin-stoop, and that, though he never came inside the cabin, knew what went on inside their brains.

"Listen to that, will you!" the dog-musher exclaimed at supper one night.

Weedon Scott listened. Through the door came a low, anxious whine, like a sobbing under the breath that has just grown audible. Then came the long sniff, as White Fang reassured himself that his god was still inside and had not yet taken himself off in mysterious and solitary flight.

"I do believe that wolf's on to you," the dog-musher said.

Weedon Scott looked across at his companion with eyes that almost pleaded, though this was given the lie by his words.

"What the devil can I do with a wolf in California?" he demanded.

"That's what I say," Matt answered. "What the devil can you do with a wolf in California?"

But this did not satisfy Weedon Scott. The other seemed to be judging him in a non-committal sort of way.

"White-man's dogs would have no show against him," Scott went on.

"He'd kill them on sight. If he didn't bankrupt me with damage suits, the authorities would take him away from me and electrocute him."

"He's a downright murderer, I know," was the dog-musher's comment.

Weedon Scott looked at him suspiciously.

"It would never do," he said decisively.

"It would never do," Matt concurred. "Why, you'd have to hire a man 'specially to take care of 'm."

The other's suspicion was allayed. He nodded cheerfully. In the silence that followed, the low, half-sobbing whine was heard at the door and then the long, questing sniff.

"There's no denyin' he thinks a hell of a lot of you," Matt said.

The other glared at him in sudden wrath. "Damn it all, man! I know my own mind and what's best!"

"I'm agreein' with you, only . . ."

"Only what?" Scott snapped out.

"Only . . ." the dog-musher began softly, then changed his mind and betrayed a rising anger of his own. "Well, you needn't get so allfired het up about it. Judgin' by your actions one'd think you didn't know your own mind."

Weedon Scott debated with himself for a while, and then said more gently: "You are right, Matt. I don't know my own mind, and that's what's the trouble."

"Why, it would be rank ridiculousness for me to take that dog along," he broke out after another pause.

"I'm agreein' with you," was Matt's answer, and again his employer was not quite satisfied with him.

"But how in the name of the great Sardanapalus he knows you're goin' is what gets me," the dog-musher continued innocently.

"It's beyond me, Matt," Scott answered, with a mournful shake of the head.

Then came the day when, through the open cabin door, White Fang saw the fatal grip on the floor and the love-master packing things into it. Also, there were comings and goings, and the erstwhile placid atmosphere of the cabin was vexed with strange perturbations and unrest. Here was indubitable evidence. White Fang had already sensed it. He now reasoned it. His god was preparing for another flight. And since he had not taken him with him before so, now, he could look to be left behind.

That night he lifted the long wolf-howl. As he had howled, in his puppy days, when he fled back from the Wild to the village to find it vanished and naught but a rubbish-heap to mark the site of Gray Beaver's tepee, so now he pointed his muzzle to the cold stars and told to them his woe.

Inside the cabin the two men had just gone to bed.

"He's gone off his food again," Matt remarked from his bunk.

There was a grunt from Weedon Scott's bunk, and a stir of blankets.

"From the way he cut up the other time you went away, I wouldn't wonder this time but what he died."

The blankets in the other bunk stirred irritably.

"Oh, shut up!" Scott cried out through the darkness. "You nag worse than a woman."

"I'm agreein' with you," the dog-musher answered, and Weedon Scott was not quite sure whether or not the other had snickered.

The next day White Fang's anxiety and restlessness were even more pronounced. He dogged his master's heels whenever he left the cabin, and haunted the front stoop when he remained inside. Through the open door he could catch glimpses of the luggage on the floor. The grip had been joined by two large canvas bags and a box. Matt was rolling the master's blankets and fur robe inside a small tarpaulin. White Fang whined as he watched the operation.

Later on, two Indians arrived. He watched them closely as they shouldered the luggage and were led off down the hill by Matt, who carried the bedding and the grip. But White Fang did not follow them. The master was still in the cabin. After a time, Matt returned. The master came to the door and called White Fang inside.

"You poor devil," he said gently, rubbing White Fang's ears and tapping his spine. "I'm hitting the long trail, old man, where you cannot follow. Now give me a growl—the last, good, goodby growl."

But White Fang refused to growl. Instead, and after a wistful, searching look, he snuggled in, burrowing his head out of sight between the master's arm and body.

"There she blows!" Matt cried. From the Yukon arose the hoarse bellowing of a river steamboat. "You've got to cut it short. Be sure and lock the front door. I'll go out the back. Get a move on!"

The two doors slammed at the same moment, and Weedon Scott waited for Matt to come around to the front. From inside the door came a low whining and sobbing. Then there were long, deep-drawn sniffs.

"You must take good care of him, Matt," Scott said, as they started down the hill. "Write and let me know how he gets along."

"Sure," the dog-musher answered. "But listen to that, will you!"

Both men stopped. White Fang was howling as dogs howl when their masters lie dead. He was voicing an utter woe, his cry bursting upward in great, heartbreaking rushes, dying down into quavering misery, and bursting upward again with rush upon rush of grief.

The Aurora was the first steamboat of the year for the Outside, and her decks were jammed with prosperous adventurers and broken gold seekers, all equally as mad to get to the Outside as they had been originally to get to the Inside. Near the gangplank, Scott was shaking hands with Matt, who was preparing to go ashore. But Matt's hand went limp in the other's grasp as his gaze shot past and remained fixed on something behind him. Scott turned to see. Sitting on the deck several feet away and watching wistfully was White Fang.

The dog-musher swore softly, in awe-stricken accents. Scott could only look in wonder.

"Did you lock the front door?" Matt demanded.

The other nodded, and asked, "How about the back?"

"You just bet I did," was the fervent reply.

White Fang flattened his ears ingratiatingly, but remained where he was, making no attempt to approach.

"I'll have to take 'm ashore with me."

Matt made a couple of steps toward White Fang, but the latter slid away from him. The dog-musher made a rush of it, and White Fang dodged between the legs of a group of men. Ducking, turning, doubling, he slid about the deck, eluding the other's efforts to capture him.

But when the love-master spoke, White Fang came to him with prompt obedience.

"Won't come to the hand that's fed 'm all these months," the dog-musher muttered resentfully. "And you—you ain't never fed 'm after them first days of gettin' acquainted. I'm blamed if I can see how he works it out that you're the boss."

Scott, who had been patting White Fang, suddenly bent closer and pointed out fresh-made cuts on his muzzle, and a gash between the eyes.

Matt bent over and passed his hand along White Fang's belly.

"We plumb forgot the window. He's all cut an' gouged underneath.

Must 'a' butted clean through it, b'gosh!"

But Weedon Scott was not listening. He was thinking rapidly. The Aurora's whistle hooted a final announcement of departure. Men were scurrying down the gangplank to the shore. Matt loosened the bandana from his own neck and started to put it around White Fang's. Scott grasped the dog-musher's hand.

"Goodby, Matt, old man. About the wolf—you needn't write. You see, I've . . . !"

"What!" the dog-musher exploded. "You don't mean to say . . . ?"

"The very thing I mean. Here's your bandana. I'll write,to you about him."

Matt paused halfway down the gang-plank.

"He'll never stand the climate!" he shouted back. "Unless you clip 'm in warm weather!"

The gangplank was hauled in, and the Aurora swung out from the bank. Weedon Scott waved a last good-by. Then he turned and bent over White Fang, standing by his side.

"Now growl, damn you, growl," he said, as he patted the responsive head and rubbed the flattening ears.

## CHAPTER 2

# THE SOUTHLAND

White Fang landed from the steamer in San Francisco. He was appalled. Deep in him, below any reasoning process or act of consciousness, he had associated power with godhead. And never had the white men seemed such marvellous gods as now, when he trod the slimy pavement of San Francisco. The log cabins he had known were replaced by towering buildings. The streets were crowded with peril wagons, carts, automobiles; great, straining horses pulling huge trucks; and monstrous cable and electric cars hooting and clanging through the midst, screeching their insistent menace after the manner of the lynxes he had known in the northern woods.

All this was the manifestation of power. Through it all, behind it all, was man, governing and controlling, expressing himself, as of old, by his mastery over matter. It was colossal, stunning. White Fang was awed. Fear sat upon him. As in his cubhood he had been made to feel his smallness and puniness on the day he first came in from the Wild to the village of Gray Beaver, so now, in his fullgrown stature and pride of strength, he was made to feel small and puny. And there were so many gods! He was made dizzy by the swarming of them. The thunder of the streets smote upon his ears. He was bewildered by the tremendous and endless rush and movement of things. As never before, he felt his dependence on the love-master, close at whose heels he followed, no matter what happened never losing sight of him.

But White Fang was to have no more than a nightmare vision of the city—an experience that was like a bad dream, unreal and terrible, that haunted him for long after in his dreams. He was put into a baggage-car by the master, chained in a corner in the midst of heaped trunks and valises. Here a squat and brawny god held sway, with much noise, hurling trunks and boxes about, dragging them in through the door and tossing them into the piles, or flinging them out of the door, smashing and crashing, to other gods who awaited them.

And here, in this inferno of luggage, was White Fang deserted by the master. Or at least White Fang thought he was deserted, until he smelled out the master's canvas clothes-bags alongside of him and proceeded to mount guard over them.

"'Bout time you come," growled the god of the car, an hour later, when Weedon Scott appeared at the door. "That dog of yourn won't let me lay a finger on your stuff."

White Fang emerged from the car. He was astonished. The nightmare city was gone. The car had been to him no more than a room in a house, and when he had entered it the city had been all around him. In the interval the city had disappeared. The roar of it no longer dinned upon his ears. Before him was smiling country, streaming with sunshine, lazy with quietude. But he had little time to marvel at the transformation. He accepted it as he accepted all the unaccountable doings and manifestations of the gods. It was their way.

There was a carriage waiting. A man and a woman approached the master. The woman's arms went out and clutched the master around the neck—a hostile act! The next moment Weedon Scott had torn loose from the embrace and closed with White Fang, who had become a snarling, raging demon.

"It's all right, mother," Scott was saying as he kept tight hold of White Fang and placated him. "He thought you were going to injure me, and he wouldn't stand for it. It's all right. It's all right. He'll learn soon enough."

"And in the meantime I may be permitted to love my son when his dog is not around," she laughed, though she was pale and weak from the fright.

She looked at White Fang, who snarled and bristled and glared malevolently.

"He'll have to learn, and he shall, without postponement," Scott said.

He spoke softly to White Fang until he had quieted him, then his voice became firm.

"Down, sir! Down with you!"

This had been one of the things taught him by the master, and White Fang obeyed, though he lay down reluctantly and sullenly.

"Now, mother."

Scott opened his arms to her, but kept his eyes on White Fang.

"Down!" he warned. "Down!"

White Fang, bristling silently, half-crouching as he rose, sank back and watched the hostile act repeated. But no harm came of it, nor of the embrace from the strange man-god that followed. Then the clothes-bags were taken into the carriage, the strange gods and the love-master followed, and White Fang pursued, now running vigilantly behind, now bristling up to the running horses and warning them that he was there to see that no harm befell the god they dragged so swiftly across the earth.

At the end of fifteen minutes, the carriage swung in through a stone gateway and on between a double row of arched and interlacing walnut trees. On either side stretched lawns, their broad sweep broken, here and there, by great, sturdy-limbed oaks. In the near distance, in contrast with the young green of the tended grass, sunburnt hay-fields showed tan and gold; while beyond were the tawny hills and upland pastures. From the head of the lawn, on the first soft swell from the valley-level, looked down the deep-porched, many-windowed house.

Little opportunity was given White Fang to see all this. Hardly had the carriage entered the grounds, when he was set upon by a sheep-dog, bright-eyed, sharp-muzzled, righteously indignant and angry. It was between him and the master, cutting him off. White Fang snarled no warning, but his hair bristled as he made his silent and deadly rush. This rush was never completed. He halted with awkward abruptness, with stiff forelegs bracing himself against his momentum, almost sitting down on his haunches, so desirous was he of avoiding contact with the dog he was in the act of attacking. It was a female, and the law of his kind thrust a barrier between. For him to attack her would require nothing less than a violation of his instinct.

But with the sheepdog it was otherwise. Being a female, she possessed no such instinct. On the other hand, being a sheepdog, her instinctive fear of the Wild, and especially of the wolf, was unusually keen. White Fang was to her a wolf, the hereditary marauder who had preyed upon her flocks from the time sheep were first herded and guarded by some dim ancestor of hers. And so, as he abandoned his rush at her and braced himself to avoid the contact, she sprang upon him. He snarled involuntarily as he felt her teeth in his shoulder, but beyond this made no offer to hurt her. He backed away, stifflegged with self-consciousness, and tried to go around her. He dodged this way and that, and curved and turned, but to no purpose. She remained always between him and the way he wanted to go.

"Here, Collie!" called the strange man in the carriage.

Weedon Scott laughed.

"Never mind, father. It is good discipline. White Fang will have to learn many things, and it's just as well that he begins now. He'll adjust himself all right."

The carriage drove on, and still Collie blocked White Fang's way. He tried to outrun her by leaving the drive and circling across the lawn; but she ran on the inner and smaller circle, and was always there, facing him with her two rows of gleaming teeth. Back he circled, across the drive to the other lawn, and again she headed him off.

The carriage was bearing the master away. White Fang caught glimpses of it disappearing amongst the trees. The situation was desperate. He essayed another circle. She followed, running swiftly. And then, suddenly, he turned upon her. It was his old fighting trick. Shoulder to shoulder, he struck her squarely. Not only was she overthrown. So fast had she been running that she rolled along, now on her back, now on her side, as she struggled to stop, clawing gravel with her feet and crying shrilly her hurt pride and indignation.

White Fang did not wait. The way was clear, and that was all he had wanted. She took after him, never ceasing her outcry. It was the straightaway now, and when it came to real running, White Fang could teach her things. She ran frantically, hysterically, straining to the utmost, advertising the effort she was making with every leap; and all the time White Fang slid smoothly away from her, silently, without effort, gliding like a ghost over the ground.

As he rounded the house to the *porte-cochère*, he came upon the carriage. It had stopped, and the master was alighting. At this moment, still running at top speed, White Fang became suddenly aware of an attack from the side. It was a deer-hound rushing upon him. White Fang tried to face it. But he was going too fast, and the hound was too close. It struck him on the side; and such was his forward momentum and the unexpectedness of it, White Fang was hurled to the ground and rolled clear over. He came out of the tangle a spectacle of malignancy, ears flattened back, lips writhing, nose wrinkling, his teeth clipping together as the fangs barely missed the hound's soft throat.

The master was running up, but was too far away; and it was Collie that saved the hound's life. Before White Fang could spring in and deliver the fatal stroke, and just as he was in the act of springing in,

Collie arrived. She had been out-manoeuvred and out-run, to say nothing of her having been unceremoniously tumbled in the gravel, and her arrival was like that of a tornado—made up of offended dignity, justifiable wrath, and instinctive hatred for this marauder from the Wild. She struck White Fang at right angles in the midst of his spring, and again he was knocked off his feet and rolled over.

The next moment the master arrived, and with one hand held White Fang, while the father called off the dogs.

"I say, this is a pretty warm reception for a poor lone wolf from the Arctic," the master said while White Fang calmed down under his caressing hand. "In all his life he's only been known once to go off his feet, and here he's been rolled twice in thirty seconds."

The carriage had driven away, and other strange gods had appeared from out the house. Some of these stood respectfully at a distance; but two of them, women, perpetrated the hostile act of clutching the master around the neck. White Fang, however, was beginning to tolerate this act. No harm seemed to come of it, while the noises the gods made were certainly not threatening. These gods also made overtures to White Fang, but he warned them off with a snarl, and the master did likewise with word of mouth. At such times White Fang leaned in close against the master's legs and received reassuring pats on the head.

The hound, under the command, "Dick! Lie down, sir!" had gone up the steps and lain down to one side on the porch, still growling and keeping a sullen watch on the intruder. Collie had been taken in charge by one of the woman-gods, who held arms around her neck and petted and caressed her; but Collie was very much perplexed and worried, whining and restless, outraged by the permitted presence of this wolf and confident that the gods were making a mistake.

All the gods started up the steps to enter the house. White Fang followed closely at the master's heels. Dick, on the porch, growled, and White Fang, on the steps, bristled and growled back.

"Take Collie inside and leave the two of them to fight it out," suggested Scott's father. "After that they'll be friends."

"Then White Fang, to show his friendship, will have to be chief mourner at the funeral," laughed the master.

The elder Scott looked incredulously, first at White Fang, then at Dick, and finally at his son.

"You mean that . . . ?"

Weedon nodded his head. "I mean just that. You'd have a dead Dick inside one minut-two minutes at the farthest."

He turned to White Fang. "Come on, you wolf. It's you that'll have to come inside."

White Fang walked stiff-legged up the steps and across the porch, with tail rigidly erect, keeping his eyes on Dick to guard against a flank attack, and at the same time prepared for whatever fierce manifestation of the unknown that might pounce out upon him from the interior of the house. But no thing of fear pounced out, and when he had gained the inside he scouted carefully around, looking for it and finding it not. Then he lay down with a contented grunt at the master's feet, observing all that went on, ever ready to spring to his feet and fight for life with the terrors he felt must lurk under the trap-roof of the dwelling.

## CHAPTER 3

# THE GOD'S DOMAIN

Not only was White Fang adaptable by nature, but he had travelled much, and knew the meaning and necessity of adjustment. Here, in Sierra Vista, which was the name of Judge Scott's place, White Fang quickly began to make himself at home. He had no further serious trouble with the dogs. They knew more about the ways of the Southland gods than did he, and in their eyes he had qualified when he accompanied the gods inside the house. Wolf that he was, and unprecedented as it was, the gods had sanctioned his presence, and they, the dogs of the gods, could only recognize this sanction.

Dick, perforce, had to go through a few stiff formalities at first, after which he calmly accepted White Fang as an addition to the premises. Had Dick had his way, they would have been good friends; but White Fang was averse to friendship. All he asked of other dogs was to be let alone. His whole life he had kept aloof from his kind, and he still desired to keep aloof. Dick's overtures bothered him, so he snarled Dick away. In the north he had learned the lesson that he must let the master's dogs alone, and he did not forget that lesson now. But he insisted on his own privacy and self-seclusion, and so thoroughly ignored Dick that that good-natured creature finally gave him up and scarcely took as much interest in him as in the hitching-post near the stable.

Not so with Collie. While she accepted him because it was the mandate of the gods, that was no reason that she should leave him in peace. Woven into her being was the memory of countless crimes he and his had perpetrated against her ancestry. Not in a day nor a generation were the ravaged sheepfolds to be forgotten. All this was a spur to her, pricking her to retaliation. She could not fly in the face of the gods who permitted him, but that did not prevent her from making life miserable for him in petty ways. A feud, ages old, was between them, and she, for one, would see to it that he was reminded.

So Collie took advantage of her sex to pick upon White Fang and maltreat him. His instinct would not permit him to attack her, while her persistence would not permit him to ignore her. When she rushed at him he turned his fur-protected shoulder to her sharp teeth and walked away stiff-legged and stately. When she forced him too hard, he was compelled to go about in a circle, his shoulder presented to her, his head turned from her, and on his face and in his eyes a patient and bored expression. Sometimes, however, a nip on his hind-quarters hastened his retreat and made it anything but stately. But as a rule he managed to maintain a dignity that was almost solemnity. He ignored her existence whenever it was possible, and made it a point to keep out of her way. When he saw or heard her coming, he got up and walked off.

There was much in other matters for White Fang to learn. Life in the Northland was simplicity itself when compared with the complicated affairs of Sierra Vista. First of all, he had to learn the family of the master. In a way he was prepared to do this. As Mit-sah and Kloo-kooch had belonged to Gray Beaver, sharing his food, his fire, and his blankets, so now, at Sierra Vista, belonged to the love-master all the denizens of the house.

But in this matter there was a difference, and many differences. Sierra Vista was a far vaster affair than the tepee of Gray Beaver. There were many persons to be considered. There was Judge Scott, and there was his wife. There were the master's two sisters, Beth and Mary. There was his wife, Alice, and then there were his children, Weedon and Maud, toddlers of four and six. There was no way for anybody to tell him about all these people, and of blood-ties and relationship he knew nothing whatever and never would be capable of knowing. Yet he quickly worked it out that all of them belonged to the master. Then, by observation, whenever opportunity offered, by study of action, speech, and the very intonations of the voice, he slowly learned the intimacy and the degree of favour they enjoyed with the master. And by this ascertained standard, White Fang treated them accordingly. What was of value to the master he valued; what was dear to the master was to be cherished by White Fang and guarded carefully.

Thus it was with the two children. All his life he had disliked children. He hated and feared their hands. The lessons were not tender that he had learned of their tyranny and cruelty in the days of the Indian villages. When Weedon and Maud had first approached him, he growled warningly and looked malignant. A cuff from the master and a sharp word had then compelled him to permit their caresses, though he growled and growled under their tiny hands, and in the growl there was no crooning note. Later, he observed that the boy and girl were of great value in the master's eyes. Then it was that no cuff nor sharp word was necessary before they could pat him.

Yet White Fang was never effusively affectionate. He yielded to the master's children with an ill but honest grace, and endured their fooling as one would endure a painful operation. When he could no longer endure, he would get up and stalk determinedly away from them. But after a time, he grew even to like the children. Still he was not demonstrative. He would not go up to them. On the other hand, instead of walking away at sight of them, he waited for them to come to him. And still later, it was noticed that a pleased light came into his eyes when he saw them approaching, and that he looked after them with an appearance of curious regret when they left him for other amusements.

All this was a matter of development, and took time. Next in his regard, after the children, was Judge Scott. There were two reasons, possibly, for this. First, he was evidently a valuable possession of the master's, and next, he was undemonstrative. White Fang liked to lie at his feet on the wide porch when he read the newspaper, from time to time favouring White Fang with a look or a word—untroublesome tokens that he recognized White Fang's presence and existence. But this was only when the master was not around. When the master appeared, all other beings ceased to exist so far as White Fang was concerned.

White Fang allowed all the members of the family to pet him and make much of him; but he never gave to them what he gave to the master. No caress of theirs could put the love-croon into his throat, and, try as they would, they could never persuade him into snuggling against them. This expression of abandon and surrender, of absolute trust, he reserved for the master alone. In fact, he never regarded the members of the family in any other light than possessions of the love-master.

Also White Fang had early come to differentiate between the family and the servants of the household. The latter were afraid of him, while he merely refrained from attacking them. This because he considered that they were likewise possessions of the master. Between White Fang and them existed a neutrality and no more. They cooked for the master and washed the dishes and did other things, just as Matt had done up in the Klondike. They were, in short, appurtenances of the household.

Outside the household there was even more for White Fang to learn. The master's domain was wide and complex, yet it had its metes and bounds. The land itself ceased at the county road. Outside was the common domain of all gods—the roads and streets. Then inside other fences were the particular domains of other gods. A myriad laws governed all these things and determined conduct; yet he did not know the speech of the gods, nor was there any way for him to learn save by experience. He obeyed his natural impulses until they ran him counter to some law. When this had been done a few times, he learned the law and after that observed it.

But most potent in his education were the cuff of the master's hand, the censure of the master's voice. Because of White Fang's very great love, a cuff from the master hurt him far more than any beating Gray Beaver or Beauty Smith had ever given him. They had hurt only the flesh of him; beneath the flesh the spirit had still raged, splendid and invincible. But with the master the cuff was always too light to hurt the flesh. Yet it went deeper. It was an expression of the master's disapproval, and White Fang's spirit wilted under it.

In point of fact, the cuff was rarely administered. The master's voice was sufficient. By it White Fang knew whether he did right or not. By it he trimmed his conduct and adjusted his actions. It was the compass by which he steered and learned to chart the manners of a new land and life.

In the Northland, the only domesticated animal was the dog. All other animals lived in the Wild, and were, when not too formidable, lawful spoil for any dog. All his days White Fang had foraged among the live things for food. It did not enter his head that in the Southland it was otherwise. But this he was to learn early in his residence in Santa Clara Valley. Sauntering around the corner of the house in the early morning, he came upon a chicken that had escaped from the chicken-yard. White Fang's natural impulse was to eat it. A couple of bounds, a flash of teeth and a frightened squawk, and he had scooped in the adventurous fowl. It was farm-bred and fat and tender; and White Fang licked his chops and decided that such fare was good.

Later in the day, he chanced upon another stray chicken near the stables. One of the grooms ran to the rescue. He did not know White

Fang's breed, so for weapon he took a light buggy-whip. At the first cut of the whip, White Fang left the chicken for the man. A club might have stopped White Fang, but not a whip. Silently, without flinching, he took a second cut in his forward rush, and as he leaped for the throat the groom cried out, "My God!" and staggered backward. He dropped the whip and shielded his throat with his arms. In consequence, his forearm was ripped open to the bone.

The man was badly frightened. It was not so much White Fang's ferocity as it was his silence that unnerved the groom. Still protecting his throat and face with his torn and bleeding arm, he tried to retreat to the barn. And it would have gone hard with him had not Collie appeared on the scene. As she had saved Dick's life, she now saved the groom's. She rushed upon White Fang in frenzied wrath. She had been right. She had known better than the blundering gods. All her suspicions were justified. Here was the ancient marauder up to his old tricks again.

The groom escaped into the stables, and White Fang backed away before Collie's wicked teeth, or presented his shoulder to them and circled round and round. But Collie did not give over, as was her wont, after a decent interval of chastisement. On the contrary, she grew more excited and angry every moment, until, in the end, White Fang flung dignity to the winds and frankly fled away from her across the fields.

"He'll learn to leave chickens alone," the master said. "But I can't give him the lesson until I catch him in the act."

Two nights later came the act, but on a more generous scale than the master had anticipated. White Fang had observed closely the chicken-yards and the habits of the chickens. In the night-time, after they had gone to roost, he climbed to the top of a pile of newly hauled lumber. From there he gained the roof of a chicken-house, passed over the ridgepole and dropped to the ground inside. A moment later he was inside the house, and the slaughter began.

In the morning, when the master came out on to the porch, fifty white Leghorn hens, laid out in a row by the groom, greeted his eyes. He whistled to himself, softly, first with surprise, and then, at the end, with admiration. His eyes were likewise greeted by White Fang, but about the latter there were no signs of shame nor guilt. He carried himself with pride, as though, forsooth, he had achieved a deed praiseworthy and meritorious. There was about him no consciousness of sin. The master's lips tightened as he faced the disagreeable task. Then he talked harshly to the unwitting culprit, and in his voice there was nothing but godlike wrath. Also, he held White Fang's nose down to the slain hens, and at the same time cuffed him soundly.

White Fang never raided a chicken-roost again. It was against the law, and he had learned it. Then the master took him into the chicken-yards. White Fang's natural impulse, when he saw the live food fluttering about him and under his very nose, was to spring upon it. He obeyed the impulse, but was checked by the master's voice. They continued in the yards for half an hour. Time and again the impulse surged over White Fang, and each time, as he yielded to it, he was checked by the master's voice. Thus it was he learned the law, and ere he left the domain of the chickens, he had learned to ignore their existence.

"You can never cure a chicken-killer." Judge Scott shook his head sadly at the luncheon table, when his son narrated the lesson he had given White Fang. "Once they've got the habit and the taste of blood . . ." Again he shook his head sadly.

But Weedon Scott did not agree with his father.

"I'll tell you what I'll do," he challenged finally. "I'll lock White Fang in with the chickens all afternoon."

"But think of the chickens," objected the Judge.

"And furthermore," the son went on, "for every chicken he kills, I'll pay you one dollar gold coin of the realm."

"But you should penalize father, too," interposed Beth.

Her sister seconded her, and a chorus of approval arose from around the table. Judge Scott nodded his head in agreement.

"All right." Weedon Scott pondered for a moment. "And if, at the end of the afternoon, White Fang hasn't harmed a chicken, for every ten minutes of the time he has spent in the yard, you will have to say to him, gravely and with deliberation, just as if you were sitting on the bench and solemnly passing judgment, 'White Fang, you are smarter than I thought.'"

From hidden points of vantage the family watched the performance. But it was a fizzle. Locked in the yard and there deserted by the master, White Fang lay down and went to sleep. Once he got up and walked over to the trough for a drink of water. The chickens he calmly ignored. So far as he was concerned they did not exist. At four o'clock he executed a running jump, gained the roof of the chicken house and leaped to the ground outside, whence he sauntered gravely to the house. He had learned the law. And on the porch, before the delighted family, Judge Scott, face to face with White Fang, said slowly and solemnly, sixteen times, "White Fang, you are smarter than I thought."

But it was the multiplicity of laws that befuddled White Fang and often brought him into disgrace. He had to learn that he must not touch the chickens that belonged to other gods. Then there were cats, and rabbits, and turkeys; all these he must let alone. In fact, when he had but partly learned the law, his impression was that he must leave all live things alone. Out in the back-pasture, a quail could flutter up under his nose unharmed. All tense and trembling with eagerness and desire, he mastered his instinct and stood still. He was obeying the will of the gods.

And then, one day, again out in the back-pasture, he saw Dick start a jackrabbit and run it. The master himself was looking on and did not interfere. Nay, he encouraged White Fang to join in the chase. And thus he learned that there was no taboo on jackrabbits. In the end he worked out the complete law. Between him and all domestic animals there must be no hostilities. If not amity, at least neutrality must obtain. But the other animal the squirrels, and quail, and cottontails, were creatures of the Wild who had never yielded allegiance to man. They were the lawful prey of any dog. It was only the tame that the gods protected, and between the tame deadly strife was not permitted. The gods held the power of life and death over their subjects, and the gods were jealous of their power.

Life was complex in the Santa Clara Valley after the simplicities of the Northland. And the chief thing demanded by these intricacies of civilization was control, restraint—a poise of self that was as delicate as the fluttering of gossamer wings and at the same time as rigid as steel. Life had a thousand faces, and White Fang found he must meet them all—thus, when he went to town, in to San Jose, running behind the carriage or loafing about the streets when the carriage stopped. Life flowed past him, deep and wide and varied, continually impinging upon his senses, demanding of him instant and endless adjustments and correspondences, and compelling him, almost always, to suppress his natural impulses.

There were butcher-shops where meat hung within reach. This meat he must not touch. There were cats at the houses the master visited that must be let alone. And there were dogs everywhere that snarled at him and that he must not attack. And then, on the crowded sidewalks, there were persons innumerable whose attention he attracted. They would stop and look at him, point him out to one another, examine him, talk to him, and, worst of all, pat him. And these perilous contacts from all these strange hands he must endure. Yet this endurance he achieved. Furthermore he got over being awkward and self-conscious. In a lofty way he received the attentions of the multitudes of strange gods. With condescension he accepted their condescension. On the other hand, there was something about him that prevented great familiarity. They patted him on the head and passed on, contented and pleased with their own daring.

But it was not all easy for White Fang. Running behind the carriage in the outskirts of San Jose, he encountered certain small boys who made a practice of flinging stones at him. Yet he knew that it was not permitted him to pursue and drag them down. Here he was compelled to violate his instinct of self-preservation, and violate it he did, for he was becoming tame and qualifying himself for civilization.

Nevertheless, White Fang was not quite satisfied with the arrangement. He had no abstract ideas about justice and fair play. But there is a certain sense of equity that resides in life, and it was this sense in him that resented the unfairness of his being permitted no defence against the stone-throwers. He forgot that in the covenant entered into between him and the gods they were pledged to care for him and defend him. But one day the master sprang from the carriage, whip in hand, and gave the stone-throwers a thrashing. After that they threw stones no more, and White Fang understood and was satisfied.

One other experience of similar nature was his. On the way to town, hanging around the saloon at the cross-roads, were three dogs that made a practice of rushing out upon him when he went by. Knowing his deadly method of fighting, the master had never ceased impressing upon White Fang the law that he must not fight. As a result, having learned the lesson well, White Fang was hard put whenever he passed the cross-roads saloon. After the first rush, each time, his snarl kept the three dogs at a distance, but they trailed along behind, yelping and bickering and insulting him. This endured for some time. The men at the saloon even urged the dogs on to attack White Fang. One day they openly sicked the dogs on him. The master stopped the carriage.

"Go to it," he said to White Fang.

But White Fang could not believe. He looked at the master, and he looked at the dogs. Then he looked back eagerly and questioningly at the master.

The master nodded his head. "Go to them, old fellow. Eat them up."

White Fang no longer hesitated. He turned and leaped silently among his enemies. All three faced him. There was a great snarling and growling, a clashing of teeth and a flurry of bodies. The dust of the road arose in a cloud and screened the battle. But at the end of several minutes two dogs were struggling in the dirt and the third was in full flight. He leaped a ditch, went through a rail fence, and fled across a field. White Fang followed, sliding over the ground in wolf fashion and with wolf speed, swiftly and without noise, and in the centre of the field he dragged down and slew the dog.

With this triple killing his main troubles with dogs ceased. The word went up and down the valley, and men saw to it that their dogs did not molest the Fighting Wolf.

## CHAPTER 4

# THE CALL OF KIND

The months came and went. There was plenty of food and no work in the Southland, and White Fang lived fat and prosperous and happy. Not alone was he in the geographical Southland, for he was in the Southland of life. Human kindness was like a sun shining upon him, and he flourished like a flower planted in good soil.

And yet he remained somehow different from other dogs. He knew the law even better than did the dogs that had known no other life, and he observed the law more punctiliously; but still there was about him a suggestion of lurking ferocity, as though the Wild still lingered in him and the wolf in him merely slept.

He never chummed with other dogs. Lonely he had lived, so far as his kind was concerned, and lonely he would continue to live. In his puppyhood, under the persecution of Lip-lip and the puppy-pack, and in his fighting days with Beauty Smith, he had acquired a fixed aversion for dogs. The natural course of his life had been diverted, and, recoiling from his kind, he had clung to the human.

Besides, all Southland dogs looked upon him with suspicion. He aroused in them their instinctive fear of the Wild, and they greeted him always with snarl and growl and belligerent hatred. He, on the other hand, learned that it was not necessary to use his teeth upon them. His naked fangs and writhing lips were uniformly efficacious, rarely failing to send a bellowing on-rushing dog back on its haunches.

But there was one trial in White Fang's life—Collie. She never gave him a moment's peace. She was not so amenable to the law as he. She defied all efforts of the master to make her become friends with White Fang. Ever in his ears was sounding her sharp and nervous snarl. She had never forgiven him the chicken-killing episode, and persistently held to the belief that his intentions were bad. She found him guilty before the act, and treated him accordingly. She became a pest to him, like a policeman following him around the stable and the grounds, and, if he even so much as glanced curiously at a pigeon or chicken, bursting into an outcry of indignation and wrath. His favorite way of ignoring her was to lie down, with his head on his fore-paws, and pretend sleep. This always dumbfounded and silenced her.

With the exception of Collie, all things went well with White Fang. He had learned control and poise, and he knew the law. He achieved a staidness, and calmness, and philosophic tolerance. He no longer lived in a hostile environment. Danger and hurt and death did not lurk everywhere about him. In time, the unknown, as a thing of terror and menace ever impending, faded away. Life was soft and easy. It flowed along smoothly, and neither fear nor foe lurked by the way.

He missed the snow without being aware of it. "An unduly long summer" would have been his thought had he thought about it, as it was, he merely missed the snow in a vague, subconscious way. In the same fashion, especially in the heat of summer when he suffered from the sun, he experienced faint longings for the Northland. Their only effect upon him, however, was to make him uneasy and restless without his knowing what was the matter.

White Fang had never been very demonstrative. Beyond his snuggling and the throwing of a crooning note into his love-growl, he had no way of expressing his love. Yet it was given him to discover a third way. He had always been susceptible to the laughter of the gods. Laughter had affected him with madness, made him frantic with rage. But he did not have it in him to be angry with the love-master, and when that god elected to laugh at him in a good-natured, bantering way, he was nonplused. He could feel the pricking and stinging of the old anger as it strove to rise up in him, but it strove against love. He could not be angry; yet he had to do something. At first he was dignified, and the master laughed the harder. Then he tried to be more dignified, and the master laughed harder than before. In the end, the master laughed him out of his dignity. His jaws slightly parted, his lips lifted a little, and a quizzical expression that was more love than humour came into his eyes. He had learned to laugh.

Likewise he learned to romp with the master, to be tumbled down and rolled over, and be the victim of innumerable rough tricks. In return he feigned anger, bristling and growling ferociously, and clipping his teeth together in snaps that had all the seeming of deadly intention. But he never forgot himself. Those snaps were always delivered on the empty air. At the end of such a romp, when blow and cuff and snap and snarl were fast and furious, they would break off suddenly and stand several feet apart, glaring at each other. And then, just as suddenly, like the sun rising on a stormy sea, they would begin to laugh. This would always culminate with the master's arms going around White Fang's neck and shoulders while the latter crooned and growled his love-song.

But nobody else ever romped with White Fang. He did not permit it. He stood on his dignity, and when they attempted it, his warning snarl and bristling mane were anything but playful. That he allowed the master these liberties was no reason that he should be a common dog, loving here and loving there, everybody's property for a romp and good time. He loved with single heart and refused to cheapen himself or his love.

The master went out on horseback a great deal, and to accompany him was one of White Fang's chief duties in life. In the Northland he had evidenced his fealty by toiling in the harness; but there were no sleds in the Southland, nor did dogs pack burdens on their backs. So he rendered fealty in the new way, by running with the master's horse. The longest day never played White Fang out. His was the gait of the wolf, smooth, tireless, and effortless, and at the end of fifty miles he would come in jauntily ahead of the horse.

It was in connection with the riding, that White Fang achieved one other mode of expression—remarkable in that he did it but twice in all his life. The first time occurred when the master was trying to teach a spirited thoroughbred the method of opening and closing gates without the rider's dismounting. Time and again and many times he ranged the horse up to the gate in the effort to close it, and each time the horse became frightened and backed and plunged away. It grew more nervous and excited every moment. When it reared, the master put the spurs to it and made it drop its forelegs back to earth, whereupon it would begin kicking with its hindlegs. White Fang watched the performance with increasing anxiety until he could contain himself no longer, when he sprang in front of the horse and barked savagely and warningly.

Though he often tried to bark thereafter, and the master encouraged him, he succeeded only once, and then it was not in the master's presence. A scamper across the pasture, a jackrabbit rising suddenly under the horse's feet, a violent sheer, a stumble, a fall to earth, and a broken leg for the master were the cause of it. White Fang sprang in a rage at the throat of the offending horse, but was checked by the master's voice.

"Home! Go home!" the master commanded, when he had ascertained his injury.

White Fang was disinclined to desert him. The master thought of writing a note, but searched his pockets vainly for pencil and paper. Again he commanded White Fang to go home.

The latter regarded him wistfully, started away, then returned and whined softly. The master talked to him gently but seriously, and he cocked his ears and listened with painful intentness.

"That's all right, old fellow, you just run along home," ran the talk. "Go on home and tell them what's happened to me. Home with you, you wolf. Get along home!"

White Fang knew the meaning of "home," and though he did not understand the remainder of the master's language, he knew it was his will that he should go home. He turned and trotted reluctantly away. Then he stopped, undecided, and looked back over his shoulder.

"Go home!" came the sharp command, and this time he obeyed.

The family was on the porch, taking the cool of the afternoon, when White Fang arrived. He came in among them, panting, covered with dust.

"Weedon's back," Weedon's mother announced.

The children welcomed White Fang with glad cries and ran to meet him. He avoided them and passed down the porch, but they cornered him against a rocking-chair and the railing He growled and tried to push by them. Their mother looked apprehensively in their direction.

"I confess, he makes me nervous around the children," she said. "I have a dread that he will turn upon them unexpectedly some day."

Growling savagely, White Fang sprang out of the corner, overturning the boy and the girl. The mother called them to her and comforted them, telling them not to bother White Fang.

"A wolf if a wolf," commented Judge Scott. "There is no trusting one."

"But he is not all wolf," interposed Beth, standing for her brother in his absence.

"You have only Weedon's opinion for that," rejoined the Judge. "He merely surmises that there is some strain of dog in White Fang; but as he will tell you himself, he knows nothing about it. As for his appearance—"

He did not finish the sentence. White Fang stood before him, growling fiercely.

"Go away! Lie down, sir!" Judge Scott commanded

White Fang turned to the love-master's wife. She screamed with fright as he seized her dress in his teeth and dragged on it till the frail fabric tore away. By this time he had become the centre of interest. He had ceased from his growling and stood, head up, looking into their faces. His throat worked spasmodically, but made no sound, while he struggled with all his body, convulsed with the effort to rid himself of the incommunicable something that strained for utterance

"I hope he is not going mad," said Weedon's mother. "I told Weedon that I was afraid the warm climate would not agree with an Arctic animal."

"He's trying to speak, I do believe," Beth announced.

At this moment speech came to White Fang, rushing up in a great burst of barking.

"Something has happened to Weedon," his wife said decisively.

They were all on their feet, now, and White Fang ran down the steps, looking back for them to follow. For the second and last time in his life he had barked and made himself understood.

After this event he found a warmer place in the hearts of the Sierra Vista people, and even the groom whose arm he had slashed admitted that he was a wise dog even if he was a wolf. Judge Scott still held to the same opinion, and proved it to everybody's dissatisfaction by measurements and descriptions taken from the encyclopaedia and various works on natural history.

The days came and went, streaming their unbroken sunshine over the Santa Clara Valley. But as they grew shorter and White Fang's second winter in the Southland came on, he made a strange discovery. Collie's teeth were no longer sharp. There was a playfulness about her nips and a gentleness that prevented them from really hurting him. He forgot that she had made life a burden to him, and when she disported herself around him he responded solemnly, striving to be playful and becoming no more than ridiculous.

One day she led him off on a long chase through the back-pasture and into the woods. It was the afternoon that the master was to ride, and White Fang knew it. The horse stood saddled and waiting at the door. White Fang hesitated. But there was that in him deeper than all the law he had learned, than the customs that had moulded him, than his love for the master, than the very will to live of himself; and when, in the moment of his indecision, Collie nipped him and scampered off, he turned and followed after. The master rode alone that day; and in the woods, side by side, White Fang ran with Collie, as his mother, Kiche, and old One Eye had run long years before in the silent Northland forest.

# CHAPTER 5

# THE SLEEPING WOLF

It was about this time that the newspapers were full of the daring escape of a convict from San Quentin prison. He was a ferocious man. He had been ill-made in the making. He had not been born right, and he had not been helped any by the moulding he had received at the hands of society. The hands of society are harsh, and this man was a striking example of its handiwork. He was a beast—a human beast, it is true, but nevertheless so terrible a beast that he can best be characterized as carnivorous.

In San Quentin prison he had proved incorrigible. Punishment failed to break his spirit. He could die dumb-mad and fighting to the last, but he could not live and be beaten. The more fiercely he fought, the more harshly society handled him, and the only effect of harshness was to make him fiercer. Straitjackets, starvation, and beatings and clubbings were the wrong treatment for Jim Hall; but it was the treatment he received. It was the treatment he had received from the time he was a little pulpy boy in a San Francisco slum-soft clay in the hands of society and ready to be formed into something.

It was during Jim Hall's third term in prison that he encountered a guard that was almost as great a beast as he. The guard treated him unfairly, lied about him to the warden, lost him his credits, persecuted him. The difference between them was that the guard carried a bunch of keys and a revolver. Jim Hall had only his naked hands and his teeth. But he sprang upon the guard one day and used his teeth on the other's throat just like any jungle animal.

After this, Jim Hall went to live in the incorrigible cell. He lived there three years. The cell was of iron, the floor, the walls, the roof. He never left this cell. He never saw the sky nor the sunshine. Day was a twilight and night was a black silence. He was in an iron tomb, buried alive. He saw no human face, spoke to no human being. When his food was shoved in to him, he growled like a wild animal. He hated all things. For days and nights he bellowed his rage at the universe. For weeks and months he never made a sound, in the black silence eating his very soul. He was a man and a monstrosity, as fearful a thing of fear as ever gibbered in the visions of a maddened brain.

And then, one night, he escaped. The warden said it was impossible, but nevertheless the cell was empty, and half in half out of it lay the body of a dead guard. Two other dead guards marked his trail through the prison to the outer walls, and he had killed with his hands to avoid noise.

He was armed with the weapons of the slain guards—a live arsenal that fled through the hills pursued by the organized might of society. A heavy price of gold was upon his head. Avaricious farmers hunted him with shotguns. His blood might pay off a mortgage or send a son to college. Public-spirited citizens took down their rifles and went out after him. A pack of bloodhounds followed the way of his bleeding feet. And the sleuth-hounds of the law, the paid fighting animals of society, with telephone, and telegraph, and special train, clung to his trail night and day.

Sometimes they came upon him, and men faced him like heroes, or stampeded through barb-wire fences to the delight of the commonwealth reading the account at the breakfast table. It was after such encounters that the dead and wounded were carted back to the towns, and their places filled by men eager for the man-hunt.

And then Jim Hall disappeared. The bloodhounds vainly quested on the lost trail. Inoffensive ranchers in remote valleys were held up by armed men and compelled to identify themselves; while the remains of Jim Hall were discovered on a dozen mountainsides by greedy claimants for blood-money.

In the meantime the newspapers were read at Sierra Vista, not so much with interest as with anxiety. The women were afraid. Judge Scott pooh-poohed and laughed, but not with reason, for it was in his last days on the bench that Jim Hall had stood before him and received sentence. And in open courtroom, before all men, Jim Hall had proclaimed that the day would come when he would wreak vengeance on the judge that sentenced him.

For once, Jim Hall was right. He was innocent of the crime for which he was sentenced. It was a case, in the parlance of thieves and police, of 'railroading." Jim Hall was being "railroaded" to prison for a crime he had not committed. Because of the two prior convictions against him, Judge Scott imposed upon him a sentence of fifty years.

Judge Scott did not know all things, and he did not know that he was party to a police conspiracy, that the evidence was hatched and perjured, that Jim Hall was guiltless of the crime charged. And Jim Hall, on the other hand, did not know that Judge Scott was merely ignorant. Jim Hall believed that the judge knew all about it and was hand in glove with the police in the perpetration of the monstrous injustice. So it was, when the doom of fifty years of living death was uttered by Judge Scott, that Jim Hall, hating all things in the society that misused him, rose up and raged in the courtroom until dragged down by half a dozen of his blue-coated enemies. To him, Judge Scott was the keystone in the arch of injustice, and upon Judge Scott he emptied the vials of his wrath and hurled the threats of his revenge yet to come. Then Jim Hall went to his living death . . . and escaped.

Of all this White Fang knew nothing. But between him and Alice, the master's wife, there existed a secret. Each night, after Sierra Vista had gone to bed, she arose and let in White Fang to sleep in the big hall. Now White Fang was not a house-dog, nor was he permitted to sleep in the house; so each morning, early, she slipped down and let him out before the family was awake.

On one such night, while all the house slept, White Fang awoke and lay very quietly. And very quietly he smelled the air and read the message it bore of a strange god's presence. And to his ears came sounds of the strange god's movements. White Fang burst into no furious outcry. It was not his way. The strange god walked softly, but more softly walked White Fang, for he had no clothes to rub against the flesh of his body. He followed silently. In the Wild he had hunted live meat that was infinitely timid, and he knew the advantage of surprise.

The strange god paused at the foot of the great staircase and listened, and White Fang was as dead, so without movement was he as he watched and waited. Up that staircase the way led to the love-master and to the love-master's dearest possessions. White Fang bristled, but waited. The strange god's foot lifted. He was beginning the ascent.

Then it was that White Fang struck. He gave no warning, with no snarl anticipated his own action. Into the air he lifted his body in the spring that landed him on the strange god's back. White Fang clung with his fore-paws to the man's shoulders, at the same time burying his fangs into the back of the man's neck. He clung on for a moment, long enough to drag the god over backward. Together they crashed to the floor. White Fang leaped clear, and, as the man struggled to rise, was in again with the slashing fangs.

Sierra Vista awoke in alarm. The noise from downstairs was as that of a score of battling fiends. There were revolver shots. A man's voice screamed once in horror and anguish. There was a great snarling and growling, and over all arose a smashing and crashing of furniture and glass.

But almost as quickly as it had arisen, the commotion died away. The struggle had not lasted more than three minutes. The frightened household clustered at the top of the stairway. From below, as from out an abyss of blackness, came up a gurgling sound, as of air bubbling through water. Sometimes this gurgle became sibilant, almost a whistle. But this, too, quickly died down and ceased. Then naught came up out of the blackness save a heavy panting of some creature struggling sorely for air.

Weedon Scott pressed a button, and the staircase and downstairs hall were flooded with light. Then he and Judge Scott, revolvers in hand, cautiously descended. There was no need for this caution. White Fang had done his work. In the midst of the wreckage of overthrown and smashed furniture, partly on his side, his face hidden by an arm, lay a man. Weedon Scott bent over, removed the arm, and turned the man's face upward. A gaping throat explained the manner of his death.

"Jim Hall," said Judge Scott, and father and son looked significantly at each other.

Then they turned to White Fang. He, too, was lying on his side. His eyes were closed, but the lids slightly lifted in an effort to look at them as they bent over him, and the tail was perceptibly agitated in a vain effort to wag. Weedon Scott patted him, and his throat rumbled an acknowledging growl. But it was a weak growl at best, and it quickly ceased. His eyelids drooped and went shut, and his whole body seemed to relax and flatten out upon the floor.

"He's all in, poor devil," muttered the master.

"We'll see about that," asserted the Judge, as he started for the telephone.

"Frankly, he has one chance in a thousand," announced the surgeon, after he had worked an hour and a half on White Fang.

Dawn was breaking through the windows and dimming the electric lights. With the exception of the children, the whole family was gathered about the surgeon to hear his verdict.

"One broken hind-leg," he went on. "Three broken ribs, one at least of which has pierced the lungs. He has lost nearly all the blood in his body. There is a large likelihood of internal injuries. He must have been jumped upon. To say nothing of three bullet holes clear through him. One chance in a thousand is really optimistic. He hasn't a chance in ten thousand."

"But he mustn't lose any chance that might be of help to him," Judge Scott exclaimed. "Never mind expense. Put him under the X-ray—anything. Weedon, telegraph at once to San Francisco for Doctor Nichols. No reflection on you, doctor, you understand; but he must have the advantage of every chance."

The surgeon smiled indulgently. "Of course I understand. He deserves all that can be done for him. He must be nursed as you would nurse a human being, a sick child. And don't forget what I told you about temperature. I'll be back at ten o'clock again."

White Fang received the nursing. Judge Scott's suggestion of a trained nurse was indignantly clamoured down by the girls, who themselves undertook the task. And White Fang won out on the one chance in ten thousand denied him by the surgeon.

The latter was not to be censured for his misjudgment. All his life he had tended and operated on the soft humans of civilization, who lived sheltered lives and had descended out of many sheltered generations. Compared with White Fang, they were frail and flabby, and clutched life without any strength in their grip. White Fang had come straight from the Wild, where the weak perish early and shelter is vouchsafed to none. In neither his father nor his mother was there any weakness, nor in the generations before them. A constitution of iron and the vitality of the Wild were White Fang's inheritance, and he clung to life, the whole of him and every part of him, in spirit and in flesh, with the tenacity that of old belonged to all creatures.

Bound down a prisoner, denied even movement by the plaster casts and bandages, White Fang lingered out the weeks. He slept long hours and dreamed much, and through his mind passed an unending pageant of Northland visions. All the ghosts of the past arose and were with him. Once again he lived in the lair with Kiche, crept trembling to the knees of Gray Beaver to tender his allegiance, ran for his life before Lip-lip and all the howling bedlam of the puppy-pack.

He ran again through the silence, hunting his living food through the months of famine; and again he ran at the head of the team, the gut-whips of Mit-sah and Gray Beaver snapping behind, their voices crying "Raa! Raa!" when they came to a narrow passage and the team closed together like a fan to go through. He lived again all his days with Beauty Smith and the fights he had fought. At such times he whimpered and snarled in his sleep, and they that looked on said that his dreams were bad.

But there was one particular nightmare from which he suffered—the clanking, clanging monsters of electric cars that were to him colossal screaming lynxes. He would lie in a screen of bushes, watching for a squirrel to venture far enough out on the ground from its tree-refuge. Then, when he sprang out upon it, it would transform itself into an electric car, menacing and terrible, towering over him like a mountain, screaming and clanging and spitting fire at him. It was the same when he challenged the hawk down out of the sky. Down out of the blue it would rush, as it dropped upon him changing itself into the ubiquitous electric car. Or again, he would be in the pen of Beauty Smith. Outside the pen, men would be gathering, and he knew that a fight was on. He watched the door for his antagonist to enter. The door would open, and thrust in upon him would come the awful electric car. A thousand times this occurred, and each time the terror it inspired was as vivid and great as ever.

Then came the day when the last bandage and the last plaster cast were taken off. It was a gala day. All Sierra Vista was gathered around. The master rubbed his ears, and he crooned his love-growl. The master's wife called him the "Blessed Wolf," which name was taken up with acclaim and all the women called him the Blessed Wolf.

He tried to rise to his feet, and after several attempts fell down from weakness. He had lain so long that his muscles had lost their cunning, and all the strength had gone out of them. He felt a little shame because of his weakness, as though, forsooth he were failing the gods in the service he owed them. Because of this he made heroic efforts to arise, and at last he stood on his four legs, tottering and swaying back and forth.

"The Blessed Wolf!" chorused the women.

Judge Scott surveyed them triumphantly.

"Out of your own mouths be it," he said. "Just as I contended right along. No mere dog could have done what he did. He's a wolf."

"A Blessed Wolf," amended the Judge's wife.

"Yes, Blessed Wolf," agreed the Judge. "And henceforth that shall be my name for him."

"He'll have to learn to walk again," said the surgeon; "so he might as well start in right now. It won't hurt him. Take him outside."

And outside he went, like a king, with all Sierra Vista about him and tending on him. He was very weak, and when he reached the lawn he lay down and rested for a while.

Then the procession started on, little spurts of strength coming into White Fang's muscles as he used them and the blood began to surge through them. The stables were reached, and there in the doorway lay Collie, a half-dozen pudgy puppies playing about her in the sun.

White Fang looked on with a wondering eye. Collie snarled warningly at him, and he was careful to keep his distance. The master with his toe helped one sprawling puppy toward him. He bristled suspiciously, but the master warned him that all was well. Collie, clasped in the arms of one of the women, watched him jealously and with a snarl warned him that all was not well.

The puppy sprawled in front of him. He cocked his ears and watched it curiously. Then their noses touched, and he felt the warm little tongue of the puppy on his jowl. White Fang's tongue went out, he knew not why, and he licked the puppy's face.

Hand-clapping and pleased cries from the gods greeted the performance. He was surprised, and looked at them in a puzzled way. Then his weakness asserted itself, and he lay down, his ears cocked, his head on one side, as he watched the puppy. The other puppies came sprawling toward him, to Collie's great disgust; and he gravely permitted them to clamber and tumble over him. At first, amid the applause of the gods, he betrayed a trifle of his old self-consciousness and awkwardness. This passed away as the puppies' antics and mauling continued, and he lay with half-shut, patient eyes, drowsing in the sun.

CHILDREN'S CLASSICS

ROBERT LOUIS STEVENSON

# The Strange Case of Dr Jekyll and Mr Hyde

ROBERT LOUIS STEVENSON

# The Strange Case of Dr Jekyll and Mr Hyde

PARRAGON

Dr Jekyll and Mr Hyde
A Parragon Classic

---

This is a Siena Book
Siena is an imprint of Parragon

First published in 1886

This edition published in 1999 by
Parragon
13 Whiteladies Road
Clifton
Bristol BS8 1PB



Printed and bound in the UK

## STORY OF THE DOOR

Mr Utterson the lawyer was a man of a rugged countenance, that was never lighted by a smile; cold, scanty and embarrassed in discourse; backward in sentiment; lean, long, dusty, dreary and yet somehow lovable. At friendly meetings, and when the wine was to his taste, something eminently human beaconed from his eye; something indeed which never found its way into his talk, but which spoke not only in these silent symbols of the after-dinner face, but more often and loudly in the acts of his life. He was austere with himself; drank gin when he was alone, to mortify a taste for vintages; and though he enjoyed the theatre, had not crossed the doors of one for twenty years. But he had an approved tolerance for others; sometimes wondering, almost with envy, at the high pressure of spirits involved in their misdeeds; and in any extremity inclined to help rather than to reprove. 'I incline to Cain's heresy,' he used to say quaintly: 'I let my brother go to the devil in his own way.' In this character, it was frequently his fortune to be the last reputable acquaintance and the last good influence in the lives of down-going men. And to such as these, so long as they came about his chambers, he never marked a shade of change in his demeanour.

No doubt the feat was easy to Mr Utterson; for he was undemonstrative at the best, and even his friendships seemed to be founded in a similar catholicity of good-nature. It is the mark of a modest man to accept his friendly circle ready-made from the hands of opportunity; and that was the lawyer's way. His friends were those of his own blood or those whom he had known the longest; his affections, like ivy, were the growth of time, they implied no aptness in the object. Hence, no doubt, the bond that united him to Mr Richard Enfield, his distant kinsman, the well-known man about town. It was a nut to crack for many, what these two could see in each other or what subject they could find in common. It was reported by those who encountered them in their Sunday walks, that they said nothing, looked singularly dull, and would hail with obvious relief the appearance of a friend. For all that, the two men put the greatest store by these excursions, counted them the chief jewel of each week, and not only set aside occasions of pleasure, but even resisted the calls of business, that they might enjoy them uninterrupted.

It chanced on one of these rambles that their way led them down a by-street in a busy quarter of London. The street was small and what is called quiet, but it drove a thriving trade on the week-days. The inhabitants were all doing well, it seemed, and all emulously hoping to do better still, and laying out the surplus of their gains in coquetry; so that the shop fronts stood along that thoroughfare with an air of invitation, like rows of smiling saleswomen. Even on Sunday, when it veiled its more florid charms and lay comparatively empty of passage, the street shone out in contrast to its dingy neighbourhood, like a fire in a forest; and with its freshly painted shutters, well-polished brasses and general cleanliness and gaiety of note, instantly caught and pleased the eye of the passenger.

Two doors from one corner, on the left hand going east, the line was broken by the entry of a court; and just at that point, a certain sinister block of building thrust forward its gable on the street. It was two storeys high; showed no window, nothing but a door on the lower storey and a blind forehead of discoloured wall on the upper; and bore in every feature, the marks of prolonged and sordid negligence. The door, which was equipped with neither bell nor knocker, was blistered and distained. Tramps slouched into the recess and struck matches on the panels; children kept shop upon the steps; the schoolboy had tried his knife on the mouldings;

and for close on a generation, no one had appeared to drive away these random visitors or to repair their ravages.

Mr Enfield and the lawyer were on the other side of the by-street; but when they came abreast of the entry, the former lifted up his cane and pointed.

'Did you ever remark that door?' he asked; and when his companion had replied in the affirmative, 'It is connected in my mind,' added he, 'with a very odd story.'

'Indeed?' said Mr Utterson, with a slight change of voice, 'and what was that?'

'Well, it was this way,' returned Mr Enfield: 'I was coming home from some place at the end of the world, about three o'clock of a black winter morning, and my way lay through a part of town where there was literally nothing to be seen but lamps. Street after street, and all the folks asleep—street after street, all lighted up as if for a procession and all as empty as a church—till at last I got into that state of mind when a man listens and listens and begins to long for the sight of a policeman. All at once, I saw two figures: one a little man who was stumping along eastward at a good walk, and the other a girl of maybe eight or ten who was running as hard as she was able down a cross street. Well, sir, the two ran into one another naturally enough at the corner; and then came the horrible part of the thing; for the man trampled calmly over the child's body and left her screaming on the ground. It sounds nothing to hear, but it was hellish to see. It wasn't like a man; it was like some damned Juggernaut. I gave a view halloa, took to my heels, collared my gentleman, and brought him back to where there was already quite a group about the screaming child. He was perfectly cool and made no resistance, but gave me one look, so ugly that it brought out the sweat on me like running. The people who had turned out were the girl's own family; and pretty soon, the doctor, for whom she had been sent, put in his appearance. Well, the child was not much the worse, more frightened, according to the Sawbones; and there you might have supposed would be an end to it. But there was one curious circumstance. I had taken a loathing to my gentleman at first sight. So had the child's family, which was only natural. But the doctor's case was what struck me. He was the usual cut and dry apothecary, of no particular age and colour, with a strong Edinburgh accent, and about as emotional as a bagpipe. Well, sir, he was like the rest of us; every time he looked at my prisoner, I saw that Sawbones turn sick and white with the desire to kill him. I knew what was in his mind, just as he knew what was in mine; and killing being out of the question, we did the next best. We told the man we could and would make such a scandal out of this, as should make his name stink from one end of London to the other. If he had any friends or any credit, we undertook that he should lose them. And all the time, as we were pitching it in red hot, we were keeping the women off him as best we could, for they were as wild as harpies. I never saw a circle of such hateful faces; and there was the man in the middle, with a kind of black, sneering coolness—frightened too, I could see that—but carrying it off, sir, really like Satan. 'If you choose to make capital out of this accident,' said he, 'I am naturally helpless. No gentleman but wishes to avoid a scene,' says he. 'Name your figure.' Well, we screwed him up to a hundred pounds for the child's family; he would have clearly liked to stick out; but there was something about the lot of us that meant mischief, and at last he struck. The next thing was to get the money; and where do you think he carried us but to that place with the door?— whipped out a key, went in, and presently came back with the matter of ten pounds in gold and a cheque for the balance on Coutts's, drawn payable to bearer and signed with a name that I can't mention, though it's one of the points of my story, but it was a name at least very well known and often printed. The figure was stiff; but the signature was good for more than that, if it was only genuine. I took the liberty of pointing out to my gentleman that the whole business looked apocryphal, and that a man does not, in real life, walk into a cellar door at four in the morning and come out of it with another man's cheque for close upon a hundred pounds. But he was quite easy and sneering. 'Set your mind at rest,' says he, 'I will stay with you till the banks open and cash the cheque myself.' So we all set off, the doctor, and the child's father, and our friend and myself, and passed the rest of the night in my chambers; and next day, when we had breakfasted, went in a body to the bank. I gave in the cheque myself, and said I had every reason to believe it was a forgery. Not a bit of it. The cheque was genuine.

'Tut-tut,' said Mr Utterson.

'I see you feel as I do,' said Mr Enfield. 'Yes, it's a bad story. For my man was a fellow that nobody could have to do with, a really damnable man; and the person that drew the cheque is the very pink of the proprieties, celebrated too, and (what makes it worse) one of your fellows who do what they call good. Black mail, I suppose; an honest man paying through the nose for some of the capers of his youth. Black Mail House is what I call that place with the door, in consequence. Though even that, you know, is far from explaining all,' he added, and with the words fell into a vein of musing.

From this he was recalled by Mr Utterson asking rather suddenly: 'And you don't know if the drawer of the cheque lives there?'

'A likely place isn't it?' returned Mr Enfield. 'But I happen to have noticed his address; he lives in some square or other.'

'And you never asked about—the place with the door?' said Mr Utterson.

'No, sir: I had a delicacy,' was the reply. 'I feel very strongly about putting questions; it partakes too much of the style of the day of judgment. You start a question, and it's like starting a stone. You sit quietly on the top of a hill; and away the stone goes, starting others; and presently some bland old bird (the last you would have thought of) is knocked on the head in his own back garden and the family have to change their name. No, sir, I make it a rule of mine: the more it looks like Queer Street, the less I ask.'

'A very good rule, too,' said the lawyer.

'But I have studied the place for myself,' continued Mr Enfield. 'It seems scarcely a house. There is no other door, and nobody goes in or out of that one but, once in a great while, the gentleman of my adventure. There are three windows looking on the court on the first floor; none below; the windows are always shut but they're clean. And then there is a chimney which is generally smoking so somebody must live there. And yet it's not so sure; for the buildings are so packed together about that court, that it's hard to say where one ends and another begins.'

The pair walked on again for a while in silence; and then 'Enfield,' said Mr Utterson, 'that's a good rule of yours.'

'Yes, I think it is,' returned Enfield.

'But for all that,' continued the lawyer, 'there's one point I want to ask: I want to ask the name of that man who walked over the child.'

'Well,' said Mr Enfield, 'I can't see what harm it would do. It was a man of the name of Hyde.'

'Hm,' said Mr Utterson. 'What sort of a man is he to see?'

'He is not easy to describe. There is something wrong with his appearance; something displeasing, something downright detestable. I never saw a man I so disliked, and yet I scarce know why. He must be deformed somewhere; he gives a strong feeling of deformity, although I couldn't specify the point. He's an extraordinary looking man, and yet I really can name nothing out of the way. No, sir; I can make no hand of it; I can't describe him. And it's not want of memory; for I declare I can see him this moment.'

Mr Utterson again walked some way in silence and obviously under a weight of consideration.

'You are sure he used a key?' he inquired at last.

'My dear sir . . .' began Enfield, surprised out of himself.

'Yes, I know,' said Utterson; 'I know it must seem strange. The fact is, if I do not ask you the name of the other party, it is because I know it already. You see, Richard, your tale has gone home. If you have been inexact in any point, you had better correct it.'

'I think you might have warned me,' returned the other with a touch of sullenness. 'But I have been pedantically exact, as you call it. The fellow had a key; and what's more, he has it still. I saw him use it, not a week ago.'

Mr Utterson sighed deeply but said never a word; and the young man presently resumed. 'Here is another lesson to say nothing,' said he. 'I am ashamed of my long tongue. Let us make a bargain never to refer to this again.'

'With all my heart,' said the lawyer. 'I shake hands on that, Richard.'

# SEARCH FOR MR HYDE

That evening, Mr Utterson came home to his bachelor house in sombre spirits and sat down to dinner without relish. It was his custom of a Sunday, when this meal was over, to sit close by the fire, a volume of some dry divinity on his reading desk, until the clock of the neighbouring church rang out the hour of twelve, when he would go soberly and gratefully to bed. On this night, however, as soon as the cloth was taken away, he took up a candle and went into his business room. There he opened his safe, took from the most private part of it a document endorsed on the envelope as Dr Jekyll's Will, and sat down with a clouded brow to study its contents. The will was holograph, for Mr Utterson, though he took charge of it now that it was made, had refused to lend the least assistance in the making of it; it provided not only that, in case of the decease of Henry Jekyll, M.D., D.C.L., LL.D., F.R.S., &c., all his possessions were to pass into the hands of his 'friend and benefactor Edward Hyde,' but that in case of Dr Jekyll's 'disappearance or unexplained absence for any period exceeding three calendar months,' the said Edward Hyde should step into the said Henry Jekyll's shoes without further delay, and free from any burthen or obligation, beyond the payment of a few small sums to the members of the doctor's household. This document had long been the lawyer's eyesore. It offended him both as a lawyer and as a lover of the sane and customary sides of life, to whom the fanciful was the immodest. And hitherto it was his ignorance of Mr Hyde that had swelled his indignation; now, by a sudden turn, it was his knowledge. It was already bad enough when the name was but a name of which he could learn no more. It was worse when it began to be clothed upon with detestable attributes; and out of the shifting, insubstantial mist that had so long baffled his eye, there leaped up the sudden, definite presentment of a fiend.

'I thought it was madness,' he said, as he replaced the obnoxious paper in the safe, 'and now I begin to fear it is disgrace.'

With that he blew out his candle, put on a great coat and set forth in the direction of Cavendish Square, that citadel of medicine, where his friend, the great Dr Lanyon, had his house and received his crowding patients. 'If anyone knows, it will be Lanyon,' he had thought.

The solemn butler knew and welcomed him; he was subjected to no stage of delay, but ushered direct from the door to the dining-room where Dr Lanyon sat alone over his wine. This was a hearty, healthy, dapper, red-faced gentleman, with a shock of hair prematurely white, and a boisterous and decided manner. At sight of Mr Utterson, he sprang up from his chair and welcomed him with both hands. The geniality, as was the way of the man, was somewhat theatrical to the eye; but it reposed on genuine feeling. For these two were old friends, old mates both at school and college, both thorough respecters of themselves and of each other, and, what does not always follow, men who thoroughly enjoyed each other's company.

After a little rambling talk, the lawyer led up to the subject which so disagreeably preoccupied his mind.

'I suppose, Lanyon,' said he, 'you and I must be the two oldest friends that Henry Jekyll has?'

'I wish the friends were younger,' chuckled Dr Lanyon. 'But I suppose we are. And what of that? I see little of him now.'

'Indeed?' said Utterson. 'I thought you had a bond of common interest.'

'We had,' was the reply. 'But it is more than ten years since Henry Jekyll became too fanciful for me. He began to go wrong, wrong in mind; and though of course I continue to take an interest in him for old sake's sake as they say, I see and I have seen devilish little of the man. Such unscientific balderdash,' added the doctor, flushing suddenly purple, 'would have estranged Damon and Pythias.'

This little spirit of temper was somewhat of a relief to Mr Utterson. 'They have only differed on some point of science,' he thought; and being a man of no scientific passions (except in the matter of conveyancing) he even added: 'It is nothing worse than that!' He gave his friend a few seconds to recover his composure, and then approached the question he had come to put. 'Did you ever come across a protege of his—one Hyde?' he asked.

'Hyde?' repeated Lanyon. 'No. Never heard of him. Since my time.'

That was the amount of information that the lawyer carried back with him to the great, dark bed on which he tossed to and fro, until the small hours of the morning began to grow large. It was a night of little ease to his toiling mind, toiling in mere darkness and besieged by questions.

Six o'clock struck on the bells of the church that was so conveniently near to Mr Utterson's dwelling, and still he was digging at the problem. Hitherto it had touched him on the intellectual side alone; but now his imagination also was engaged or rather enslaved; and as he lay and tossed in the gross darkness of the night and the curtained room, Mr Enfield's tale went by before his mind in a scroll of lighted pictures. He would be aware of the great field of lamps of a nocturnal city; then of the figure of a man walking swiftly; then of a child running from the doctor's; and then these met, and that human Juggernaut trod the child down and passed on regardless of her screams. Or else he would see a room in a rich house, where his friend lay asleep, dreaming and smiling at his dreams; and then the door of that room would be opened, the curtains of the bed plucked apart, the sleeper recalled, and lo! there would stand by his side a figure to whom power was given, and even at that dead hour, he must rise and do its bidding. The figure in these two phases haunted the lawyer all night; and if at any time he dozed over, it was but to see it glide more stealthily through sleeping houses, or move the more swiftly and still the more swiftly, even to dizziness, through wider labyrinths of lamplighted city, and at every street corner crush a child and leave her screaming. And still the figure had no face by which he might know it; even in his dreams, it had no face, or one that baffled him and melted before his eyes; and thus it was that there sprang up and grew apace in the lawyer's mind a singularly strong, almost an inordinate, curiosity to behold the features of the real Mr Hyde. If he could but once set eyes on him, he thought the mystery would lighten and perhaps roll altogether away, as was the habit of mysterious things when well examined. He might see a reason for his friend's strange preference or bondage (call it which you please) and even for the startling clauses of the will. And at least it would be a face worth seeing: the face of a man who was without bowels of mercy: a face which had but to show itself to raise up, in the mind of the unimpressionable Enfield, a spirit of enduring hatred.

From that time forward, Mr Utterson began to haunt the door in the by-street of shops. In the morning before office hours, at noon when business was plenty and time scarce, at night under the face of the fogged city moon, by all lights and at all hours of solitude or concourse, the lawyer was to be found on his chosen post.

'If he be Mr Hyde,' he had thought, 'I shall be Mr Seek.'

And at last his patience was rewarded. It was a fine dry night; frost in the air; the streets as clean as a ballroom floor; the lamps, unshaken by any wind, drawing a regular pattern of light and shadow. By ten o'clock, when the shops were closed, the by-street was very solitary and, in spite of the low growl of London from all round, very silent. Small sounds carried far; domestic sounds out of the houses were clearly audible on either side of the roadway; and the rumour of the approach of any passenger preceded him by a long time. Mr Utterson had been some minutes at his post, when he was aware of an odd, light footstep drawing near. In the course of his nightly patrols, he had long grown accustomed to the quaint effect with which the footfalls of a single person, while he is still a great way off, suddenly spring out distinct from the vast hum and clatter of the city. Yet his attention had never before been so sharply and decisively arrested; and it was with a strong, superstitious prevision of success that he withdrew into the entry of the court.

The steps drew swiftly nearer, and swelled out suddenly louder as they turned the end of the street. The lawyer, looking forth from the entry, could soon see what manner of man he had to deal with. He was small and very plainly dressed, and the look of him, even at that distance, went somehow strongly against the watcher's inclination. But he made straight for the door, crossing the roadway to save time; and as he came, he drew a key from his pocket like one approaching home.

Mr Utterson stepped out and touched him on the shoulder as he passed. 'Mr Hyde, I think?'

Mr Hyde shrank back with a hissing intake of the breath. But his fear was only momentary; and though he did not look the lawyer in the face, he answered coolly enough: 'That is my name. What do you want?'

'I see you are going in,' returned the lawyer. 'I am an old friend of Dr Jekyll's—Mr Utterson of Gaunt Street—you must have heard my name; and meeting you so conveniently, I thought you might admit me.'

'You will not find Dr Jekyll; he is from home,' replied Mr Hyde, blowing in the key. And then suddenly, but still without looking up, 'How did you know me?' he asked.

'On your side,' said Mr Utterson, 'will you do me a favour?'

'With pleasure,' replied the other. 'What shall it be?'

'Will you let me see your face?' asked the lawyer.

Mr Hyde appeared to hesitate, and then, as if upon some sudden reflection, fronted about with an air of defiance; and the pair stared at each other pretty fixedly for a few seconds. 'Now I shall know you again,' said Mr Utterson. 'It may be useful.'

'Yes,' returned Mr Hyde, 'it is as well we have met; and *a propos*, you should have my address.' And he gave a number of a street in Soho.

'Good God!' thought Mr Utterson, 'can he too have been thinking of the will?' But he kept his feelings to himself and only grunted in acknowledgement of the address.

'And now,' said the other, 'how did you know me?'

'By description,' was the reply.

'Whose description?'

'We have common friends,' said Mr Utterson.

'Common friends?' echoed Mr Hyde, a little hoarsely. 'Who are they?'

'Jekyll, for instance,' said the lawyer.

'He never told you,' cried Mr Hyde, with a flush of anger. 'I did not think you would have lied.'

'Come,' said Mr Utterson, 'that is not fitting language.'

The other snarled aloud into a savage laugh; and the next moment, with extraordinary quickness, he had unlocked the door and disappeared into the house.

The lawyer stood awhile when Mr Hyde had left him, the picture of disquietude. Then he began slowly to mount the street, pausing every step or two and putting his hand to his brow like a man in mental perplexity. The problem he was thus debating as he walked, was one of a class that is rarely solved. Mr Hyde was pale and dwarfish, he gave an impression of deformity without any nameable malformation, he had a displeasing smile, he had borne himself to the lawyer with a sort of murderous mixture of timidity and boldness, and he spoke with a husky, whispering and somewhat broken voice; all these were points against him, but not all of these together could explain the hitherto unknown disgust, loathing and fear with which Mr Utterson regarded him. 'There must be something else,' said the perplexed gentleman. 'There is something more, if I could find a name for it. God bless me, the man seems hardly human! Something troglodytic, shall we say? or can it be the old story of Dr Fell? or is it the mere radiance of a foul soul that thus transpires through, and transfigures, its clay continent? The last, I think; for O my poor old Harry Jekyll, if ever I read Satan's signature upon a face, it is on that of your new friend.'

Round the corner from the by-street, there was a square of ancient, handsome houses, now for the most part decayed from their high estate and let in flats and chambers to all sorts and conditions of men: map-engravers, architects, shady lawyers and the agents of obscure enterprises. One house, however, second from the corner, was still occupied entire; and at the door of this, which wore a great air of wealth and comfort, though it was now plunged in darkness except for the fan-light, Mr Utterson stopped and knocked. A well-dressed, elderly servant opened the door.

'Is Dr Jekyll at home, Poole?' asked the lawyer.

'I will see, Mr Utterson,' said Poole, admitting the visitor, as he spoke, into a large, low-roofed, comfortable hall, paved with flags, warmed (after the fashion of a country house) by a bright, open fire, and furnished with costly cabinets of oak. 'Will you wait here by the fire, sir? or shall I give you a light in the dining-room?'

'Here, thank you,' said the lawyer, and he drew near and leaned on the tall fender. This hall, in which he was now left alone, was a pet fancy of his friend the doctor's; and Utterson himself was wont to speak of it as the pleasantest room in London. But to-night there was a shudder in his blood; the face of Hyde sat heavy on his memory; he felt (what was rare with him) a nausea and distaste of life; and in the gloom of his spirits, he seemed to read a menace in the flickering of the firelight on the polished cabinets and the uneasy starting of the shadow on the roof. He was ashamed of his relief, when Poole presently returned to announce that Dr Jekyll was gone out.

'I saw Mr Hyde go in by the old dissecting room door, Poole,' he said. 'Is that right, when Dr Jekyll is from home?'

'Quite right, Mr Utterson, sir,' replied the servant. 'Mr Hyde has a key.'

'Your master seems to repose a great deal of trust in that young man, Poole,' resumed the other musingly.

'Yes, sir, he do indeed,' said Poole. 'We have all orders to obey him.'

'I do not think I ever met Mr Hyde?' asked Utterson.

'O, dear no, sir. He never *dines* here,' replied the butler. 'Indeed we see very little of him on this side of the house; he mostly comes and goes by the laboratory.'

'Well, good night, Poole.'

'Good night, Mr Utterson.'

And the lawyer set out homeward with a very heavy heart. 'Poor Harry Jekyll,' he thought, 'my mind misgives me he is in deep waters! He was wild when he was young; a long while ago to be sure; but in the law of God, there is no statute of limitations. Ay, it must be that; the ghost of some old sin, the cancer of some concealed disgrace; punishment coming, *pede claudo*, years after memory has forgotten and self-love condoned the fault.' And the lawyer, scared by the thought, brooded awhile on his own past, groping in all the corners of memory, lest by chance some Jack-in-the-Box of an old iniquity should leap to light there. His past was fairly blameless; few men could read the rolls of their life with less apprehension; yet he was humbled to the dust by the many ill things he had done, and raised up again into a sober and fearful gratitude by the many that he had come so near to doing, yet avoided. And then by a return on his former subject, he conceived a spark of hope. 'This Master Hyde, if he were studied,' thought he, 'must have secrets of his own: black secrets, by the look of him; secrets compared to which poor Jekyll's worst would be like sunshine. Things cannot continue as they are. It turns me cold to think of this creature stealing like a thief to Harry's bedside; poor Harry, what a wakening! And the danger of it; for if this Hyde suspects the existence of the will, he may grow impatient to inherit. Ay, I must put my shoulder to the wheel—if Jekyll will but let me,' he added, 'if Jekyll will only let me.' For once more he saw before his mind's eye, as clear as a transparency, the strange clauses of the will.

# DR JEKYLL WAS QUITE AT EASE

A fortnight later, by excellent good fortune, the doctor gave one of his pleasant dinners to some five or six old cronies, all intelligent, reputable men and all judges of good wine; and Mr Utterson so contrived that he remained behind after the others had departed. This was no new arrangement, but a thing that had befallen many scores of times. Where Utterson was liked, he was liked well. Hosts loved to detain the dry lawyer, when the light-hearted and the loose-tongued had already their foot on the threshold; they liked to sit awhile in his unobtrusive company, practising for solitude, sobering their minds in the man's rich silence after the expense and strain of gaiety. To this rule, Dr Jekyll was no exception; and as he now sat on the opposite side of the fire—a large, well-made, smooth-faced man of fifty, with something of a slyish cast perhaps, but every mark of capacity and kindness—you could see by his looks that he cherished for Mr Utterson a sincere and warm affection.

'I have been wanting to speak to you, Jekyll,' began the latter. 'You know that will of yours?'

A close observer might have gathered that the topic was distasteful; but the doctor carried it off gaily. 'My poor Utterson,' said he, 'you are unfortunate in such a client. I never saw a man so distressed as you were by my will; unless it were that hide-bound pedant, Lanyon, at what he called my scientific heresies. O, I know he's a good fellow—you needn't frown—an excellent fellow, and I always mean to see more of him; but a hide-bound pedant for all that; an ignorant, blatant pedant. I was never more disappointed in any man than Lanyon.

'You know I never approved of it,' pursued Utterson, ruthlessly disregarding the fresh topic.

'My will? Yes, certainly, I know that,' said the doctor, a trifle sharply. 'You have told me so.'

'Well, I tell you so again,' continued the lawyer. 'I have been learning something of young Hyde.'

The large handsome face of Dr Jekyll grew pale to the very lips, and there came a blackness about his eyes. 'I do not care to hear more,' said he. 'This is a matter I thought we had agreed to drop.'

'What I heard was abominable,' said Utterson.

'It can make no change. You do not understand my position,' returned the doctor, with a certain incoherency of manner. 'I am painfully situated, Utterson; my position is a very strange—a very strange one. It is one of those affairs that cannot be mended by talking.'

'Jekyll,' said Utterson, 'you know me: I am a man to be trusted. Make a clean breast of this in confidence; and I make no doubt I can get you out of it.'

'My good Utterson,' said the doctor, 'this is very good of you, this is downright good of you, and I cannot find words to thank you in. I believe you fully; I would trust you before any man alive, ay, before myself, if I could make the choice; but indeed it isn't what you fancy; it is not so bad as that; and just to put your good heart at rest, I will tell you one thing: the moment I choose, I can be rid of Mr Hyde. I give you my hand upon that; and I thank you again and again; and I will just add one little word, Utterson, that I'm sure you'll take in good part: this is a private matter, and I beg of you to let it sleep.'

Utterson reflected a little looking in the fire.

'I have no doubt you are perfectly right,' he said at last, getting to his feet.

'Well, but since we have touched upon this business, and for the last time I hope,' continued the doctor, 'there is one point I should like you to understand. I have really a very great interest in poor Hyde. I know you have seen him; he told me so; and I fear he was rude. But I do sincerely take a great, a very great interest in that young man and if I am taken away, Utterson, I wish you to promise me that you will bear with him and get his rights for him. I think you would, if you knew all; and it would be a weight off my mind if you would promise.'

'I can't pretend that I shall ever like him,' said the lawyer.

'I don't ask that,' pleaded Jekyll, laying his hand upon the other's arm; 'I only ask for justice; I only ask you to help him for my sake, when I am no longer here.'

Utterson heaved an irrepressible sigh. 'Well,' said he. 'I promise.'

## THE CAREW MURDER CASE

Nearly a year later, in the month of October 18—, London was startled by a crime of singular ferocity and rendered all the more notable by the high position of the victim. The details were few and startling. A maid servant living alone in a house not far from the river, had gone upstairs to bed about eleven. Although a fog rolled over the city in the small hours, the early part of the night was cloudless, and the lane, which the maid's window overlooked, was brilliantly lit by the full moon. It seems she was romantically given, for she sat down upon her box, which stood immediately under the window, and fell into a dream of musing. Never (she used to say, with streaming tears, when she narrated that experience) never had she felt more at peace with all men or thought more kindly of the world. And as she so sat she became aware of an aged and beautiful gentleman with white hair, drawing near along the lane; and advancing to meet him, another and very small gentleman, to whom at first she paid less attention. When they had come within speech (which was just under the maid's eyes) the older man bowed and accosted the other with a very pretty manner of politeness. It did not seem as if the subject of his address were of great importance; indeed, from his pointing, it sometimes appeared as if he were only inquiring his way; but the moon shone on his face as he spoke, and the girl was pleased to watch it, it seemed to breathe such an innocent and old-world kindness of disposition, yet with something high too, as of a well-founded self-content. Presently her eye wandered to the other, and she was surprised to recognize in him a certain Mr Hyde, who had once visited her master and for whom she had conceived a dislike. He had in his hand a heavy cane, with which he was trifling; but he answered never a word, and seemed to listen with an ill-contained impatience. And then all of a sudden he broke out in a great flame of anger, stamping with his foot, brandishing the cane, and carrying on (as the maid described it) like a madman. The old gentleman took a step back, with the air of one very much surprised and a trifle hurt; and at that Mr Hyde broke out of all bounds and clubbed him to the earth. And next moment, with ape-like fury, he was trampling his victim under foot, and hailing down a storm of blows, under which the bones were audibly shattered and the body jumped upon the roadway. At the horror of these sights and sounds, the maid fainted.

It was two o'clock when she came to herself and called for the police. The murderer was gone long ago; but there lay his victim in the middle of the lane, incredibly mangled. The stick with which the deed had been done, although it was of some rare and very tough and heavy wood, had broken in the middle under the stress of this insensate cruelty; and one splintered half had rolled in the neighbouring gutter—the other, without doubt, had been carried away by the murderer. A purse and a gold watch were found upon the victim; but no cards or papers, except a sealed and stamped envelope, which he had been probably carrying to the post, and which bore the name and address of Mr Utterson.

This was brought to the lawyer the next morning, before he was out of bed; and he had no sooner seen it, and been told the circumstances, than he shot out a solemn lip. 'I shall say nothing till I have seen the body,' said he; 'this may be very serious. Have the kindness to wait while I dress.' And with the same grave countenance he hurried through his breakfast and drove to the police station, whither the body had been carried. As soon as he came into the cell, he nodded.

'Yes,' said he, 'I recognize him. I am sorry to say that this is Sir Danvers Carew.'

'Good God, sir,' exclaimed the officer, 'is it

possible?' And the next moment his eye lighted up with professional ambition. 'This will make a deal of noise,' he said. 'And perhaps you can help us to the man.' And he briefly narrated what the maid had seen, and showed the broken stick.

Mr Utterson had already quailed at the name of Hyde; but when the stick was laid before him, he could doubt no longer: broken and battered as it was, he recognized it for one that he had himself presented many years before to Henry Jekyll.

'Is this Mr Hyde a person of small stature?' he inquired.

'Particularly small and particularly wicked-looking, is what the maid calls him,' said the officer.

Mr Utterson reflected; and then, raising his head, 'If you will come with me in my cab,' he said, 'I think I can take you to his house.'

It was by this time about nine in the morning, and the first fog of the season. A great chocolate-coloured pall lowered over heaven, but the wind was continually charging and routing these embattled vapours; so that as the cab crawled from street to street, Mr Utterson beheld a marvellous number of degrees and hues of twilight; for here it would be dark like the back-end of evening; and there would be a glow of a rich, lurid brown, like the light of some strange conflagration; and here, for a moment, the fog would be quite broken up, and a haggard shaft of daylight would glance in between the swirling wreaths. The dismal quarter of Soho seen under these changing glimpses, with its muddy ways, and slatternly passengers, and its lamps, which had never been extinguished or had been kindled afresh to combat this mournful reinvasion of darkness, seemed, in the lawyer's eyes, like a district of some city in a nightmare. The thoughts of his mind, besides, were of the gloomiest dye; and when he glanced at the companion of his drive, he was conscious of some touch of that terror of the law and the law's officers, which may at times assail the most honest.

As the cab drew up before the address indicated, the fog lifted a little and showed him a dingy street, a gin palace, a low French eating house, a shop for the retail of penny numbers and twopenny salads, many ragged children huddled in the doorways, and many women of many different nationalities passing out, key in hand, to have a morning glass; and the next moment the fog settled down again upon that part, as brown as umber, and cut him off from his blackguardly surroundings. This was the home of Henry Jekyll's favourite; of a man who was heir to a quarter of a million sterling.

An ivory-faced and silvery-haired old woman opened the door. She had an evil face, smoothed by hypocrisy; but her manners were excellent. Yes, she said, this was Mr Hyde's, but he was not at home; he had been in that night very late, but had gone away again in less than an hour; there was nothing strange in that; his habits were very irregular, and he was often absent; for instance, it was nearly two months since she had seen him till yesterday.

'Very well then, we wish to see his rooms,' said the lawyer; and when the woman began to declare it was impossible, 'I had better tell you who this person is,' he added. 'This is Inspector Newcomen of Scotland Yard.'

A flash of odious joy appeared upon the woman's face. 'Ah!' said she, 'he is in trouble! What has he done?'

Mr Utterson and the inspector exchanged glances. 'He don't seem a very popular character,' observed the latter. 'And now, my good woman, just let me and this gentleman have a look about us.'

In the whole extent of the house, which but for the old woman remained otherwise empty, Mr Hyde had only used a couple of rooms; but these were furnished with luxury and good taste. A closet was filled with wine; the plate was of silver, the napery elegant; a good picture hung upon the walls, a gift (as Utterson supposed) from Henry Jekyll, who was much of a connoisseur; and the carpets were of many piles and agreeable in colour. At this moment, however, the rooms bore every mark of having been recently and hurriedly ransacked; clothes lay about the floor, with their pockets inside out; lockfast drawers stood open; and on the hearth there lay a pile of grey ashes, as though many papers had been burned. From these embers the inspector disinterred the butt end of a green cheque book, which had resisted the action of the fire; the other half of the stick was found behind the door; and as this clinched his suspicions, the officer declared himself delighted. A visit to the bank, where several thousand pounds were found to be lying to the murderer's credit, completed his gratification.

'You may depend upon it, sir,' he told Mr Utterson: 'I have him in my hand. He must have lost his head, or he never would have left the stick or, above all, burned the cheque book. Why, money's life to the man. We have nothing to do but wait for him at the bank, and get out the handbills.'

This last, however, was not so easy of accomplishment; for Mr Hyde had numbered few familiars—even the master of the servant maid had only seen him twice; his family could nowhere be traced; he had never been photographed; and the few who could describe him differed widely, as common observers will. Only on one point, were they agreed; and that was the haunting sense of unexpressed deformity with which the fugitive impressed his beholders.

## INCIDENT OF THE LETTER

It was late in the afternoon, when Mr Utterson found his way to Dr Jekyll's door, where he was at once admitted by Poole, and carried down by the kitchen offices and across a yard which had once been a garden, to the building which was indifferently known as the laboratory or the dissecting rooms. The doctor had bought the house from the heirs of a celebrated surgeon; and his own tastes being rather chemical than anatomical, had changed the destination of the block at the bottom of the garden. It was the first time that the lawyer had been received in that part of his friend's quarters; and he eyed the dingy windowless structure with curiosity, and gazed round with a distasteful sense of strangeness as he crossed the theatre, once crowded with eager students now lying gaunt and silent, the tables laden with chemical apparatus, the floor strewn with crates and littered with packing straw, and the light falling dimly through the foggy cupola. At the further end, a flight of stairs mounted to a door covered with red baize; and through this Mr Utterson was at last received into the doctor's cabinet. It was a large room, fitted round with glass presses, furnished, among other things, with a cheval-glass and a business table, and looking out upon the court by three dusty windows barred with iron. The fire burned in the grate; a lamp was set lighted on the chimney shelf, for even in the houses the fog began to lie thickly; and there, close up to the warmth, sat Dr Jekyll, looking deadly sick. He did not rise to meet his visitor, but held out a cold hand and bade him welcome in a changed voice.

'And now,' said Mr Utterson, as soon as Poole had left them, 'you have heard the news?'

The doctor shuddered. 'They were crying it in the square,' he said. 'I heard them in my dining room.'

'One word,' said the lawyer. 'Carew was my client, but so are you, and I want to know what I am doing. You have not been mad enough to hide this fellow?'

'Utterson, I swear to God,' cried the doctor, 'I swear to God I will never set eyes on him again. I bind my honour to you that I am done with him in this world. It is all at an end. And indeed he does not want my help; you do not know him as I do; he is safe, he is quite safe; mark my words, he will never more be heard of.'

The lawyer listened gloomily; he did not like his friend's feverish manner. 'You seem pretty sure of him,' said he; 'and for your sake, I hope you may be right. If it came to a trial, your name might appear.'

'I am quite sure of him,' replied Jekyll; 'I have grounds for certainty that I cannot share with anyone. But there is one thing on which you may advise me. I have—I have received a letter; and I am at a loss whether I should show it to the police. I should like to leave it in your hands, Utterson; you would judge wisely I am sure; I have so great a trust in you.'

'You fear, I suppose, that it might lead to his detection?' asked the lawyer.

'No,' said the other. 'I cannot say that I care what becomes of Hyde; I am quite done with him. I was thinking of my own character, which this hateful business has rather exposed.'

Utterson ruminated awhile; he was surprised at his friend's selfishness, and yet relieved by it. 'Well,' said he, at last, 'let me see the letter.'

The letter was written in an odd, upright hand and signed 'Edward Hyde': and it signified, briefly enough, that the writer's benefactor, Dr Jekyll, whom he had long so unworthily repaid for a thousand generosities, need labour under no alarm for his safety as he had means of escape on which he placed a sure dependence. The lawyer liked this letter well enough; it put a better colour on the intimacy than he had looked for; and he blamed himself for some of his past suspicions.

'Have you the envelope?' he asked.

'I burned it,' replied Jekyll, 'before I thought what I was about. But it bore no postmark. The note was handed in.'

'Shall I keep this and sleep upon it?' asked Utterson.

'I wish you to judge for me entirely,' was the reply. 'I have lost confidence in myself.'

'Well, I shall consider,' returned the lawyer. 'And now one word more: it was Hyde who dictated the terms in your will about that disappearance?'

The doctor seemed seized with a qualm of faintness; he shut his mouth tight and nodded.

'I knew it,' said Utterson. 'He meant to murder you. You have had a fine escape.'

'I have had what is far more to the purpose,' returned the doctor solemnly: 'I have had a lesson—O God, Utterson, what a lesson I have had!' And he covered his face for a moment with his hands.

On his way out, the lawyer stopped and had a word or two with Poole. 'By the by,' said he, 'there was a letter handed in to-day: what was the messenger like?' But Poole was positive nothing had come except by post; 'and only circulars by that,' he added.

This news sent off the visitor with his fears renewed. Plainly the letter had come by the laboratory door; possibly, indeed, it had been written in the cabinet; and if that were so, it must be differently judged, and handled with the more caution. The newsboys, as he went, were crying themselves hoarse along the footways: 'Special edition. Shocking murder of an M.P.' That was the funeral oration of one friend and client; and he could not help a certain apprehension lest the good name of another should be sucked down in the eddy of the scandal. It was, at least, a ticklish decision that he had to make; and self-reliant as he was by habit, he began to cherish a longing for advice. It was not to be had directly; but perhaps, he thought, it might be fished for.

Presently after, he sat on one side of his own hearth, with Mr Guest, his head clerk, upon the other, and midway between, at a nicely calculated distance from the fire, a bottle of a particular old wine that had long dwelt unsunned in the foundations of his house. The fog still slept on the wing above the drowned city, where the lamps glimmered like carbuncles; and through the muffle and smother of these fallen clouds, the procession of the town's life was still rolling in through the great arteries with a sound as of a mighty wind. But the room was gay with firelight. In the bottle the acids were long ago resolved; the imperial dye had softened with time, as the colour grows richer in stained windows; and the glow of hot autumn afternoons on hillside vineyards, was ready to be set free and to disperse the fogs of London. Insensibly the lawyer melted. There was no man from whom he kept fewer secrets than Mr Guest; and he was not always sure that he kept as many as he meant. Guest had often been on business to the doctor's; he knew Poole; he could scarce have failed to hear of Mr Hyde's familiarity about the house; he might draw conclusions: was it not as well, then, that he should see a letter which put that mystery to rights? and above all since Guest, being a great student and critic of handwriting, would consider the step natural and obliging? The clerk, besides, was a man of counsel; he would scarce read so strange document without dropping a remark; and by that remark Mr Utterson might shape his future course.

'This is a sad business about Sir Danvers,' he said.

'Yes, sir, indeed. It has elicited a great deal of public feeling,' returned Guest. 'The man, of course, was mad.'

'I should like to hear your views on that,' replied Utterson. 'I have a document here in his handwriting; it is between ourselves, for I scarce know what to do about it; it is an ugly business at the best. But there it is; quite in your way: a murderer's autograph.'

Guest's eyes brightened, and he sat down at once and studied it with passion. 'No, sir,' he said; 'not mad; but it is an odd hand.'

'And by all accounts a very odd writer,' added the lawyer.

Just then the servant entered with a note.

'Is that from Doctor Jekyll, sir?' inquired the clerk. 'I thought I knew the writing. Anything private, Mr Utterson?'

'Only an invitation to dinner. Why? do you want to see it?'

'One moment. I thank you, sir;' and the clerk laid the two sheets of paper alongside and sedulously compared their contents. 'Thank you, sir,' he said at last, returning both; 'it's a very interesting autograph.'

There was a pause, during which Mr Utterson struggled with himself. 'Why did you compare them, Guest?' he inquired suddenly.

'Well, sir,' returned the clerk, 'there's a rather singular resemblance; the two hands are in many points identical: only differently sloped.'

'Rather quaint,' said Utterson.

'It is, as you say, rather quaint,' returned Guest.

'I wouldn't speak of this note, you know,' said the master.

'No, sir,' said the clerk. 'I understand.'

But no sooner was Mr. Utterson alone that night, than he locked the note into his safe where it reposed from that time forward. 'What!' he thought. 'Henry Jekyll forge for a murderer!' And his blood ran cold in his veins.

# REMARKABLE INCIDENT OF DOCTOR LANYON

Time ran on; thousands of pounds were offered in reward, for the death of Sir Danvers was resented as a public injury; but Mr Hyde had disappeared out of the ken of the police as though he had never existed. Much of his past was unearthed, indeed, and all disreputable: tales came out of the man's cruelty, at once so callous and violent, of his vile life, of his strange associates, of the hatred that seemed to have surrounded his career; but of his present whereabouts, not a whisper. From the time he had left the house in Soho on the morning of the murder, he was simply blotted out; and gradually, as time drew on, Mr Utterson began to recover from the hotness of his alarm, and to grow more at quiet with himself. The death of Sir Danvers was, to his way of thinking, more than paid for by the disappearance of Mr Hyde. Now that that evil influence had been withdrawn, a new life began for Dr Jekyll. He came out of his seclusion, renewed relations with his friends, became once more their familiar guest and entertainer; and whilst he had always been known for charities, he was now no less distinguished for religion. He was busy, he was much in the open air, he did good; his face seemed to open and brighten, as if with an inward consciousness of service; and for more than two months, the doctor was at peace.

On the 8th of January Utterson had dined at the doctor's with a small party; Lanyon had been there; and the face of the host had looked from one to the other as in the old days when the trio were inseparable friends. On the 12th, and again on the 14th, the door was shut against the lawyer. 'The doctor was confined to the house,' Poole said, 'and saw no one.' On the 15th, he tried again, and was again refused; and having now been used for the last two months to see his friend almost daily, he found this return of solitude to weigh upon his spirits. The fifth night, he had in Guest to dine with him; and the sixth he betook himself to Doctor Lanyon's.

There at least he was not denied admittance; but when he came in, he was shocked at the change which had taken place in the doctor's appearance. He had his death-warrant written legibly upon his face. The rosy man had grown pale; his flesh had fallen away; he was visibly balder and older; and yet it was not so much these tokens of a swift physical decay that arrested the lawyer's notice, as a look in the eye and quality of manner that seemed to testify to some deep-seated terror of the mind. It was unlikely that the doctor should fear death; and yet that was what Utterson was tempted to suspect. 'Yes,' he thought; 'he is a doctor, he must know his own state and that his days are counted; and the knowledge is more than he can bear.' And yet when Utterson remarked on his ill-looks, it was with an air of great firmness that Lanyon declared himself a doomed man.

'I have had a shock,' he said, 'and I shall never recover. It is a question of weeks. Well, life has been pleasant; I liked it; yes, sir, I used to like it. I sometimes think if we knew all, we should be more glad to get away.'

'Jekyll is ill, too,' observed Utterson. 'Have you seen him?'

But Lanyon's face changed, and he held up a trembling hand. 'I wish to see or hear no more of Doctor Jekyll,' he said in a loud, unsteady voice. 'I am quite done with that person; and I beg that you will spare me any allusion to one whom I regard as dead.'

'Tut-tut,' said Mr Utterson; and then after a considerable pause, 'Can't I do anything?' he inquired. 'We are three very old friends, Lanyon; we shall not live to make others.'

'Nothing can be done,' returned Lanyon; 'ask himself.'

'He will not see me,' said the lawyer.

'I am not surprised at that,' was the reply. 'Some day, Utterson, after I am dead, you may perhaps come to learn the right and wrong of this. I cannot tell you. And in the meantime, if you can sit and talk with me of other things, for God's sake, stay and do so; but if you cannot keep clear of this accursed topic, then, in God's name, go, for I cannot bear it.'

As soon as he got home, Utterson sat down and wrote to Jekyll, complaining of his exclusion from the house, and asking the cause of this unhappy break with Lanyon; and the next day brought him a long answer, often very pathetically worded, and sometimes darkly mysterious in drift. The quarrel with Lanyon was incurable. 'I do not blame our old friend,' Jekyll wrote, 'but I share his view that we must never meet. I mean from henceforth to lead a life of extreme seclusion; you must not be surprised, nor must you doubt my friendship, if my door is often shut even to you. You must suffer me to go my own dark way. I have brought on myself a punishment and a danger that I cannot name. If I am the chief of sinners, I am the chief of sufferers also. I could not think that this earth contained a place for sufferings and terrors so unmanning; and you can do but one thing, Utterson, to lighten this destiny, and that is to respect my silence.' Utterson was amazed; the dark influence of Hyde had been withdrawn, the doctor had returned to his old tasks and amities; a week ago, the prospect had smiled with every promise of a cheerful and an honoured age; and now in a moment, friendship, and peace of mind and the whole tenor of his life were wrecked. So great and unprepared a change pointed to madness; but in view of Lanyon's manner and words, there must lie for it some deeper ground.

A week afterwards Dr Lanyon took to his bed, and in something less than a fortnight he was dead. The night after the funeral, at which he had been sadly affected, Utterson locked the door of his business room, and sitting there by the light of a melancholy candle, drew out and set before him an envelope addressed by the hand and sealed with the seal of his dead friend. 'PRIVATE: for the hands of J. G. Utterson ALONE and in case of his predecease to be destroyed unread,' so it was emphatically superscribed; and the lawyer dreaded to behold the contents. 'I have buried one friend to-day,' he thought: 'what if this should cost me another?' And then he condemned the fear as a disloyalty, and broke the seal. Within there was another enclosure, likewise sealed, and marked upon the cover as 'not to be opened till the death or disappearance of Dr Henry Jekyll.' Utterson could not trust his eyes. Yes, it was disappearance; here again, as in the mad will which he had long ago restored to its author, here again were the idea of a disappearance and the name of Henry Jekyll bracketed. But in the will, that idea had sprung from the sinister suggestion of the man Hyde; it was set there with a purpose all too plain and horrible. Written by the hand of Lanyon, what should it mean? A great curiosity came on the trustee, to disregard the prohibition and dive at once to the bottom of these mysteries; but professional honour and faith to his dead friend were stringent obligations; and the packet slept in the inmost corner of his private safe.

It is one thing to mortify curiosity, another to conquer it; and it may be doubted if, from that day forth, Utterson desired the society of his surviving friend with the same eagerness. He thought of him kindly; but his thoughts were disquieted and fearful. He went to call indeed; but he was perhaps relieved to be denied admittance; perhaps, in his heart, he preferred to speak with Poole upon the doorstep and surrounded by the air and sounds of the open city, rather than to be admitted into that house of voluntary bondage, and to sit and speak with its inscrutable recluse. Poole had, indeed, no very pleasant news to communicate. The doctor, it appeared, now more than ever confined himself to the cabinet over the laboratory, where he would sometimes even sleep; he was out of spirits, he had grown very silent, he did not read; it seemed as if he had something on his mind. Utterson became so used to the unvarying character of these reports, that he fell off little by little in the frequency of his visits.

## INCIDENT AT THE WINDOW

It chanced on Sunday, when Mr Utterson was on his usual walk with Mr Enfield, that their way lay once again through the bystreet; and that when they came in front of the door, both stopped to gaze on it.

'Well,' said Enfield, 'that story's at an end at least. We shall never see more of Mr Hyde.'

'I hope not,' said Utterson. 'Did I ever tell you that I once saw him, and shared your feeling of repulsion?'

'It was impossible to do the one without the other,' returned Enfield. 'And by the way what an ass you must have thought me, not to know that this was a back way to Dr Jekyll's! It was partly your own fault that I found it out, even when I did.'

'So you found it out, did you?' said Utterson. 'But if that be so, we may step into the court and take a look at the windows. To tell you the truth, I am uneasy about poor Jekyll; and even outside, I feel as if the presence of a friend might do him good.'

The court was very cool and a little damp, and full of premature twilight, although the sky, high up overhead, was still bright with sunset. The middle one of the three windows was half way open; and sitting close beside it, taking the air with an infinite sadness of mien, like some disconsolate prisoner, Utterson saw Dr Jekyll.

'What! Jekyll!' he cried. 'I trust you are better.'

'I am very low, Utterson,' replied the doctor drearily, 'very low. It will not last long, thank God.'

'You stay too much indoors,' said the lawyer. 'You should be out, whipping up the circulation like Mr Enfield and me. (This is my cousin—Mr Enfield—Dr Jekyll.) Come now; get your hat and take a quick turn with us.'

'You are very good,' sighed the other. 'I should like to very much; but no, no, no, it is quite impossible; I dare not. But indeed, Utterson, I am very glad to see you; this is really a great pleasure; I would ask you and Mr Enfield up, but the place is really not fit.'

'Why then,' said the lawyer, good-naturedly, 'the best thing we can do is to stay down here and speak with you from where we are.

'That is just what I was about to venture to propose,' returned the doctor with a smile. But the words were hardly uttered, before the smile was struck out of his face and succeeded by an expression of such abject terror and despair, as froze the very blood of the two gentlemen below.

They saw it but for a glimpse, for the window was instantly thrust down; but that glimpse had been sufficient and they turned and left the court without a word. In silence, too, they traversed the bystreet; and it was not until they had come into a neighbouring thoroughfare, where even upon a Sunday there were still some stirrings of life, that Mr Utterson at last turned and looked at his companion. They were both pale; and there was an answering horror in their eyes.

'God forgive us, God forgive us,' said Mr Utterson.

But Mr Enfield only nodded his head very seriously, and walked on once more in silence.

# THE LAST NIGHT

Mr Utterson was sitting by his fireside one evening after dinner, when he was surprised to receive a visit from Poole.

'Bless me, Poole, what brings you here?' he cried; and then taking a second look at him, 'What ails you?' he added, 'is the doctor ill?'

'Mr Utterson,' said the man, 'there is something wrong.'

'Take a seat, and here is a glass of wine for you,' said the lawyer. 'Now, take your time, and tell me plainly what you want.'

'You know the doctor's ways, sir,' replied Poole, 'and how he shuts himself up. Well, he's shut up again in the cabinet; and I don't like it, sir—I wish I may die if I like it. Mr Utterson, sir, I'm afraid.'

'Now, my good man,' said the lawyer, 'be explicit. What are you afraid of?'

'I've been afraid for about a week,' returned Poole, doggedly disregarding the question; 'and I can bear it no more.'

The man's appearance amply bore out his words; his manner was altered for the worse; and except for the moment when he had first announced his terror, he had not once looked the lawyer in the face. Even now, he sat with the glass of wine untasted on his knee, and his eyes directed to a corner of the floor. 'I can bear it no more,' he repeated.

'Come,' said the lawyer, 'I see you have some good reason, Poole; I see there is something seriously amiss. Try to tell me what it is.'

'I think there's been foul play,' said Poole, hoarsely.

'Foul play!' cried the lawyer, a good deal frightened and rather inclined to be irritated in consequence. 'What foul play? What does the man mean?'

'I daren't say, sir,' was the answer; 'but will you come along with me and see for yourself?'

'Mr Utterson's only answer was to rise and get his hat and great coat; but he observed with wonder the greatness of the relief that appeared upon the butler's face, and perhaps with no less, that the wine was still untasted when he set it down to follow.

It was a wild, cold, seasonable night of March, with a pale moon, lying on her back as though the wind had tilted her, and a flying wrack of the most diaphanous and lawny texture. The wind made talking difficult, and flecked the blood into the face. It seemed to have swept the streets unusually bare of passengers, besides; for Mr

Utterson thought he had never seen that part of London so deserted. He could have wished it otherwise; never in his life had he been conscious of so sharp a wish to see and touch his fellow-creatures; for struggle as he might, there was borne in upon his mind a crushing anticipation of calamity. The square, when they got there, was all full of wind and dust, and the thin trees in the garden were lashing themselves along the railing. Poole, who had kept all the way a pace or two ahead, now pulled up in the middle of the pavement, and in spite of the biting weather, took off his hat and mopped his brow with a red pocket-handkerchief. But for all the hurry of his coming, these were not the dews of exertion that he wiped away, but the moisture of some strangling anguish; for his face was white and his voice, when he spoke, harsh and broken.

'Well, sir,' he said, 'here we are, and God grant there be nothing wrong.'

'Amen, Poole,' said the lawyer.

Thereupon the servant knocked in a very guarded manner; the door was opened on the chain; and a voice asked from within, 'Is that you, Poole?'

'It's all right,' said Poole. 'Open the door.'

The hall, when they entered it, was brightly lighted up; the fire was built high; and about the hearth the whole of the servants, men and women, stood huddled together like a flock of sheep. At the sight of Mr Utterson, the housemaid broke into hysterical whimpering; and the cook, crying out 'Bless God! it's Mr Utterson,' ran forward as if to take him in her arms.

'What, what? Are you all here?' said the lawyer peevishly. 'Very irregular, very unseemly; your master would be far from pleased.'

'They're all afraid,' said Poole.

Blank silence followed, no one protesting; only the maid lifted up her voice and now wept loudly.

'Hold your tongue!' Poole said to her, with a ferocity of accent that testified to his own jangled nerves; and indeed, when the girl had so suddenly raised the note of her lamentation, they had all started and turned towards the inner door with faces of dreadful expectation. 'And now,' continued the butler, addressing the knife-boy, 'reach me a candle, and we'll get this through hands at once.' And then he begged Mr Utterson to follow him, and led the way to the back garden.

'Now, sir,' said he, 'you come as gently as you can. I want you to hear, and I don't want you to be heard. And see here, sir, if by any chance he was to ask you in, don't go.'

Mr Utterson's nerves, at this unlooked-for termination, gave a jerk that nearly threw him from his balance; but he re-collected his courage and followed the butler into the laboratory building and through the surgical theatre, with its lumber of crates and bottles, to the foot of the stair. Here Poole motioned him to stand on one side and listen; while he himself, setting down the candle and making a great and obvious call on his resolution, mounted the steps and knocked with a somewhat uncertain hand on the red baize of the cabinet door.

'Mr Utterson, sir, asking to see you,' he called; and even as he did so, once more violently signed to the lawyer to give ear.

A voice answered from within: 'Tell him I cannot see anyone,' it said complainingly.

'Thank you, sir,' said Poole, with a note of something like triumph in his voice; and taking up his candle, he led Mr Utterson back across the yard and into the great kitchen, where the fire was out and the beetles were leaping on the floor.

'Sir,' he said, looking Mr Utterson in the eyes, 'was that my master's voice?'

'It seems much changed,' replied the lawyer, very pale, but giving look for look.

'Changed? Well, yes, I think so,' said the butler. 'Have I been twenty years in this man's house, to be deceived about his voice? No, sir; master's made away with; he was made away with, eight days ago, when we heard him cry out upon the name of God: and who's in there instead of him, and why it stays there, is a thing that cries to Heaven, Mr Utterson!'

'This is a very strange tale, Poole; this is rather a wild tale, my man,' said Mr Utterson, biting his finger. 'Suppose it were as you suppose, supposing Dr Jekyll to have been—well, murdered, what could induce the murderer to stay? That won't hold water; it doesn't commend itself to reason.'

'Well, Mr Utterson, you are a hard man to satisfy, but I'll do it yet,' said Poole. 'All this last week (you must know) him, or it, or whatever it is that lives in that cabinet, has been crying night and day for some sort of medicine and cannot get it to his mind. It was sometimes his way—the master's, that is—to write his orders on a sheet of paper and throw it on the stair. We've had nothing else this week back; nothing but papers, and a closed door, and the very meals left there to be smuggled in when nobody was looking. Well, sir, every day, ay, and twice and thrice in the same day, there have been orders and complaints, and I have been sent flying to all the wholesale chemists in town. Every time I brought the stuff back, there would be another paper telling me to return it, because it was not pure, and another order to a different firm. This drug is wanted bitter bad, sir, whatever for.'

'Have you any of these papers?' asked Mr Utterson.

Poole felt in his pocket and handed out a crumpled note, which the lawyer, bending nearer to the candle, carefully examined. Its contents ran thus: 'Dr Jekyll presents his compliments to Messrs. Maw. He assures them that their last sample is impure and quite useless for his present purpose. In the year 18—, Dr J. purchased a somewhat large quantity from Messrs. M. He now begs them to search with the most sedulous care, and should any of the same quality be left, to forward it to him at once. Expense is no consideration. The importance of this to Dr J. can hardly be exaggerated.' So far the letter had run composedly enough, but here with a sudden splutter of the pen, the writer's emotion had broken loose. 'For God's sake,' he had added, 'find me some of the old.'

'This is a strange note,' said Mr Utterson; and then sharply, 'How do you come to have it open?'

'The man at Maw's was main angry, sir, and he threw it back to me like so much dirt,' returned Poole.

'This is unquestionably the doctor's hand, do you know?' resumed the lawyer.

'I thought it looked like it,' said the servant

rather sulkily; and then, with another voice, 'But what matters hand of write,' he said. 'I've seen him!'

'Seen him?' repeated Mr Utterson. 'Well?'

'That's it!' said Poole. 'It was this way. I came suddenly into the theatre from the garden. It seems he had slipped out to look for this drug or whatever it is; for the cabinet door was open, and there he was at the far end of the room digging among the crates. He looked up when I came in, gave a kind of cry, and whipped upstairs into the cabinet. It was but for one minute that I saw him, but the hair stood upon my head like quills. Sir, if that was my master, why had he a mask upon his face? If it was my master, why did he cry out like a rat, and run from me? I have served him long enough. And then . . .' the man paused and passed his hand over his face.

'These are all very strange circumstances,' said Mr Utterson, 'but I think I begin to see daylight. Your master, Poole, is plainly seized with one of those maladies that both torture and deform the sufferer; hence, for aught I know, the alteration of his voice; hence the mask and his avoidance of his friends; hence his eagerness to find this drug, by means of which the poor soul retains some hope of ultimate recovery— God grant that he be not deceived! There is my explanation; it is sad enough, Poole, ay, and appalling to consider;

but it is plain and natural, hangs well together and delivers us from all exorbitant alarms.'

'Sir,' said the butler, turning to a sort of mottled pallor, 'that thing was not my master, and there's the truth. My master'—here he looked round him and began to whisper—'is a tall fine build of a man, and this was more of a dwarf.' Utterson attempted to protest. 'O, sir,' cried Poole, 'do you think I do not know my master after twenty years? do you think I do not know where his head comes to in the cabinet door, where I saw him every morning of my life? No, sir, that thing in the mask was never Doctor Jekyll—God knows what it was, but it was never Doctor Jekyll; and it is the belief of my heart that there was murder done.'

'Poole,' replied the lawyer, 'if you say that, it will become my duty to make certain. Much as I desire to spare your master's feelings, much as I am puzzled by this note which seems to prove him to be still alive, I shall consider it my duty to break in that door.'

'Ah, Mr Utterson, that's talking!' cried the butler.

'And now comes the second question,' resumed Utterson: 'Who is going to do it?'

'Why, you and me, sir,' was the undaunted reply.

'That is very well said,' returned the lawyer; 'and whatever comes of it, I shall make it my business to see you are no loser.'

'There is an axe in the theatre,' continued Poole; 'and you might take the kitchen poker for yourself.'

The lawyer took that rude but weighty instrument into his hand, and balanced it. 'Do you know, Poole,' he said, looking up, 'that you and I are about to place ourselves in a position of some peril?'

'You may say so, sir, indeed,' returned the butler.

'It is well, then, that we should be frank,' said the other. 'We both think more than we have said; let us make a clean breast. This masked figure that you saw, did you recognize it?'

'Well, sir, it went so quick, and the creature was so doubled up, that I could hardly swear to that,' was the answer. 'But if you mean, was it Mr Hyde?—why, yes, I think it was! You see, it was much of the same bigness; and it had the same quick light way with it; and then who else could have got in by the laboratory door? You have not forgot, sir, that at the time of the murder he had still the key with him? But that's not all. I don't know, Mr Utterson, if ever you met this Mr Hyde?'

'Yes,' said the lawyer, 'I once spoke with him.'

'Then you must know as well as the rest of us that there was something queer about that gentleman—something that gave a man a turn—

I don't know rightly how to say it, sir, beyond this: that you felt it in your marrow kind of cold and thin.'

'I own I felt something of what you describe,' said Mr Utterson.

'Quite so, sir,' returned Poole. 'Well, when that masked thing like a monkey jumped from among the chemicals and whipped into the cabinet, it went down my spine like ice. O, I know it's not evidence, Mr Utterson; I'm book-learned enough for that; but a man has his feelings, and I give you my bible-word it was Mr Hyde!'

'Ay, ay,' said the lawyer. 'My fears incline to the same point. Evil, I fear, founded—evil was sure to come—of that connection. Ay, truly, I believe you; I believe poor Harry is killed; and I believe his murderer (for what purpose, God alone can tell) is still lurking in his victim's room. Well, let our name be vengeance. Call Bradshaw.'

The footman came at the summons, very white and nervous.

'Pull yourself together, Bradshaw,' said the lawyer. 'This suspense, I know, is telling upon all of you; but it is now our intention to make an end of it. Poole, here, and I are going to force our way into the cabinet. If all is well, my shoulders are broad enough to bear the blame. Meanwhile, lest anything should really be amiss, or any malefactor seek to escape by the back, you and the boy must go round the corner with a pair of good sticks, and take your post at the laboratory door. We give you ten minutes, to get to your stations.'

As Bradshaw left, the lawyer looked at his watch. 'And now, Poole, let us get to ours,' he said; and taking the poker under his arm, he led the way into the yard. The scud had banked over the moon, and it was now quite dark. The wind, which only broke in puffs and draughts into that deep well of building, tossed the light of the candle to and fro about their steps, until they came into the shelter of the theatre, where they sat down silently to wait. London hummed solemnly all around; but nearer at hand, the stillness was only broken by the sound of a footfall moving to and fro along the cabinet floor.

'So it will walk all day, sir,' whispered Poole; 'ay, and the better part of the night. Only when a new sample comes from the chemist there's a bit of a break. Ah, it's an ill-conscience that's such an enemy to rest! Ah, sir, there's blood foully shed in every step of it! But hark again, a little closer—put your heart in your ears, Mr Utterson, and tell me, is that the doctor's foot?'

The steps fell lightly and oddly, with a certain swing, for all they went so slowly; it was different indeed from the heavy creaking tread of Henry Jekyll. Utterson sighed. 'Is there never anything else?' he asked.

Poole nodded. 'Once,' he said. 'Once I heard it weeping!'

'Weeping? how that?' said the lawyer, conscious of a sudden chill of horror.

'Weeping like a woman or a lost soul,' said the butler. 'I came away with that upon my heart, that I could have wept too.'

But now the ten minutes drew to an end. Poole disinterred the axe from under a stack of packing straw; the candle was set upon the nearest table to light them to the attack; and they drew near with bated breath to where that patient foot was still going up and down, up and down, in the quiet of the night.

'Jekyll,' cried Utterson, with a loud voice, 'I demand to see you.' He paused a moment, but there came no reply. 'I give you fair warning, our suspicions are aroused, and I must and shall see you,' he resumed; 'if not by fair means then by foul—if not of your consent, then by brute force!'

'Utterson,' said the voice, 'for God's sake, have mercy!'

'Ah, that's not Jekyll's voice—it's Hyde's!' cried Utterson. 'Down with the door, Poole.'

Poole swung the axe over his shoulder; the blow shook the building, and the red baize door leaped against the lock and hinges. A dismal screech, as of mere animal terror, rang from the cabinet. Up went the axe again, and again the panels crashed and the frame bounded; four times the blow fell; but the wood was tough and the fittings were of excellent workmanship; and it was not until the fifth, that the lock burst in sunder and the wreck of the door fell inwards on the carpet.

The besiegers, appalled by their own riot and the stillness that had succeeded, stood back a little and peered in. There lay the cabinet before their eyes in the quiet lamplight, a good fire glowing and chattering on the hearth, the kettle singing its thin strain, a drawer or two open, papers neatly set forth on the business table, and nearer the fire, the things laid out for tea; the quietest room, you would have said and, but for the glazed presses full of chemicals, the most commonplace that night in London.

Right in the midst there lay the body of a man sorely contorted and still twitching. They drew near on tiptoe, turned it on its back and beheld the face of Edward Hyde. He was dressed in clothes far too large for him, clothes of the doctor's bigness; the cords of his face still moved with a semblance of life, but life was quite gone; and by the crushed phial in the hand and the strong smell of kernels that hung upon the air, Utterson knew that he was looking on the body of a self-destroyer.

'We have come too late,' he said sternly, 'whether to save or punish. Hyde is gone to his account; and it only remains for us to find the body of your master.'

The far greater proportion of the building was occupied by the theatre, which filled almost the whole ground story and was lighted from above, and by the cabinet, which formed an upper story at one end and looked upon the court. A corridor joined the theatre to the door on the bystreet; and with this, the cabinet communicated separately by a second flight of stairs. There were besides a few dark closets and a spacious cellar. All these they now thoroughly examined. Each closet needed but a glance, for all were empty and all, by the dust that fell from their doors, had stood long unopened. The cellar, indeed, was filled with crazy lumber, mostly dating from the times of the surgeon who was Jekyll's predecessor; but even as they opened the door, they were advertised of the uselessness of further search, by the fall of a perfect mat of cobweb which had for years sealed up the entrance. Nowhere was there any trace of Henry Jekyll, dead or alive.

Poole stamped on the flags of the corridor. 'He must be buried here,' he said, hearkening to the sound.

'Or he may have fled,' said Utterson, and he

turned to examine the door in the bystreet. It was locked; and lying near by on the flags, they found the key, already stained with rust.

'This does not look like use,' observed the lawyer.

'Use!' echoed Poole. 'Do you not see, sir, it is broken? much as if a man had stamped on it.'

'Ay,' continued Utterson, 'and the fractures, too, are rusty.' The two men looked at each other with a scare. 'This is beyond me, Poole,' said the lawyer. 'Let us go back to the cabinet.'

They mounted the stair in silence, and still with an occasional awestruck glance at the dead body, proceeded more thoroughly to examine the contents of the cabinet. At one table, there were traces of chemical work, various measured heaps of some white salt being laid on glass saucers, as though for an experiment in which the unhappy man had been prevented.

'That is the same drug that I was always bringing him,' said Poole; and even as he spoke, the kettle with a startling noise boiled over.

This brought them to the fireside, where the easy chair was drawn cosily up, and the tea things stood ready to the sitter's elbow, the very sugar in the cup. There were several books on a shelf; one lay beside the tea things open, and Utterson was amazed to find it a copy of a pious work, for which Jekyll had several times expressed a great esteem, annotated, in his own hand, with startling blasphemies.

Next, in the course of their review of the chamber, the searchers came to the cheval glass, into whose depths they looked with an involuntary horror. But it was so turned as to show them nothing but the rosy glow playing on the roof, the fire sparkling in a hundred repetitions along the glazed front of the presses, and their own pale and fearful countenances stooping to look in.

'This glass has seen some strange things, sir,' whispered Poole.

'And surely none stranger than itself,' echoed the lawyer in the same tones. 'For what did Jekyll'—he caught himself up at the word with a start, and then conquering the weakness: 'what could Jekyll want with it?' he said.

'You may say that!' said Poole.

Next they turned to the business table. On the desk among the neat array of papers, a large envelope was uppermost, and bore, in the doctor's hand, the name of Mr Utterson. The lawyer unsealed it, and several enclosures fell to the floor. The first was a will, drawn in the same eccentric terms as the one which he had returned six months before, to serve as a testament in case of death and as a deed of gift in case of disappearance; but in place of the name of Edward

Hyde, the lawyer, with indescribable amazement, read the name of Gabriel John Utterson. He looked at Poole, and then back at the paper, and last of all at the dead malefactor stretched upon the carpet.

'My head goes round,' he said. 'He has been all these days in possession; he had no cause to like me; he must have raged to see himself displaced; and he has not destroyed this document.'

He caught up the next paper; it was a brief note in the doctor's hand and dated at the top. 'O Poole!' the lawyer cried, 'he was alive and here this day. He cannot have been disposed of in so short a space, he must be still alive, he must have fled! And then, why fled? and how? and in that case, can we venture to declare this suicide? O, we must be careful. I foresee that we may yet involve your master in some dire catastrophe.'

'Why don't you read it, sir?' asked Poole.

'Because I fear,' replied the lawyer solemnly. 'God grant I have no cause for it!' And with that he brought the paper to his eyes and read as follows.

'My dear Utterson,—When this shall fall into your hands, I shall have disappeared, under what circumstances I have not the penetration to foresee, but my instinct and all the circumstances of my nameless situation tell me that the end is sure and must be early. Go then, and first read the narrative which Lanyon warned me he was to place in your hands; and if you care to hear more, turn to the confession of:

'Your unworthy and unhappy friend,

'HENRY JEKYLL.'

'There was a third enclosure?' asked Utterson.

'Here, sir,' said Poole, and gave into his hands a considerable packet sealed in several places.

The lawyer put it in his pocket. 'I would say nothing of this paper. If your master has fled or is dead, we may at least save his credit. It is now ten; I must go home and read these documents in quiet; but I shall be back before midnight, when we shall send for the police.'

They went out, locking the door of the theatre behind them; and Utterson, once more leaving the servants gathered about the fire in the hall, trudged back to his office to read the two narratives in which this mystery was now to be explained.

# DOCTOR LANYON'S NARRATIVE

On the ninth of January, now four days ago, I received by the evening delivery a registered envelope, addressed in the hand of my colleague and old school-companion, Henry Jekyll. I was a good deal surprised by this; for we were by no means in the habit of correspondence; I had seen the man, dined with him, indeed, the night before; and I could imagine nothing in our intercourse that should justify the formality of registration. The contents increased my wonder; for this is how the letter ran:

'10th December, 18—

'Dear Lanyon,—You are one of my oldest friends; and although we may have differed at times on scientific questions, I cannot remember, at least on my side, any break in our affection. There was never a day when, if you had said to me, "Jekyll, my life, my honour, my reason, depend upon you," I would not have sacrificed my fortune or my left hand to help you. Lanyon, my life, my honour, my reason, are all at your mercy; if you fail me to-night, I am lost. You might suppose, after this preface, that I am going to ask you for something dishonourable to grant. Judge for yourself.

'I want you to postpone all other engagements for to-night—ay, even if you were summoned to the bedside of an emperor; to take a cab, unless your carriage should be actually at the door; and with this letter in your hand for consultation, to drive straight to my house. Poole, my butler, has his orders; you will find him waiting your arrival with a locksmith. The door of my cabinet is then to be forced; and you are to go in alone; to open the glazed press (letter E) on the left hand, breaking the lock if it be shut; and to draw out, *with all its contents as they stand*, the fourth drawer from the top or (which is the same thing) the third from the bottom. In my extreme distress of mind, I have a morbid fear of misdirecting you; but even if I am in error, you may know the right drawer by its contents: some powders, a phial and a paper book. This drawer I beg of you to carry back with you to Cavendish Square exactly as it stands.

'That is the first part of the service: now for the second. You should be back, if you set out at once on the receipt of this, long before midnight; but I will leave you that amount of margin, not only in the fear of one of those obstacles that can neither be prevented nor foreseen, but because an hour when your servants are in bed is to be preferred for what will then remain to do. At midnight, then, I have to ask you to be alone in your consulting room, to admit with your own hand into the house a man who will present himself in my name, and to place in his hands the drawer that you will have brought with you from my cabinet. Then you will have played your part and earned my gratitude completely. Five minutes, afterwards, if you insist upon an explanation, you will have understood that these arrangements are of capital importance; and that by the neglect of one of them, fantastic as they must appear, you might have charged your conscience with my death or the shipwreck of my reason.

'Confident as I am that you will not trifle with this appeal, my heart sinks and my hand trembles at the bare thought of such a possibility. Think of me at this hour, in a strange place, labouring under a blackness of distress that no fancy can exaggerate, and yet well aware that, if you will but punctually serve me, my troubles will roll away like a story that is told. Serve me, my dear Lanyon, and save 'Your friend,

'H. J.

'P.S. I had already sealed this up when a fresh terror struck upon my soul. It is possible that the post office may fail me, and this letter not come into your hands until to-morrow morning. In that case, dear Lanyon, do my errand when it shall be most convenient for you in the course of the day, and once more expect my messenger at midnight. It may then already be too late; and if that passes without event, you will know that you have seen the last of Henry Jekyll.'

Upon the reading of this letter, I made sure my colleague was insane; but till that was proved beyond the possibility of doubt, I felt bound to do as he requested. The less I understood of this farrago, the less I was in a position to judge of its importance; and an appeal so worded could not be set aside without a grave responsibility. I rose accordingly from table, got into a hansom, and drove straight to Jekyll's house. The butler was awaiting my arrival; he had received by the same post as mine a registered letter of instruction and had sent at once for a locksmith and a carpenter. The tradesmen came while we were yet speaking; and we moved in a body to old Dr Denman's surgical theatre from which (as you are doubtless aware) Jekyll's private cabinet is most conveniently entered. The door was very strong, the lock excellent; the carpenter avowed he would have great trouble and have to do much damage, if force were to be used; and the locksmith was near despair. But this last was a handy fellow, and after two hours' work, the door stood open. The press marked E was unlocked; and I took out the drawer, had it filled up with straw and tied in a sheet, and returned with it to Cavendish Square.

Here I proceeded to examine its contents. The powders were neatly enough made up, but not with the nicety of the dispensing chemist; so that it was plain they were of Jekyll's private manufacture; and when I opened one of the wrappers, I found what seemed to me a simple, crystalline salt of a white colour. The phial, to which I next turned my attention, might have been about half-full of a blood-red liquor, which was highly pungent to the sense of smell and seemed to me to contain phosphorus and some volatile ether. At the other ingredients, I could make no guess. The book was an ordinary version book and contained little but a series of dates. These covered a period of many years, but I observed that the entries ceased nearly a year ago and quite abruptly. Here and there a brief remark was appended to a date, usually no more than a single word: 'double' occurring perhaps six times in a total of several hundred entries; and once very early in the list and followed by several marks of exclamation, 'total failure!!!' All this, though it whetted my curiosity, told me little that was definite. Here were a phial of some tincture, a paper of some salt, and the record of a series of experiments that had led (like too many of Jekyll's investigations) to no end of practical usefulness. How could the presence of these articles in my house affect either the honour, the sanity, or the life of my flighty colleague? If his messenger could go to one place, why could he not go to another? And even granting some impediment, why was this gentleman to be received by me in secret? The more I reflected, the more convinced I grew that I was dealing with a case of cerebral disease; and though I dismissed my servants to bed, I loaded an old revolver that I might be found in some posture of self-defence.

Twelve o'clock had scarce rung out over London, ere the knocker sounded very gently on the door. I went myself at the summons, and found a small man crouching against the pillars of the portico.

'Are you come from Dr Jekyll?' I asked.

He told me 'yes' by a constrained gesture; and when I had bidden him enter, he did not obey me without a searching backward glance into the darkness of the square. There was a policeman not far off, advancing with his bull's eye open; and at the sight, I thought my visitor started and made greater haste.

These particulars struck me, I confess, disagreeably; and as I followed him into the bright light of the consulting room, I kept my hand ready on my weapon. Here, at last, I had a chance of clearly seeing him. I had never set eyes on him before, so much was certain. He was small, as I have said; I was struck besides with the shocking expression of his face, with his remarkable combination of great muscular activity and great apparent debility of constitution, and—last but not least—with the odd, subjective disturbance caused by his neighbourhood. This bore some resemblance to incipient rigor, and was accompanied by a marked sinking of the pulse. At the time, I set it down to some idiosyncratic, personal distaste, and merely wondered at the acuteness of the symptoms; but I have since had reason to believe the cause to lie much deeper in the nature of man, and to turn on some nobler hinge than the principle of hatred.

This person (who had thus, from the first moment of his entrance, struck in me what I can only describe as a disgustful curiosity) was dressed in a fashion that would have made an ordinary person laughable: his clothes, that is to say, although they were of rich and sober fabric, were enormously too large for him in every measurement—the trousers hanging on his legs and rolled up to keep them from the ground, the waist of the coat below his haunches, and the collar sprawling wide upon his shoulders. Strange to relate, this ludicrous accoutrement was far from moving me to laughter. Rather, as there was something abnormal and misbegotten in the very essence of the creature that now faced me—something seizing, surprising and revolting—this fresh disparity seemed but to fit in with and to reinforce it; so that to my interest in the man's nature and character, there was added a curiosity as to his origin, his life, his fortune and status in the world.

These observations, though they have taken so great a space to be set down in, were yet the work of a few seconds. My visitor was, indeed, on fire with sombre excitement.

'Have you got it?' he cried. 'Have you got it?' And so lively was his impatience that he even laid his hand upon my arm and sought to shake me.

I put him back, conscious at his touch of a certain icy pang along my blood. 'Come, sir,' said I. 'You forget that I have not yet the pleasure of your acquaintance. Be seated, if you please.' And I showed him an example, and sat down myself in my customary seat and with as fair an imitation of my ordinary manner to a patient, as the lateness of the hour, the nature of my preoccupations, and the horror I had of my visitor, would suffer me to muster.

'I beg your pardon, Dr Lanyon,' he replied civilly enough. 'What you say is very well founded; and my impatience has shown its heels to my politeness. I come here at the instance of your colleague, Dr Henry Jekyll, on a piece of business of some moment; and I understood . . .' he paused and put his hand to his throat, and I could see, in spite of his collected manner, that he was wrestling against the approaches of the hysteria—'I understood, a drawer . . .'

But here I took pity on my visitor's suspense, and some perhaps on my own growing curiosity.

'There it is, sir,' said I, pointing to the drawer, where it lay on the floor behind a table and still covered with the sheet.

He sprang to it, and then paused, and laid his hand upon his heart; I could hear his teeth grate with the convulsive action of his jaws; and his face was so ghastly to see that I grew alarmed both for his life and reason.

'Compose yourself,' said I.

He turned a dreadful smile to me, and as if with the decision of despair, plucked away the sheet. At sight of the contents, he uttered one loud sob of such immense relief that I sat petrified. And the next moment, in a voice that was already fairly well under control, 'Have you a graduated glass?' he asked.

I rose from my place with something of an effort and gave him what he asked.

He thanked me with a smiling nod, measured out a few minims of the red tincture and added one of the powders. The mixture, which was at first of a reddish hue, began, in proportion as the crystals melted, to brighten in colour, to effervesce audibly, and to throw off small fumes of vapour. Suddenly and at the same moment, the ebullition ceased and the compound changed to a dark purple, which faded again more slowly to a watery green. My visitor, who had watched these metamorphoses with a keen eye, smiled, set down the glass upon the table, and then turned and looked upon me with an air of scrutiny.

'And now,' said he, 'to settle what remains. Will you be wise? will you be guided? will you suffer me to take this glass in my hand and to go forth from your house without further parley? or has the greed of curiosity too much command of you? Think before you answer, for it shall be done as you decide. As you decide, you shall be left as you were before, and neither richer nor wiser, unless the sense of service rendered to a man in mortal distress may be counted as a kind of riches of the soul. Or, if you shall so prefer to choose, a new province of knowledge and new avenues to fame and power shall be laid open to you, here, in this room, upon the instant; and your sight shall be blasted by a prodigy to stagger the unbelief of Satan.'

'Sir,' said I, affecting a coolness that I was far from truly possessing, 'you speak enigmas, and you will perhaps not wonder that I hear you with no very strong impression of belief. But I have gone too far in the way of inexplicable services to pause before I see the end.'

'It is well,' replied my visitor. 'Lanyon, you remember your vows: what follows is under the seal of our profession. And now, you who have so long been bound to the most narrow and material views, you who have denied the virtue of transcendental medicine, you who have derided your superiors—behold! '

He put the glass to his lips and drank at one gulp. A cry followed; he reeled, staggered, clutched at the table and held on, staring with injected eyes, gasping with open mouth; and as I looked there came, I thought, a change—he seemed to swell—his face became suddenly black and the features seemed to melt and alter—and the next moment, I had sprung to my feet and leaped back against the wall, my arm raised to shield me from that prodigy, my mind submerged in terror.

'O God!' I screamed, and 'O God!' again and again; for there before my eyes—pale and shaken, and half fainting, and groping before him with his hands, like a man restored from death—there stood Henry Jekyll!

What he told me in the next hour, I cannot bring my mind to set on paper. I saw what I saw, I heard what I heard, and my soul sickened at it; and yet now when that sight has faded from my eyes, I ask myself if I believe it, and I cannot answer. My life is shaken to its roots; sleep has left me; the deadliest terror sits by me at all hours of the day and night; I feel that my days are numbered, and that I must die; and yet I shall die incredulous. As for the moral turpitude that man unveiled to me, even with tears of penitence, I cannot, even in memory, dwell on it without a start of horror. I will say but one thing, Utterson, and that (if you can bring your mind to credit it) will be more than enough. The creature who crept into my house that night was, on Jekyll's own confession, known by the name of Hyde and hunted for in every corner of the land as the murderer of Carew.

Hastie Lanyon.

# HENRY JEKYLL'S FULL STATEMENT OF THE CASE

I was born in the year 18— to a large fortune, endowed besides with excellent parts, inclined by nature to industry, fond of the respect of the wise and good among my fellow-men, and thus, as might have been supposed, with every guarantee of an honourable and distinguished future. And indeed the worst of my fault was a certain impatient gaiety of disposition, such as has made the happiness of many, but such as I found it hard to reconcile with my imperious desire to carry my head high, and wear a more than commonly grave countenance before the public. Hence it came about that I concealed my pleasures; and that when I reached years of reflection, and began to look round me and take stock of my progress and position in the world, I stood already committed to a profound duplicity of life. Many a man would have even blazoned such irregularities as I was guilty of; but from the high views that I had set before me, I regarded and hid them with an almost morbid sense of shame. It was thus rather the exacting nature of my aspirations than any particular degradation in my faults, that made me what I was and, with even a deeper trench than in the majority of men, severed in me those provinces of good and ill which divide and compound man's dual nature. In this case, I was driven to reflect deeply and inveterately on that hard law of life, which lies at the root of religion and is one of the most plentiful springs of distress. Though so profound a double-dealer, I was in no sense a hypocrite; both sides of me were in dead earnest; I was no more myself when I laid aside restraint and plunged in shame, than when I laboured, in the eye of day, at the furtherance of knowledge or the relief of sorrow and suffering. And it chanced that the direction of my scientific studies, which led wholly towards the mystic and the transcendental, reacted and shed a strong light on this consciousness of the perennial war among my members. With every day, and from both sides of my intelligence, the moral and the intellectual, I thus drew steadily nearer to that truth, by whose partial discovery I have been doomed to such a dreadful shipwreck: that man is not truly one, but truly two. I say two, because the state of my own knowledge does not pass beyond that point. Others will follow, others will outstrip me on the same lines; and I hazard the guess that man will be ultimately known for a mere polity of multifarious, incongruous and independent denizens. I for my part, from the nature of my life, advanced infallibly in one direction and in one direction only. It was on the moral side, and in my own person, that I learned to recognize the thorough and primitive duality of man; I saw that, of the two natures that contended in the field of my consciousness, even if I could rightly be said to be either, it was only because I was radically both; and from an early date, even before the course of my scientific discoveries had begun to suggest the most naked possibility of such a miracle, I had learned to dwell with pleasure, as a beloved daydream, on the thought of the separation of these elements. If each, I told myself, could but be housed in separate identities, life would be relieved of all that was unbearable; the unjust might go his way, delivered from the aspirations and remorse of his more upright twin; and the just could walk steadfastly and securely on his upward path, doing the good things in which he found his pleasure, and no longer exposed to disgrace and penitence by the hands of this extraneous evil. It was the curse of mankind that these incongruous faggots were thus bound together—that in the agonized womb of consciousness, these polar twins should be continuously struggling. How, then, were they dissociated?

I was so far in my reflections when, as I have said, a side light began to shine upon the subject from the laboratory table. I began to perceive more deeply than it has ever yet been stated, the trembling immateriality, the mist-like transience, of this seemingly so solid body in which we walk attired. Certain agents I found to have the power to shake and to pluck back that fleshly vestment, even as a wind might toss the curtains of a pavilion. For two good reasons, I will not enter deeply into this scientific branch of my confession. First, because I have been made to learn that the doom and burthen of our life is bound forever on man's shoulders, and when the attempt is made to cast it off, it but returns upon us with more unfamiliar and more awful pressure. Second, because as my narrative will make alas! too evident, my discoveries were incomplete. Enough, then, that I not only recognized my natural body for the mere aura and effulgence of certain of the powers that made up my spirit, but managed to compound a drug by which these powers should be dethroned from their supremacy, and a second form and countenance substituted, none the less natural to me because they were the expression, and bore the stamp, of lower elements in my soul.

I hesitated long before I put this theory to the test of practice. I knew well that I risked death; for any drug that so potently controlled and shook the very fortress of identity, might by the least scruple of an overdose or at the least inopportunity in the moment of exhibition, utterly blot out that immaterial tabernacle which I looked to it to change. But the temptation of a discovery so singular and profound, at last overcame the suggestions of alarm. I had long since prepared my tincture; I purchased at once, from a firm of wholesale chemists, a large quantity of a particular salt which I knew, from my experiments, to be the last ingredient required; and late one accursed night, I compounded the elements, watched them boil and smoke together in the glass, and when the ebullition had subsided, with a strong glow of courage, drank off the potion.

The most racking pangs succeeded: a grinding in the bones, deadly nausea, and a horror of the spirit that cannot be exceeded at the hour of birth or death. Then these agonies began swiftly to subside, and I came to myself as if out of a great sickness. There was something strange in my sensations, something indescribably new and, from its very novelty, incredibly sweet. I felt younger, lighter, happier in body; within I was conscious of a heady recklessness, a current of disordered sensual images running like a mill race in my fancy, a solution of the bonds of obligation, an unknown but not an innocent freedom of the soul. I knew myself, at the first breath of this new life, to be more wicked, tenfold more wicked, sold a slave to my original evil; and the thought, in that moment, braced and delighted me like wine. I stretched out my hands, exulting in the freshness of these sensations; and in the act, I was suddenly aware that I had lost in stature.

There was no mirror, at that date, in my room; that which stands beside me as I write, was brought there later on and for the very purpose of these transformations. The night, however, was far gone into the morning—the morning, black as it was, was nearly ripe for the conception of the day—the inmates of my house were locked in the most rigorous hours of slumber; and I determined, flushed as I was with hope and triumph, to venture in my new shape as far as to my bedroom. I crossed the yard, wherein the constellations looked down upon me, I could have thought, with wonder, the first creature of that sort that their unsleeping vigilance had yet disclosed to them; I stole through the corridors, a stranger in my own house; and coming to my room, I saw for the first time the appearance of Edward Hyde.

I must here speak by theory alone, saying not that which I know, but that which I suppose to be most probable. The evil side of my nature, to which I had now transferred the stamping efficacy, was less robust and less developed than the good which I had just deposed. Again, in the course of my life, which had been, after all, nine tenths a life of effort, virtue and control, it had been much less exercised and much less exhausted. And hence, as I think, it came about that Edward Hyde was so much smaller, slighter and younger than Henry Jekyll. Even as good shone upon the countenance of the one, evil was written broadly and plainly on the face of the other. Evil besides (which I must still believe to be the lethal side of man) had left on that body an imprint of deformity and decay. And yet when I looked upon that ugly idol in the glass, I was conscious of no repugnance, rather of a leap of welcome. This, too, was myself. It seemed natural and human. In my eyes it bore a livelier image of the spirit, it seemed more express and single, than the imperfect and divided countenance, I had been hitherto accustomed to call mine. And in so far I was doubtless right. I have observed that when I wore the semblance of Edward Hyde, none could come near to me at first without a visible misgiving of the flesh. This, as I take it, was because all human beings, as we meet them, are commingled out of good and evil: and Edward Hyde, alone in the ranks of mankind, was pure evil.

I lingered but a moment at the mirror: the second and conclusive experiment had yet to be attempted; it yet remained to be seen if I had lost my identity beyond redemption and must flee before daylight from a house that was no longer mine; and hurrying back to my cabinet, I once more prepared and drank the cup, once more suffered the pangs of dissolution, and came to myself once more with the character, the stature and the face of Henry Jekyll.

That night I had come to the fatal cross roads. Had I approached my discovery in a more noble spirit, had I risked the experiment while under the empire of generous or pious aspirations, all must have been otherwise, and from these agonies of death and birth, I had come forth an angel instead of a fiend. The drug had no discriminating action; it was neither diabolical nor divine; it but shook the doors of the prisonhouse of my disposition; and like the captives of Philippi, that which stood within ran forth At that time my virtue slumbered; my evil, kept awake by ambition, was alert and swift to seize the occasion; and the thing that was projected was Edward Hyde. Hence, although I had now two characters as well as two appearances, one was wholly evil, and the other was still the old Henry Jekyll, that incongruous compound of whose reformation and improvement I had already learned to despair. The movement was thus wholly toward the worse.

Even at that time, I had not yet conquered my aversion to the dryness of a life of study. I would still be merrily disposed at times; and as my pleasures were (to say the least) undignified, and I was not only well known and highly considered, but growing towards the elderly man, this incoherency of my life was daily growing more unwelcome. It was on this side that my new power tempted me until I fell in slavery. I had but to drink the cup, to doff at once the body of the noted professor, and to assume, like a thick cloak, that of Edward Hyde. I smiled at the notion; it seemed to me at the time to be humorous; and I made my preparations with the most studious care. I took and furnished that house in Soho, to which Hyde was tracked by the police; and engaged as housekeeper a creature whom I well knew to be silent and unscrupulous. On the other side, I announced to my servants that a Mr Hyde (whom I described) was to have full liberty and power about my house in the square; and to parry mishaps, I even called and made myself a familiar object, in my second character. I next drew up that will to which you so much objected; so that if anything befell me in the person of Doctor Jekyll, I could enter on that of Edward Hyde without pecuniary loss. And thus fortified, as I supposed, on every side, I began to profit by the strange immunities of my position.

Men have before hired bravos to transact their crimes, while their own person and reputation sat under shelter. I was the first that ever did so for his pleasures. I was the first that could thus plod in the public eye with a load of genial respectability, and in a moment, like a schoolboy, strip off these lendings and spring headlong into the sea of liberty. But for me, in my impenetrable mantle, the safety was complete. Think of it—I did not even exist! Let me but escape into my laboratory door, give me but a second or two to mix and swallow the draught that I had always standing ready; and whatever he had done, Edward Hyde would pass away like the stain of breath upon a mirror; and there in his stead, quietly at home, trimming the midnight lamp in his study, a man who could afford to laugh at suspicion, would be Henry Jekyll.

The pleasures which I made haste to seek in my disguise were, as I have said, undignified; I would scarce use a harder term. But in the hands of Edward Hyde, they soon began to turn towards the monstrous. When I would come back from these excursions, I was often plunged into a kind of wonder at my vicarious depravity. This familiar that I called out of my own soul, and sent forth alone to do his good pleasure, was a being inherently malign and villainous; his every act and thought centered on self; drinking pleasure with bestial avidity from any degree of torture to another; relentless like a man of stone. Henry Jekyll stood at times aghast before the acts of Edward Hyde; but the situation was apart from ordinary laws, and insidiously relaxed the grasp of conscience. It was Hyde, after all, and Hyde alone, that was guilty. Jekyll was no worse; he woke again to his good qualities seemingly unimpaired; he would even make haste, where it was possible, to undo the evil done by Hyde. And thus his conscience slumbered.

Into the details of the infamy at which I thus connived (for even now I can scarce grant that I committed it) I have no design of entering; I mean but to point out the warnings and the successive steps with which my chastisement approached. I met with one accident which, as it brought on no consequence, I shall no more than mention. An act of cruelty to a child aroused against me the anger of a passer by, whom I recognized the other day in the person of your kinsman; the doctor and the child's family joined him; there were moments when I feared for my life; and at last, in order to pacify their too just resentment, Edward Hyde had to bring them to the door, and pay them in a cheque drawn in the name, of Henry Jekyll. But this danger was easily eliminated from the future, by opening an account at another bank in the name of Edward Hyde himself; and when, by sloping my own hand backward, I had supplied my double with a signature, I thought I sat beyond the reach of fate.

Some two months before the murder of Sir Danvers, I had been out for one of my adventures, had returned at a late hour, and woke the next day in bed with somewhat odd sensations. It was in vain I looked about me; in vain I saw the decent furniture and tall proportions of my room in the square; in vain that I recognized the pattern of the bed curtains and the design of the mahogany frame; something still kept insisting that I was not where I was, that I had not wakened where I seemed to be, but in the little room in Soho where I was accustomed to sleep in the body of Edward Hyde. I smiled to myself, and, in my psychological way, began lazily to inquire into the elements of this illusion, occasionally, even as I did so, dropping back into a comfortable morning doze. I was still so engaged when, in one of my more wakeful moments, my eye fell upon my hand. Now the hand of Henry Jekyll (as you have often remarked) was professional in shape and size: it was large, firm, white and comely. But the hand which I now saw, clearly enough, in the yellow light of a mid-London morning, lying half shut on the bed clothes, was lean, corded, knuckly, of a dusky pallor and thickly shaded with a swart growth of hair. It was the hand of Edward Hyde.

I must have stared upon it for near half a minute, sunk as I was in the mere stupidity of wonder, before terror woke up in my breast as sudden and startling as the crash of cymbals; and bounding from my bed, I rushed to the mirror. At the sight that met my eyes, my blood was changed into something exquisitely thin and icy. Yes, I had gone to bed Henry Jekyll, I had awakened Edward Hyde. How was this to be explained? I asked myself; and then, with another bound of terror—how was it to be remedied? It was well on in the morning; the servants were up; all my drugs were in the cabinet—a long journey, down two pair of stairs, through the back passage, across the open court and through the anatomical theatre, from where I was then standing horror-struck. It might indeed be possible to cover my face; but of what use was that, when I was unable to conceal the alteration in my stature? And then with an overpowering sweetness of relief, it came back upon my mind that the servants were already used to the coming and going of my second self. I had soon dressed, as well as I was able, in clothes of my own size: had soon passed through the house, where Bradshaw stared and drew back at seeing Mr Hyde at such an hour and in such a strange array; and ten minutes later, Dr Jekyll had returned to his own shape and was sitting down, with a darkened brow, to make a feint of breakfasting.

Small indeed was my appetite. This inexplicable incident, this reversal of my previous experience, seemed, like the Babylonian finger on the wall, to be spelling out the letters of my judgment; and I began to reflect more seriously than ever before on the issues and possibilities of my double existence. That part of me which I had the power of projecting, had lately been much exercised and nourished; it had seemed to me of late as though the body of Edward Hyde had grown in stature, as though (when I wore that form) I were conscious of a more generous tide of blood; and I began to spy a danger that, if this were much prolonged, the balance of my nature might be permanently overthrown, the power of voluntary change be forfeited, and the character of Edward Hyde become irrevocably mine. The power of the drug had not been always equally displayed. Once, very early in my career, it had totally failed me; since then I had been obliged on more than one occasion to double, and once, with infinite risk of death, to treble the amount; and these rare uncertainties had cast hitherto the sole shadow on my contentment. Now, however, and in the light of that morning's accident, I was led to remark that whereas, in the beginning, the difficulty had been to throw off the body of Jekyll, it had of late, gradually but decidedly transferred itself to the other side. All things therefore seemed to point to this: that I was slowly losing hold of my original and better self, and becoming slowly incorporated with my second and worse.

Between these two, I now felt I had to choose. My two natures had memory in common, but all other faculties were most unequally shared between them. Jekyll (who was composite) now with the most sensitive apprehensions, now with a greedy gusto, projected and shared in the pleasures and adventure of Hyde; but Hyde was indifferent to Jekyll, or but remembered him as the mountain bandit remembers the cavern in which he conceals himself from pursuit. Jekyll had more than a father's interest; Hyde had more than a son's indifference. To cast in my lot with Jekyll, was to die to those appetites which I had long secretly indulged and had of late begun to pamper. To cast it in with Hyde, was to die to a thousand interests and aspirations, and to become, at a blow and forever, despised and friendless. The bargain might appear unequal; but there was still another consideration in the scales; for while Jekyll would suffer smartingly in the fires of abstinence, Hyde would be not even conscious of all that he had lost. Strange as my circumstances were, the terms of this debate are as old and commonplace as man; much the same inducements and alarms cast the die for any tempted and trembling sinner; and it fell out with me, as it falls with so vast a majority of my fellows, that I chose the better part and was found wanting in the strength to keep to it.

Yes, I preferred the elderly and discontented doctor, surrounded by friends and cherishing honest hopes; and bade a resolute farewell to the liberty, the comparative youth, the light step, leaping pulses and secret pleasures, that I had enjoyed in the disguise of Hyde. I made this choice perhaps with some unconscious reservation, for I neither gave up the house in Soho, nor destroyed the clothes of Edward Hyde, which still lay ready in my cabinet. For two months, however, I was true to my determination; for two months, I led a life of such severity as I had never before attained to, and enjoyed the compensations of an approving conscience. But time began at last to obliterate the freshness of my alarm; the praises of conscience began to grow into a thing of course; I began to be tortured with throes and longings, as of Hyde struggling after freedom; and at last, in an hour of moral weakness, I once again compounded and swallowed the transforming draught.

I do not suppose that, when a drunkard reasons with himself upon his vice, he is once out of five hundred times affected by the dangers that he runs through his brutish, physical insensibility; neither had I, long as I had considered my position, made enough allowance for the complete moral insensibility and insensate readiness to evil, which were the leading characters of Edward Hyde. Yet it was by these that I was punished. My devil had been long caged, he came out roaring. I was conscious, even when I took the draught, of a more unbridled, a more furious propensity to ill. It must have been this, I suppose, that stirred in my soul that tempest of impatience with which I listened to the civilities of my unhappy victim; I declare at least, before God, no man morally sane could have been guilty of that crime upon so pitiful a provocation; and that I struck in no more reasonable spirit than that in which a sick child may break a plaything. But I had voluntarily stripped myself of all those balancing instincts, by which even the worst of us continues to walk with some degree of steadiness among temptations; and in my case, to be tempted, however slightly, was to fall.

Instantly the spirit of hell awoke in me and raged. With a transport of glee, I mauled the unresisting body, tasting delight from every blow; and it was not till weariness had begun to succeed, that I was suddenly, in the top fit of my delirium, struck through the heart by a cold thrill of terror. A mist dispersed; I saw my life to be forfeit; and fled from the scene of these excesses, at once glorying and trembling, my lust of evil gratified and stimulated, my love of life screwed to the topmost peg. I ran to the house in Soho, and (to make assurance doubly sure) destroyed my papers; thence I set out through the lamplit streets, in the same divided ecstasy of mind, gloating on my crime, light-headedly devising others in the future, and yet still hastening and still hearkening in my wake for the steps of the avenger. Hyde had a song upon his lips as he compounded the draught, and as he drank it, pledged the dead man. The pangs of transformation had not done tearing him, before Henry Jekyll, with streaming tears of gratitude and remorse, had fallen upon his knees and lifted his clasped hands to God. The veil of self-indulgence was rent from head to foot, I saw my life as a whole: I followed it up from the days of childhood, when I had walked with my father's hand, and through the self-denying toils of my professional life, to arrive again and again, with the same sense of unreality, at the damned horrors of the evening. I could have screamed aloud; I sought with tears and prayers to smother down the crowd of hideous images and sounds with which my memory swarmed against me; and still, between the petitions, the ugly face of my iniquity stared into my soul. As the acuteness of this remorse began to die away, it was succeeded by a sense of joy. The problem of my conduct was solved. Hyde was thenceforth impossible; whether I would or not, I was now confined to the better part of my existence; and oh, how I rejoiced to think it! with what willing humility, I embraced anew the restrictions of natural life! with what sincere renunciation, I locked the door by which I had so often gone and come, and ground the key under my heel!

The next day, came the news that the murder had been overlooked, that the guilt of Hyde was patent to the world, and that the victim was a man high in public estimation. It was not only a crime, it had been a tragic folly. I think I was glad to know it; I think I was glad to have my better impulses thus buttressed and guarded by the terrors of the scaffold. Jekyll was now my city of refuge; let but Hyde peep out an instant, and the hands of all men would be raised to take and slay him.

I resolved in my future conduct to redeem the past; and I can say with honesty that my resolve was fruitful of some good. You know yourself how earnestly in the last months of last year, I laboured to relieve suffering; you know that much was done for others, and that the days passed quietly, almost happily for myself. Nor can I truly say that I wearied of this beneficent and innocent life; I think instead that I daily enjoyed it more completely; but I was still cursed with my duality of purpose; and as the first edge of my penitence wore off, the lower side of me, so long indulged, so recently chained down, began to growl for license. Not that I dreamed of resuscitating Hyde; the bare idea of that would startle me to frenzy: no, it was in my own person, that I was once more tempted to trifle with my conscience; and it was as an ordinary secret sinner, that I at last fell before the assaults of temptation.

There comes an end to all things; the most capacious measure is filled at last; and this brief condescension to my evil finally destroyed the balance of my soul. And yet I was not alarmed; the fall seemed natural, like a return to the old days before I had made my discovery. It was a fine, clear, January day, wet under foot where the frost had melted, but cloudless overhead; and the Regent's park was full of winter chirruppings and sweet with Spring odours. I sat in the sun on a bench; the animal within me licking the chops of memory; the spiritual side a little drowsed, promising subsequent penitence, but not yet moved to begin. After all, I reflected I was like my neighbours; and then I smiled, comparing myself with other men, comparing my active goodwill with the lazy cruelty of their neglect. And at the very moment of that vainglorious thought, a qualm came over me, a horrid nausea and the most deadly shuddering. These passed away, and left me faint; and then as in its turn the faintness subsided, I began to be aware of a change in the temper of my thoughts, a greater boldness, a contempt of danger, a solution of the bonds of obligation. I looked down; my clothes hung formlessly on my shrunken limbs; the hand that lay on my knee was corded and hairy. I was once more Edward Hyde. A moment before I had been safe of all men's respect, wealthy, beloved—the cloth laying for me in the dining room at home; and now I was the common quarry of mankind, hunted, houseless, a known murderer, thrall to the gallows.

My reason wavered, but it did not fail me utterly. I have more than once observed that, in my second character, my faculties seemed sharpened to a point and my spirits more tensely elastic; thus it came about that, where Jekyll perhaps might have succumbed, Hyde rose to the importance of the moment. My drugs were in one of the presses of my cabinet; how was I to reach them? That was the problem that (crushing my temples in my hands) I set myself to solve. The laboratory door I had closed. If I sought to enter by the house, my own servants would consign me to the gallows. I saw I must employ another hand, and thought of Lanyon. How was he to be reached? how persuaded? Supposing that I escaped capture in the streets, how was I to make my way into his presence? and how should I, an unknown and displeasing visitor, prevail on the famous physician to rifle the study of his colleague, Dr Jekyll? Then I remembered that of my original character, one part remained to me: I could write my own hand; and once I had conceived that kindling spark, the way that I must follow became lighted up from end to end.

Thereupon, I arranged my clothes as best I could, and summoning a passing hansom, drove to an hotel in Portland street, the name of which I chanced to remember. At my appearance (which was indeed comical enough, however tragic a fate these garments covered) the driver could not conceal his mirth. I gnashed my teeth upon him with a gust of devilish fury; and the smile withered from his face—happily for him—yet more happily for myself, for in another instant I had certainly dragged him from his perch. At the inn, as I entered, I looked about me with so black a countenance as made the attendants tremble; not a look did they exchange in my presence; but obsequiously took my orders, led me to a private room, and brought me wherewithal to write. Hyde in danger of his life was a creature new to me: shaken with inordinate anger, strung to the pitch of murder, lusting to inflict pain. Yet the creature was astute; mastered his fury with a great effort of the will; composed his two important letters, one to Lanyon and one to Poole; and that he might receive actual evidence of their being posted, sent them out with directions that they should be registered.

Thenceforward, he sat all day over the fire in the private room, gnawing his nails; there he dined, sitting alone with his fears, the waiter visibly quailing before his eye; and thence, when the night was fully come, he set forth in the corner of a closed cab, and was driven to and fro about the streets of the city. He, I say—I cannot say, I. That child of Hell had nothing human; nothing lived in him but fear and hatred. And when at last, thinking the driver had begun to grow suspicious, he discharged the cab and ventured on foot, attired in his misfitting clothes, an object marked out for observation, into the midst of the nocturnal passengers, these two base passions raged within him like a tempest. He walked fast, hunted by his fears, chattering to himself, skulking through the less frequented thoroughfares, counting the minutes that still divided him from midnight. Once a woman spoke to him, offering, I think, a box of lights. He smote her in the face, and she fled.

When I came to myself at Lanyon's, the horror of my old friend perhaps affected me somewhat:

I do not know; it was at least but a drop in the sea to the abhorrence with which I looked back upon these hours. A change had come over me. It was no longer the fear of the gallows, it was the horror of being Hyde that racked me. I received Lanyon's condemnation partly in a dream; it was partly in a dream that I came home to my own house and got into bed. I slept after the prostration of the day, with a stringent and profound slumber which not even the nightmares that wrung me could avail to break. I awoke in the morning shaken, weakened, but refreshed. I still hated and feared the thought of the brute that slept within me, and I had not of course forgotten the appalling dangers of the day before; but I was once more at home, in my own house and close to my drugs; and gratitude for my escape shone so strong in my soul that it almost rivalled the brightness of hope.

I was stepping leisurely across the court after breakfast, drinking the chill of the air with pleasure, when I was seized again with those indescribable sensations that heralded the change; and I had but the time to gain the shelter of my cabinet, before I was once again raging and freezing with the passions of Hyde. It took on this occasion a double dose to recall me to myself; and alas, six hours after, as I sat looking sadly in the fire, the pangs returned, and the drug had to be re-administered. In short, from that day forth it seemed only by a great effort as of gymnastics, and only under the immediate stimulation of the drug, that I was able to wear the countenance of Jekyll. At all hours of the day and night, I would be taken with the premonitory shudder; above all, if I slept, or even dozed for a moment in my chair, it was always as Hyde that I awakened. Under the strain of this continually impending doom and by the sleeplessness to which I now condemned myself, ay, even beyond what I had thought possible to man, I became, in my own person, a creature eaten up and emptied by fever, languidly weak both in body and mind, and solely occupied by one thought: the horror of my other self. But when I slept, or when the virtue of the medicine wore off, I would leap almost without transition (for the pangs of transformation grew daily less marked) into the possession of a fancy brimming with images of terror, a soul boiling with causeless hatreds, and a body that seemed not strong enough to contain the raging energies of life. The powers of Hyde seemed to have grown with the sickliness of Jekyll. And certainly the hate that now divided them was equal on each side. With Jekyll, it was a thing of vital instinct. He had now seen the full deformity of that creature that shared with him some of the phenomena of consciousness, and was co-heir with him to death: and beyond these links of community, which in themselves made the most poignant part of his distress, he thought of Hyde, for all his energy of life, as of something not only hellish but inorganic. This was the shocking thing; that the slime of the pit seemed to utter cries and voices; that the amorphous dust gesticulated and sinned; that what was dead, and had no shape, should usurp the offices of life. And this again, that that insurgent horror was knit to him closer than a wife, closer than an eye; lay caged in his flesh, where he heard it mutter and felt it struggle to be born; and at every hour of weakness, and in the confidence of slumber, prevailed against him, and deposed him out of life. The hatred of Hyde for Jekyll, was of a different order. His terror of the gallows drove him continually to commit temporary suicide, and return to his subordinate station of a part instead of a person; but he loathed the necessity, he loathed the despondency into which Jekyll was now fallen, and he resented the dislike with which he was himself regarded. Hence the apelike tricks that he would play me, scrawling in my own hand blasphemies on the pages of my books, burning the letters and destroying the portrait of my father;' and indeed, had it not been for his fear of death, he would long ago have ruined himself in order to involve me in the ruin.

But his love of life is wonderful; I go further: I, who sicken and freeze at the mere thought of him, when I recall the abjection and passion of this attachment, and when I know how he fears my power to cut him off by suicide, I find it in my heart to pity him.

It is useless, and the time awfully fails me, to prolong this description; no one has ever suffered such torments, let that suffice; and yet even to these, habit brought—no, not alleviation—but a certain callousness of soul, a certain acquiescence of despair; and my punishment might have gone on for years, but for the last calamity which has now fallen, and which has finally severed me from my own face and nature. My provision of the salt, which had never been renewed since the date of the first experiment, began to run low. I sent out for a fresh supply, and mixed the draught; the ebullition followed, and the first change of colour, not the second; I drank it and it was without efficiency. You will learn from Poole how I have had London ransacked; it was in vain; and I am now persuaded that my first supply was impure, and that it was that unknown impurity which lent efficacy to the draught.

About a week has passed, and I am now finishing this statement under the influence of the last of the old powders. This, then, is the last time, short of a miracle, that Henry Jekyll can think his own thoughts or see his own face (now how sadly altered!) in the glass. Nor must I delay too long to bring my writing to an end; for if my narrative has hitherto escaped destruction, it has been by a combination of great prudence and great good luck. Should the throes of change take me in the act of writing it, Hyde will tear it in pieces; but if some time shall have elapsed after I have laid it by, his wonderful selfishness and circumscription to the moment will probably save it once again from the action of his apelike spite. And indeed the doom that is closing on us both, has already changed and crushed him. Half an hour from now, when I shall again and forever reindue that hated personality, I know how I shall sit shuddering and weeping in my chair, or continue, with the most strained and fearstruck ecstasy of listening, to pace up and down this room (my last earthly refuge) and give ear to every sound of menace. Will Hyde die upon the scaffold? or will he find the courage to release himself at the last moment? God knows; I am careless; this is my true hour of death, and what is to follow concerns another than myself. Here then, as I lay down the pen and proceed to seal up my confession, I bring the life of that unhappy Henry Jekyll to an end.